KINGSTON

AND THE

MAGICIAN'S LOST AND FOUND

KINGSTON

— AND THE —

MAGICIAN'S LOST AND FOUND

RUCKER MOSES
AND THEO GANGI

putnam

G. P. PUTNAM'S SONS

G. P. PUTNAM'S SONS

An imprint of Penguin Random House LLC, New York

Copyright © 2021 by Craig S. Phillips and Harold Hayes, Jr.
Map and interior illustrations © 2021 by Sienne Josselin

Penguin supports copyright. Copyright fuels creativity, encourages diverse voices, promotes free speech, and creates a vibrant culture. Thank you for buying an authorized edition of this book and for complying with copyright laws by not reproducing, scanning, or distributing any part of it in any form without permission.You are supporting writers and allowing Penguin to continue to publish books for every reader.

G. P. Putnam's Sons is a registered trademark of Penguin Random House LLC.

Visit us online at penguinrandomhouse.com

Library of Congress Cataloging-in-Publication Data
Names: Moses, Rucker, author. | Gangi, Theo, author. | Josselin, Sienne, illustrator.
Title: Kingston and the magician's lost and found / Rucker Moses and Theo Gangi; map and interior illustrations by Sienne Josselin.
Description: New York: G. P. Putnam's Sons, [2020] | Summary: Returning to Brooklyn, where his magician father disappeared years before, twelve-year-old Kingston learns that magic is real and that if he enters the Realm, he might get his father back.
Identifiers: LCCN 2020027059 (print) | LCCN 2020027060 (ebook)
ISBN 9780525516866 (hardcover) | ISBN 9780525516873 (ebook)
Subjects: CYAC: Magic—Fiction. | Missing persons—Fiction. | Family life—Brooklyn (New York, N.Y.)—Fiction. | Magicians—Fiction. | African Americans—Fiction. | Brooklyn—New York (State)—Brooklyn—Fiction. | Mystery and detective stories.
Classification: LCC PZ7.1.M67725 Kin 2020 (print) | LCC PZ7.1.M67725 (ebook)
DDC [Fic]—dc23
LC record available at https://lccn.loc.gov/2020027059
LC ebook record available at https://lccn.loc.gov/2020027060

Printed in the United States of America
ISBN 9780525516866
1 3 5 7 9 10 8 6 4 2

Design by Suki Boynton • Text set in Warnock Pro

This book is a work of fiction. Any references to historical events, real people, or real places are used fictitiously. Other names, characters, places, and events are products of the author's imagination, and any resemblance to actual events or places or persons, living or dead, is entirely coincidental.

To my two favorite lefties

and my fellow Purple Gum Ball.

—C.S.P.

To Frederick.

—H.H. Jr.

To the Black Gangis.

—T.G.

MY FATHER WAS famous. He was the greatest magician in Echo City. And he made himself disappear.

Disappear. Like, here one second, gone the next.

Not *disappear* like he went out for milk and eggs and never came back, like the bullies at school used to say. He wasn't abducted by aliens or kidnapped by the mob. He doesn't have another family and he isn't dead.

He's alive. I know he is. No one else thinks so, but I know.

Ma says not to sit around waiting for him. That I'll just be disappointed. She's afraid I'll be like him, that I'll get lost in magic and she'll lose me like she lost him. I promise her I won't get lost. Sometimes she believes me.

Sometimes I mean it.

It's been four years, six months, and seven days since he's been gone. I was eight years old then. That's also four years and five months since we left Brooklyn, and today we're moving back to Pop's old home in Echo City, Brooklyn. Ma says the James Family Brownstone, aka 52 Ricks Street, will go back to the bank if we don't. She taught me a nasty-sounding word, *foreclosure*. It's like *closed* but times *four* and with a *ure* at the end in case you didn't know that the word meant business. Ma says it means banks take your house when you run out of money. So now she wants to open up a café, which is her lifelong dream.

But she's still nervous about moving. She doesn't say so, only I can tell by how she's driving. Inching along the hot summer streets and peeking at signs like a cat. Sighing at every red light. Squinting out the window at the street corners and row houses. She keeps tapping angry fingers at Google Maps on her phone screen. She thinks she knows Brooklyn, but it's been a while.

"I don't understand," she says, frustrated. "This thing has us jumping all over the streets."

Ma pulls the car over and flicks on the hazard lights of our rental SUV. She takes the phone off the dash mount, fingernails clicking on the screen as she stares with photon-beam focus. Mom believes in the power of apps and phone maps to get us places. The one thing she isn't doing is looking out the windows. But that's okay, I'm looking out for the both of us.

"How did our blue dot just land us in the middle of the Brooklyn Navy Yard?" she says. "Does it look like we're in the middle of the Navy Yard? Oh, wait now . . . now we're in the East River? We are literally in a body of water?"

I'm waiting for the car horns to start blaring at us, like they usually do when we stop and check directions, but there's no one around at all. It's like we found this one abandoned block in Brooklyn. I see a stop sign. There's a word scribbled underneath.

MAGIK

It makes me smile. Brooklyn and magic have always gone together for me. When we lived here with Dad, our lives were full of magic. Tricks, shows, and convos about the all-time great magicians filled our home back then. Before Dad disappeared and we left Brooklyn, and magic along with it. And Ma got so sick and tired of magic she didn't even want to hear about it anymore.

Then I realize the word *magik* is under the stop sign for a reason. It's a message.

STOP
MAGIK

"Well. Would you look at that," says Mom.

"Yeah. I know. 'Stop magik' sounds like good advice to you, right?"

Mom looks at me like she has no idea what I'm talking about.

"No—well, sure, I guess, but King, look—"

Before she can point her finger, I see it.

Looming right there above us like an elephant on the sidewalk.

The Mercury Theater.

We're quiet for a moment. I'm not sure how Mom will react.

I don't even know how I'm reacting, honestly.

Most times, when you visit a place you haven't seen in years, it seems small. Not the Mercury. And for sure I've grown a ton since I was here. But somehow the old theater is as huge as it ever was. It's like the dinosaur of buildings. Bigger than everything around it, and from another time.

Mom takes a deep breath and I hear her tremble on the exhale. My heartbeat is jacked up quick like I just hit the fast-forward button a couple times. I remember how sad she was, back when Pop never came home that first night. When she filled out the missing person report. How we held each other and cried.

I wonder if she's going to hit the gas and drive off, like she did the day we left Echo City. Like when she stashed all the pictures of Pops and his magic shows in a box down in the basement. I wonder if she's going to make a comment that cuts about magic and fools and leaving things in the past.

But she doesn't do any of that.

She opens her door and just stands there in the heat. Taking it in.

I hop out of the car and stand next to her. She doesn't look away from the theater, but her hand finds my shoulder.

There's a hole in the dome of the theater, with pigeons flying in and out. There are carvings of vines and grapes all up and down the columns and in patterns surrounding the windows, elaborate, with carved birds here and there fluttering at the stems. There are two gargoyles with mouths open and fangs tilted to the sky at the foot of the dome, like they're trying to shout to the world about the fire. Even now, all these years later, you can see the charred marks of that blaze.

To look at the marquee, you might think the theater was just down for a week between shows. Random letters are scattered around like they're waiting to be reassembled and make sense. But look at the glass front doors and those rusty chains, and you know that the shows, the crowds, the magic are all a distant memory. The ticket booth is boarded up with cheap plywood that couldn't even keep out the rain. The underside of the marquee is lined with busted-out light bulbs with shards like the stalactites of a cave.

Ma takes my hand. Crazy how many things she can say with a touch—things like, *I miss him, too, We're going to be okay*, and *I love you* and *You still better not be thinking about doing magic.*

But she doesn't say a word. And believe me, Ma can talk when she wants to.

We just stand there, holding hands, at the last place in this world anyone ever saw my father alive.

MOM GIVES MY hand one last squeeze and I understand it's time to get back in the car and move along.

Only I'm not ready. I'm *here*—Echo City, Brooklyn, the Mercury Theater—and I think of all the times I've fantasized about this place, all the late nights of imagining the theater in EC, BK, like it was some land of make-believe. In school I'd zone out and sketch that dome in the margin of my notebook without realizing. I'd remember the gargoyles in different poses and the vine carvings circling the windows like snakes.

I drift closer to the theater doors and I see my own reflection in the glass. Black eyes like little hovering planets.

Long cheeks and a double dimple like Pops. Hair tight at the sides, growing in free twists up top, several inches in the air like a volcano midblast. I've got a quiet face, I've been told. It stares back from the glass.

"King? King!"

Just a peek, I'm thinking.

Maybe there's a phantom crowd in there. Maybe the ghosts relive that night we lost him, over and over, like I do in my head. Maybe Pop left me some bread crumbs to follow. Maybe he left me a sign. Something to explain why he had to go.

"King!"

I use my hand like a visor and press the side of my palm against the glass and all the sun vanishes. I can just make out the inside.

Some corner of my mind thinks, *Maybe he's there.* Waiting, all these years. To reappear like this was all an elaborate trick, like, *ta-da.*

It's dark in there. Crazy dark. And behind all that dark there's . . . nothing. A whole lot of it.

"King! Get away from there, let's go!"

"It's fine, Ma!" I call back. "I'm coming!"

I linger there for a cool second that drags into a cool

five seconds and just as I'm ready, sorta, to pull myself away, I think I see something.

A dark figure in a Prince Albert coat.

I nearly leap out of my shoes.

It's just the outline of his shape in the reflection. It's a man. But he isn't in the theater. It's almost like he's trapped in the glass itself. I can't see his face in the dark. Just the coat, buttoned beneath the breast and cut off just before the knees, like something straight out of an old-school magic poster.

Is that him? In a throwback magician getup? Is it Pops?

"King? What is it? Will you get away from there?"

I glance at my mom. Then I press back against the glass, cupping my hands around my eyes to block out the sunlight.

Only, I don't see anything but the dark anymore. I stare as hard as I can at the nothing until Ma has her hand on my shoulder again, not quite so gentle this time. She spins me around to look at her.

"King, I said let's go. What are you doing?" Her eyes are wide with worry.

"Nothing, Ma. I just wanted to see."

"See what?"

See him.

"Nothing," I say.

"Please don't tell me I'm making a huge mistake bringing you back here," she says.

"No, Ma. It's good. I'm good. We good."

"Come on, King. Get in the car."

She looks at me with that side-eye and headshake like, *Look at this kid.*

Nuts like his father.

As we drive away from the Mercury, I keep staring out the back window. The theater doesn't appear abandoned anymore—not exactly. Before, I thought the chains kept the world *out*, but now I think they keep something *in*. Something alive. As Mom takes a turn and the theater passes out of sight, I think the chains expand for a second like the ribs of a caged beast, breathing.

Now that we've found the Mercury, Mom knows exactly how to get to our old brownstone. A few quick turns and we pull up in front of the three-story town house. I haven't seen this place since I was eight. It's not how I remember it. Our stoop is overgrown with vines. We used to decorate the windows of the storefront "like a magician's Macy's," Pops would say. Now they're covered in old newspaper and the glass is cracked like spiderwebs. Tree roots carve up the sidewalk where my cousin Veronica used to school me at hopscotch.

The ground floor is a half-abandoned storefront. A rusty sign reads: SECOND SIGHT. A handwritten note is taped to a soiled window: Possibly on Vacation. There's a hodgepodge of locks on the door. Dead bolts, latches, chains, and a dozen or so knockers.

Mom sighs. "Well, we got three months to get this operation straight or the whole brownstone belongs to the Bank of Cities," she says.

"Sure, Ma, I know."

"And your uncles . . . ," she starts in. I've heard this one before.

"They're not really good at . . . *work*," we say at the same time.

"And 'Second Sight'?" Mom continues. "Is this a magic shop or are they selling eyeglasses here?"

"It's a reference," I say, and regret it right away.

"Do tell." Mom's eyes are wide.

I know I shouldn't explain. Mom gets tired of my magic history lessons. But I want to explain.

I close my eyes and speak extra fast. "Magician

Jean-Eugène Robert-Houdin's famous two-person mind-reading trick."

"Even a non-magic mom like me has heard of Houdini, you know."

"Not *Houdini*, it's Hou*din*," I correct her.

"So there's two *Houdies* now?" She chuckles.

"Houdini named himself after Houdin, that's all. He's only the father of modern magic."

"Why, thank you for the Kingsplanation." Her voice is dry.

"Yeah." I shrug. "I know stuff, is all."

"Yeah, you sure do. You even know a ton of stuff that *isn't* about magic. I'd love to hear about that stuff, too, sometime, how does that sound?"

"Sure, Ma." I do this sorta shrug-nod thing that Ma says looks like I got the hiccups.

"Welp, might as well try these knockers," she says, and taps one of the half dozen.

No answer.

I try my luck with a lion-faced knocker. The door rattles *rat-tat-tat*, with still no answer.

Ma spots a doorbell behind some overgrown ivy. But before her finger can find the button, the door swings open.

We're looking at the point of a sword blade.

Ma gasps.

A burnished-metal medieval helmet with grim eye slits glares from behind the curved blade.

"Aunt Nina?" a muffled voice echoes inside the helmet. "King?"

The warrior lowers the sword and raises the helmet visor.

It's my fourteen-year-old cousin, Veronica. Her soft brown eyes gaze at us. She pries the helmet from her head, which takes some effort, and shakes her hair out. Buzzed on one side and long the rest of the way around. Black with ash-blond streaks at the edges.

"I'm so sorry, I forgot you were coming today!"

"Veronica, if I may ask, you forgot we were coming, and you greeted us as if we were . . . *customers*?"

Veronica chuckles. "Oh. Those. Figured you were intruders. But customers—interesting. Suppose that's theoretically possible. Anyway, come in, come in! Experience the wonder," she says, oozing sarcasm.

My eyes adjust to the gloom as we enter a small room with red satin walls. It's all dusty. More like a museum than a shop. Masks and wands are set out on display. Shelves are lined with magic boxes, gag tricks, ornate coins, and top hats. I see a tuxedoed mannequin holding a fanned-out deck of cards. There's a set of fancy canes with brass handles in the shapes of different animal heads. Two taxidermy owls are mounted one on either side of a shelf: one perched, one in flight. There's photos of famous magicians on the walls. I recognize Dad's hero, Black Herman, as well as Jean-Eugène Robert-Houdin and the Martinka brothers, who opened the most famous magic shop in NYC. But this place is no Martinka & Company.

My Uncle Crooked Eye saunters into the room in an unbuttoned pink shirt with a greasy tank top underneath. His belly looks like it's made a nice home for pints of ice cream. He used to warm up the crowds for my pop with his Crooked Eye routine. He could move his wonky eyes in two different directions at the same time. He dubbed himself the "Ultimate Lookout."

I'm waiting for a trick to appear in his hand, or for his eyes to spaz out in whatever direction for a quick laugh. But he remains composed. "Nina! Darling, it's so good to see you."

"Heyward, it's good to see you, too," she says.

My uncle pauses. "Heyward," he repeats, like he's tasting the sound of it. "Well, I'll be, been years since anyone used my government name."

"Hi, Uncle Crooked Eye!" I announce.

His eyes roll around like a couple of cue balls until his pupils find me. Then they hit a split in opposite directions.

"Young King!"

He holds out a hand for me to slap and pulls me in for a hug. He crouches down and gives me a good once-over that lasts so long it's more of a twice-over.

"Well, well, looking more and more like him every day, Nephew," he says, almost to himself. Then he seems to remember that my mom is right there, and he buttons up like he didn't mean to mention Dad like that. "Except, you better looking, 'cause you look like your mama, too."

Mom chuckles at the lame attempt. "Smooth, Heyward."

She paces around the magic shop, eyeing the posters of old magic acts hung on the walls. There's an empty space between posters for Magician Mulholland and Okito the Great. Ma stops and stares.

"Now, I'm no detective," she says, "but how does dust settle on every inch of this place except for that perfectly rectangular bit on the wall right there?"

"Told you," says Veronica.

"That was Preston's poster, huh?" Ma asks Uncle Crooked.

I look to the empty spot on the wall and try to imagine my father's face there, drawn in full color like all those retro magic posters. I'm kind of disappointed that they took the poster down. I was looking forward to seeing King Preston the Great, at least in pictures, with that double-dimpled smile we share. Mom kept all our pics of Dad boxed up in the basement, where no one could see them. I wonder, *Doesn't anyone want to remember him?* Seems like even here in Brooklyn, in his old home in his hometown, folks want to pretend like he didn't exist.

Uncle Crooked tries to explain: "Well, Nina, thing is, we figured, you know, with you being away so long, that don't nobody want to be reminded of the past like that."

"It was discussed," says Veronica. "Whether to take it down or not. I thought you could handle it. I was overruled."

Ma smiles at Uncle Crooked. "Heyward, that's very considerate of you. But I'm okay. I can handle it. So can King. I mean, don't get me wrong, this place is heavy with the past. But we wouldn't have come back here if we weren't ready to face up to it," Mom continues. "My only question for you is—are you ready to let go?"

Uncle Crooked looks around the shop. He eyes every dusty trick, every old deck of cards with a look of love.

"Translation: he's not ready," says Veronica.

"How about you?" Mom asks her. "You up for helping turn this spot into the sweetest café in Echo City?"

"So ready, Auntie Nina. No offense, Uncle, but it's time to put this place to bed. Like, way past bedtime."

"Careful your father doesn't hear you talk like that," warns Uncle Crooked.

"Where is your brother? Is he around?" asks my mom, talking about my other uncle, Long Fingers, Veronica's father.

Veronica and Crooked Eye exchange a look.

"He's around," says Veronica.

"Let's just say he's attached to the . . . *magic* of this place," Crooked Eye explains carefully.

"Look, I get how much magic and this shop mean to you and your brother," says my mom. "But seriously, when was the last time you had a customer?"

"I can answer that for ya," Veronica says like she's about to enjoy this. She pulls a big dusty book from behind the counter and thumbs through the pages, half of them falling out of the binding. "Our last sale was March twentieth."

"Four months ago?" Mom asks.

"Actually . . . that was March twentieth of last year," Veronica says, looking more closely at the book.

Crooked Eye shrugs. "Was a good March."

"Heyward. It's time," says Ma.

Uncle Crooked sighs.

And I feel him. There's so much history in this store, these cards, books, and tricks. So many memories of Pop. Now Ma wants to clean him out of his old home. Like, I get that it's important to move on and all. But why does Mom have to be so good at it?

"Ma, can't we try and make the magic store work?" I ask. "I mean, maybe it needs a cleanup and to get some, you know, buzz or something?"

"Bees don't buzz that much," says Veronica.

"Thanks, Young King," Uncle Crooked says. "But your ma is right. In life, change is the one constant. Birth, death, life. Tide's in, tide's out. I appreciate what you're doing for us, Nina. I know you didn't have to come back here to save this place. But honestly, I can't imagine losing our home. On behalf of the James family, you have our thanks."

I touch the pocket watch that's hanging from my neck beneath my shirt.

It's a funny pocket watch that Pop left me. It's brass and old-fashioned and it goes all the way up to 13.

I touch it when I want to remember him.

Sometimes, I want to remember him most when I'm afraid he'll be forgotten forever.

MEET MY NEW room. Same as my old room.

I mean, literally the same room I grew up in.

Same mirror on the closet door as when I was eight.

There's something scary about mirrors. The way they make the world into more worlds.

My father disappeared into a mirror.

I know, that sounds weird. But it's true. I watched it happen and so did everyone else.

I knew in that moment that magic was real. Really real.

But then we moved out of Echo City and Mom started pretending that magic's not real. At school, they'd say that magic is not real. One time I got mad and told a teacher that I know magic is real, because my pop did magic and vanished through a mirror. Next thing I knew, Mom had to come meet the principal after school. I had to sit down with Gary, a counselor with curly hair and a beard, to "talk about my feelings." All we did was play chess, and I learned to pretend that Pops disappeared just like regular pops disappear.

Now that we're back in Brooklyn, I can stop pretending. I can be around my pop's folks, people like my uncles and V, who won't make me pretend and won't treat me like I'm crazy.

We're done moving in our boxes and stuff from the rental car, and Mom has lain down. I'm crazy restless and things are quiet—too quiet. I can almost hear the Mercury calling to me. I think about that figure in the Prince Albert coat in the dark, and I want to go back so bad it's like an ache in my neck. But there's no cool way to do it. No way to get out without Ma phoning missing persons for the second time in her life. No way to explore the city on my own.

So instead, I explore the house. Because if magic is hiding anywhere in this world, it's in a dusty old brownstone like this one, that's had a family of magicians living in it for decades.

In the kitchen, I find the wall where we used to mark how much I'd grown each year. I compare myself now to how short I was when I was eight. I've grown by about one full head—two if you count the twists in my hair. I was always on the tall side for my class, but not like Pop—he's the tallest of his brothers by far. When I first started growing out my twists, I liked how it made me taller, more like Pop.

The James Family Brownstone is basically how we left it. Most of the furniture is the same, but older. The one difference is that every spare space is stacked with books. Old books, new books, books with covers stripped off, books with crumbling bindings, or with titles so faded you can barely read them. Stacks and stacks of them load the hallways, windowsills, and half the upstairs bathtub. I'm searching the house looking for magic, and instead my neck hurts from holding my head sideways trying to read all the titles of these books on and about magic, like *Black Herman's Secrets of Magic, Mystery and Legerdemain*, and *The Fourth Book of Occult Philosophy*. The bookcase in the living room is also loaded with books, but here they're all ordered neatly, covering the entire back wall, floor to ceiling, with a rolling ladder like in a legit library. I scan the bindings—*Picatrix, Testament of Solomon*—and recognize one title in particular, *The Four Elements of Magic*, by Anonymous.

I remember Pops used to read that book so much, Mom would make comments like, "*The Four Elements of Magic*? Much as you read that book, more like *The Fourth Member of Our Family*." I wish I had asked Pops about the elements. Maybe I was just too young, or before he disappeared I wasn't as curious about magic.

Cracks run down the faded leather spine like the lines on my palm. I try to pull the book from the shelf but feel this strange tension, like a pair of fingers is holding the book from the other side. I pull against the resistance, and the book slides halfway off the shelf as a hinge somewhere inside the wall seems to move. I hear a crank and grinding of gears and at first I think I've broken something.

Then the entire bookcase rattles in its grooves and slowly turns inward, revealing an opening.

Wow, I think, and I wonder, *Was this always here?*

Did Pops use this passage, and I never knew?

I step into a small foyer that's the shape of a hexagon. There's the entrance to my back, the other side of the bookcase that closes behind me. There's a hallway in front of me. And on the four walls to my right and my left, there's nothing but pictures and clippings of Pop.

It's like a shrine. Three of the walls are dedicated to

his best tricks. There's Hooker's Vanishing Deck on one wall, the trick where he could make cards disappear and reappear, and that no one could ever figure out. There's the Skull of Balsamo—that creepy, hovering human skull with a brass jaw that could see into the past and speak to the dead. Then there's William Tell's Pistol, the act with the old-style handgun that shot a bullet Pop could catch like a fastball. The fourth wall is all clippings about his strange disappearance, and photos of the Mirror.

Looking at these walls, I realize how much Pop is missed. He's not just missed by that old, forgotten magic store out front—he's like the glue that held this place together. And I finally get to look at pictures of him. I scan every feature in every frame, looking for faces that I make and poses that I hit, too.

The doorway that leads to the hallway has an inscription hung over top:

THE FOUR ELEMENTS OPEN THE WAY.

I shrug. Guess I figured out that one on my own.

I walk through and there's some lived-in rooms. There's a sofa with a kitchen at the back.

Through another doorway, I find the jackpot.

Well, not *the* jackpot. But *a* jackpot. Not real magic exactly, but a real magician's workshop.

The walls are lined with shelves overflowing with screws, light bulbs, springs, bolts, crystals, bones, cigar boxes, magician's wax, bent cards, and old newspapers. Projects are everywhere. Half-finished or half-abandoned, depending on your point of view. Half-completed sketches. Over a half dozen moldy coffee cups. Neon lights in odd shapes cast a strange color across the room.

And my Uncle Long Fingers sits right in the center of it all, working on something that's covered beneath a giant tarp.

I stay quiet and watch him work, though I can't make out what's under there. Uncle Long still hasn't noticed me, he's so into his project, fingers bent around a screwdriver like spider legs. The focus he pours into the end of his working fingertips is a physical force. Probably has its own gravitational field.

Uncle Long Fingers has let himself go. He sports a matted 'fro like a shrub that needs a gardener. His bushy salt-and-pepper beard is speckled with crumbs. His body is soft and sunken as a beanbag chair. But his mind—you can see the intelligence, wild in his eyes like an electric storm.

I inch closer, trying to get a look at what he's working

with, what he's screwing or unscrewing or fixing or taking apart.

Something familiar catches my eye. A pocket watch dangles from a hook that's attached to a plaque. I look closer and realize it's just like the watch my dad left me—it goes all the way up to 13. There's a bunch of random letters scrawled on the wall above the plaque:

Ybbx Sbejneq naq Onpxjneq, Vg'f Nyy gur Fnzr

"What's up, Nephew?" His gruff voice startles me nearly out of my skin.

"H—hi, Uncle," I say, and wave a hand.

But waving at him is pointless. He still hasn't looked up at me.

"You lost?" he asks.

"No," I say firmly. My eyes fall back to the scrawl of letters that looks like total gibberish—or, I should say, the code. *Look Forward and Backward, It's All the Same*," I recite.

He strokes the crumbs from his beard and runs his fingers over the hodgepodge of letters like he's impressed. "You can decode those letters that fast?" he asks.

I reach for the chain around my neck and show him the watch.

"My dad taught it to me. He left me one just like the one you got here."

Long Fingers takes both watches in his hands and examines them together. "Well, I'll be. That's Preston's old watch, all right," he says with a whisper. Then he glances at me and recovers his gruff expression. "Never knew he gave this to you."

"He used to write me notes in that code to see how long it would take me to figure it out. He told me how time is just a construct of the mind. The ability to slow down and speed up time is the magician's greatest asset. A trained magician can see the smallest blink of an eye. The key is thirteen," I say, and point to the number 13 on the watch.

"Oh yeah?" He smirks. "So you got it all figured it out?"

"It's a simple code. You take a letter, and substitute it with another letter that's thirteen letters forward or thirteen letters back. You get the same letter whether you go forward or backward."

I grab a piece of paper and a pencil from his messy desk and write it out.

"So take the letter *A*, right? In the code, the letter *A*

is repped by the letter N, because an N is thirteen ahead of A," I say, scribbling down letters and numbers. "Or you can count thirteen back and start with Z. It's all the same. A is always N. It doesn't matter, because, *Look forward and backward . . ."*

"It's all the same." Long Fingers finishes the phrase. "Not bad, kid. Time is the key. Look forward and backward *in time."*

He reaches to the plaque and removes a wood-grain slat, revealing two circular sets of letters surrounding the clockface. Clearly, he made this plaque just to mount his or my dad's Watch of 13. The alphabet runs in two concentric circles around the numbers on the clockface, showing how the code works. The first set starts with an *A* over the 1 on the clock, the second set starts with an *N* over the 1.

"Wow, this thing has been around my neck for four years and I never knew that trick. My dad always made me do the math."

"I suspect that was part of your daddy's point. We came up with that little code back in the day, passing notes to each other. But you knew that phrase already. You didn't decode it that fast, did you?" he asks, genuinely curious.

I shrug with a wink. "Magician's secret."

But of course he's right.

"Okay, Nephew, color me impressed. You know the code, you figured out the bookcase and made it to my little lab here. So what brings you snooping around this old house?"

"Magic."

"Magic? Haven't you heard? We gettin' rid of that stuff so we can serve coffee and biscuits," he says with a bitter growl.

"I don't mean that magic. Not those tricks out there. Anyone with a few bucks can buy those. I mean real magic."

"What makes you think there's any such thing as real magic?"

"'Cause I seen it," I say. I give him a cold look so he knows what I mean.

"Ah. Yeah, well, I think you seen enough of that stuff to last a lifetime."

"No. I want to see more."

"Maybe you don't know what it is you want."

"Of course I don't know. How could I know? My ma doesn't want me talking or thinking about magic. She just wants me to be a normal boy. But I don't think there's any such thing as that, and if there was, normal boys don't see their fathers vanish into mirrors."

He shrugs. "Maybe not."

"I have questions, Uncle."

"Well, you can ask them, but just so we clear, that don't mean I got to answer them."

"Fine."

I want to ask about the Mercury and the figure in the Prince Albert coat—but I've made lists of questions, all for a moment like this, and a random one awkwardly jumps out at me. "If magic is real, why don't we magic the dishes clean every night?"

He laughs. "That's the best you got?"

"How come we don't magic the house out of fore-closure?"

He pauses and gives me a serious look. "Clearly, it doesn't work like that, 'cause you here with your mama, isn't that right, Nephew?"

"How come we don't magic Pop back?"

Uncle Long shakes his head and goes back to his work. "Go find your mama before I tell her you back here shoving wet fingers in electrical sockets."

"You can't say? Or you don't know?"

"I said *get*," he growls.

"Does that mean we can't do it? Or we can, but you don't want to?"

"Get!" he barks like an old dog about to bite.

I take a couple last looks at his workshop on my way out.

But nothing's floating, glowing, burning, shattering, reassembling, vanishing, or reappearing.

Just a bunch of broken-down parts and half-baked tricks.

No magic.

At least none that I can see.

5

THE NEXT DAY, Saturday, from the crack of dawn, Ma has her trusty vacuum cleaner humming. I call the machine Ole Betsy. Sounds like she's gargling lug nuts in a cast-iron throat, as usual.

I open my bedroom door to find Ma running Ole Betsy on the hallway carpet.

"Oh, King, good, you're up," she says.

"Huh?" I cup my hand to my ear.

Ma gets the idea and shuts off Betsy. "How'd you sleep?" she asks.

"Okay, I guess."

I see over her shoulder into her room. Her bed is

already made up all perfect, corners tucked crazy tight like they do in hotels.

"How about you?"

When Ma is worried about stuff, she likes to keep busy and work. That's how I know she must be worried. About the café or just being here with all these memories, I can't say.

"Wanna help make breakfast?" she asks.

We go from making breakfast with Uncle Crooked to cleaning the kitchen with V and waiting for Long Fingers to come down and eat (he never does) to clearing the table to unpacking all our moving boxes and right into boxing up the magic shop in those same boxes. It's tough for Uncle Crooked Eye, but Mom tries to be as gentle as she can. Uncle Crooked is at one point standing in the corner, arms full of tricks he can't possibly part with, like a kid clutching his favorite stuffed animals. Veronica gets him to demonstrate this trick where he blindfolds himself, and Ma and I are able to work.

By 3:00 p.m. it's scorching hot both inside and out. The AC unit chugs in the corner but isn't much help. We all retreat to the kitchen and break for a snack. But I'm still starving. Around 4:30 p.m., the air conditioner goes out. V and I make such a fuss about the heat that Ma lets me go out for some pizza. Veronica doesn't need to beg or even ask permission, but for some reason she does anyway, almost like she wants to. Ma makes a crack about how us "young ones can't take the heat" and gives me a couple bucks for a slice.

AT 5:00 P.M., when we get outside, the sun is still intense. Sunset is a long ways off on our block.

Looking around Ricks Street, I remember Pop all over this place. On our stoop with his collar open, in linen pants and a porkpie hat. Ma always called him "timeless." He didn't dress like anyone else on the block. He also didn't let me waste the day away on an iPad. Sundays were for learning magic. Coins, cards, watches, we'd sit outside and do it all. Pops knew everyone. I remember him by the gate asking the neighbors about their older folks (Mom would ask about the babies). I see the NO PARKING sign where my bike was stolen one time, and Pop just had to say a couple words to a couple people and, by the morning, the bike reappeared chained to that same post. I see the bodega where they'd save newspapers or flyers with Dad's shows.

The sidewalk is a patchwork of odd rectangles, from spackled gray to black tar to blond concrete, with sprouts of yellow grass in the cracks between. The gaps get even bigger by the trees, where the roots beneath crack the concrete and stone. I remember Pop would put a hand over those special stones, rising from the earth like the undead, and say, "There's more life under there. There's magic under there," with that wink like maybe he was joking.

I notice some words written in pink and yellow chalk on the concrete. They read:

Are you hurting?

Are you helping?

Am I hurting? Am I helping? The questions worm into my mind.

Then I realize I'm not exactly sure what the questions mean.

"Hey, V," I say, and point to the sidewalk. "You think that means *Are you hurting?* like, are you sort of hurting others, like other people? Or you think it means *Are you hurting?* like, are you in pain?"

She looks, reads, and smiles. "Maybe it's however you take it to mean. Like, it depends on the person."

We walk some more in silence and pass more faded chalk letters on the sidewalk, too faded to read. Veronica has a hand on her sore hip from all that work at the house. She was always older and bigger than me, but now she's a teenager and has, like, teenage muscles and this walk that makes me think she could beat me up if she wanted. I realize how little I know about her these days. If she was hurting about something, other than her hip, I'd have no idea what it was.

"Well, what does it mean for you?" I ask.

"It means both, I guess. If you're in pain, you're probably hurting someone else. And if you're helping yourself, you're probably helping others. But it's interesting, how everyone takes it different. How'd you take it?" she asks. "Like, what's the first thing you thought when you first read the questions?"

"Oh, I don't really remember."

"You don't remember? It was seven seconds ago. What was your first thought?" she asks.

"Um . . ."

"Your very first thought," she says rapid-fire, "right away—go!"

"Okay, well, honestly, my first thought, my very first thought, before I thought about what the words really mean, was, like, it's great being back here, but I miss Pop. And it hurts."

"Oh," she says. "Sorry."

"Yeah. It's okay. You asked."

"Lots of reminders of him?"

"Yup. Everywhere I look," I admit. "It's thick with him around here."

"Okay, well, let me ask you this. Are you helping?"

"Well, sure, I helped unpack and organize and—"

"No, I mean, are you helping yourself feel better about missing your pop?" she asks.

I open my mouth to answer before I realize I have no idea what to say. I want to say, *Why, yes, I'm helping in all of these helpful ways,* but I got nothing.

I say, "To be honest, I don't even know what helping would look like. Unless I went back in time and stopped him before he went through the Mirror at the Mercury."

"What?" she says, her eyebrows bent like crowbars. "No, I mean, helping yourself, like, to not miss him so much."

"How is that even possible? Like, I miss him. That's how I feel."

"Right, but we can help ourselves still, right? Sorta help ourselves not feel so bad about things we can't change."

"Only thing that would make me feel better is if he were here," I say.

Veronica wants to say something else, probably about accepting things the way they are, but I think my tone tells her not to bother.

"So what," she says, "you expect him to just appear out of thin air?"

I shrug. "He disappeared into thin air. Why not? I mean, V—you ever go by that old theater?"

"Why would I go over there?"

"I don't know. Is it really abandoned?" I ask.

"Well, I think there's some pigeons squatting in the hole in the roof. Does that count?"

"I mean . . . I don't know. It's stupid. Forget I said anything."

"Done. 'Cause you didn't say anything," she says, and looks at me like I've got five heads.

"What I mean to say is, does any magic stuff sorta happen over there? Or anywhere, in general, I guess."

Veronica laughs. "'Does any magic stuff sorta happen?'" She imitates me, but I know my voice doesn't sound that squeaky. "King, cuzzo, what sorta magic stuff are you imagining?" Now she's really cheesing.

I realize how close that smile is to mine, and Pop's.

"Why are you acting like this is some crazy question? Like, we know my pops vanished in a mirror. That's what

I'm imagining, V. Magic stuff like what we all saw with our own eyes."

Her smirk softens and her smile is genuine. "Listen, I feel for you, I really do. I mean, I was raised without my mom, and that's really hard sometimes. And my dad won't tell me anything about her, just that she didn't care enough to raise me."

"Ouch. That's what he says?"

"That's exactly how he says it, too." Veronica bites her lower lip and it disappears beneath her teeth. I remember how she used to make that worried face a lot when she was much younger. "But *her*—I miss her sometimes, is that weird? Like, how can you miss someone you can't even remember? But I do."

We walk in silence for a while, missing our missing parents.

But I'm also thinking about how she didn't answer my question.

I **REMEMBER WALKING** up and down Thurston Avenue with Dad. We had a routine. First the French Drop—a coffee shop with all these strange taxidermied animals mounted to the walls. It's another bodega now. Then we'd hit Harry's Handcuffs Hardware and buy what most people considered junk. Pops said it was a gold mine. He usually had a list from Long Fingers, always the weirdest stuff: doorknobs, mannequins, springs, fabric, circuit boards, old gutted TVs, car parts, even pigeons. The last stop was Not Not Ray's Pizza, best (and only) slice in Echo City.

Pop would explain how there's like one thousand Ray's Pizza places all around NYC. Famous Ray's, Original Ray's, Famous Original Ray's Pizza. So somebody opened a spot in Brooklyn called Not Ray's Pizza. So when Matteo Spinelli opened his spot in Echo City, he called it Not Not Ray's Pizza. To avoid confusion.

As we stroll the block, I see that Not Not Ray's has stood the test of time.

This place. I remember the heat-crust-and-cheese smell of the oven wafting outside. Smells so good it hits your toes. We enter and in the back there's dough being tossed in the air like flying saucers. But I can barely see Matteo Spinelli because there's this really tall kid there standing in the way. He's all rods and elbows, like scaffolding.

"Come on, Matty-o, just a couple of those pepperonis. I got you for them tomorrow."

The kid's voice sounds strangely familiar . . .

"First of all, my ginormous friend, it's pronounced *Matteo*," he says in a strong Brooklyn-Italian accent, "and you still owe me for the extra sausage from last week."

"Come on, Matty—*Matteo*—I'm a growing boy, my body needs those toppings."

"And my cash register needs that dollar fifty. Look at you, you've had enough toppings, you bang yer head in my doorway every other day."

"Yes, and that reminds me that you, sir, will be hearing from my personal injurious lawyer. Or I can accept a settlement of six to seven pepperonis on this slice right here."

"Next?" Matteo says to us. "Hi, Veronica. Can I help you?"

The tall kid turns around and I recognize his face. He lights up with a one-thousand-gigawatt smile.

"King! The King is back!" he shouts.

He holds out an open hand, fingers long as ski poles.

"Eddie?" I say.

"They call me Too Tall nowdays," he says.

I get a pain in my neck looking up at him.

"Oh yeah?" I say, blocking the light fixture from my eyes. "What they call you that for?"

"Um . . . ," he says, and taps a finger to his lips.

Then he sees my expression and busts out laughing.

"My man, Young King!" he says, and slaps my palm and pats my back. He holds my hand and looks at me like he's seeing a ghost.

My hand disappears inside his massive one like a coin trick.

Coin trick . . . Makes me think of something.

"Kingston?" asks Matteo Spinelli.

Matteo Spinelli is just as I remember him. The only

43

thing he liked better than pizza was a good magic trick. Show him one he hadn't seen, and you could snag a free slice.

"Matteo, you remember my cousin?" asks Veronica.

"Of course I do, Preston's kid. Welcome back!"

"Matteo, you still giving out slices for a good magic trick?" I ask him.

"I don't know, my friend. I haven't seen a trick in four years."

I have these trick white magician's gloves that Uncle Crooked Eye let me hold, since they fit me so well. I slide them out of my back pocket and pull them on. Too Tall Eddie's coins sit on the counter. I scoop them up in these white gloves and cup my hands over them and start shaking them like maracas.

"Eddie—"

"Too Tall," he corrects me.

"Too Tall, how much money was here before?"

"Two dollars, twenty-five cents," he says.

"Matteo, is that right?" I ask, still shaking the coins in my gloved hands.

"Yup. A dollar fifty short for a pepperoni slice."

Too Tall rolls his eyes.

Veronica, onto what I'm up to, winks at Matteo.

"Okay. Matteo, hold out your hands, please?"

I dump the coins into Matteo's palms.

The pizza shop owner counts the coins twice, three times, and nods, impressed, as he slides them into his register. "One pepperoni, coming right up, and a free slice for the young magician!"

Too Tall's eyes *wow* in amazement. He points a finger at my chest as a smile expands across his face. "You, my man, you are magic. You are a magical little individual."

"So, Too Tall—"

"King, you can call me Tall, for short," he says with a warm, pepperoni-filled grin. Too Tall, Veronica, and I are all sitting in a booth with our slices.

"I ain't calling you nothin' for *short*," I say with a snort.

"Good one!" he says.

Veronica shakes her head. "How did you two dorks survive without each other all these years?"

"That's a good question," Tall says, taking her words at face value. "I played a lot of basketball. Got going on my sneaker collection, and when I couldn't afford a slice at Not Not Ray's, I ate a lot of peanut-butter-and-honey sandwiches."

"Really?" I say. "Interesting. Honey, you say?"

"Honey." He nods. "Jelly is not a necessary condiment. The important thing is the sweet, mixed with the nut butter." He chef-kisses his fingertips.

"Well, how does this sound?" I suggest. "Jelly-with-cream-cheese sandwiches."

Too Tall's eyes go wide.

"On cinnamon-raisin bread," I add.

"Mind. Blown."

Veronica hits an eye roll strong enough to flip the checkered pizza table. "Okay, you two are the worst. I thought boy talk would be more interesting than this."

"Thought wrong, cuzzo," I say with a satisfying bite of Not Not Ray's finest.

"So what you been up to all these years?" asks Tall.

"Just, you know, going to school, and working on my magic."

"Working on your magic? Like, how you work on a jump shot?"

"Sorta like that, I guess."

"Like—magic *tricks*?" Tall asks.

"No, not stupid magic *tricks*." Veronica jumps in with eyes of mischief. "Real magic. Right, King?"

"What? No, Tall was right, magic tricks—"

Veronica goes on: "So what were you asking me about just now? About the Mercury and magic 'stuff'?"

"Well, yeah, that's different—"

"*Real magic*, right, King? That's what you were wondering about?"

I set my slice down on the wax paper and wipe the grease from the corners of my mouth. Too Tall's and Veronica's eyes are on me. I remember their faces from years before, how they used to look. Veronica's eyes were wider then, her cheeks chubbier, her smile was full of teeth too big for her mouth. Too Tall—we used to call him "Skinny Eddie"—and, well, there's about twice as much of him now. That was also a different me then, and I start thinking about time, and how different I was four years ago before the fire at the Mercury. Before Dad vanished. Before I knew for certain that magic was really real.

"I was asking Veronica about the Mercury Theater. Where they had the fire. Where my dad disappeared. I mean, you been around Echo City all this time. You ever seen anything go down over there?"

"Any *magic* stuff?" Veronica chimes in with that sarcastic grin.

Too Tall thinks this over. "You mean that old building with the big dome and those gargoyles?"

"That's the one."

"Well . . . this is going to sound weird, but . . ." Tall hesitates.

"Tall, my father disappeared through a mirror four years ago and never came back. You're not going to out-weird me."

Too Tall is startled to hear this. "What? What do you mean, *through a mirror*?"

This leaves me speechless.

I always figured that everyone knew that Dad was gone, but it never occurred to me that everyone might not know *how* Dad had gone.

Maybe the real story went around—but who would believe that?

"He's not lying," says Veronica, sincere for once. "I was there. Everyone saw it, right there onstage. Kingston's dad jumped in that creepy Mirror and was just *gone*. There was a big crash, and then that fire everywhere. Last time anybody saw him."

"Whoa," says Too Tall. "So when you left? Okay . . . Wow."

The expression on his face seems to work out a whole lot of missing information about a whole lot of missing years.

"So what were you going to say?" I ask. "About the Mercury?"

"Oh, the theater? Nothing. Just I heard, my one cousin told my other cousin and he told—"

"Told you?" asks V.

"No, he told this kid I ball with on the playground, and he told my closest cousin, who told me that one of those gargoyles ate a pigeon one time. But you were right. Your story, that's way weirder."

"A gargoyle ate a pigeon?" I ask.

"Well, either that or the pigeon just flew away. The details get lost in translation. But go back to the part about your pops and the Mirror. I'd heard that he got a show in Vegas and you guys all left, after the fire."

"Who told you that?" asks Veronica.

"One of my cousins. I can't remember which one." Tall shakes his head. "*Man*, I'm sorry to hear you had to go through that. You ever think he might come back? I mean, if he could disappear, why not reappear, you know?"

Veronica nods. "I think that's why he was asking about the Mercury. Is that right, King?"

"Yeah," I admit. "I mean, he's a magician, right? And all magicians' great tricks have a finale. It's called the Prestige, where they show the audience the card they pulled, or—"

"Or the rabbit they pulled out of the hat?" Tall chimes in helpfully.

"Sure. There's that moment when the audience is wowed and the magician—he stands there and takes a bow. And there was this old magician named Black Herman. He did this trick where he'd bury himself alive and then, three weeks later, folks would buy tickets to watch him dig himself out, then follow him to the stage for a show. And he was one of my pop's heroes. I just can't help but think maybe . . ." I let my words trail off. For some reason I can't bring myself to say the rest out loud.

Veronica steps in. "Maybe this is a disappear-reappear trick, with a four-year delay on the Prestige?"

Hearing her say the words makes me wince. I look at Too Tall, though, and he doesn't think it sounds so strange.

"Maybe your father's doing the Black Herman move?" he suggests.

"Maybe?" I say.

"Well, there's one way to find out, li'l King. Now, I'm as creeped out by burnt-up old-timey theaters with daddy-stealing mirrors as anyone, but let's go check this place out, and see if there isn't a magic Pops waiting to appear onstage."

"For real?" I say.

"For reals. Tired of running these fools in pickup games at the playground all day anyway. Plus, it's too hot for that mess. Let's go check out this theater."

I'm looking at Veronica. I expect her to shoot down our stupid idea and send us back to Ma.

But instead she says, "Hey, tall guy, let me ask you something. Are you hurting, or are you helping?"

Too Tall is confused by her question. "I have hurt exactly no one. Why? What have you heard?"

Veronica shrugs and says to me, "I don't know, King. He sounds guilty about something."

Too Tall looks bewildered. He turns and says to me, "King, what is she talking about?"

"Somebody wrote *Are you hurting? Are you helping?* on the sidewalk by our house," I say. "And now she's asking people, I guess?"

"You were the one obsessed with it," V grumbles.

"I'm helping!" Tall insists.

"I believe you," I say to Tall.

"Good. You should," he says.

"How about you, V?" I ask. "You helping, or hurting? Are you coming, or staying?"

She holds up her hands in surrender. "You gonna finish that crust before we go or nah?"

WE'RE UNDER THE marquee in front of the once-majestic entrance of the Mercury Theater. The chains roped around the doors seem to grind and tighten. The shade beneath the sign feels like the sort of gloom where ghosts gather. The shattered glass bulbs hang above us like they could drop at any moment. I step up to the glass and peer through. I'm looking for that figure in the Prince Albert coat. All I see is darkness.

"One thing I never understand is creepy gargoyles," says Too Tall. "Like, why would anyone put those crazy-lookin' demon-monsters up there in the first place?"

I look up to the stone-carved creatures. Their eyes

are round and bulging above snarling fangs and forked tongues, long like frozen snakes. "I don't know," I say.

"I like them," says Veronica.

"You do?" asks Tall.

"Yeah. They look like they dine on human hearts or something," she says like that's a good thing.

"Just what I was thinking," Too Tall mumbles.

I'm waiting for one to spring to life. "Maybe they're supposed to be, like, guarding something."

My eyes then drift to the random letters left splashed on the marquee. Something feels off about them.

"Why do you suppose those letters are like that?" I ask.

Veronica squints up. She reads, "*O-E-V-P-X . . . J-N-Y-Y . . .* Seems pretty good and nonsensical to me."

"Yeah. I mean, isn't that weird?" I say. "Shouldn't it say something like 'Magic Show,' but with letters missing?"

"Like, 'Mgi how'?" says Tall.

"Yeah. Or something. I mean, why those letters?"

Veronica stares at the sign. "Like, I can't tell what the sign ever said. Strange, since the theater hasn't been touched since the fire."

"Exactly," I say. "It's almost like somebody got up there and put those letters—specifically those letters—like that. I wonder? Nah, it's too crazy."

"You wonder what, King?" says Veronica.

"*Look forward and backward, it's all the same,*" I say, almost to myself.

"Um, you want to try making some sense to us here on the planet Earth?" says V.

"There's this code my dad taught me. In fact, your dad told me they came up with it together."

"You talked to my dad?" Veronica asks, astonished.

"Well, yeah. I found his workshop, you know? And he had this watch there." I take out the pocket watch from around my neck. "It goes up to the number thirteen, just like mine."

Tall and Veronica check out the numbers going all the way around.

"It's kind of cool, how it looks like a normal watch face, then it's like, no, the numbers go to thirteen, not twelve, and that knocks the three, six, and nine off-center," says Too Tall.

"See, thirteen—it's like half of twenty-six, the number of letters in the alphabet. So to crack the code, you take the numeric value of each letter, and either add or subtract by thirteen. Then that's the decoded letter. Make sense?"

"Not really," says Tall.

"And your father taught you this?" asks Veronica.

"Well, yeah. You ever see that watch to thirteen your dad has in his workshop?"

"Honestly, I never go in there. Like, never."

"My pops used to write me notes in the code," I say, and I take in the random letters on the marquee once more. "Anybody have a pen and paper?" I ask.

"We're in the middle of the street, dude, not class," says Too Tall. "I got a phone, that help?"

"I don't think so. Think I need to draw on something."

"How about this?" Veronica digs in her pocket and comes up with two ground-down sticks of chalk, one pink, one yellow.

"Okay, wait a minute . . . ," I say. "*You* write that stuff on the sidewalk?"

She shrugs. "Keeps people honest."

"Okay, wow. Well, why didn't you say anything?"

"It was fun watching you think it through when you thought it was a message from beyond. Now come on, cuz, show me this code."

I take the chalk and draw a circle on the sidewalk. I don't think anyone will mind. Then I imagine the circle like my watch and put the number 13 at the top, and draw each number counting all the way around. "Okay, so here's the Watch of 13. With me so far?"

"Right there with you," says Tall.

"Then you go around with the alphabet," I continue, and I write an *A* beside the 1, a *B* beside the 2, and all the way to the *M* beside the 13.

"Okay," says Tall, "looks like you ran out of numbers for letters."

Veronica smirks like she's getting it.

"Right, then you finish the alphabet around the circle like this," I say, and keep writing another row of letters around the last row. So now the *A* has an *N* beside it, the *B* has an *O* beside it, all the way to the *M* that has a *Z* beside it, above the number 13. "The code works where you just sub one letter for the one beside it. So the first letter on the marquee is *O*, so sub that with a—"

"*B!*" Tall says, looking

at the sidewalk drawing, and he shoots a fist up like he hit a buzzer beater.

"Not bad, cuzzo," says Veronica. *"Look forward and backward."* She repeats the phrase I mentioned earlier.

"It's all the same," I say. "Right. If you go clockwise or counterclockwise, the code letter is thirteen letters away, forward or backward. It's all the same."

"Okay, okay, I like this now," says Tall. "Next?"

We decode the rest of the letters, and Too Tall types them up on his cell phone as we go.

O = B
E = R
V = I
P = C
X = K

As the first word begins to form, my fingers tremble with adrenaline.

O-E-V-P-X from the marquee becomes *B-R-I-C-K.*

"Brick," says Veronica.

"Brick?" says Tall.

"Brick," I repeat. "Well, it makes more sense than *oevpx*, anyway. Let's keep going."

The last four letters:

J = W
N = A
Y = L
Y = L

W-A-L-L.

"Looks like we've hit a brick wall," Too Tall cracks.

"Ba-dum-bum," says Veronica.

I stare at the words Too Tall has typed up on his screen.

"This is crazy," says Veronica. "I mean, you realize what this means?"

"That someone who knows the code put those letters up there like that? Yeah, V. That's, like, all I can think of. I mean, the only people who know that code are my father and yours. And Crooked Eye, I suppose."

"That we know of . . . ," says V.

"True . . . But then, what's this message mean?"

"Has to mean something," says Veronica.

I pace and tap a finger to my skull.

"Does putting your finger on your head really help you think or nah?" asks Veronica.

But I ignore her.

Brick wall . . . Brick wall . . . must be a reference . . .

"Got it!" I shout. "It's a trick!"

"What's a trick? It's not really a brick wall?" says Too Tall.

"Sorta. It's a classic Houdini trick. Houdini's Brick Wall. He'd fool the audience into thinking he'd walked through a solid brick wall by escaping through a trapdoor covered by a carpet in front."

And there I see it—a little ways down from the chained-up doors, there's a moldy old rug lying by the exterior wall.

I rush to it and throw it back.

There's a small chute tunneling under the theater.

"Pop," I whisper.

"You're not for real going down in there, right, King?" Too Tall asks in a shaky voice.

By the time he finishes his question, he's got his answer.

I slide in, feetfirst.

The light from the summer city day vanishes as I plunge down the throat of the chute.

THE CHUTE TAKES me down a ways, then switches directions, like gears somewhere have moved the chamber around. There's a sudden drop directly down, and I finally land in absolute darkness.

I call out to Veronica and Too Tall.

I hear bodies sliding down the chute above me, and muffled yells. Gears move again from the upper levels. I step out of the way, hoping they'll come after me, but they never show.

Then it's quiet again.

I wonder if the chute took them somewhere different.

Wish I had Tall's phone.

Wish Ma had let me have a phone already.

Wish I had light, I mean any sort of light.

And eventually, I think, *What am I even doing here?*

I shout some more for Tall and Veronica, but my words seem to bounce right back, like wherever I am, there's layers of hard, old metalwork that likes sound about as much as it likes light.

I turn and try to climb back up the chute, but the opening is closed now. I press my fingers against the grime of metal and there's no give.

It seems there's only one way to go, and that's forward.

Once, I would have been so psyched to be in the bowels of the Mercury Theater, free to explore. But this dark is so dark it's *weird*. I hold my hand out in front of my face, waiting for my eyes to adjust and hoping to make out the shape of my fingers—the fingers I know are right there . . .

But nothing. I can't even see my own hand.

So I walk, and trust—no, hope—that my outstretched hand will stop anything from hitting my face before my face hits it.

The floor feels uneven beneath my feet, gravelly and dusty. I kick something squishy and hope it doesn't have fur, a tail, and a heartbeat. I blink and blink and begin to see things. Or think I see things.

My hand hits something. An old metal rod, by the feel of it—rusty, but sturdy, like a fire escape. It's hovering at about eye level. I give the rod a good shake, and the structure it's attached to rattles. I reach up higher and find another rod—or, rung—to the ladder I'm pretty certain I've just discovered.

I climb up, trusting, hoping the next rung will be there as I reach, one at a time, up to an old wooden trapdoor, and I heave my shoulder into it. The hatch opens and light spills in, and I'm backstage at the Mercury.

A sunbeam slants through the hole in the roof above like a spotlight. The rest of the dome is in darkness. A pigeon passes through the light from outside and casts a long, bat-like shadow. It flaps into the heart of the dome and vanishes. Suddenly a chorus of flaps sets off, one after the other, fluttering in fury and echoing like the old theater is a bat cave.

I look around. There's no color anywhere. Just long shadows that ripple and breathe. Ash layers everything, gray and bumpy like I imagine the surface of the moon. I remember backstage, how it once was. The endless velvet curtains that hung. The spiderweb of ropes that were strung up on pulleys to the rafters, all of them gone. There's a set of old levers where a stagehand could, I guess, work the pulleys and traps that once made the show go on.

I make my way to center stage and look out at where the audience would be. The auditorium is stark and still as an old black-and-white photograph. Rows of seats line the walls all around like a cylinder up to the dome. They watch like frozen spectators—or *specters* . . . I wonder why those two words are so close. Is it because what ghosts really do is watch?

But I can hear something. Not sure what it is. Like the phantom of a thousand sounds that never died all the way out. Applause, overtures, whistles, shouts all pour down.

I see the seat in the front row where I sat the last time I ever saw my father.

I think of my father standing right here, and imagine what he looked out on before he vanished. The hundreds of astonished faces. His brothers. Mom. Me.

Something tells me to *turn around* and there's something that wasn't there before.

I think—*There's people behind me*—

But no. It's a mural on the back wall. My father and the Maestro are squared off in graphic, bright colors.

There's a strange backdrop. A dark landscape with mist

rolling over end-of-the-world cliffs. A branch of lightning splits clouds that billow in midstorm. Even the pitch-black empty spaces have depth, like I could step inside and walk there forever.

Pop is in his all-black suit, hands summoning light. I see myself in his face. There's my cheekbones, my dimple. I raise a hand, almost to say *Hi*.

My stomach grows cold when I look over at Maestro.

The magician's half-mirrored mask covers the left side of his otherwise plain face. Eyes like he's peering into a universe that's darker than the one we know.

I hate him.

It's his fault my dad's gone.

Pops disappeared going after Maestro. Vanished into the same Mirror before it shattered on the stage.

It was all set to be an amazing night. Magic Duel of the Century. I was there, in the audience, just eight years old. The memory feels new. Maybe not like it was yesterday but last week at the latest. The best and brightest of Echo City were there. Brooklyn glitz and style and swagger, all enchanted like.

But it went bad.

Pop—he owned the crowd with his routine. His floating light bulb trick. His vanishing, reappearing cards that no magician could ever figure out. That old creepy skull he had that let him read people's thoughts.

Then Maestro's turn. His assistant rolls out three large cabinets. Urma Tan, with eyes like frost and blond hair so pale it's almost white. Dressed in all black, with red fingernails long and curling like small serpents. They do Maestro's famous teleportation trick, where he would vanish Urma Tan from one cabinet to appear in another.

But then Maestro revealed his new trick. Urma Tan wheeled out the Mirror.

The Mirror was set in an elaborate carved-wood frame with a serpent eating its tail at the top, but the glass was what stood out to me. The surface didn't just reflect the world. It *was* another world, if that makes sense. The audience reflected in the Mirror was us, but wasn't us. It moved less like how a reflection moves and more like how a shadow moves, just a step behind its maker.

Maestro was looking into it like he was obsessed. Like he had forgotten all about the audience. Dad looked worried and I knew something was wrong.

Then Maestro walked toward the Mirror. Some energy was surging from within. A blue light appeared deep within the glass that grew and glimmered like a star.

Then Urma Tan dove into the Mirror.

You expected a crash, but she was gone. Just like that, without a sound.

It seemed like part of the act at first. The audience was impressed.

But Maestro looked devastated. Then he dove in right after her. Headfirst, like into a swimming pool. I braced myself for the crash, but again none came. He was just gone.

A beam of blue light flashed from the depths of the Mirror and shined somewhere backstage, behind the curtain. Sparks popped from the Mirror in every direction. The Mirror spat them out like sunflower seeds. They popped like exploding coal on the velvet curtains. The fire flared and spread.

And then, faster than I could think, like his mind had long been made up, Pop glanced to me and Mom with the faintest magical wink and jumped in after Maestro.

And he was gone, too.

Then the Mirror crashed to the floor in a thousand pieces.

I SLIDE MY feet along the dusty stage and think about the shards of glass. There's still black burn marks on the floor from the fire, but no glass. Not even glass dust. Someone must have come and swept it up. Maybe whoever painted that mural? Who would take the time to do something like that, paint a mural with so much care and detail where no one would ever see it?

And really, who would rearrange the letters on the marquee?

Wind gusts through the hole in the dome and swirls debris on center stage. The hairs along my arm tingle. I think about the Mirror and I make out the shape of a trapdoor on the stage floor. I clear the dust and ash with big sweeps of my feet. Magicians were famous for using these kinds of trapdoors in stages for all sorts of tricks. With this and the one I came down, the Mercury must be full of them. I give the stage a few stomps, then remember the levers backstage.

I jet over to them and pull every lever there—the up ones down, and the down ones up.

I hear the sound of old hinges grinding and the slap of the wooden hatch opening.

There, on center stage, the trapdoor hangs open.

I hustle over to it. Thinking, *What if it was all a trick? Like Black Herman's burial?*

What if he's just . . . been down there *all these years?*

Just as I'm starting to worry about how he's been eating, and am wondering if he's starving or a skeleton or what, I peer down into the open hatch.

The sunbeam from the hole in the roof has a pink-orange glow. It hits just the right spot to light up the chamber below. There's an old Houdini-style trunk, like the ones he used to chain himself up in and pop out of moments later.

I hop down and barely feel the impact on my feet.

Sure, the chest is a little small for a whole person, but Dad is a great magician and could fold himself up and I'm sure he's fine in there . . .

I knock on the old wood and say, "Dad? Dad? It's me." I try not to be distracted by how I don't hear anything in response or by thoughts of how anyone could actually be alive after all these years. I just focus on *how to get this old thing open.*

There are chains wrapped around the trunk and an old padlock. The chains are just for show, I'm sure—the lock is the key to getting the thing open. The padlock has four rotating rings of digits, requiring a four-digit code. Then I see, carved into the wall above the chest, some familiar letters:

Ybbx Sbejneq naq Onpxjneq, Vg'f Nyy gur Fnzr

The same letters from the Watch of 13 plaque in Long Fingers's workshop. *Look forward and backward, it's all the same.*

Forward and backward, it's all the same . . .

My fingers trembling, knowing this *has* to be a message *meant for me*, knowing what the numbers are as I flick the padlock to 1 . . . 3 . . . 1 . . . 3 . . .

Forward and backward, it's all the same.

The numbers that you count forward and backward on the Watch of 13 are . . .

13, 13!

The padlock clicks open. My hands are a blur as I strip the chains from around the chest, open it up, thinking, *Pop, I'm coming, Pop!*

But there's no person inside the trunk.

When I come to my senses, I am relieved he's not actually in there. I mean, he would be a four-year-old skeleton if he were.

There's just one small thing at the bottom of the trunk.

It's a box.

Just a box.

It *is* a nice box.

Mahogany, well made. Each side has a carving on it. A deck of cards on one, a pistol on another, a skull on the third side, and a square on the fourth. The designs are elaborate, with swirls and flourishes like the box was made way back in the day. But unlike this old theater, the box hasn't aged at all. There's no dust, no scratches, no nicks, or any damage at all. I try to open it but there's no give. The thing feels solid as a log.

I don't know how long I spend turning the box over, examining it, prodding it, and thinking about how to get in. There's a complicated brass piece connecting the top of the box to the body, and it looks like some kind of locking mechanism. There's a circular opening that reveals layers of gears within, like the inside of a clock.

After a quick hesitation, I rotate the top and it moves real smooth, like somebody just hit it with WD-40. As the hole in the top of the box turns, the gears on the inside follow, and those curved brass bars oscillate around and around until the segments all align to form another circle just within the box. A number is revealed in brass in the recesses of the gears that you couldn't see before: 13. I judge the size of the circle that the curved brass bars just formed and . . .

Could it be?

I take the pocket watch out from around my neck and set it in the circle, just over the brass number 13. It fits like the last piece of a jigsaw puzzle.

There's a *click* as the lock releases and the clock hands start moving. The lid of the box parts like lips about to whisper.

Pop, I think. *You wanted me to find this.*

OR DID HE, *though?*

My blood is pounding, like I can feel my pulse with each tick of the clock hand running the circle of numbers, all the way into my fingertips as I raise the lid of the box.

I warn myself not to get carried away.

Maybe other people know about the Watch of 13.

Long Fingers knows.

Others must know.

But another voice says, *This is a message from Dad, he's reaching out to me, from wherever he is, like I always knew he would—*

Then I snap out of it as what's in the box comes into focus.

There's a sheet of paper, but not like you'd see at school. It looks old, like something in a museum.

And it's floating.

Right in the center of the box, hovering like a hummingbird in midair.

I'm looking for the strings, the magnets, the part that would explain *how this is possible*, but there's just this levitating piece of folded-up paper.

I'm scared to touch it. What if it's some kind of trap? Who knows who's been here since my dad disappeared?

I try to slow my thoughts and take in my surroundings. It's a small space, the sort of spot a magician might hide in after they've disappeared onstage. The box isn't hidden behind some fake wall or bookcase. It's right here in the open. How has nobody found this thing? Or maybe they have, and I'm just the first one to figure out how to open it?

The first one to come here with this Watch of 13.

So maybe, I think, *whatever is in this box* is *meant for me.*

And I wonder what the paper says. I *have* to see what's on it.

I snatch the page out lightning quick, and then wait a moment with my eyes shut for spikes to fly from the wall or a giant boulder to crush me from above.

When nothing happens, I open the paper to reveal a map.

Looks like a map of Echo City, drawn by hand.

Just a map.

No *X*s marking any spots.

I reach my hand back into the box. I feel around the felt-lined bottom and corners for vents or magnets or strings or something to explain the hovering map, and I hear—

"*Yooo—*"

And somebody crashes into me.

A sudden blue light flashes from the box and fills the trap like a light bulb popping.

My face hits the floor. The light hurts my eyes. The box is stuck underneath me. I feel like I just took a clown-size shoe to the back. There is a body on top of me. So much body it can really only be one person.

"King?" Too Tall says, relieved to see it's me. "Wha—what happened? I'm sorry, my dude, you okay?"

Too Tall's words sound distant. The wind is knocked out of me. It takes a few breaths for everything to come back into focus. I try to push myself up, but my left hand is *stuck in the box.*

How is that even possible?

Too Tall is saying, "Am I glad to see you! We went down that chute after you and next thing I know, I'm totally lost and alone. No you, no Veronica. Wandering around, like, man, this place gives me the creeps. And then—I see this mural, I'm backtracking and *wham* I fall down a hole in the stage! But you already knew that. Need a hand?"

Too Tall is on his feet in a crouch, offering to help me up.

I yank my hand from the box to take his—

—and it's gone—

Too Tall's mouth opens but he doesn't make a sound.

My left hand is gone.

There is nothing there.

There's no stump. No bones. No blood. Just no hand. There's a faint blue glow where my wrist ends and the rest of my hand has vanished, like it's been erased. It's like those Bunsen burners from science class, just a blue vapor and then nothing.

But I can still feel my hand.

Can't I?

I hold it up to my face but I just see Too Tall, jaw hanging on for dear life.

"Th-th-there's no . . ." His words come out at half the speed as normal.

"*Shh,*" I say, holding a finger to my lips. I realize I can actually feel my finger against my lips.

I can't see my hand, but I can feel it?

"*Shh*?" Tall repeats. "Why *shhh*? You don't have a hand and you're worried about me talking?"

"Sorry! I just didn't want to hear the words *don't have a hand.*"

"What else is there to say right now? What other words of all the words would I say? You don't have a hand!"

"I—I—" I close my eyes.

Calm. Breathe.

Just because Tall is saying I don't have a hand and I don't exactly *see* a hand at the end of my wrist doesn't mean I don't have a hand. Maybe if I open my eyes, I *will* see my hand, and Too Tall and I were just hilariously mistaken . . .

I open my eyes. No dice. No hand. No hand at all.

Then I realize—Too Tall is by himself.

"Wait—where's Veronica?"

"I don't know, dude, I was saying before. We all got separated at the chute."

"You think she's okay?" I ask.

"Dude—is *she* okay? Are *you* okay?"

"Am I?"

Am I okay? I repeat in my head. And then again, *Am I okay? Am I?*

"I don't know, Tall. This is beyond insane." I stare at the empty space that my hand used to occupy.

"Bananas," he says. "King. What happened?"

I catch my breath and tell him about the chest all chained up, about the code and the box.

"This box here," I say, and reach for it on the floor. First with my right hand. Then I decide to try to pick it up with my left, my ghosted hand. I grab the box and the sensation of my fingers is there. Thumb, pointer, pinkie, and the others—I can feel them all. The wood is smooth and dense and the metal of the Watch of 13 lodged in the lock is cool.

I glance over at Too Tall and realize by his horrified look that to him the box appears to be floating in the air by the end of my wrist.

"H-how are you doing that?" he asks, spooked out of his mind.

"I—I don't know. I mean, I'm just holding it. But I can't see my hand. I can feel it—I just can't see it."

"That makes two of us."

I offer the box to Tall. He hesitates to take it.

"What?" I ask.

"I don't know. That box cost you your hand," he says, taking a step back into a corner of grime. "So you found a strange box in an abandoned theater and thought, hey, let me just shove my hand in there?"

"It's not just some strange box. Well, maybe it is, but Tall, I'm thinking my dad wanted me to find this box. I mean, it was the watch he left me that opened it."

"Your dad," says Tall. "The one that disappeared?"

"Yeah . . ."

"That vanished? Ghosted? Went and got *gone*?"

"Yeah," I say, my voice shrinking.

What if the rest of me disappears, too? What if the hand is just the beginning? What if this is what happened to Pops?

In all my fantasies of coming to the Mercury, of reliving that night Pops disappeared, it's always me who stops Pop from vanishing. *I'm* the one who brings *him* back. Never, not once, did I disappear, too.

But Pop vanished and *so could I.*

"Stay with me, King," Too Tall says.

"I—I'm trying, but what if I can't help it? What if I go, too?"

"Don't talk like that. You feel strange? You feel, I don't know, vanish-y?"

"I don't know. I don't know what that feels like. I want my hand back. I'd feel better with my hand back."

"I hear you. But the rest of you. Still here, yeah?"

I put my hand to my face—lips, eyes, cheeks—then the rest of me. Neck. Elbows. Chest. Everything checks out. My heart, beating like a jackhammer. My tummy, turning with the grease from the pizza.

"Everything else's where it's supposed to be," I say.

Tall takes my wrist, braves the weirdness of it, and plants his very visible palm into my vanished one. Our palms collide with a *pop*. His fingers collapse around my phantom knuckles. He's gripping my hand—but we can only see his, alone, like a pantomime handshake.

"You still here, King," he says, "you still here all right."

NEW VOICES CRASH into the theater. They hoot and echo in chaos and I can't make out what they're saying. The theater suddenly sounds like a playground at recess. Could be anywhere from six to twenty noisy kids running down the aisles.

Too Tall's eyes go wide, like, *What now?*

Then a thin, commanding voice slices through the noise above like a razor blade.

"Spread out," it says. "Find them."

And just those words ghost all that ruckus. Footsteps rush down the aisles toward the stage.

I wonder, *Did they get in through the front doors?*

Or the chute?

And I remember that I left the code written out on the sidewalk in chalk. Could they have figured out how to read the code and found the brick wall?

I turn to Too Tall in panic. I open my mouth to say something about the code but he puts a finger to his lips.

I nod and keep quiet as a church mouse.

But I look at the sunbeam from above that spotlights center stage and realize it won't matter. This trap will be the first place they look.

And I remember those white magician's gloves that Crooked Eye gave me.

I take them out of my backpack and slide one on my ghosted hand. I worry again for a moment that the hand is really gone, but the glove fits right over it and you'd never know . . .

What? That you don't have but sorta still have a hand? That Ma is going to be like, "King, I know I gave birth to a kid with two hands. Now what in god's name have you done with the other one?"

I tell myself to breathe.

To *calm down.*

And after a couple deep breaths I think, *How did*

these kids just happen to show up now? I get a bad feeling that this is no coincidence. They could have been hiding nearby, waiting for me to find this box. They could even know I have the Watch of 13. The timing is too close together. So I slip the box into my backpack and strap it on my shoulders.

"Uh-oh, King," says Tall.

There's a kid sitting in the open trapdoor with his legs dangling above us. He has a pair of intense green eyes, and he looks *rough*.

There's a scar etched across his neck like a barbed-wire choke collar. He's a little older than me, definitely a teenager, but beyond that I couldn't tell his age. Maybe it's the strange lighting, or the dust and ash surrounding us, but his face is this gray color that looks barely human. There are scars on his cheeks, scribbled symbols like doodles you sketch in the margins of your math textbook. His pupils are tiny pinpricks in the bright meadow green of his eyes. He smiles like a creature that doesn't smile but has heard about smiles.

He holds out a hand. His boys gather around. They all have that strange ash-gray color to their skin, like you can't even tell if they're black or white or what.

"Give me the Lost and Found," he orders.

I'm speechless. I don't even know what he's talking

about. *Does he want the box? Did he see me put it in my backpack?* I can't say for sure.

"Get outta here, Mint," says Too Tall. He tries to puff up his chest but his voice is shaky. "How about *you* get lost . . . and found."

Mint makes a *tried-this-the-easy-way* face and simply says, "Smoke them out."

I hear the flick of a light and something metal lands in our chamber and bounces around, hissing. Too Tall and I watch as two cola cans with lit fuses roll to a stop on the floor between us, spitting out sparks like makeshift smoke bombs.

"Who walks around with *smoke bombs*?" Tall shrieks before covering his face with his fitted cap.

The cans unleash clouds of smoke that flood the trap. I try to cover up, but smoke streams through my fingers and eyelids, tears stinging my face. I squeeze my eyes shut in blinding pain.

"We got to get outta here!" Tall coughs.

"Now come up," I hear Mint's voice. "Or I'll shut this trap and let you two steam like a couple lobsters."

"Okay," says Tall. "You win, let us out!"

I hate to admit it, but he's right. We're helpless down here, both of us.

"Take my hand," Mint says as I blindly reach up for it. "Closer," he says, "closer," until I feel his stiff grip. He pulls me up and out of the trap. As soon as I get back onstage, his boys grab me and pin my arms behind my back.

"Give me the box," orders Mint.

"Too Tall"—I cough—"get him out." I can barely open my eyes. The sting is still so sharp.

"Yo, Mint!" I hear Tall shout from below the stage. "Come on, man!"

I squint to see smoke billowing from the trapdoor behind Mint as he glares like a demon. His faceless crew tightens their grip on me.

"I'll make you a deal," says Mint. "Give me the box and I'll help your friend."

"Help him out now!" I say. If I just hand over the box, how do I know he'll do what he says?

"What, help him out of here?" Mint says with a nasty snicker.

My vision clears up just enough to watch him reach down into the smoke and pull the trapdoor closed with a *thud*.

"No!" I shout.

Too Tall hollers from under the stage, hoarse and desperate. There's snickers and laughter from all around. I lunge at Mint but his minions hold me back. My blood goes hot. I pull and yank and claw in rage.

Suddenly, the trapdoor opens again and smoke shoots up and Too Tall shouts with relief. "Whoa, that's better! Now get me outta here!"

Mint looks confused by the door having opened.

Who did that? Somebody must have worked the back-stage levers. *Veronica?* I wonder.

"Give me that bag," Mint snaps, and grabs my back-pack strap and yanks hard. I hook my arm to it and hold on for dear life, hold on with everything, thinking, *This box is mine, my dad wanted me to have this—*

And I feel this strange energy suddenly course through my hand—the ghosted hand—almost like it's heating up like a kettle until it reaches a point where the hand can't contain all that hot anymore and I swing it at Mint and—

I look up to see all the smoke, every curling, steaming inch of it, has gathered beneath the roof into the shape of a giant fist. A smoke-made fist the size of a wrecking ball. My fist and the smoke fist both speed toward Mint and—

—boom—

The bag goes slack. No one is pulling on it anymore.

I open my eyes. I can see again.

The smoke fist is gone, now the stage is covered in fog, and there's a large puff of smoke coming from the stage trap. Completely normal and not at all in the shape of a giant fist.

All those bodies that were surrounding me are gone.

Mint is gone.

Then I realize they aren't *gone* gone. Not *Dad* gone. They've just moved a ways back.

Mint has fallen clean off the stage and is spread out somewhere between the third- and fourth-row orchestra seats. Like about ten to fifteen feet away.

The rest of his crew isn't far from him. They were all blasted off the stage. They writhe around the seats and aisles, dazed but awake. I'm standing center stage, alone.

"Tall!" I rush to the trapdoor. "Tall!" I shout down into the thick layers of smoke. I can barely make out his shape through the gray curtain.

"Yo, King!" I'm relieved to hear his voice—at least he sounds with-it. "What in the world is going on up there?" He coughs.

"You okay, man? I'm getting you out!" I say. I drop to my knees and reach my gloved hand into the trap. "Come toward me!"

And as soon as I speak, I feel Too Tall's hand collide

with mine. "Whoa!" he says, like he's as surprised as I am. I brace myself to pull him up, but I'm amazed by how easy it is—he practically floats up the chamber by the tug of my hand, and then he's beside me onstage.

He's still holding his hat over his face. When he removes it, his eyes are red and teary, but he looks okay.

"How—did you do that?" he asks.

"I—I don't really know. I don't know how I did any of it. You good, Tall?" I ask.

"Yeah, I think so," he says, staring at my gloved hand.

I follow his gaze. The white glove is lit up with a faint blue glow like a colored light bulb with fingers.

"My man, how are you doing that?"

"I don't know!"

"And look at this," he says, and shows me a clear crystal about the size of a dinner knife.

"What's that?" I ask.

"No clue. I slipped on it down there when the smoke was everywhere."

"That thing was just down there? I swear it wasn't there before," I say, and examine the crystal. It reflects the blue glow from my hand. My hand . . .

"Did you see the fist?" I ask him. "The fist made of smoke?"

"What smoke fist?"

Before I can answer, a voice shouts from behind me, "King, come on, let's go!"

And I remember how the trapdoor opened. Like someone had worked the lever backstage . . .

It's Veronica. She's all the way stage left, pointing, and it seems like she knows what she's saying and where she's going.

I wonder how long she's been waiting and watching, and I am *so* glad to see her.

WE FOLLOW VERONICA to a set of stairs that leads us one level down, and then to another trap that leads to a ladder. The ladder leads us to the sewers.

"V—you knew this was here?" I ask, descending the metal rungs.

"The chute from out front. It led me here," she says. "I climbed back up this way to get to the theater."

I touch my foot to a long tunnel made of dark, wet bricks.

"Make sure you shut that door!" she calls to Too Tall.

There are two walking platforms, one on either side of the running filth and sludge.

"Come on," says V. "They'll try to follow. Look alive."

She's moving fast, ducking past rusty pipes. I hurry after her. She's found another ladder on the side of the tunnel. Veronica climbs without a word. It's even darker up the ladder than it is in the tunnel.

"Can you guys help me?" she calls. "This manhole cover is too heavy."

She comes back down and Too Tall quickly climbs up and starts pushing and forcing the underside of the manhole cover, but the thing is really heavy. As I watch Tall struggle, I think about what's just happened. I hold my hand up and watch it ripple with blue light beneath the glove. *I moved all those boys. I made a fist out of smoke,* I think, *and then I moved Too Tall. I put him back onstage like it was nothing. With this.*

"Tall," I say, "let me try something."

I wave my hand at the manhole and concentrate like I'm trying to push, like the round iron lid is right there in my hand.

It opens. Streetlight suddenly beams into the shaft. Too Tall slides the cover along the sidewalk with a scrape and we're free.

The street is quiet as we step into an alley. Folks walk by on the avenue like it's just another ordinary evening in ordinary ole Echo City.

Veronica grabs me by the shoulders and spins me around to look at her.

"Now, what in the world was that?"

"I—uh, um . . ."

Where do I even start?

"His hand," says Too Tall, giving me up. "His hand, like, disappeared but it's still there actually and it's just pure magic or something. And I think it kinda moved that manhole cover, 'cause it was too heavy for me."

I give Tall a long stare.

He shrugs. Then elbows me. "What, you think you're gonna figure this out on your own? Show her!"

He may have a point.

"Yeah, King, show me." Veronica's eyes are tired and her hair is mussed up. There's a little pulse popping behind her jaw that I've only seen when she's really worried about something.

I pull the glove off my hand.

"To be honest," I say, "there's not a lot to see."

She gets the point. She puts her fingers to her astonished lips.

"And you're saying your hand is still there somehow?" she asks.

I reach to touch her. She flinches at first, just like Too

Tall did, then relaxes as I take her hand in mine. I feel her warm flesh, clammy with sweat. "See? Still there."

"I see," she says, squeezing my hand as she stares at her own hand gripped around nothing. "Or I don't see. I mean, I get . . . I mean, *wow*."

"Can I ask you, V? How long were you watching us?"

"Long enough," she says.

I ask, "Long enough to see the smoke form the shape of a fist?"

She looks at me like I'm nuts. "It's not exactly something you miss," she says.

"*I* missed it!" Tall whips his head back to V. "*You* saw it?"

"How did you *do* that?" she grills me, like she's more worried than impressed.

I think: *How did I do that?*

"Those guys were all over me. I mean, I was surrounded, Mint had my backpack, I could barely see anything, I was upset about how they trapped Too Tall, and then—my hand—well, you saw. You tell me. What did it look like?"

"It was like . . . all the smoke suddenly woke up and changed direction and gathered up into a giant fist, like a smoke ring, but with knuckles."

"*Wow*," says Too Tall.

"Yeah," I say. "That's what I saw, too. Tell me, you think it looked like, I dunno, *my* hand?"

"I don't know, King! Maybe? Who notices how a giant smoke hand looks?"

"I'm just wondering, that's all."

"Well, you're messing with some scary stuff. Powerful stuff. It wasn't just the smoke hand, King—that wasn't the scariest part. It crashed down like your fist was *controlling the smoke fist*. Your left hand was glowing blue and that fist and the smoke fist synchronized and *wham*. There was this *blast*. Those boys went flying, I bet you broke some bones. Mint—I mean, he *flew*. It was . . . the craziest thing I've ever seen," she says like she never expected to say that phrase and actually mean it.

I glance at Too Tall. He can't stop tapping his giant feet. I can't tell if he's nervous or excited. "You saved me, though," he says, and takes my hand and holds it fast, like he means it. "I won't forget that. Not ever."

"Thank Veronica, too," I say. "She's the one that opened the trapdoor when Mint closed it on you, so you could breathe."

"You did that for me?" Tall says, touching a closed fist over his heart. "Thank you, V. They could have caught you backstage. You didn't have to do that."

"Don't mention it," she says, like she's a little uncomfortable with the attention. "Mint is just terrible. I don't understand what happened to him. He didn't use to be like that."

"I know. He even looks different," says Tall. "All of those boys do. Like they're, I don't know, what's the reverse of a suntan? Anyway, we better get moving. Don't want to see them again."

But Veronica has her attention back on my hand. "How did this happen?" she asks me.

I tell her about the trunk beneath the stage, how I opened the lock and found this strange box, and how Too Tall fell on me and my hand went *through* the box somehow, and there was a blast of light from the box, and how Tall found that crystal down there after that . . .

"That kid with the green eyes—he called this box the 'Lost and Found' or something," I say. "They came into the theater for it, I think."

"But you still have it?"

"Yeah." I put my glove back on and take the box out for her to see.

She examines the pocket watch still lodged in the locking mechanism. "Wow. Your dad's watch . . ."

"Look. It's running now. It's never worked before, but

once I put the watch in the lock, the hands started moving."

She thinks this over but says nothing. Traffic passes by on the street outside the alley. It's getting late.

"And there's a map inside," I say.

She opens the box and looks at the map. "It's Echo City," she says.

"V, you know why those kids would want that box? Or is it the map they want? You think they knew I got it open somehow?"

"I don't know, King. I really don't. Mint and those kids—they hang around that weird house on Torrini."

"Where the She-Wizard of Torrini Boulevard lives?" says Too Tall, and makes the sign of the cross.

"I guess?" says Veronica. "They're into some weird cult stuff, daring each other to jump off buildings and break police car windows, crazy as a bag of cats. They're the type of kids that pull the legs off a spider 'cause they're bored. I stay away from them. You should, too," she warns.

"Gladly. But what if they come looking for me? I mean, they know I've got the box and I'm not exactly hard to find."

She sighs. "Jeez, King. You've been in town less than forty-eight hours and already stirred the hornets' nest. I mean, these guys can *sting*. I hate to say it, but you need help. You've got to tell someone."

"Tell my mom? That we broke into the Mercury? She'd flip!"

She closes her eyes like she's going to regret what she's about to say. "I was actually thinking of . . . *my* parent."

VERONICA LEADS THE way to the old bookcase wall.

She's spent the last twenty minutes preparing Uncle Long Fingers for my hand situation. I spent that time being cross-examined by Mom about why we got home at 9:00 p.m. instead of 8:00. I told her about meeting Eddie "Too Tall" at Not Not Ray's. She remembered him. I said we lost track of time, hanging out. I think she bought it, but you never know. I'm actually surprised we were only an hour late.

When Ma and Crooked start cleaning the kitchen from dinner, Veronica gives me the sign. I stand beside her as she pulls the book to open the secret door.

Then she lets me go in ahead of her.

"You're not coming?"

"Listen, thanks to tonight, I have now entered that old, musty lab exactly 1.5 times, and that's 1.5 times too many. Find me when you're done. And good luck."

My uncle is exactly how he was the first time I came in here. Same ratty beard, same fried eyes, same tired expression, and I'm pretty sure he's working on the same trick or device or whatever beneath that massive tarp.

"Hey, Unc," I say.

He holds out one of those long hands he's known for. "Lemme see the box."

I give it over.

For some reason, it feels like a teacher grading my paper in red ink right in front of the whole class. He examines the box for what feels like forever. Taps it, knocks it, opens it, right side up, upside down.

As he works, I can't help but wonder, *Did he leave it there under the stage for me to find?* I know it sounds out-there, but there's only so many people who could have known the code and put it up on the marquee—my pops, and him . . . But if he did, then all this box examining is a bunch of playacting, and Uncle Long Fingers just doesn't seem the sort to mess with all of that. No, if Uncle Long had wanted me to have that box, he'd probably just have walked into my bedroom and dropped it on me and left without a word.

He sets the box down on his desk and places his hand on top.

"Well, congratulations," he says in a dry tone. "You found Preston's old box. The Magician's Lost and Found. One hundred percent authentic, not a fake or a copy." He lets out a sigh. "Now tell me how you found it."

I tell him. I don't leave anything out, at least not deliberately. I tell him about the code, the watch, and the moment I found it—

"That's when the hand . . . *happened*?" he asks.

Knew he'd get to that.

"Yeah," I say.

He holds out his hand toward me just like he had for the box.

As I give him my gloved hand, I realize that he needs to touch things to understand them. Probably how he got his nickname.

Without a word, he rolls my white magician's glove up onto my fingertips so it looks like the glove is floating like a marshmallow without the stick.

Now, I'm *still* startled to see that there's nothing there, but for whatever reason, Long Fingers isn't. He just looks like a scientist observing science stuff. He then takes my glove all the way off and holds my wrist by the faint blue glow up to his work light.

Which is about the same as just, well, looking directly at the light.

Then he gives it back to me, and hands me back the glove, and asks me to explain everything, and he means *everything*, that happened.

And I do.

And he asks me to repeat the whole story, including everything, and he means *everything* . . .

And I repeat the story and try not to skip anything.

Then he asks me to focus on the part when Too Tall fell on me. When my hand went through the box.

"There was a flash of light?" he asks.

"Yeah."

"What color was it?"

"Blue light," I say.

He nods, sighs, and leans back, clearly bothered by something.

"Your uncle—my brother, as it were—Crooked Eye believes that children shouldn't know any more than they can handle. My question is, how does anyone know what they can handle until it's there to be handled? Child or no. Kids are adaptable, isn't that right, li'l King?"

"Sure."

"So I'll put it to you plainly. Your father ain't exactly gone. But he ain't never coming back."

I wasn't expecting that. I was expecting something about the box or my *invisible hand* . . .

Uncle Long goes on. "I see you're quiet for once. Good. That's wise. 'Cause there's a lot to open your mind to, and if you're busy talking or thinking up questions or what to say, you also busy not listening."

"I'm listening," I blurt.

He pauses and looks at me cross, like I'm not getting his point. "Well, what'd I just say?"

"Your father ain't exactly gone. But he ain't never coming back," I repeat.

"Well, yeah. Now you remember yesterday—what you first came in my lab here to ask me?"

"I thought you said not to think up questions—"

"Quit trying so hard to be smart, kid, you'll get a brain cramp," he snaps.

He's right. He's here trying to tell me something important. It's almost like I can't help it. Like, if I sit here and listen to what he has to tell me, I won't be a kid anymore.

"Okay. I came to ask . . ." What did I ask? About where's Pop? About why we don't magic the dishes clean every night? What was it? "I asked about real magic."

"That's right, you did. And to be honest, that impressed me. Because it's the first and most important question, out of all the stuff that your mama don't want you to know and Crooked don't want you to know. Something, I think, your daddy was close to wanting to tell you when you got a little older."

"That—?"

"That yes. Magic is real. Really real."

I nod and blink a few times. Now I already know that magic is really real, but it's still startling to hear an adult actually admit something.

"And what's happening with my hand?" I ask. "I know it's magic. But, like, do you get what's going on?"

"I'm getting to that. But it starts with your daddy, and where he's gone, and why he had to go."

"Why did he?" I ask.

"He was protecting us."

"Couldn't he protect us *and* stay? Did he have to *go*?"

My uncle's eyelids seem heavy, but I think he's more sad than sleepy. He slumps his shoulders.

"I've asked myself that question maybe a thousand times," he says. "And a thousand times, the answer is yes. He had to go."

"But why?"

"Here's where you got to understand how the whole magic thing works. Now, you've been to the aquarium, yes?"

"Which one?"

He sighs. "You've been to *an* aquarium?"

"Yes."

"Okay, you know how you're on one side, and there's this thick glass, and on the other side of the glass it's all water and aquatic life, yeah?"

"Yeah."

"That's how our world is with magic. We're protected by something like that thick glass, though you can't see it. And on the other side of that glass is magic, or a magical realm. Some folks call it the Realm. Now, say there was a fish, ended up on our side of the glass. Just to survive, they would need some of that water. Just to survive, they would be letting some of the Realm into our world. That's like cracking a hole in that glass between you and the fishes and whatnot on the other side of the aquarium, you get me?"

"I think I do. So there's a fish from the other side of the glass. And it's drawing water into our reality?"

"Exactly. Now, when glass gets too many cracks in it, what happens to it?"

I close my eyes, and think of the Mirror onstage at the Mercury. "It shatters."

"Exactly. Reality itself would explode. So Maestro's Mirror? That thing was like a hole clean through the glass. A portal that allowed Maestro to jump into the Realm. Only something was pulling the Realm into our world, too, and if Preston hadn't destroyed it?" He slowly shakes his head and draws an imaginary line across his throat. "That's all she wrote."

"But what's that mean? What would happen? Like, how could it be so bad?"

He gives me a look that's serious as a graveyard. "What happens when the glass breaks at the aquarium?"

"I'm guessing your feet get wet."

"Well, imagine all the water in the ocean is on the other side. No end to it gushing all around you, up to your ears, until the reality on the other side of that glass drowns our reality as we know it. No breathing, no thinking, no anything. Us and everything we know, gone. Replaced by whatever comes through that busted glass." He shakes his head. "Your pop saved us all."

"So why couldn't Dad have just broken the Mirror? Why did he have to jump through?"

"Here's the kicker. If he'd broken the Mirror from *our* side of things, that portal? It would remain open in *perpetuity*." He draws the word out like it has a dozen syllables. Then he pauses to make sure I understand. "No, Preston had to shatter the portal from *inside the Realm*. That was the only way to close it."

"So what's all this got to do with this box?"

"A little device of Preston's. He was always looking for a safe way to access the Realm without making a rift. When you put your hand in there, and your buddy Too Tall fell on you, you must have made a rift anyways. What with the blue light and all of that. A small rift, but a rift between worlds nonetheless. Your hand must have got stuck in the in-between. I never heard of anything like that happening. But that's the only explanation I got for your hand there, doing what it's doing."

"It's not doing a whole lot," I grumble.

"Doing a lot more than you know, being in two places at once. Part of your hand is here, in our world. That's how you can put your glove on and climb ladders and alla that. But part of your hand is *there*. In the *Realm*. And that's how you conjured a smoke fist and sent those kids flying a couple football fields."

I stare at my gloved hand, tapping each finger to my thumb. "Are you saying I can *touch* the Realm, somehow?"

"It sounds like you already did."

"So if I can touch the Realm, and Pop is *in* the Realm, can't I, like, touch him?"

"Listen, King, it's very important that you *don't try to use your hand to touch the Realm*. Remember that fish out of water I was talking about? Imagine it's more like a shark. And you're just chum. Whatever Realm power you tap into, she'll smell it like blood in the water. You copy that?"

"I copy," I repeat, though it's only a reflex. "But who is this shark you're talking about? Why'd you call her 'she'?"

For the first time since I've been down here, Long Fingers perks up. He hefts his large, lumbering body out of that chair with the grace of a forklift and walks around his worktable and over to me. He squares me up by the shoulders, then puts his hands on his knees to bend to my eye level. His eyes are little brown cocoa beans in shot glasses of milk.

"Do. Not. Try. To. Use. Your. Hand. Don't think about what it can do, and don't try and find out. I want you to leave this box with me, and I'll work on a way to get you right again. In the meantime, keep cool, wear that glove, and don't tell anyone about this. Bad enough my daughter knows, li'l Princess of Mischief, that one." He scrunches his mouth like this next bit is difficult to chew. "Now, I'd never tell you to hide anything from your ma . . ."

"But you're telling me to do that?"

"I said I'd *never* do that. You know y'all's relationship better than I do, and if you think she can hand—"

"I won't say a word, Unc."

He holds his hands up. "Your call. But listen, if you try and use that hand, and the Realm starts leaking in, and I find out, and I *will* find out, I'll smell it—I'ma have to tell her. Because it's too important. And if you won't listen to me, you for sure better listen to her."

"I won't use it. I promise."

"You sure?"

"Yeah. If we lost Pop because this Realm stuff is that

important, that's enough for me," I say, but I feel like I'm trying out the words to see how they sound. "I got one question, though. Couldn't we use, like, just enough magic to bring Dad back? And then that's it?"

He turns around and holds a pain in his lower back. "Good night, Young King. Good. Night."

I'M SITTING OUTSIDE on the stoop and I can't imagine hitting the pillow. I am wired, my heart racing like it's got enough voltage running through it to power the county grid.

At 4:00 a.m., the street is so quiet I'd believe I'm back in the suburbs. Must be how they grow trees in Brooklyn, extra thick and gnarly and lush. The leaves swish in the breeze like they're whispering secrets.

The one word that keeps playing in my head, from all the info my uncle just dumped on me, is *sacrifice* . . .

Because that's what I understand now that maybe I never understood before.

I always had a sense that Pop did what he did for the

greater good, because that's the kind of person he is . . . or *was*? *Is*? I'm still not even sure.

And when I think about my hand, and the power that's somehow at my invisible fingertips, and how I conjured a blast that scattered a handful of punks like bowling pins, the one thought that keeps me from tempting that power now is *sacrifice*.

If I lost Dad because he made a sacrifice, then I have to . . .

Also sacrifice.

I take my glove off to see if there's been any change. But nothing.

Nothing at all.

Part of my hand, I guess the part I can't see, is in the Realm . . .

And Dad is in the Realm.

Doesn't that mean I could touch him?

The door opens behind me and the light casts two silhouettes down the stoop, mine and Veronica's.

"Whatup, cuzzo."

I put the white glove back on.

Veronica sits on the top step beside me, gives my face a good once-over, and smirks. "You look like how I feel after talking to my father for an hour."

I chuckle and force a smile, but I'm just being polite.

"*Oof.* That bad, huh? Well, sorry to interrupt. I can see you're staring out at the tree-lined block all romantic and pensive and whatnot." She puts a hand on my shoulder like she's about to get up. "Happy soul searching!"

"Wait," I say. "Stay, please. Just got a lot on my mind, is all."

"I know it, I do."

"How much do you know?"

"You mean, like, about *the Realm*?" she says in a mock-spooky voice that actually does make me laugh for real.

"So you do know."

"Only because I, like, spy on my dad and my uncle sometimes. Made my dad come clean one time, last May. He told me your dad jumped into that Mirror to save, like, reality itself or something. Pretty cool." She shrugs. "Cooler than anything my dad ever did."

"V, that doesn't exactly make me feel better."

"Well, maybe you're looking at this the wrong way? I mean, sure, you lost your father. But he didn't abandon you. I mean, he had a *purpose*. That's kinda noble, don't you think? It's rare enough that people do anything good for anyone, much less for *every*one. You know, King? People are terrible. But your father, he's, like, not at all terrible."

"Wow. You've got some low expectations, huh?"

"Can you blame me? My ma gave me up to that cantankerous blob back there. No one even told me why, but I know it wasn't 'cause she was trying to save the world or anything. King, she was my *mother* and she gave me up. Like, if your mother doesn't have your back, who does?"

I see a different side of Veronica then. She looks angry. And sure, I've seen lots of versions of her being angry, but usually she wears this smirk like she knows she's got one up on all the suckers of the world. Now she looks like the opposite. Like she's missing this one piece of basic equipment that everyone else walks around with, and it's so natural that people like me don't even realize we've got it. *A mother to love you.* Wow. That's like missing a lung.

"Now, don't go feeling sorry for me or nothing like that," she warns me, maybe reading my expression. "I don't want that at all. I will leave your little mopey self out here right now," she digs at me, but her smile is gentle.

"Nah, I get it, V. Sometimes it feels like the stuff that happens to me is all that matters. But everybody goes through stuff. Is it weird, though, that, after all this talk about how noble my dad was or is or whatever, all this about how I should appreciate what he did for the greater good, it just makes me want him back, like, even more?"

"Yeah, I feel you. I mean, what can ya do?" she says, shrugging.

I feel something then, in my gloved hand. A tingling pressure that gets more and more insistent. Almost like fingertips pressing into my flesh.

"What is it?" asks Veronica.

"I—I don't know."

I take off the glove. I almost expect to see thumbs digging into my palm. But there's nothing there, of course.

Then something very different presses into my hand. A crunch, like paper, like a balled-up piece of paper tucked into my palm, and then the other pressure closes my invisible fingers around the ball.

"King, what is it? You look like you're seeing a ghost."

I'm speechless. I feel my fist clutching onto a ball of paper, but I see absolutely nothing.

Then the pressure is gone. Nothing holding my fist closed.

So I open up my hand.

Out drops a balled-up sheet of yellow legal paper.

It lands between me and Veronica on the top step.

"Okay, wow. Where did that come from?" Veronica looks up. "There a large paper pigeon above us?"

I stare at the yellow ball and put my glove back on. I'm thinking I shouldn't take it off anymore. Strange things seem to happen when I do.

"It was like someone crumpled it up and put it in my hand and closed my fist around it," I say in amazement, exploring the street for any signs of life that's not V or me. "I opened my hand, and this dropped out."

Veronica looks at the paper, dumbfounded.

"Well." She quickly recovers. "You going to look at it or what?"

I take a deep breath and pick up the paper in my flesh-and-blood right hand and begin unfolding. It's all scrunched and knotted, like someone had fun when they balled this up.

I smooth it out on my knee and make out the handwriting:

You can save him.
He is still within reach.
He will not be for long.
Once he is gone,
he is gone forever.

116

Meet me at Mandrake Meadow.
You can save him.

"You can save him," Veronica reads out loud from over my shoulder. "Whoa. That's spooky."

I stare at the words, reading them over and over:

You can save him.

Save him.

You can save him.

I can save him.

"Where's this Mandrake Meadow?" I ask.

"So you're not at all sketched out by this, um, how do I say, hands-free messaging?"

I shrug. "Got my attention, didn't it? I mean, yeah, it's spooky. But I've gotta see what this is about, don't you think?"

"But why is this note anonymous? There's just a lot of red flags. If they were trying to help, why not just come, like, in the light of day? And, like, visible?"

"There's lots of questions I need to ask, I guess. But V, I just can't help but think I *should* be able to reach him somehow. Your pops told me my hand is half trapped in the Realm. If *my hand* is in the Realm, and we know *Pops* is in the Realm, well . . ."

. . . I can save him . . .

"I hear you," says V. "Mandrake Meadow . . . That, I don't know. But it sounds kind of familiar? Like something I just heard, or saw . . . God, it's at the tip of my tongue . . ." And then something dawns on her. "King, you still have that map?"

The map. "V, I can't believe I forgot all about it! I even forgot to mention it to your dad," I say, and dig in my back pocket for the old folded-up piece of paper. I'm shaking my head at myself. "Jeez, I even tried to recount everything that happened for him, *twice*."

"Sure," V says dubiously. "You forgot all about it."

"No, really—"

"I get it, King. You wanted to keep something to yourself. I'd probably do the same thing."

Did I keep the map to myself on purpose? I wonder.

She gets her fingers on the map and tracks quickly to *Mandrake Meadow*, listed just a few blocks away from *Pocket Playground* with a little illustration of wavy lines that must represent grass or something.

"There," she says. "Strange. I don't know when this map was made, but there's no meadow there now."

I scan the names on the map. Some look familiar, but most of them don't.

"Wow," I say. "So whoever slipped me that note must know about this map, and know that we have it."

It gets so quiet between us for a moment that I swear I hear crickets, even though there's no crickets in Brooklyn.

"It just gets creepier, huh, King?" V finally speaks. "I'd tread very carefully if I were you. And don't stay out here all night. If anybody needs a decent night's sleep, it's you."

V goes to her room to either fall asleep or watch anime on her laptop. Whichever comes first, she says.

I spend another couple minutes out on the stoop before I tiptoe upstairs, doing my best not to wake Ma. I take each step in super-slow-mo, being extra quiet but also making sure I don't stub my toe or trip on anything. The steps are so noisy, it doesn't seem to matter. I hold on to the banister, but it's loose and that makes the whole stair-case creak and moan, so I rush up to the second floor like the ship's about to go down.

I hear another noise, like pipes squeaking in the dis-tance. At first, I think it's this cranky old brownstone acting up again, but as I get closer to my mom's room, it's not that. It's her. She has a light on. She's awake.

Her door is open a crack. I ease closer.

And I realize she's crying.

I can just make her out, lying under the covers.

She's all the way on her side of the king-size bed. The entire other side of the bed is untouched. Like even now, after all these years, she sleeps as if he's still there. Like he could walk through this door this instant and climb into bed with her and she wouldn't even have to move an inch.

She's crying because she misses him. And being here makes it worse.

I realize I'm not breathing. Hearing her cry just stole the breath right out my chest.

I slip into my room and close the door as gently as possible and I get in my bed and I cry, too.

Because after all this, all I went through with the Mercury and the box and the hand and learning about the Realm . . .

He's still gone.

After Ma spent years working to put food on the table and then got the strength to face Echo City and everything she's lost and come back home for her dream to run a café . . .

He's still gone.

After learning that V's mom abandoned her and that

as bad as I think I have it sometimes, others have it worse, and at least my pops was around to raise me and he was a good man and he loved me . . .

He's still gone.

At that point, nothing else matters.

He's still gone, and I have to bring him back.

And not just for me.

THE REST OF Saturday night to Sunday morning is spent trying to wrestle my squirming body and hyperactive mind into something resembling rest.

When the blinds glow with the rising sun, it's a relief that I can stop pretending to sleep.

And start thinking of a way to get out of the house.

By the time Mom comes to get me for this chore or another, she sees me wearing high-tops, ball shorts, a tank top, and exactly one white glove.

"Morning, Ma, is it cool if I go hit the playground with Too T—Eddie today?"

She's taken aback to see me so ready to go.

"W-well, sure, honey." The ends of her lips curl up in a smile.

Then I remember her last night, crying quietly on her side of the bed while that massive empty space lay next to her.

"You two made plans?" she asks.

"Yeah." The lie comes quickly. "He's coming by, I should just call him, tell him I'm ready."

"My boy, you sure are in a rush. Don't you want breakfast?"

"Breakfast—of course. Sure."

"You two are picking up right where you left off, huh?"

"Yeah, Ma. I mean, it's good to be back, you know? This place—it's weird and all, but it feels like home. You think?"

Her mouth drops open. She's probably not sure how to respond.

"I think we'll be okay," I say with a shrug. "That's all."

"Good, King . . . I'm glad." She looks like she doesn't know what's gotten into me, but she'll take it.

BREAKFAST FEELS LIKE it takes forever. Too Tall doesn't show up until close to noon. Leaves Mom plenty of time to come up with chores for me to do. By the time Too Tall gets to our door, even he's surprised by how ready I am to go.

"Okay, bye, Ma, bye, Uncle!" I say, and I'm halfway out the door before they can say anything back.

"Whoa, can I, like, say hi to your peeps, man?" says Too Tall.

"Later."

"King!" my mom calls from the top of the stairs.

I freeze in mid-dash. "Yeah, Ma?"

She hesitates like she's not sure what to say. "Be safe."

Strange how her words and that somber look land like a jackknife to the gut, but I still manage to say, "Of course," with an eye roll like I'm just *so* over it.

"And be back by five for dinner. No later."

"Hi, Miss James!" Too Tall shouts with a wave like he's signaling an airplane.

"Hi, Eddie!"

"Let's go," I hiss at him, and flee down the block.

"What's the rush, King?" asks Tall, catching up. "Pickup games won't run for real for another few hours."

I want to tell him about everything. So much has

happened even in the handful of hours since I've seen him. But all that comes out my mouth is "Stuff. A lotta big-time stuff, man, I need to update you. Let's get off of Ricks before Ma thinks of some reason I need to come back."

It's just days before the Fourth of July and I feel like I could melt into the sidewalk. The concrete and brick and asphalt all bake in the sun and you can see the heat moving through the air like opening an oven door. Heat like you're wearing another person on you at all times. I'm already sweating as we round the corner to Thurston Avenue.

The names of all the streets of Echo City are vivid in my mind after studying that map.

"Okay, tell me, tell me!" says Tall.

"On the way."

"Where to? I know Echo City like the back of my hand."

"To Mandrake Meadow."

"Huh? Where's that?"

"Thought you knew Echo City like the back of your hand," I say with a grin.

Too Tall examines the back of his hand like he just noticed it for the first time. "To be honest with you? I, like, never look at the back of my hand."

"You know what I mean."

"No, really—look at those little hairs on my knuckles. You got those?"

"Wouldn't know."

I take the map out of my pocket—those deep pockets they put in basketball shorts—and open the map in front of him.

"Okay, King-crazy, what am I supposed to be looking at?"

I tap a finger to *Mandrake Meadow*.

Too Tall scrunches up his face like he's reading the last line in an eye exam. "Okay . . . Yeah, I know where that is. But it's just, like, some old lot. Calling that a meadow— that's a stretch. You should see—it's like they demoed a building and just left the rubble laying there. Got all kinds of randos squatting, sketchy."

"Huh," I say, and reexamine the map.

"King, listen. I need you to back it up, I mean *all the way* up to the beginning."

"Okay, okay. Ready for it? I know where my pops is. My uncle told me."

"Yeah?" says Tall, keeping pace with me once again. "Wait, *what*?" he shouts when it dawns on him what I just said. "Your *pops*? That's huge, King, what'd he say?"

"He said, *Your father ain't exactly gone. But he ain't never coming back.*"

"Okay. Is that, like, some kinda riddle?"

"Well, it's hard to explain. You gotta promise this stays between us, okay?"

"Of course, my man. I already didn't tell *any* of my cousins about the fact that . . ." Tall eyes the strangers passing us on the street with suspicion. Then he mouths, *That-you-don't-have-a-hand.*

"Thanks, man. Let's walk and talk."

As I tell Tall all about the Realm, I check the map against the neighborhood, down Thurston Avenue, the main stretch of Echo City. Mandrake Meadow isn't the only thing on the map that isn't there now. All these spots on the map are different. What's called the *Red Room* on a map label is actually a dive bar. *The Double Rainbow* cashes checks. *The Flourish* is a bodega with a handful of people trying their luck on lotto tickets. *The Dead End*— an enclosed triangle with haunted houses like the Ghost Gaze, Lemur Leftovers, and the Jamaican spot, Duppy Conqueror—those ghost spots are just ghost, boarded up and abandoned. The *Devant Dollar Store* is a Family Dollar now. The *Davenport Brothers Furniture* store is a Raymour & Flanigan. *The Sawed Lady* is Bella's Beauty, and *Conjuror's Cuts* is a Supercuts. The *Eye of Agamoto* is called Sumi Sushi, *Fu Manchu Chow* is Han Dynasty, and *Marabout Middle Eastern Grill* is called Shawarma House.

Too Tall is sufficiently blown away by my explanation about the Realm, and my ability to both tell a story and check the map against the city at the same time.

"So your hand is part . . . in this *Realmy, realm-agic-y* place?"

"Yup."

"And that's where your pops went."

"That's what my uncle says."

"So in theory, you could, like, shake his hand or something?"

"See, that's what I'm thinking! Only I don't think my uncle wants me to try or anything."

"What makes you say that?"

"Well, he said, like, don't do that. Or anything with the hand or the Realm at all. He said he'd smell it. He's working on fixing it so I get my normal hand back."

"Boring."

"Agree. I mean, what's the harm in a little magic, right? I used it without realizing on Mint back at the Mercury—"

"Outstanding—much respect—"

"Thank you—and nothing bad happened then. I mean, I get that opening a *big* rift between our world and the Realm would be horrendous, but I asked my uncle about using *little* bits of magic here and there, and he got all funny about it. Like he thinks I'll try it."

"Well . . ."

"Well, yeah, I might. But just to get my pops back. I mean, can you imagine that? If I could bring him back—for mom and my uncles and *us*."

"Well, sure," Tall says, and thinks this over. "But you have no idea how to actually do that."

"Ah, here's the last part of my night. The Mandrake Meadow part."

"Good. I almost forgot."

"I'm sitting there on the stoop—it's like four in the morning. And I feel someone put a balled-up piece of paper in my hand—my Realm hand—but there's no one there! I can't see a thing, until I open my hand and this falls out."

I reach in my other pocket and show Tall the hand-written note.

"*You can save him,*" Tall reads. "You *can save him*?"

"Right? I can save him!"

But Tall doesn't share my excitement. "Listen, King, this one feels a little sketchy to me."

"What do you mean?"

"First of all, this Mandrake Meadow is a sketch spot. But even this note? I don't know, man. Like, if it was on the up-and-up, why not just come to you, straight-up? Why all the hocus-pocus? Why didn't somebody sign the note?"

"Yeah, that's what Veronica said. I'm thinking, only one way to find out."

"King, I know you been out of Brooklyn for a few years now, but you got to be more suspicious about, well, most things. Especially strange things, like this. It could be a—"

"Don't say it could be a trap."

"It *could* be a trap. And we already *know* Mint and them are gunning for you. Mint seems like a tricky type, maybe he slipped you that note?"

"Tall, whoever gave me that note slipped it in my *Realm* hand. That means they got some kinda Realm power, or access at least. You really think Mint got it like that?"

"Look, this is all over my head. I'm just saying, it's over yours, too. You got to be careful."

Everyone's caution is frustrating me. *Does no one understand how important this is?*

"But what if what the note says is true? What if I can save him? And what about the part in the middle? *He is still within reach,*" I recite. "*He will not be for long. Once he is gone, he is gone forever.* Tall, my uncle explained some things, but there's so much I don't understand about where my father is and what he's doing. If there's a chance, even a small chance, that note is true, then I need to find out."

He nods like he hears what I'm saying and takes a deep breath.

"We'll find out soon enough. We're here."

MANDRAKE MEADOW IS just as Too Tall described, though if a building were demoed here, I've never seen one so thoroughly pulverized before. The whole field is just *dust*. I can't even make out the shape of a brick or anything. It's just fine, dark gray grains that slope in mounds like a beach in the dead of night.

"I knew you couldn't keep away," says a familiar voice from behind us.

Veronica walks up in a baggy pair of ripped-up jeans and her hands in her pockets. She squints at me and shakes her head. "Let me ask you this. What would you do if I *didn't* cancel my plans to clean out the old chess masters at Pocket Playground, just to come watch your back? Don't answer that," she says before I could anyway. "I know. That's why I came."

"Thanks, V. I'm not gonna lie, I'm glad you're here," I say.

"Can I maybe try one more time to talk you out of, well, whatever terrible idea you're up to?"

I think about how to explain how important this is to me, without sounding childish.

Veronica sighs. "Save it. I get it. At least you brought along some muscle." She looks Too Tall up and down. "Mr., um, Appropriately Tall, was it?"

"Uh, it's Too Tall, actually," he mumbles.

"Okay, King," she says, and looks at the barren field. "We going to check this 'meadow' out or what?"

"Not much to check out," says Tall, his head swiveling, on the lookout.

We all scan the dusty lot.

"You guys don't remember anything else ever being here? Like a building?" I ask.

Too Tall and Veronica shrug.

"There had to be something. I mean, look, there's a bit of a wall over there—right?"

A short section of wall—or something like it—stands over on the other side of the field of dust.

"I guess . . . ," Tall says as he squints.

"Welp, only one way to know for sure," I say, and set out across the field.

V shrugs, following me. "Okay. Let's do it." Too Tall hesitates.

"It's okay, Tall," I call. "We'll check it out and be right back."

"Man . . . You lucky I'm rocking my beater shoes," he complains, but follows behind. "You don't know Mint and them like I do. Those dudes took a bad turn. Got, like, nothing to live for. I don't trust them. Just wish you wouldn't take these chances."

"You sound like my ma," I say.

"She sounds like a smart lady," says Veronica.

The wall stands like a ruin against the sky. The gray dust gets all in our shoe soles, laces, and even leaves a layer of film on my ankles. It smells like the stale debris around a construction site. As we get closer, I can make out a mural painted on what's left of the wall.

It's a painting of a meadow so vivid it could be a photograph. Green slopes, tall grass, reeds and dandelions restless in the wind. There are patches of flowers that look like angry black roses. V says those look like mandrakes maybe. The whole meadow feels like it's moving, only you just missed it. Like you can feel the twitch of a blade of grass in the corner of your eye. There's charcoal clouds that shift like a coming storm.

I stare and stare. Feels like I could stare forever. Like the green slopes keep unfolding deeper and deeper.

"*Wow*," says Too Tall. "Whoever's painting these is, like, *good*."

"Like the one back at the Mercury," I say.

"Yeah. The one I was staring at when I fell on you . . ."

"Of my father and Maestro. But look at that . . ."

There's an object on one of the sloping green patches of grass. It's a hat. I get all the way up to it and look carefully. A porkpie hat. With a card in the band.

It's . . . "That's my dad's hat!"

"Wow," says Veronica.

"What's that, now?" says Tall.

"Right there—look!" I say.

"How do you know that's your dad's?" asks Tall.

"Because look at the card there, tucked in the band. You see the insignia, with the bear's head? That's the Joker from Hooker's Vanishing Deck! It's one of my dad's old tricks."

"Well, how do you suppose your pop's hat got in this here meadow?"

Something to be said for Too Tall—instead of trying to tell me that it's not real, it's just a painting, he wants to know how the hat got there.

"I mean, Dad was wearing that hat when he jumped through the Mirror."

"Whoa," says Tall.

Could that hat be in the Realm? Does that mean this meadow is showing us the Realm somehow?

What if . . .

As crazy as the idea seems, I pull the glove off my ghost hand.

"King—didn't my dad say not to use that hand?" shoots Veronica. "At least, that's what he told me."

Too Tall realizes what I'm doing and covers his mouth.

I reach with my phantom fingers to the mural, right on the image of the hat . . .

And my hand hits a solid wall.

"Okay. Maybe I got carried away," I admit.

Too Tall shrugs. "Worth a shot, I guess."

"Right idea," says a voice from nowhere. "Wrong equipment."

Too Tall told me so.

Mint steps out from behind the wall.

MINT IS PALE and washed-out like he's made of gray construction paper, though his green eyes are even brighter in the sun.

"I told you, King," says Tall. "It's a goose chase. We outta here."

Mint raises his hands like he means no harm. "No goose. No chase. No clown. No jokes." His voice is steady, like how he spoke to his crew back at the Mercury, *Smoke them out.* Like it was nothing. Like talking to us now is nothing.

"What do you want, Mint?" asks Veronica in a bored tone.

Mint fixes his eyes on me. "My boss wants you," he says.

"Who's your boss?"

"You'll find out when you come with me."

Veronica and Too Tall fold their arms like a pair of bodyguards.

"That don't cut it, chief," says Too Tall.

"Do better," says Veronica.

"Can he speak for himself?" asks Mint.

"He can. But we're, like, his lawyers on this side of King's County," says Tall.

"Why doesn't your boss come here himself?" I say. "And why do you have a boss anyway? Is bugging me, like, your job somehow?"

Mint holds out his hands. "I got no answers for you. I'm just an escort today."

"Mint, I know we barely know each other," says Veronica. "Just around the neighborhood here and there. But take it from me. You look terrible."

Mint blinks like a lizard and looks at me.

Tall says to me under his breath, "He's bad news, King. Bet you anything he wants to take you to that creepy spot on Torrini Boulevard. My cousin warned me not to go near that house. Says kids go in and don't ever come back out."

"What does your boss want?" I ask.

"Says the note should speak for itself," answers Mint.

"Well, if the boss is not here, why'd the note say to come here?"

"Isn't it obvious?" he asks, and then turns to admire the mural, with the porkpie hat on the sloping grass. "Boss thought you'd recognize this."

I keep my poker face as flat as his tone. *Reveal nothing.*

"*You* painted this?" asks Too Tall.

"Me? Do I look like that freak?" Mint chuckles without smiling. His laughter sounds strange, like trying to start a car when the engine won't turn over. "May not be CCTV, but it's as close as we get."

Too Tall is puzzled. "CC . . . TV?" he repeats, squinting at the mural.

"If you Einsteins need it spelled out for you, take a class. I'm here for Kingston. You coming or not?"

Veronica holds up a finger in front of Mint's face like an exclamation point. " 'Scuse us. We need a word with our client. King, sidebar."

She hooks one of my arms and one of Tall's and takes

us out of Mint's earshot. She whispers, "Okay. You're not seriously considering going with him, are you?"

One look at me and she knows the answer.

"King!" says Tall. "For one, you're crazy."

"I know this is all a bit creepy," I say.

"There has got to be a creepier word than *creepy* to describe how creepy this all is," says Veronica.

"What's for two?" I ask Tall.

"Huh?"

"You said, 'King, for one, you're crazy.' So what's 'for two'?" I say.

"For two, this is *all* crazy!" says Tall. "I mean, that dude's neck scar over there? Looks like somebody went and killed that dude but he forgot to die! That could be this 'boss,' for all we know."

"Right—for all we know. But we don't know. I came this far, Tall, I need to find out. Listen, if I don't come back—"

"What?" says Veronica.

"I'm saying, if I don't come back—"

"Oh no. That's not how this works," she says, and doubles back to Mint. "Okay, green eyes. King is coming. But so are we. So you and your boss got to deal. Deal?"

"I'll have to ask," says Mint.

"Fine, ask your supervisor for permission. But if you want King, you get us, too."

An old three-story building stands out on Torrini Boulevard, separated by narrow alleyways on either side from the other buildings. Usually in Echo City, the buildings line up right next to one another, but not this one. There's a yard out front with yellow grass, dirt patches, and crunchy leaves that've laid here dead since last fall. There's an overgrown driveway and a car that probably hasn't been used in decades, but it looks like it's been centuries. The metal wheels bite the dirt and the tires droop in the dead grass like puddles.

I hear Too Tall's lungs heaving by my ear. I look up at the house and I almost lose my nerve. We approach the front door. It's huge and towers over even Too Tall. There's a crystal mounted atop the entrance. I point to the crystal and look at Tall. He nods. It's just like the crystal he had back at the theater. I wonder if he's still got it, but I don't want to ask in front of Mint.

There are white columns on either side like a pair of

fangs. The white paint is chipped and the panels are decaying. Ivy covers the building like some tentacled monster. Mint pounds a fist on the door and slips inside. We shoot nervous glances at one another.

"Thank you guys," I whisper, and part of me wishes they weren't here. I'm glad they are, but if anything bad happens to them? I'd never forgive myself.

The door opens up like a slow yawn and Mint's voice tells us to "Come in."

We take uneasy steps through the gloomy archway. It smells like wet, rotten wood mixed with old washed-up-actress perfume.

Urma Tan is at the top of the stairway in front of us. Maestro's assistant. The one who went through the Mirror that night at the Mercury.

Last time I saw her was the last time I saw my dad.

19

My mouth drops open. I can't believe my eyes.

She should not be here. She should be in the Realm, with Maestro and my father.

But she *is* here. It's her, there's no mistaking. She looks older, of course, but it's her. Same pale eyes and pale skin. Her hair is all the way white now. She takes a step down the stairs in a nightgown and it looks like she's floating.

"*The She-Wizard . . . ,*" Too Tall whispers.

"Is that . . . ," asks Veronica, her question trailing off.

"Welcome," Urma says, and extends a hand, her long, pale fingernails like a drawn blade.

"You—you're Urma Tan," I manage to say.

I give her hand an awkward half squeeze.

"I am."

"But . . . you're not supposed to be here. You're supposed to be gone, with my dad," I say.

"Hello, Kingston. Veronica." She takes the hand of my cousin, who also looks dumbfounded. "And who is this?"

Too Tall introduces himself.

"Thank you all for coming. I'm sure you have questions, and I'm happy to explain. Come," she says. "Have a seat."

Mint leaves us as Urma leads the way into a sitting room that feels like no one has sat in for years. There's a thick shag carpet and a couple of couches, and all of it is beige. The couch cushions look comfortable but have these springs that stick you where you sit.

"Some tea?" she offers. There's a little teapot on a silver tray on the coffee table. I feel like I'm at my grandma's. Too Tall looks at it like it's a tray full of rat poison.

"No thanks. Um, where's my dad?" I ask.

She purses her thin lips. "I don't know," she says with regret in her voice.

"But you both went through that Mirror," I say.

"Kingston, I think you ought to listen to what I have to say. Then maybe you'll understand where I've been and what I'm doing here. Tell me, first, what do you know about the Realm?"

Too Tall gives me a wary look that says, *Don't give anything away.*

I almost say *I know my dad is there*—thinking, I don't know much else, I don't know what he's doing there, or what actually *is* there—but Veronica cuts me off.

"Wait, King." She turns to Urma Tan. "Lady, with all due respect, you asked him here. You're the one that *went* to the Realm. You slipped him that note somehow, into his Realm hand. Neat trick and all, but you're the one that should be telling us about the Realm."

"Fair point," says Urma, clicking her teeth. "It's hard to know where to begin."

"Maybe start with how you got back to our reality?" I say.

"One can get from the Realm and back with a portal, like Maestro's Mirror. Creating a portal is difficult, but not impossible."

"And I can do it? I can bring my dad back?" I ask, trying to keep the excitement out of my voice.

"Yes," she says. "And I can help you."

"How?" asks Veronica. "And why? I mean, what's in it for you?"

"I can help you make the portal. That requires some doing. And as for what's in it for me, well, that's a longer story. In order to understand why I need your help, you must understand the nature of the Realm."

"Okay, so what is it?" I ask.

"And don't just say it will wreck reality as we know it if we open a portal," says Veronica. "We get it."

"I would never tell you that," says Urma. "In order to understand the Realm, first you must understand the nature of magic. You see, real magic can do anything you could possibly dream. Only, magic doesn't dream. It doesn't imagine, or think, or anything we people do. It can't. Magic is not people. However, it *likes* people. Without people, who would care about magic? Without people, who would dream up the impossible? Without people, magic doesn't really know what to do. So you could say magic is dependent on people. And in that way, the Realm is very suggestible." Urma turns her pale eyes to me. I feel like I'm under a hot lamp. "When one opens a rift between worlds, the Realm absorbs all it sees. And copies it. Creates an echo. A moment in time that lives forever. Does that make sense?"

Veronica and Tall look about as lost as I feel.

"Um, sort of," I say. "So it's, like, a copy of our world? With, like, places and people and things?"

"And Not Not Ray's?" asks Too Tall. "I mean, Poppa James gotta be eating something."

I have to admit, it's nice to think my father might be in a place that resembles our reality. I realize that I've been imagining him sort of floating in a netherworld, with solar systems and shooting stars and empty space like he's alone in the universe.

"When a rift opens, the Realm copies. So if there's a rift near the pizza place, then yes. There's pizza."

"And you were *there*?" says Veronica.

"How did you get back?" I ask.

Urma stands. She opens her robe and reveals a crystal dangling around her neck by a thin chain. The crystal is big like costume jewelry with a blue light glowing in its center like a cold star.

Too Tall slaps a hand over his mouth. It looks just like the crystal he found under the stage.

"This may be hard to believe, but here's the truth. I know the Realm because the Realm made me," says Urma Tan. "I'm not the Urma you think I am. I'm not from this world."

"Huh?" comes out my mouth.

"Um, excuse me?" says V.

My uncle's words come back to me. *Say there was a fish, ended up on our side of the glass . . .*

"The night of the fire at the Mercury, the Urma of your world went through the Mirror and to the Realm with Maestro and your father." She shrugs and paces like a cat. "That wasn't me. I'm a different Urma Tan."

"Wait, what?" I sputter.

Veronica folds her arms. "Does that *not-of-this-world* bit work on Mint and those followers of yours?"

"I'm too old to play games with children," Urma says. "I'm too weak, and I don't have the time. Remember you asked if the Realm had people in it? Well, it does. I was one of them. I'm not the your-world Urma Tan. That Urma is there, somewhere, best of luck to her. I'm a copy." She flashes jazz hands. *"Ta-da."*

"You're saying that wasn't even you onstage four years ago?" I ask.

"Correct. We just did the teleportation trick, and I was hiding."

The three of us are stunned silent. I don't even know where to begin with this one.

"Maestro led me to this reality to use me in his magic act," she says like that should explain everything. Then she sees how unconvinced we are. "I know. It's a lot. I have something to show you. It might help you understand."

Urma opens a pair of cabinet doors. There's an old television set there, and a stack of homemade DVDs. She puts one in the DVD player and pokes a couple buttons on the remote.

There's a stage. It looks like the Mercury before the fire. But I can tell it's not that night. The lighting is different, like it's a matinee. Maestro waltzes out to rounds of applause in his spooky, mirrored magic-man mask. Urma is behind him. She's wearing black elbow-length gloves, a white halter top, and a bow tie.

"I look good, don't I?" says Urma in the living room, watching the screen. "Well, *she* looks good, anyways. We were identical."

She hits the fast-forward button. Maestro's act flies by on the screen. He buzzes around the stage doing illusions with metal rings, works the crowd, gets back onstage, does card tricks with a volunteer from the audience, shows him a card, pretty standard stuff.

Urma clicks a button and the DVD plays at regular speed for this next part. I recognize the setup right away; they did this trick the night of the fire.

Urma, on the stage, wheels out a tall cabinet with two doors that stands a head taller than Maestro. There's no chatter, just instrumental music that buzzes heavy with bass. Urma moves half like a dancer and half like she's showing cars at a car show. She wheels another cabinet out that's identical to the first one. Then a third cabinet that she sets between the other two. Maestro gestures for the audience to watch carefully as he enters the first cabinet on the left. Urma joins him. She pulls a rope from inside somewhere and ties Maestro's wrists up. Maestro pretends to struggle. Urma closes the cabinet doors on him. Then she steps inside the cabinet in the center and waves her arms around "magically," and the cabinets to either side of her rise off the ground (on wires; I can see the wires). She picks a white sheet up off the floor and holds it high so you can't see her. She shakes the sheet once, twice. And reveals . . . Maestro. He's standing there now, twirling the sheet, and posing in the center cabinet to applause. Urma is gone. He points to the first cabinet, where he was just tied up. The doors fly open and it's empty. He points to the third cabinet, to his left. The doors fly open and there's Urma. Posing. Cheesing.

"*Voilà*," Urma says, pausing the DVD as her old self takes a bow. "Teleportation. Maestro's best trick. None of the old magicians could figure out how he did it."

"Wait, so you're saying that's *you*? And there's *another* Urma on the stage somewhere?" I ask.

"We would switch roles. Sometimes I would be the one hiding behind the cabinet. Sometimes I'd be the girl getting the applause."

"But you could be look-alikes," Veronica says. "You could even be her twin for all we know. I'm saying, how does this all mean you're from *the Realm*?"

"My dear, I didn't believe it myself. When I first met the other Urma, *I* even thought I was the original Urma, and she the copy. But Maestro showed me it's true."

"Wait, so you're saying there's copies of *everything* in our world?" asks Too Tall. "Like, there's a Realm Kingston, there's a Realm me?"

"Certainly."

Too Tall is trying to process all this. "So it's a multiverse sort of situation?"

"Come on," says V. "You're not buying this, are you?"

"I have no reason to lie to you, Veronica," says Urma.

"I bet you do," V shoots back. "I bet you have some reason you lured my cousin to this house."

"You're right, Veronica. There is a reason I brought you here. And a reason I'm telling you everything I know." Urma holds the crystal around her neck in her hands. "Because I can't live without *this*."

"I found one of those under the stage," says Tall. "What is it?"

"This crystal, like me, is *of the Realm*. It enables me to live in your reality. Without it, I would wither up and expire. It's like pure Realm energy, concentrated. It's made of the stuff of my world, and it keeps me going."

"Okay," I say. "But what's that got to do with me?"

"When Maestro first brought me to this world, he had this box. It was a small box, made of wood, but enchanted in such a way that it could reach the Realm without opening a rift. Maestro would put a crystal inside and it would come out full of Realm energy. It's a small thing, but it means everything to me."

"And this box . . . ," I say.

She looks back at the television like she's remembering something. "It turned out it was Preston's box, and he took it back. The box you found at the Mercury, Kingston."

"Okay," says Veronica, losing her patience. "So you want the box King found. Is that it? Well, you can't have it. Because we don't even have it. Can we go now?"

"You don't have it?" Urma asks with a nervous chuckle. She digs her nails against the crystal around her neck. "But I'm sure you can get it, no?"

"Wait, I don't understand," I say. "If you need these crystals to survive, what have you been doing since my dad disappeared? I mean, you haven't had the box this whole time."

"It hasn't been easy. When Maestro opened the portal the night of the fire, that rift created heaps of crystal. I gathered them. I've kept them. There's crystals all around us, in this house. I'm surviving, but barely. I haven't left the house since that day four years ago, Kingston. I need that box to live. If you would bring it to me, I will show you how to retrieve your father from the Realm."

It sounds good. Too good. I want to believe she can help me. I want to believe that giving her the box would solve everything. But I have this nagging feeling. I remember my uncle's warning. *That fish out of water I was talking about? Imagine it's more like a shark. And you're just chum.*

"My uncle has the box, Miss Tan. If you can help us get my dad back, I'm sure he'll let you hold the box," I say, though I'm not exactly sure of anything my uncle will or won't do. "I can ask him," I offer.

This doesn't seem to satisfy Urma.

"But how can you be sure he'll be reasonable? Maybe," she says like the idea just occurred to her, "you can sneak it for me?"

"Are you asking me to swipe it from my uncle, to give to you?"

"We're not stealing from my father for you, lady," says Veronica.

"Of course. Of course, I understand," Urma says. "Could you do me one favor, then?"

She removes the crystal from around her neck by its chain and dangles it in front of us.

My eyes are drawn to the light in the center that looks like a tiny star.

"Look at the light."

The crystal swings.

Back . . .

And forth . . .

"Look at the light," she repeats.

And I'm so, so sleepy.

Eyelids so heavy they fall shut.

21

WAIT FOR YOUR father ...

Wait for your father ...

Wait for your father to go to sleep. Search his workshop for the Magician's Lost and Found. Bring the box and the Watch of 13 to me. Wait for your father to go to sleep. Search his workshop for the Magician's Lost and Found. Bring the box and the Watch of 13 to me. Wait for your father to go to sleep ...

My eyes open. I have to resist the urge to sleep. It's hard. I want to sleep very badly. But I can't. I know I can't. This isn't right at all.

I'm on the beige couch next to Veronica and Too Tall. Too Tall is fast asleep against the armchair next to the couch. We're surrounded by Mint and the boys from the theater. Urma Tan is in front of them, standing over us. She's dangling the crystal in front of Veronica. It's rocking back and forth, back and forth. My cousin is in some kind of trance. Urma is speaking to her.

" . . . bring the box and the Watch of 13 to me."

"He's awake!" Mint shouts.

It takes me a second to realize he's talking about me.

"What?" says Urma.

"Kingston—he's awake!" Mint repeats, pointing at me. I've never heard him sound so surprised.

Urma's pale eyes turn to me. "How in the world?" she says, almost to herself.

"His hand's glowing," growls Mint.

"Indeed," says Urma.

"You said he's not strong enough to resist yet—" says Mint.

Strong enough . . . yet? I look down, a step behind their conversation. My hand *is* glowing.

I get a jolt of awareness as everything that's going on around me clicks. Too Tall is asleep, Veronica is in a trance, I'm groggy, just waking up . . .

The crystal catches my eye. The chain sways and the light from inside the shard winks at me. It's like a star trapped in ice. I realize my hand is reaching for the light. My fingers are glowing blue beneath the glove. I feel like I'm in some sort of trance, but not the trance Urma was trying to put me in. The opposite of that. I can sense what she wants from me, but all this energy coming from my hand is resisting her. Power is gathering to my fingertips. I can detect the faintest shifts of breath on the air. It's like I can touch anything I want in the room without moving. Like I can touch the crystal . . .

It *leaps* from Urma's grasp and whips across the coffee table. I catch it as though I called it *straight to my hand.*

I stare at diamond-shaped crystal. I thought it would be cold, but it's warm to the touch.

I look up. Urma and the crew are as stunned as I am.

As I hold the crystal in my hand, away from Urma, she gasps and changes color. Her flesh turns that construction-paper gray. It happens as quick as if a rain cloud blocked the sun. Suddenly, she looks like she's not made of flesh and blood. You can see the edges of her skull beneath her skin like she's peeling. The strength leaves her body, and Mint catches her before she falls.

"V, Tall!" I shout as loud as I can. "Wake up! Run!"

They both snap to, shaking off the trance, blinking really fast.

"Wha—?" says Tall.

"What's going on?" says V.

"Run!" I shout again. I'm on my feet now.

They don't need to be told twice.

We break for the door. The crew is too stunned and confused to do anything about it.

"Kingston." I hear Urma's weak voice.

I stop at the entrance.

V and Tall burn past me, out into the yard.

I know I probably shouldn't, but I look back.

Mint and one of his boys hold Urma up beneath her arms. She looks so weak, a strong breeze could crush her.

"Please. Help me," she says. "And I can help you save him."

I look down at the crystal in my hand.

My thoughts collide in my mind.

King, you can't trust her. She tried to hypnotize you.

But she needs it to live . . .

Can she really open a portal?

Like the one my dad sacrificed himself to close?

But can I really save him?

The thoughts come too fast and I'm stuck not knowing what to do.

"King!" Veronica shouts from outside. "Come on, let's go!"

I take one more look at Urma, and I can see that she's suffering. That part is real.

I drop the crystal at my feet by the door and I'm gone.

———◆———

ONCE I CATCH up to Tall and my cousin, we all jog together like we're fleeing a crime scene. I can tell everyone is really shaken up, because no one wants to be the first to talk about what just happened. I don't know how we decided where to go, or whether we even decided at all, or if the smell of comfort food, of baking crust and cheese drew us to Not Not Ray's on its own.

We don't even say a word until we're all sitting down with hot pizza.

"I mean, what's she even doing with *children* there?" Veronica blurts as she takes a bite out of her sausage-and-peppers slice.

"I don't know. It was so strange," I say, relieved to be able to talk about it.

"Too strange for me," says Tall. "King, you want to tell

us what went down back there? I can't remember much. Only that it got very weird, very quickly."

"She held out that crystal," I say. "Next thing I knew, we were all asleep."

Then my hand was glowing. That's what woke me up.

It stopped glowing when we hit Thurston Avenue, about when we were out of range of Urma.

"What was she doing to us?" Veronica asks, and she sounds concerned.

"She was telling you, over and over, to steal the box from your dad and bring it to her," I say. "The box, and the Watch of 13."

"Are you serious?" Veronica scowls in outrage. "So that nutty lady put programs inside my mind? King, that is the worst thing I've ever heard."

"But maybe I stopped it? I mean, I think I stopped it," I say.

"How can you know?" she asks.

"Yeah, did they program me, too, King?" asks Tall.

"I honestly don't know. I was out cold. They seemed really surprised when I woke up, even," I say. "I think my Realm hand, like, snapped me out of it."

"Maybe she's hypnotizing those kids," says Tall. "I

mean, why would they hang around her like that? What's she doing for them?"

It hadn't occurred to me. But he's got a point.

"But why?" asks V. "What does she get out of it?"

"And if she's such a master hypnotist, then why try and talk to me at all? Why tell us all that about the Realm and being a copy? Why not just start with the hypnosis?"

"It's not that easy," says V. "Hypnotists—they have to make you drop your guard. You can't just walk into a room with a crystal on a chain."

"Did you guys see what happened when the crystal *flew* to me?" I ask. "I mean, can we talk about that for a sec?"

"Yeah, I wasn't sure if I dreamed that. It's very hazy," says Tall.

"What, like, it came to you?" asks V.

"Yeah, guys, this hand is, like, breaking all kinds of laws of physics. I guess you were in a trance at the time. The crystal popped right out of her hand and into mine. And did you see what happened next? She collapsed. She turned gray. Like, grayer than Mint, her whole body. I thought her face was going to fall off."

"Yeah," says V. "So what?"

"Maybe she was telling the truth?"

"The truth about what, now?" asks Tall.

"About needing the energy from the crystals to survive. About the Realm. About . . . creating a portal to bring Dad back," I say. "I think she was maybe telling the truth, is all."

"King, you sound kinda desperate," says V.

"What? I don't mean I'm going to give her the box. I just mean, maybe she's telling the truth. That we can make a portal."

"*We* can make a portal?"

"Well, whoever. I mean, doesn't it make sense? If Maestro could do it, why can't we? That's the part where I feel like she was telling the truth. And it's just the kind of thing your father wouldn't want to tell me, thinking I'll do something stupid."

"Well, in fairness to my dad, you *are* doing stupid things. Maestro was a master magician. He studied for a lifetime in order to be able to make that Mirror." Veronica releases a breath. "Should we tell my dad about all this?"

"I don't know, V."

"Not that I'm saying we should—but why not?" she asks.

"Because he won't let me do it. He probably thinks

something bad will happen if I try to get Pop back, just 'cause I'm a kid."

"So you want to do this on your own? Without Urma's help or my dad's help?"

"You think I should trust Urma Tan?"

"Well, it seems like you sorta kinda are, if you don't want to talk to my dad about it. You're taking her word at face value."

"Not at face value. Not exactly. I don't want to give her the box."

"But you think the rest of what she said was true? What if she made all that up just to get this box from you?"

"It's possible. Of course it's possible. I just wish we knew more."

"What about those murals?" says Tall. "I mean, whoever's painting those can, like, *see* the Realm somehow. We've got to find *them*. 'Cause, Urma? Urma Tan is lying," says Tall.

"Right," says Veronica.

"Well, like we said, since we don't know exactly *what* she's lying about, it's a good idea. I mean, even she says those murals show the Realm," I say.

"Is there proof, though?" asks Tall. "Is there any other

proof that these murals are of the Realm, other than Urma 'Suspect' Tan's word?"

I shrug. "My dad's hat?"

"You mentioned that before," says V. "Why do you think it's in the Realm?"

"He wore that hat when he performed at the Mercury. Remember? When he jumped through the Mirror."

"Okay," says Tall. "So, Operation Find Us a Muralist is officially in effect."

"Great," I say.

"Matteo!" Too Tall calls.

"Yes, my friend?" Matteo is knuckles deep in a round heap of dough.

"You know who's been doing those murals around town?"

"Murals . . . Like the one of the graveyard over by the Dead End?"

"Yeah," says Tall with a quick wink to us. "That's the one." Though I'm pretty sure he's just playing along.

"That mural is incredible. My son almost turned and walked into it! Spooky," he says.

"You know who does those?"

He shrugs. "No clue," he says, and goes back to his dough.

"Okay," says Veronica. "So what's our first stop?"

"Let me ask you guys this. Is there an art supply store in Echo City?" I suggest. "I'm saying, whoever this muralist is, they go through a ton of paint. Something tells me it's local."

CLEOPATRA'S ART SUPPLIES is a makeshift storefront on the ground floor of a warehouse. A little bell chimes when we open the door, but for now, we're the only ones in the store. Too Tall, Veronica, and I walk the aisles, scanning the drafting pencils, different sizes and types of paper, and all the spray cans of paint. Everything feels half done. A stack of sketch pads separates two aisles. The back of the store is just a hanging tarp.

"Wow, they just leave the spray paint cans out like that?" observes Too Tall. "Maybe our muralist just swipes them."

Veronica asks, "What makes you say that?"

"Well, it's like King said. Those murals we saw? That's a lot of paint to go through. Paint costs money. Unless it don't, you feel me?"

The art store smells like plaster dust, warehouse debris, and pencil shavings.

"Look back here!" Too Tall holds one of the hanging tarps in the back aside. "You're going to want to see this, I think."

I duck through the opening. There's another tarped-off area, but this space has paintings hung up on the walls. They're all of street scenes from Echo City, with the same sort of strong outlines and colors as the murals. It's the old nightlife from years ago, people out and about in cuff links and jazzman hats and frilly dresses and pearls and silver heels in front of bright storefronts and neon signs splashing color into each frame. As I'm looking at each painting, the storefront signs begin to feel familiar . . . *The Red Room, The Double Rainbow, The Flourish, Lemur Leftovers, The Sawed Lady Salon* . . . I quickly pull the old map out of my shorts pocket and match the names.

I gaze at the paintings some more as it hits me that this is the Thurston Avenue from my map.

"Um, can I help you?" a voice intrudes.

We're all caught off guard. I turn to see a bald, serious-looking Black girl, maybe fourteen or fifteen, staring at us like she's caught us all shoplifting.

"We were just admiring your artwork," says Veronica, the first of us to recover.

"This isn't my work. And this area is private."

"Right. Er, sorry," says Veronica.

"The art supplies are all out front," says the girl.

I take one last look at the paintings as we file back out through the tarp.

Too Tall clears his throat and puts on a smile so big it's like an instant light show. "We were wondering if you knew the person doing these incredibly fly murals around the neighborhood," he says in a smooth delivery.

"Can't say I do," the girl says in a bored voice. "Can I help you find some supplies?"

"Do you know the murals we're talking about?" I ask. "They're kind of amazing."

"Lots of murals in Brooklyn," she says.

I smell something funny about her reaction. Like she isn't even asking which murals or where they are or anything. Like she just wants us to go away.

"Well, could you tell us who did those paintings of Thurston Avenue back there?" I ask, with a little more firmness in my voice.

She looks at me then, as if for the first time, and something about my face seems to startle her. She lets out a tiny gasp and her eyes twitch wide for a second.

She recovers fast, but her reaction was obvious.

"What? Did you paint those?" I ask.

"N-no," she says. "The owner paints those." Her mouth opens like she wants to ask me something, and then she changes her mind.

"Can we talk to him?" I ask.

"Or *her*?" Veronica says, darting a look at me before winking at the girl.

But she isn't feeling the love from V, either. "No. You can't."

"Listen. I know this may sound silly, but it's *really* important that we talk to whoever is doing these paintings," I say in my best pleading voice.

Veronica chimes in. "We have reason—I mean, *good* reason—to think that the person who does these paintings can help us figure out some really tough stuff that we can't figure out any other way."

She's listening. She's not bought in, but she's listening. And I like her face when she's listening to us.

"It's about my father," I say. "He's gone now. But I need to know if he's safe."

"Who's your father?" she asks.

"Preston James. I'm Kingston, this is my cousin Veronica. That there is Too Tall."

"Howdy," says Tall.

She nods to each of us. "I'm Sula. Preston was your father?"

"He *is* my father."

"Huh," Sula says, still with that good hard look at me. "And that's your face," she says, almost to herself.

I shrug. "Only face I got."

Sula sighs like she's about to do something she will regret. "I think you'd better follow me."

She turns on a dime and heads toward the back.

Veronica, Too Tall, and I all hesitate.

"You coming?" asks Sula.

She holds the tarp open, and waves.

We follow her down a hallway and up a temporary staircase to a platform. I notice her arms are muscular and she moves like an athlete. We turn another corner and enter a big room, lit by a lone bulb.

There's a wall with a just-finished mural.

Everyone is speechless.

There, painted on the wall, is *me*.

My face.

No question.

And I know exactly when it was.

Yesterday. I'm in the trapdoor chamber below the stage at the Mercury Theater. My hand is in the box. The Magician's Lost and Found, at least that's what Urma Tan called it, is painted huge. Like the box is falling toward the viewer. I'm behind the box with my hair crazy and my eyes bugging out. I'm stumbling over the box, my wrist disappeared inside.

Too Tall stares at the mural from inches away like he's just putting it together. "I was there," he whispers, and points to the corner where his sneaker just makes it into the frame.

There's a boy sitting at a table in front of the mural. He's covered in paint, and eating cereal. He's also bald, and his face is a dead ringer for Sula's.

"This is my brother, Sol," says Sula with a hand on his shoulder. "Sol, this is Kingston James. Preston's son." Her heavy-lidded eyes land on me. "Kingston, Maestro was our father."

IT TAKES A good minute for everything that's happening to sink in.

I'm looking from Sula to Sol, comparing them to my memories of Maestro's face.

Too Tall is still staring at the mural, paying special attention to the footwear in the background.

Sula is pacing and shaking her head. Worried about something.

Sol is staring at me even harder than I'm staring at him.

I realize it's weird to just look at another person's face for whole seconds on end, but in that moment, I don't care. Sol doesn't seem to care, either.

Maestro's children, I think. *Does the rivalry pass on from parent to child?*

And then I think, *But who could understand what I'm going through better than them?*

"Man, this mural is, like, good," says Too Tall. "I mean, really good. Kid even got the stitching right on my Concord 11s."

"How did you see this?" I ask Sol. "This just happened. Like, yesterday."

His eyes go wide. His dark pupils glimmer in the light like a pair of blackberries.

"How did you know I was there? When did you paint—" And I realize by his blank look that he's not going to answer, or say anything. "When did he paint this?" I turn to Sula.

"Yesterday. He was sleeping all day, which he does a lot, and then he woke up about six and he just started painting. Didn't stop for three hours," she says.

Veronica asks, "Your brother does all of these murals around the neighborhood?"

Sula glances at Veronica like she's trying to figure out friend from foe.

"I'm Veronica. Kingston's cousin. My father isn't

a magician like you guys, though. He's a trick builder. Which may be the only thing worse than a magician."

Sula breaks a grin. "Maybe. We'll have to compare notes sometime. But yes—my brother is Echo City's little phantom muralist. Where you may just see a wall, he sees a field of flowers."

I point to the mural. "I was there, yesterday, right when you said he woke up. That happened under the stage at the Mercury. Sula, everything in your brother's mural happened yesterday, to us."

Sula nods, taking it in.

"Well, to him everything he paints is really happening, whether it happens here or there," she says.

"You mean the Realm, don't you? You know about it?" I say.

"Do I know about the Realm?" Sula paces around the paint cans. "Does a butcher's kid know about a T-bone?" she asks me.

I shrug. "My dad never told me anything about it."

"Maybe. Or maybe you know more than you realize."

"I don't know. My dad was kinda big on protecting us."

"Can't say the same," says Sula. "But I didn't get the worst of it. My brother takes that honor."

I look into the kid's blackberry eyes, wondering what they've seen.

"I'm not sure if you already know this," Sula says carefully. "I feel I should tell you. You opened a rift to the Realm yesterday. Did you know that?"

"I . . . No," I say. "I did not know that."

Veronica shakes her head along with Too Tall.

"Oh," says Sula. "Yikes. That's all my brother paints. Scenes he sees in the Realm. So you didn't mean to do that?"

I look back up at the painting. "Does it look like I know what I'm doing?" I ask.

"To be honest with you, no. Guess I was hoping you did. It can be bad news, to mess with the Realm when you don't know what you're doing. Or even when you do know what you're doing, really. Nothing good ever happens."

"How does your brother see into the Realm?" asks Veronica.

"He just does. He's not what you'd call normal."

"This day is not what I'd call normal," Too Tall mutters.

"Listen, it's a long story. I've got some chocolate milkshakes in the fridge. I can shut down the store. You got time?"

We all nod. It's a better offer than we expected.

"So you *know* about the two Urmas? *Wow,*" Sula says, taking a sip of chocolate milkshake. We all sit on empty plaster buckets on the warehouse floor. We've spent the last hour or so talking. Turns out Sol and Sula are both thirteen years old, Sol just looks younger. We told her about our trip to Urma's house on Torrini Boulevard. "That's going to make this story way easier to tell. Basically, we're both Maestro's kids," Sula says simply. "The real Urma Tan is my mother. The Realm Urma—the one you met earlier today, apparently—that's Sol's mother."

"Wait, what?" I say.

"That's a new one on me," says V.

Too Tall examines Sol's face.

"I don't know, bud. I think you look like your daddy," says Tall.

"So your mom *and* dad are in the Realm, just like my dad?" I say. "Realm Urma said that she can help us make a portal and bring them home."

There's a look of fear in Sula's eye as she shakes her head. "You *can't* trust her," she says.

"Right." Too Tall and V agree with Sula on that one.

"No, you don't understand. She isn't human." Sula turns to Veronica. "She only seems like a real person."

"You mean how she's some kinda Realm zombie?" asks Too Tall. "No offense," he says to Sol.

"Call her what you like. Trust me, he's not offended. I'm more of a mom to him than she ever was," says Sula. "She uses the power in those crystals to control and drain the children around her. It's how she stays looking like herself. Without feeding off their youth, she'd look as gray as those kids."

"I wondered what was happening to them," says Veronica, understanding.

"Mint and the rest of them all think they're learning some ancient magic, meanwhile she's just feeding off them. But she's running out of time, her Realm energy is depleted. It's been four years since anyone's opened the Realm, started a new echo. That is, until you showed up," she says, cutting her eyes at me.

"Why kids?" asks V.

"It's their youth, I think, that sustains her. Most of the kids come off the street around here, no family. She teaches them about crystals and shows off her 'powers.' Those crystals are the only thing keeping her alive. Somehow, they hold energy longer with the kids around. She has this *thirst*, like a vampire from another reality. She, like, drinks your life force. And you don't even know it's happening," says Sula.

"It happened to you?" asks V.

"And Sol. Look, I know you guys probably think you had a weird childhood, with magicians and trick builders and everything. But imagine there's two of your mom, and you have to pretend one doesn't exist."

"Okay," I say. "You win."

"We always wondered why Sol was sick a lot, and he had that gray look, you know, how the boys around her now look. That's how Sol used to look, too."

Sol flashes a healthy grin and pinches his own cheek, like, *Look how hearty I am these days.* He gets a smile out of me, V, and Tall.

"Just before the night of the Mercury, I told my father that Realm Urma was draining Sol," says Sula. "He didn't believe me, at first. But I think he was trying to return her to the Realm, before everything went wrong."

"Why do you say that?" I ask.

"Maestro—my father—I think made that portal that night to send Realm Urma back to the Realm, where she belongs. But somehow it was *my* mom that went through the Mirror. The rest is history. I think *she* pushed my mom through with her magic, somehow," says Sula. There's no doubt who *she* refers to.

"*She* hypnotized me to get me to steal from my father for her," says V. "Or, she tried to. Still not sure if it worked." She shrugs.

"I'm so sorry. She's hurt a lot of people, especially her own son. Sol was born with a gift and a curse. Sol gets these visions, and they're so intense they only go away if he paints them. It's like he needs to obsess over the image, and spend days with it, then it leaves him alone."

"You think it's because his mother is a Realm echo of the real Urma?"

"I think so," says Sula. "Kid's lucky to be here, whatever that means. It's like his body is here, but his mind is in the Realm. Like he's in two places at once."

Sol startles me for a second. He's pulled his headphones off and he's tugging at the white glove on my left hand.

I think I get it. He wants me to take the glove off.

He was listening the whole time. He knows about my hand, without even seeing it. Maybe he does see it.

Maybe I shouldn't, I think. *But what have I really got to lose?*

I yank off the glove, and watch as their mouths drop in awe.

"Think I know how your brother feels. I'm sorta in two places at once, myself. Except my mind is here, and my hand, I guess, is in the Realm."

"Okay . . . ," says Sula. "How did this happen exactly?"

"It's all in that mural up there."

I explain yesterday's mission to the Mercury, and how I found that box—the Magician's Lost and Found—and how my hand slipped inside.

As I talk, her eyes seem to see three times more than what I'm saying. I'm distracted by how pretty she is. Eyebrows thick like two perfect caterpillars, eyes round and big with eyelids heavy like a set of curtains in front of the whole universe, like if she opens them all the way you'll be lost in space.

"So you went to the theater looking for your dad?" Sula asks.

"Well, not exactly. Just hoping I'd find some clue about how to get him back."

"But King, *you made* a new breach. Remember, the

Realm is echoes of our world, copies made the moment there's a breach. The last breach before yesterday was four years ago, at the Mercury."

"How do you know that?" asks V.

"Because I *see* the Realm all the time, I know each echo pretty well by now. My brother is always painting them. *This* is the first new echo in four years." She points back up at the mural. That moment is looming over us in more ways than one.

"Okay," I say. "And that's a problem?"

"Don't you know how the Realm works?" she asks.

"I don't. Don't know what I'm doing. Feels like we covered this."

"Look, the Realm is made of echoes of our world, right? When you cause a rift, open a portal, whatever you want to call it, you start a new echo. But the old echoes are pushed back as soon as a new one is created. And eventually, you can't get back to those old echoes. They're out of reach from our reality. You follow me?"

"So you're saying . . ."

"That this place your dad's in—this echo, he may be stuck there forever soon. When you opened the Lost and Found, you put your dad's echo on the clock. Your dad—

and my dad and mom—are in that echo that's fading further away from our reality. It's only a matter of time. His echo could be lost in the Realm."

"Oh no," I say. "How long? How long do we have?"

Sol goes and digs through some piles of boards and canvas and comes back with a small dry-erase board attached to a chain, and a marker.

He writes on the board the number 13.

"Thirteen what?" I ask. "Thirteen hours? Thirteen days? What?"

He keeps on writing, another 13 below that.

"Look forward and backward, it's all the same," says Sula. "The Realm cycles in hours of thirteen. After two cycles"—she snaps her fingers—"time's up."

"WHAT TIME *WAS* it?" I realize that's the most important question. "What time was it when I found the box?"

I look from Too Tall to Veronica as if they might know the answer immediately.

They just shrug.

"I don't know, cuz," says V.

"Quick! We've got to figure it out!"

"Um, wait!" says Tall. "Why do we need to know that, exactly?"

I press my palms into my forehead.

"Because," Veronica says patiently. "When Kingston put his hand in the box, he made something happen in the

Realm. From that moment, we've got twenty-six hours—two cycles of thirteen—before his dad's echo is gone for good. At least, that's what I got."

I nod to her. "That's what I got, too."

We look to Sula. She nods. "Yes. I think that's right."

"Ah," says Tall. "Okay, let me think. What time was it? Phones keep time. And phones keep track of everything. Did we use any phones? Send any texts?"

I snap my fingers. "You made a note on your notepad, about the code."

"Yes!" Too Tall says, and thumbs through his phone. "That note was made . . . yesterday at 6:18 p.m."

"Okay, and then we wandered around that old theater for a while. Say I found the box, I don't know, twenty minutes later?"

"Call it 6:30, to be safe," says Veronica.

"Okay, so 6:30 p.m. yesterday plus twenty-six hours is—"

"It's 8:30 p.m. this evening," says V.

"Right. And the time now?" I ask.

"It's 5:03 p.m.," Tall reads from his phone.

Three hours . . .

"Hey, not so bad! Three whole hours!" says Too Tall.

I can't even tell if he's trying to be supportive or if he really thinks that's plenty of time. I just groan.

Three hours.

The thought makes me dizzy.

"So. What now?" he says.

"What now? I don't have the slightest idea! I don't have a clue how to make a portal or pull Dad through or even find Dad—I don't know!"

"Okay, big guy," says Tall. "I'm with ya. Take it easy now, I'm one of the good guys."

V puts a gentle hand on my shoulder.

"Right. Sorry," I say.

Sol writes something on the board where he'd written 13 twice. Only now, there's just one 13 written there. He takes the marker between the 1 and the 3 and draws a simple + sign.

"One plus three," says Veronica.

"Four," says Too Tall. "Right. Four."

"What's he mean?" I ask.

Sula shrugs.

"Great," says Too Tall. "More riddles and numbers. My favorite."

"Can you help us?" I ask Sula.

"Listen, I wish you good luck and all. But nothing

good happens when you mess with the Realm." Sol suddenly gives his sister a look. She reads his expression and nods. "Sol wants to help you, Kingston. But I don't know how to open a portal in the next three hours. I don't know how to open a portal at all, to tell you the truth. I know it's not easy, which is why no one has pulled it off in the last four years. I think there was some reason that my father had to open the portal when your dad was onstage. But to be completely honest, I'd rather Sol didn't go near the Realm, Urma, or anything having to do with any of it."

I nod when she's done talking. But my mind feels like the dome of the Mercury right now. Like there's a gaping hole in my skull and pigeons are flying in and out. I don't know what to do. Usually if I feel like this, I go to Mom. And if Mom's not there, I go to Dad. Well, not the real Dad, but the Dad Voice in my head. Even though Dad's been gone for years, I still can remember his voice so well that sometimes I can hear what he would say, even though he's not around to say it. Dad Voice would say something like, *Kid, you better look after that muralist,* or, *You better be nice to your mom and tell her the truth.*

It was always *you better.* But not like *you better do this or else,* it was more like *you better* be *a better you.* Pop was there to help me see how I could be better at being me.

But now I'm trying to hear what he would tell me to do, only it's not there. No Dad Voice. I close my eyes and listen, but there's nothing.

Like what will happen when his reality fades and he's gone for good.

"Whoa, King," says Veronica, seeing the dead look in my eyes. "Don't go too dark, now. Hang in there."

"What do we do, V?"

"Forgive me for suggesting this again, but don't you think it's time we talk to my dad?"

"You sure?"

"What's the worst he could do?"

"He could stop us," I say.

"Stop us from doing what?"

She's got me there.

Veronica goes on: "I'm just saying, we don't know what we're doing. And maybe my dad doesn't know about the fading echo. Maybe if we tell him, he'll want to help."

THE WALK BACK home takes exactly twelve minutes. Along the way, I think about how to tell Uncle Long Fingers everything we've been up to, from Urma Tan's hypnosis to Sol's painting of me. I wonder how much he already knows.

When we get home, I'm so ready to talk to Long Fingers that I'm actually shocked that my mother is the first person I see.

"Oh, hi, King!" she says.

She's sweaty in a tank top and her braids are pulled up in a high ponytail. She's hard at work clearing out the ground floor to turn the space into a café. She's made some progress. The walls are bare of any and all posters and signs of magic.

The shelving units are pushed to a wall. The velvet curtain that separated the front area is gone, and when you stand near the entrance, you can just about see all the way to the back room and the windows that look out on the backyard.

"Hi, Miss James!" says Too Tall.

"Welcome to the future King's Cup!" Ma returns his bright smile. "Would you all like a tour? Full disclosure, it may require some imagination."

"King's . . . Cup?" I repeat.

"You like it?" she asks with a wink.

"Well, yeah," I say.

"Okay, over here to my right," she says, and waves an open hand along the wall where the shelves are stacked, "will be the countertop. We'll serve the drinks here. We'll have all your milks and sugars and napkins and such. Behind that wall will be the kitchen. We're going to stain—yes, stain—this brick wall here. It'll be all nice and warm and red and exposed. Then here, here, there, and outside, this will all be seating areas . . ."

I start to zone out as Mom walks us through each part of her dream café. All I can think about is Pop. How can she stand there and yap away about this when we have *less than three hours* to save him?

Because she doesn't know, I remind myself. *Because you won't tell her.*

"King, are you okay?" she asks.

The seconds feel like an eternity as Too Tall, Veronica, and my mom all watch me.

Tell her, some voice urges from the back of my mind. *Tell her everything. She has a right to know.*

"I'm fine, Ma," I say.

"You don't like the name?"

"No, I love it. I appreciate it. Like, a lot."

"Okay. You don't sound too sure."

"Ma—I just need to talk to Uncle Long Fingers, really quick."

"Oh? That's so strange, because he just left."

"He *left*?" I almost shriek.

Mom shrugs. "I was as surprised as you. Him and Crooked Eye. They just took off. They wheeled this huge contraption out the back. Whole thing covered in a tarp. Wouldn't say where they were going, or when they're coming back. King, you sure you're okay?"

"It's just . . . this *game* we were going to play. Long Fingers, he had, like, the rules."

Mom looks at me like I have five heads. Then she scans

Veronica and Too Tall, who smile and nod like, *Exactly what King said.*

I'm so relieved when Ma finally nods back and goes to work. Not that I got away with anything. She'll ask later, why I'm acting so strange. But right now, we have under *three hours* and counting, and it looks like we'll have to try and pull something off without my uncle's help.

"He *left*?" Veronica says in amazement as we take the stairs up to the second floor. "Wow."

"What's so strange about that?" asks Too Tall.

"Nothing, if he were anyone else in the world," says V as we gather in the doorway to my room. "But my dad doesn't leave this place. Wild horses couldn't get him out the front door."

"Must be serious," I say.

"So what's the next move?" asks Tall.

"We got to hit Long Fingers's workshop," I say, ready to do just that. "Maybe we can figure out what he was building, and where he went or something." A plan is kicking into overdrive in my head. *And see if he left the Lost and Found behind.*

Because Urma came through a rift to the Realm. She knows how to do it.

And if I bring her the box, she will help me get him back.

The hard truth is, I would trade this box for my dad. Any day.

I lead the way through the doorway to the room with the wall of books.

"His lab is right back there. You'll like this, Tall. Watch this sick bookcase move," I say, and point to it. *"Whoops—"*

The book *The Four Elements of Magic* leans back on its spine and the wall rumbles and turns to reveal the opening passageway.

I'm standing about twelve feet away, looking at my Realm hand. Just by thinking about moving the book, I moved the book from across the room.

Too Tall covers his amazed mouth with his hands, like he saw a celebrity but knows it's not the time to shout their name.

I shrug. "I didn't mean to do that. I mean, I meant to go do that the normal way."

Finally he says, *"Ba-NA-nas."*

"I'd really like to understand the powers of that hand of yours better," says Veronica.

"Me too," I say.

Okay, I realize as I step into the passageway. *I'm moving books from across the room by accident.* My focus is so strong, it's almost out of my control. Glad Mom wasn't around to see that. I'd have some explaining to do.

My eyes adjust to the dim light and the red glow in the foyer. It's the old shrine to my father, with the pictures and clippings of him and his tricks. V reads the sign hanging over the doorway.

"*The Four Elements Open the Way.* Huh."

"What?" I ask.

"No, it's nothing. Just, four, like the number Sol showed us."

"*Four* Elements of Magic," I say.

"And these four walls here," she says.

I look from one wall to the next in the hexagonal room—six sides: one entrance, one exit, and four walls. "A wall for Dad's three best tricks . . . and one for the Mirror."

"Okay, that is a lot of fours. So what's it mean?" asks Too Tall, looming behind us in the tight space.

"I'm just thinking, those four elements, right? See, I know how my dad's mind works. *The Four Elements Open the Way.* Very clever. I bet you anything that's not about the book and this passageway. It's about the *actual* four elements, whatever those are."

"You mean like the four walls here?" asks Too Tall.

V smiles at me.

The pictures on each wall are each devoted to a different object. Three are of my dad's best-known tricks: Hooker's Vanishing Deck, the Skull of Balsamo, and William Tell's Pistol. The fourth wall is all pictures of Maestro's Mirror. Could each trick represent an element?

"The way these pictures are organized. It's no coincidence," I say. "Four tricks, four elements . . ."

Like Dad's book . . . More like the fourth member of our family . . .

Realizing there's one clue that's been right under our noses, I head back out the way we came.

"Where you going, King?" asks Tall.

"About time we checked out my dad's old book."

26

BACK OUT AT the wall of books, V removes *The Four Elements of Magic* from its wall contraption with a screwdriver from her dad's workshop.

The book is so old, pages are falling out as I leaf through. Tall bends to pick a couple off the floor.

I'm not gonna lie, the book is crazy hard to read. *F*s and *E*s are thrown into words in bizarre places, and some phrasing just sounds beyond odd. I stop at a passage that reads:

> *The third kinde of Magick containeth the whole Philofophy of Nature which bringeth to light the inmoft vertues, and extracleth them out of Natures hidden bofome to humane ufe;*

"Whoa," says Tall. "Is that even English?"

"It's Old English. Like old before spelling was a thing, I guess," says Veronica.

I keep paging through, searching for something I can understand. Then I stop at a page full of Dad's handwriting. "Here!" I say, and get a warm rush at the sight of the familiar script. Looping *L*s and bold *D*s in the handwriting that used to fill the pages of yellow legal pads stacked around the house.

"You can understand *that*?" says Tall.

"The Four Elements," I say as I decipher my dad's handwriting. "He's talking about the four elements. Just like the Magician's Lost and Found."

Tall looks at me, puzzled.

"The top of the box, it had the same *four* signs. The Pistol. The Deck of Cards. The Skull of Balsamo. And the Mirror."

"*The Four Elements Open the Way*," says Veronica. "Your dad was using three of them in his act every night."

"Yup. The William Tell's Pistol gag, Hooker's Vanishing Deck, and the Skull of Balsamo," I say excitedly. "Those were his go-tos."

"And Maestro's was the Mirror," Veronica says.

"It says here they each represent a different school of

magic, the Pistol is Force, the Cards are Illusion, the Skull is Mystic, and the Mirror is Sorcery."

"So they're like parts of a magic puzzle or something," Tall jumps in.

"Bingo," I say. "The box must bring the four elements together?"

Too Tall shrugs. "Maybe it's in the wood? Wish we had that thing. You think there's any chance your dad left the box in his workshop?"

"Only one way to find out," says Veronica. She has this determined look that makes me smile.

LONG FINGERS'S LAB looks very different without the man himself sitting in the middle of it all. I can actually see to the back wall without that big thing under the tarp in the middle. I look around, wondering how he and Crooked even got that thing out of here. There's some of the stuff from the magic store—the canes and mannequin hands—that my uncles stashed here. The taxidermy owls are high on a shelf, keeping watch. There's a bunch of blueprints tacked to the walls with handwriting scribbled all over them. There's a giant map of the world with dates scribbled across different places: Ancient Egypt, 2594 BC; Carthage, 146 BC; Ancient Rome, 44 BC; Britannia, 420; Paris, 1312; Florence, 1492; Edo, 1603; Budapest, 1881; West Africa, 1901; Louisville, 1934. There's a stack of mirrored shards. Each shard is cut in the shape of a lightning bolt. I find more and more of them as I look around for the box, all about the same size.

"He sure did leave in a hurry," Too Tall says, holding his hand to a warm coffee mug sitting on the desk.

"I don't see it here," I say. "Anyone?"

"Nothing," says V.

"Nada," says Tall.

"Hmm," I say. "Think Long Fingers took it with him?"

"Possible, I guess," says V. "Well, hey, look at that."

"What?" Tall and I say at the same time.

V runs her fingers alongside a cabinet about the size of a mini-fridge. The wood is stained blond and it has a five-pointed star tooled into the center of each side.

"My dad, he built this for me," she says.

"I'm all about a good trip down memory lane, but I think we're on the clock here," Tall says.

V ignores him and traces her finger along the five-pointed star.

"A five-sided star is also five *V*s joined together." She

bends to pull the cabinet away from the wall. "*Whoa*, this thing got heavy," she says as she turns it around.

The side she reveals has a metal latch and lock bolted to it. There's a four-digit number combination beside the lock.

Tall face-palms. "I mean enough already, it's like this family does everything in code."

V starts playing with the combination.

"You think you can figure it out?" I ask.

"Like I said, I know how my dad's mind works," she says, turns the last number wheel, and unlatches the lock. She opens the lid of the cabinet and it releases air with a hiss. "Five *V*s. Or, five fives. In other words, five to the fifth power," V explains. "Five to the fifth power equals 3,125." She shrugs. "That's the code: 3125."

The inside of the cabinet is lined with steel chrome, like a real safe.

There at the bottom, looking like a buried treasure, is the Magician's Lost and Found.

"Why you smiling like that?" Tall asks V.

"No, it's nothing. He knows that I would guess that code. Didn't know he trusted me like that."

"I'm so glad he did," I say, and pick up the Lost and Found.

The Watch of 13 is even still in the locking mechanism. I notice the watch hand is on the 11. Are the watch hands clicking toward Dad's fading echo? I look at my own watch. It's 6:25 p.m.; we're about two hours away from the 13.

"What, King?" asks V.

"Two hours and counting," I say, and open up the Lost and Found, hoping for a clue, some direction, anything to help get Pops back before it's too late.

There's a handwritten note floating near the top. I'd know that handwriting anywhere.

It's my dad's.

THIS NOTE WASN'T *here before. He wrote this. Recently.*

Not four years ago, gathering dust.

He wrote this now. Like, in the present. He's alive, he has a hand, and that hand held a pen and wrote this note. And now it's in my hands.

I realize this is the closest I've been to my dad in nearly four years.

Tall prods, "What's it say?" like he can't take the suspense anymore.

I read it to them:

"Message received, big brother. Will be at appointed place by thirteenth hour. The elements await you in Black

Herman's grave, but you'll have to pull a Henry Brown to get them."

In the silence that follows, I read the words over and over again.

"Wow," says V. "That's a lot."

"Yeah," I agree.

"So the note was meant for my father?" she observes.

"Apparently," I say.

"It sounds like my dad is trying to save your dad after all, huh?"

"Yeah, I think so."

She leans in to read the note herself. "What's this, 'appointed place'?"

"I have no idea. Must be something they worked out between the two of them." Still, something about all of this is bothering me.

"King, why do you sound so glum? Isn't this good news?"

"I dunno, V. It's just, we're running out of time, and Long Fingers didn't even see this note yet, obviously. You see this reference to Black Herman's grave?"

"I did notice that," says V.

"Tall, is there a graveyard in Echo City?"

"Not that I know of."

"I thought so." I dig in my shorts pocket for the map and lay it out. "I'm pretty sure I remember seeing some sort of grave reference on here . . . *There*. Look," I say, and point to a spot on the map by Algernon Lane and Broken Jade Junction. *Graveyard Gate*, it says. "I'm going." I start packing up the map.

"Whoa, whoa, King, not so fast," says V.

I turn on a dime. "*Yes*, so fast. Matter-of-fact, not nearly fast enough. The clock is ticking, V. We don't even know what we're doing or whether we're on the right track. But I got to try something. And this makes the most sense. Come or stay, but I'm going."

I stop at my room to strap on my backpack after I slide the Lost and Found inside and zip up. Then I lead the way back downstairs and to the front door as quickly as possible.

"Leaving us already?" My mom intercepts us. She has a rag in hand like she's just scrubbed all of Echo City by herself. She can't seem to decide whether to be concerned or playful.

"Um, yeah, Ma, it's that game we were playing," I say.

"The one that Uncle Long Fingers knows the rules to?" asks Mom, eyes squinted in suspicion.

"Yeah. That one. And it's like, we got to go back outside . . ."

"Outside, huh? Well, that sounds nice. I was going to ask if you wanted to go for a walk, I haven't been out all day," says Ma.

"Um, well, the thing is . . ." I'm trying to think of a reason she can't come, but I'm coming up blank.

My hesitation isn't lost on Ma. "Are you ducking me, King?" she asks.

"No, Ma, I swear."

"I'm only kidding," she says, and then tilts her head. "Sorta."

"Let's spend time together tomorrow, okay, Ma? Tomorrow, I promise, I'll help out with the house and everything. All day, I'm here."

Maybe with Pop, I think. *Maybe we'll all be here and we can get back all that lost time.*

"Okay," she says. "Veronica, you're playing this game, too?"

"Sure am, Auntie," she says. "Tons of fun."

"Okay. Well, don't have too much fun. Keep an eye on King, V. Please, for me. King's not exactly used to the big city these days. Don't let him get too carried away."

Veronica pauses awkwardly. "I—I won't let him. I

mean, I'll keep both eyes on him, Auntie. Not to worry."

"I'll try not to. Good to see you, Eddie. See you later, King. Love you."

"See you, Ma."

As soon as she nods, we're out the door.

It isn't until I take the steps down to the sidewalk that I realize I didn't say *I love you* back.

THE SHADOWS FALL heavy and stretch long on the sidewalk as time inches closer to the thirteenth hour.

"So tell me, what's up with the rest of that note?" Tall asks me.

"Which part?"

"Well, whose grave are we going to, for one?"

"Black Herman," says Veronica. "Famous old magician from back in the day. He was like a hero to our dads."

"Oh yeah, you mentioned him yesterday. He was the one that would fake his own death and come back?"

"He had this old saying," I explain. "*The Great Black Herman Returns Every Seven Years.* Had it printed on all his old posters and everything."

Veronica says, "Yeah, he'd, like, bury himself alive, and days later be dug up. Then he'd lead a crowd to the local theater and do a show."

"Okay, not bad," says Tall. "Think he'd charge for the burial and the show, like, sell two separate tickets?"

Veronica scoffs. "Probably. In between, he'd even go to nearby towns and be buried alive there, too. Then he'd just keep it going. He'd tour the whole country. Think that was the deal with the whole *Returns Every Seven Years* thing. Took a while to get around back then."

"Sure, maybe that's it," I say. "But everything we learned about magic, we learned before we knew that magic was real. Maybe those stories aren't so straight-forward."

"You think he really died and came back to life?" V says with a sarcastic grin.

"I'm just saying, we don't know anything, for real. I mean, was he from Virginia, like history says? Or was he born in a town in West Africa, like his book says?"

"Um, I'm gonna go with what history says, King," says V with a chuckle. "That book is full of nonsense so he could make money. Like you really think he went to Egypt, India, China, and Paris? *Pfft*. If there was anything magic about that guy, it was how he could turn a profit. Even after he died, they sold tickets to see his body."

"Well, he faked his death for most of his career. No one believed it when he actually died."

Too Tall nods, impressed. "You two really know a lot about this guy, huh?"

"Sure," says V. "In a house like ours, full of Black magicians? Black Herman is like the Black Houdini, only no one's heard of him."

"He was a good man, too, Tall. He supported his community. He'd give loans to Black businesses, scholarships to students, and do free performances to help struggling churches. He never turned his back on his people."

"And what was the other name on there?" asks Tall.

This one I'm less sure about. "It was Henry Brown. Some old magician, I guess. Don't remember his act."

"Henry 'Box' Brown," says Veronica. "Was a slave, in Virginia. He mailed himself north, to Philadelphia, and freedom." She taps my backpack, knuckle rapping the wood of the Magician's Lost and Found. "In a small wooden box."

We walk in silence for a while, and I wonder if this small wooden box can help free my pops, wherever he may be.

TURNS OUT "GRAVEYARD Gate" isn't a graveyard, exactly, but a mural of one. The painting runs half the length of an Echo City block on the forgotten wall of an abandoned car wash. There's a ladder propped up against the wall. Sol is standing toward the top of the ladder, painting something.

Veronica, Too Tall, and I shrug all at once. Sol doesn't seem to notice us, and we don't want to disturb him. He's so focused on his craft, it feels wrong.

We take in the mural. The painted gates are the first thing I notice. The bars are black and high, curling into spirals at the top. There's a hill at the center of the mural and there's a mausoleum at the summit. Sol is painting something inside the mausoleum. Something very small that I can't see.

Gravestones line the way along the sloping hill. Some stand tall and proud with names and phrases declared in bold letters, but none I can actually read. Some are small like rocks, and a couple are made of wood. I try to get close enough to read the names, but the closer I get, the less sense the letters make, like trying to read in a dream.

Sol slides down the ladder with ease and looks at us like he knew we were there all this time.

"Hey, Sol. Where's your sister?" I ask.

He has his dry-erase board hanging on a chain around his neck. He writes something in marker:

The more you look the less you see.

"This kid sure is expert with the cryptic scribbles," says Too Tall, reading the board.

Sol just looks at me and nods, like it all makes perfect sense.

"He's *amazing*," says Veronica, gazing at the graveyard mural with awe. "How long did this take you?"

Sol shrugs.

He's looking at my backpack now with that eerie glare of his. He touches the box through the canvas.

"Um, yeah," I say, very confused. What do I tell him? I

think he's trying to help me. In fact, I'm pretty sure if Sula had her way, he wouldn't be here with us now.

"I've got the Lost and Found," I tell him.

The kid's eyes go round and wide and he nods.

"You want me to take it out?"

He nods some more.

I take the Lost and Found out of my backpack. I open it up, check around the edges, and press against the felt lining. There's nothing there.

Sol's eyes widen when he sees the box. I let him hold it.

I point to the mural. "Which one of these is Black Herman's grave?" I ask him.

He glances at me, and then returns his attention to the box like I never said a word. He runs his fingers around its edges carefully, like he's memorizing every detail.

"Hey," I say, pointing to a stone in the mural. "You painted these, right? Well, I can't read the names on the gravestones. Which one is Black Herman's?"

Not that I'd have a clue what to do next.

He takes me by the hand and steps up to the graveyard gates. He takes the box and sets it against where the handle is painted.

"You want me to put my hand in there?" I ask.

"Oh, you've got to be kidding me," says Veronica.

Sol shakes his head.

"That kid don't look like he's joking," says Tall.

Sol waves me to come closer, and nods in a way that says, *It's okay. Trust me.*

I let him take me by the wrist of my gloved hand and guide it toward the box.

"Okay, I think I get it," I say.

I open the lid of the box and feel a waft of cold air.

Then he tugs the fabric of my white glove and shakes his head.

"No good?" I ask.

He shakes his head some more.

"Sure thing, I gotcha." I take off the glove.

I'm still not quite used to having no visible hand. Even as I wiggle my invisible fingers, I expect to see them.

Sol's smile is full of tiny teeth. He sets his feet and holds the box steady like a catcher who just called a pitch.

I reach my hand through the box.

And my hand keeps going. Past the bottom of the box, past where the wall should be, until I feel the hard metal of a handle in my palm, cool to the touch.

My expression must be crazy because Sol just smiles at me like, *See?*

He nods.

Keep going.

My heart is beating a million miles an hour. There's no visible explanation for what's happening. My hand is *through the box* and *through the wall* somehow.

And now I'm holding the handle to a painted gate, and the handle is cool and hard as iron.

I turn the handle and feel its rusty creak.

Nervous laughter bursts through my teeth.

There's a rush of cold air.

"This is *ama*—"

Fog consumes me. Thick, gushing fog that fills my mouth and throat and surprises the breath out of me. I'm blinded by the cool gray like I've just walked into a cloud.

"V? Tall?" I say, but my voice is muffled by the fog. "Hello? Sol? Anyone?" But the words bounce right back.

The fog clears in front of me. I see the bars of the gates to the graveyard. The handle is still in my hand. But the painted grass behind it is . . . *actual* grass.

Where in holy Houdini am I?

I PUSH THE gate open and the metal scrapes the earth. My heart is pounding so hard it rattles my chest. I look behind me, but there's a wall of fog so thick it might as well be made of cement. Veronica, Tall, and Sol are gone.

It's just me, the graveyard, and the box.

I let go of the handle once I'm in the gates, and I take the box in both hands and press it close to my chest. I'm hoping it'll keep the bad things away.

When I look down, I notice something shocking.

I have *two* visible hands.

Amazed, I hold my left hand up in front of me. I take in every little detail, every line in my palm.

Where am I? I wonder again. *Am I in the Realm?*

Seems there's nowhere to go but forward, so that's where I go. One step after the next in the chilly, wet grass.

A shiver runs down my spine, and it's not just from wearing short sleeves in the sudden cold. It's the blackout darkness of the sky. The fog breaking like waves over the edges of gravestones. The stone monuments and statues of people in frock coats with blank eyes. The brambles and bushes cluttered on top of one another.

"The more you look the less you see," I hum to myself.

I stop at each stone to look at the names. I can read them now. One stone slab that's half buried in fallen leaves reads, *Doctor Peter.* Next to that are a few prickly plants, like cedars and yuccas. A collection of seashells marks another grave. Some graves are marked by workers' objects like an iron pipe and a slab of maybe railroad iron. There's a large statue of a man, carved head to toe in dark bronze. He's wearing a tuxedo jacket with tails and a bow tie and he's holding a skull in his hands. He stands on a platform with the words *In Memory of the Celebrated Ventriloquist Who Died Sept. 20, 1825.* I realize it's Richard Potter, America's first Black magician.

"He wasn't just the first Black magician, you know," says a voice.

"Who's there?"

I snap my head right and left, up and down, my heart racing.

But I don't see anyone.

"He was America's first *magician*, full stop," the voice continues.

"Who's talking?" I say, my own voice shaking. "Come out!"

"Oh. Sorry. Wait for it," he says—I can't see him yet, but I'm pretty sure it's a he. His voice wobbles like a preacher-performer.

The black clouds drift apart and a moonbeam cuts through the darkness.

A man emerges in the moonbeam like a spotlight. He's like a sketch, only half drawn. He's made up of shades and shadows and empty space and pale light. He smiles and winks like he made the clouds move and the moon shine all by himself. He's tall and handsome, and he wears a pyramid-shaped medallion and a Prince Albert coat.

"You . . . *you're*—no, it's not possible."

"Ah, but my boy, I specialize in the impossible."

"I saw you. Back at the Mercury. That was you, wasn't it?"

"Indeed it was."

I can see his face clearer than ever before. He looks just like he does in the old magic posters.

"You're Black Herman," I say.

He grins as though he's pleased to be recognized. "I go by a lot of names. I'm most proud of the Great Black Herman, Master of Legerdemain."

I blink and blink to adjust to the strange way he appears in the moonlight, like a hologram of a black-and-white photo. As he moves, some parts of him vanish, like the outline of his strong jawline, or the lapels of his coat. The parts of him that would be in shadow just simply aren't there. "But what happened to the rest of you?" I ask him. "Are you some kinda ghost?"

"Not exactly. But I don't mind if you call me a ghost, if a ghost is how you see me. But I never did die. At least, not in the normal sense. I took too many trips to the Realm. Just didn't quite make it back in one piece."

"I don't understand. Are we in the Realm?"

"Well, I'm not sure *we* are anywhere."

"What do you mean? Is this the Realm?" I ask.

"My own little corner of it, yes."

"I thought the Realm was just echoes of reality."

"There are so many little realms in what we call the Realm. Most of them are echoes. 'Cause the folks that made them didn't have any idea what they was doing. But young man, I am the Master of Legerdemain and this here is my own little realm within the Realm, gloomy though it may be. I made this. And I made it to my liking."

"You . . . *made* this place?"

"That I did. Welcome to 'Black Herman's Private Graveyard.' A place for all us Black magicians to rest. Honor us the way we'd want to be honored—each in our own way. Those plants right there are for the old Obeah doctors and healers, straight from West Africa. You see Richard Potter got himself a nice fancy statue—he did well for himself, so he got a right to enjoy it. That there is Isaac Willis—the Great Boomsky—"

I see where he's pointing and look at the gravestone. The letters read:

The More You Look the Less You See.

So *that's* why Sol wrote those words when I was trying to read the stones on the mural.

"This one here is Professor J. Herman Moore, the Prince of Mystery. Did you know I was—"

"His assistant?"

Black Herman smiles and looks astonished.

I nod and play it cool. Not every day you surprise a two-hundred-year-old legendary ghost. Or Realm spirit. Or whatever he is.

"Well, I'll be. Didn't think folks still spoke about me nowadays."

"My dad told me all about you. You're his hero."

"Well, heroes are funny things. Wait a minute," he says, and drifts closer, examining me. "Heh, well, look at that. You favor him, you know. I know your dad. He came here."

"He did?" I nearly shriek.

"He sure did. More than once. In fact, last visit he paid me was just a short while ago."

"So I just missed him?"

"Only just."

"Wait, so if he walked in here, and I walked in here, can't he come back and meet me? Can't he just leave with me?"

"Leave with you?" Black Herman repeats with a hefty chuckle. "Son, what makes you think you're actually *here*?"

"What do you mean?"

"Hate to break it to you, but you are not, as it were, here."

"I'm not here? But you're like a ghost—you're not here!"

"Far as I can tell, I am here for the foreseeable. No, if you really were in this place, you'd have a heck of a time getting back. Look for yourself. You cast a shadow?"

I look down and realize no, there's no shadow at all. I wave my hand in the moonlight and look at where it strikes the grass, but there's nothing.

"Then how can you be here, if you don't cast a shadow?" he asks.

"But I feel the cold," I say, wondering how this is possible, how I could be here but not here. "The wet grass and the rocky ground."

"The mind is a powerful trickster. To me, you're about as real as I am to you."

"So I'm imagining all of this?"

"It's a bit more complicated than that. You must have seen this place somewhere in your world, am I right? It's about reflections and gates."

"Reflections?"

"Yeah. That's how I discovered the Realm for the first time. Your pops, too. Reflections are magic, young man."

"They make the world into more worlds," I say.

"Quite handsomely put."

"My friend painted this graveyard. It was a huge mural. That's how I found it."

"Interesting. Your friend can bring reflections to life, then. I saw my first glimpse of the Realm in a stained-glass window in a small church in Louisville. Your father told me he saw this graveyard in a reflection in a pool of rain-water by a gutter when Brooklyn got flooded one time."

"And I saw you in the reflection in the glass at the Mercury," I say, realizing I actually saw the Realm with-out realizing.

"I suppose so. But actually, physically being here? That's something different. First time your daddy came, he was dream-visiting, just like you. Eventually, he fig-ured out how to receive some gifts I left for him. This last visit, he came for real. Rode the echoes and showed up in person. Imagine my surprise when he returned those gifts for safekeeping." I remember the note Pops left for Long Fingers. *The elements await you in Black Herman's grave.* The "gifts" Black Herman is talking about must be the elements. "He left them somewhere—those gifts?"

"He did," Black Herman says with a cryptic look. "What brings *you* here?"

"My dad. I'm here to find my dad. To bring him back home."

He looks me up and down. "Some folks aren't meant to walk in just one world."

"But if he can walk into your world, he can walk back into mine."

He grins like I'm not quite following him. "I wasn't talking about your daddy."

"Me?"

"You got the look. You got faraway lands on the mind. And you're ready and willing to go places, no matter what the risk."

"I'm just here 'cause I want to find my pops."

"Sure, that's how it starts. Then you find you need to keep moving. Being in one world don't feel quite right. You start to feel stuck. You know the places you dream about be real and that knowledge be calling to you. Next thing you know, you riding echoes."

"Riding echoes?"

"That's how you get from place to place in the Realm. That's how I was born in Virginia. Then it was the jungles of West Africa. Then I made it to Egypt. India. 'Cause each trip was like I was born again."

"*The Great Black Herman Returns Every Seven Years,*" I say.

"That's right. I used to say that at every show. I'd always find my way back, you see. I set this place to give me someplace to go once I was done with it all. Faked my death one last time, and slipped out here. I let the clock run out, the portal shut, and now I don't leave here, not anymore."

"Wow," I say, thinking about how Dad might get trapped in his echo. "That sounds rough."

"It's not so bad. I was tired of running myself down, hopping from echo to echo. I miss performing sometimes. The crowds. And I miss jumping from world to world, across oceans and eras. Would you believe I visited the pharaoh's court in Egypt, met history's first magician, Dedi himself, almost five thousand years ago? Nah, you probably wouldn't believe that. But it's true. And come to find out, he wasn't the first by a long shot. In fact, we lucky to even know his name."

"Wait, so you traveled back *in time*?"

"Well, sort of. As you said, the Realm is full of echoes. Each one is a moment in time, preserved. And you can jump from one echo to the next, if you know how to do it."

"But I thought once the rift closes, you can't leave your echo anymore."

"Well, that's not quite the case. See, each echo is a twenty-six-hour loop of a moment in time. A moment centered around—"

"A rift," I say.

"Correct. Now, everything about that echo stays the same as the moment in real time, including the rift. So at the thirteenth hour, there's a rift somewhere in each echo, and if you can find it, you can jump through it, into other echoes. We call it riding echoes. But it's a dangerous pastime, young man, and you could end up stuck."

"How do you end up stuck?"

"When you ride echoes, you can miss and get stuck in the portal itself. You have to be careful."

"Mr. Herman, I'm not trying to ride echoes or anything like that. I lost my pop. I just want him back."

"But your daddy's not the type to sit still. You might have to follow him."

"I need to open a portal or a gate or something, just to pull him through before it's too late. He's coming home. I know he is. He just needs my help."

"You might be right about that. If you can open a portal, and he meets you there, you should be able to help him home, as long as there's no new echo pushing your daddy's echo out of reach. But opening a portal—that ain't exactly child's play."

"You need the four elements of magic. Right? Force, Illusion, Mystic, and Sorcery. That's how you open a portal, when all four elements come together. Right?" I ask, though I can't picture how this might work.

"Heh. Quite the magic student we got here. Well, your

daddy got three of them from me, anyway. My three best tricks. He must have got the fourth from somewhere else."

He sure did. Maestro's Mirror.

"Where?" I ask.

"I couldn't say."

"No, I mean did he get the objects from your grave?"

"You make your own daddy sound like a common grave robber. Yes, he got them from me, but he had my blessing. We talked, just like you and me are doing. And I showed him the way."

"And that's where he returned them?"

Black Herman shows a sly grin.

"Please. Show me the way."

He turns his head to the mausoleum up on top of the hill.

He winks and smiles. The clouds move and the moonlight fades and the half-lit sketch of Black Herman vanishes into the shade.

THE MAUSOLEUM IS dedicated to the life of Black
Herman. Scenes of his greatest triumphs are carved
in stone along the walls. There's him at a stadium of
thousands. Him in his study in Harlem, surrounded by
well-dressed community folks. Him at the pharaoh's
court in ancient Egypt. Him as a young man in a small
West African town. Him in a coffin, buried alive before
a crowd in America.

There's a familiar box that's set on a podium against
the back wall.

I look at the box in my hands, to make sure it's still
there.

The Lost and Found and the box against the wall are practically identical. The only difference I can see is the locking mechanism with the Watch of 13. The box in Black Herman's mausoleum doesn't have one. Otherwise, they are the same.

I reach to open Black Herman's box, but my hand goes right through. I try again, but it's like the box is only an illusion.

"That won't work. *You* not here, my boy."

I look around for Black Herman, but don't see him. It's just his voice talking to me.

"So how do I get the elements?" I ask, getting an anxious chill.

"The box, young man. The place where the fading echo meets the rising earth."

"What? That's just a riddle," I say. "Give me something I can do."

"Your daddy figured it out."

That makes me pause.

If my dad figured it out, so can I.

Black Herman must have known that would work on me. Am I that easy to see through?

The box, the box . . .

Where the fading echo meets the rising earth.

I don't know what that means. But I do know there's two boxes, one a Realm box and one a real box (though at this point I don't know which is which).

If I'm looking for the place where they meet, maybe I should introduce them to each other?

I set the box in my hands over the top of the box on the platform.

"That's it," Black Herman says.

I line up the sides of each box so there's no space between the two. I lower the Lost and Found box so it phases *through* the podium box. When the two boxes occupy the exact same space, I hold still. To my naked eye, it looks like one single box.

Only I'm afraid of what's going to happen if I let go. Will the Lost and Found keep phasing and fall through the podium and through the floor? If none of this is really here, what is there to hold it up?

I close my eyes. *Trust*, I think. *This is the spot where the fading echo meets the rising earth.*

It has to be.

I let go of the box and open my eyes.

The Lost and Found sits on top of the podium in Black Herman's mausoleum. Two boxes are now one.

I touch the wood and it feels solid, too. I open the lid, reach in, and pull out a leather sack tied with leather strings.

One by one, I remove the objects.

The deck of cards.

The pistol.

The skull.

And a shard of mirror glass in the shape of a lightning bolt.

A smile spreads across my face.

I got you, Dad. I'm coming.

I CARRY THE Lost and Found back down the hill, heavy with the four objects rattling around inside.

Getting closer, I think, hurrying to the gates. *Closer to Dad, closer to—*

Then I stop short.

I realize I don't know what's the *appointed spot,* according to Dad and Long Fingers. I don't know where to go next. Assuming I can get out of this graveyard. Which I'm hoping won't be a problem—according to Black Herman, I never left Echo City. Only my mind is here. Or something.

"Black Herman?" I say just before the tall gates.

I look around. I hope he hears me.

"If you were going to go back to reality from the Realm, where would you do it?" I ask him.

There's a moment of quiet, and then Herman says, "I'm disappointed, Kingston. I thought you could figure that out on your own. When I performed my buried-alive trick, where would I return?"

I grin. "The same spot where you left. Got it, Black Herman. Thank you for all of your help. It was a great honor meeting you. I'll never forget it. Hope to see you again, somehow."

I open the gates and step through, toward the heavy fog.

I'm waiting for something to happen, but nothing does.

"*Ahem,*" says Black Herman.

I think for a moment.

The same spot where you left . . .

"Okay, okay, I think I get it," I say.

I close the gate behind me and turn the handle with a squeaky *clang*.

I get a rush of warmth as the fog consumes me once more. My vision goes blank and there's a sound like when you cup your ear to seashells. The world starts spinning. I have to close my eyes to keep from getting dizzy . . .

I open them, and I'm at the mural of the graveyard. I'm holding the Lost and Found against the wall.

But I lose my balance and fall to the sidewalk and drop the box.

"King!" I hear the combined voices of Veronica and Too Tall.

I roll onto my back and look up.

There are three faces. My cousin looks like she might actually cry. Tall's eyes are wide. Only Sol seems pretty cool about everything.

"What happened, King? Are you okay? Please tell me you're okay," says Veronica.

"I think so, V," I say, rubbing my forehead and feeling the concrete against the back of my head like rock-hard sandpaper.

"Good," she says, recovering. "Because your mom will kill me. And that won't work for me, I like living."

"Can you get up?" asks Tall. "Or you need to lay there for a bit?"

"I'm up, I'm up," I say as though talking to an alarm clock that's gone off too many times.

I hold out my left hand for Tall to take it and help me up.

I realize my hand is gone once again. I should be

used to it by now, but after having it back, it takes me a second. *How did I have it back just now?* I wonder. *Was it real?*

Did I ever have it back? Or was that just my mind, being tricky with me?

"King? King! You there?" asks Tall. "How hard did you hit your head?"

"Tall, how long was I gone just now?"

"What do you mean, *how long were you gone*?" asks Too Tall.

I open my mouth to clarify, but something stops me. I try to imagine everything that's happening from Tall and V's perspective, and I realize I can't. I have no idea what the last few moments looked like to them.

"What did you see me do, just now?" I ask. "You saw me turn the handle through the box, right?"

"You stuck your hand through," says V, "and turned your wrist. Then you made a dreamy face. Then you turned your hand again, dropped the box, and collapsed."

So that whole trip to the graveyard happened in a fraction of time. My body never actually left, like Black Herman said.

The box—I think in a panic—*the four objects!*

I rush to where I dropped the box on the sidewalk.

It lies on its side. I turn the box upright and open it with shaking hands.

"What's *that*?" asks Tall.

The leather bag is still there.

Whew.

"I get that this sounds crazy," I say. "But just now, I was *in that graveyard*."

Sol starts chuckling.

"What's so funny, little man?" Too Tall asks with some bass in his voice.

"Listen to me. *I'm* telling you, it's true."

I explain to them about the enchanted graveyard of magic Black America, and how I met Black Herman in a Prince Albert coat, and how I saw him in a reflection before.

They're listening carefully to every word. Though I can't tell if they believe me.

So I pull out the leather bag and untie the leather strings.

"Here. I found this in the graveyard, just like Dad's note said."

I take out the Skull of Balsamo—a preserved human skull with copper lining the jawbone. That gets a *wow* out of them. Then Hooker's Vanishing Deck—looks like an ordinary deck of cards, with a bear-head insignia. Then William Tell's Pistol, an old-timey six-shooter with a long barrel. And then the shard of mirrored glass.

Too Tall and V look stunned.

"We have the four elements. You understand now?" I say.

"This is unbelievable, King," Veronica says, holding up the copper-lined skull and looking in its blank eye sockets.

"I know. I mean, thanks. I mean, what time is it? We got to go."

"Where to?" asks Tall.

"When you want to return to reality from the Realm, you got to come back the way you came."

32

THERE'S A U-HAUL truck parked behind the Mercury. The loading entrance to the theater is actually open, and the truck is wedged into the dock at an odd angle. Whoever left this here was in a hurry. We walk around the truck, and the loading entrance takes us through a tunnel and backstage.

One thing hasn't changed—the Mercury is so quiet you can hear your own heartbeat.

I check the Watch of 13 lodged in the Lost and Found. The hour hand is just past the 12 and creeping toward the thirteenth hour. One more turn of the small hand and I may never see him again.

"What time you got?" I ask V.

"7:32." She glances at the watch on her wrist. "Fifty-eight minutes, scratch that, fifty-seven. 7:33 now."

Too Tall, Veronica, Sol, and I look out from stage left.

On the stage, there's a huge object with a tarp draped over it, about seven feet tall. It's the same behemoth that Long Fingers had in his workshop. Now it stands right on top of the trapdoor where I found the Lost and Found to begin with.

"Well, I'm guessing my dad and uncle brought that thing in the U-Haul, huh? But where are they?" says Veronica.

"Hello!" I call, my voice bouncing around the old theater. "Uncle Crooked Eye? Uncle Long Fingers?"

No response.

But it does feel good to hear my own voice echo back to me. Like I've announced myself to all the phantom shows and crowds that linger in this magic-rich place.

I'm here. And I've come to bring Dad home.

We approach the tarp on center stage.

"What do you suppose it is?" asks Too Tall.

"I think I know," I say.

"Wait, King," says Veronica. "This is super creepy. Where are my dad and Uncle Crooked?"

I shrug. "I'm sure they're just on the way to the graveyard and we missed them."

"But won't they need the Lost and Found to go to the graveyard? I'm telling you, King, this is suspect," V says.

"Look, we have the box, and the elements. We can't waste any more time."

I take the tarp in hand and give it a pull with a flourish to reveal the Mirror.

"I knew it!" I say. "This is what he was working on. Your dad wanted to get his brother back just as much as I did."

Sol steps forward and stares up at the Mirror.

"Whoa," says Tall. "You mean your uncle *made* this?"

"Right under our noses," I say, and admire the craftmanship. It's an exact replica of Maestro's Mirror, right down to the snakes tooled into the wood and meeting at the very top. The only missing part is a lightning-shaped hole in the center of the glass.

"Uncle Long never gave up on Dad, though the whole world thought he did," I say, taking out one object from the Lost and Found at a time and setting them down in front of the Mirror. The skull. The cards. The pistol.

"I was wondering where the glass had gone, after the fire. It was your dad, V. He came and gathered up all the glass he could."

I take the last object out of the bag. The lightning-shaped mirror shard.

"So *that's* why all those shards in his workshop," says V.

"Yup. That shard must have gone through to the other side with Dad. At his workshop, we saw how he tried to duplicate the glass, but it needed this piece to work, all along. Dad had to pass it back. Long Fingers needed the Lost and Found."

"But King, don't you think it's a little sketch that this Mirror is just waiting here like this?"

I lower the lid of the box and I check the Watch of 13 as it ticks toward the 13.

"We're running out of time, V."

Sol points to the hole in the Mirror. He nods to me. With trembling fingers, I set the lightning-bolt-shaped shard into the empty space in the Mirror like the last piece of a jigsaw puzzle.

"Okay, what happens now?" asks Tall. "Don't you need some Gorilla Glue or something so it holds?"

He gets his answer as something clicks. Blue light

starts blazing from all four objects. The skull glows with blue in its eyes. The cards look like they're surrounded by blue flame. The pistol has a blue flame streaming from the nozzle. And a blue star appears in the depths of the Mirror.

And then it expands like a rising blue sun, pushing away our reflection.

A silhouette is in front of the blue light.

The tall shape of a man.

A figure I know so well.

He steps forward and the blinding blue recedes behind him. His features become clear. Double-dimpled smile. Salt-and-pepper stubble. The same black suit he wore the night of his last performance.

He keeps moving forward. Toward me. Toward us.

He smiles. His eyes narrow.

His open hand reaches for me, and I reach back with my Realm hand.

We did it, I think, *he's here!*

It's just me and Dad.

I forget everything else. I don't even know where the glass ends and he begins. I don't know whether I'm standing onstage or I'm inside the Mirror.

All I know is we clasp hands. His grip is strong.

His eyes smile and tear with relief. He mouths, *King.*

Then something happens. There's a loud shout. I hear my name, I think.

But I don't look away. I won't. I hold on . . .

There's an arm wrapped around me. Another arm that hooks my right elbow as a hand lands on my chest.

"Kingston, no!"

It's *Mom.*

I REALIZE MOM doesn't even *see* Pop.

I'm half inside the Mirror. She's holding me from center stage. I grip Pop's hand with my Realm hand. Mom is pulling us both back toward her. She's trying to rescue me from the Mirror. But she's actually helping me bring Dad back home.

Then there's an eruption of blue light.

Ferocious energy floods in on me like a dam broke somewhere within the Mirror. There's so much force I lose my grip and Pop's hand slips away.

No—

Something's horribly wrong.

Blue light blasts from the Mirror. I don't see Pops anymore. Tons of light and energy pour into our world.

I tumble back out of the Mirror and onto the stage floor. Mom falls with me, clutching me to her chest.

Mom gets to her feet, still clutching me. "What are you doing, King? Are you trying to toss yourself away, just like he did?"

I feel her nails bite my arm. Her hands are trembling and it's like they send an electric current through me, shaking me. "He was here," I blubber. "I had his hand in my hand, Mom! We can bring him back!"

But she doesn't hear me at all. She gets to her knees, ignoring me and the blazing blue light rushing from the Mirror. "And if this young lady hadn't come looking for her little brother, what would have happened then, Kingston?"

I notice Sula is behind her. She's got her arm around Sol, who's shaking her off like he's seriously annoyed and pointing up to the roof.

A burst of wind crashes down from above. Cold air fills the warm, humid theater as overhead beams buckle and crack.

I look to the hole in the roof. The light from the Mirror surges up there.

A voice booms. It's deep and carries through the entire place.

"The night the caterpillar's world ends . . ."

A figure floats down from the hole in the roof, spotlit by the intense beam of blue light-energy.

It's Urma Tan, gliding through the rafters, head to toe in black with crystals woven throughout her dress.

"The night the caterpillar's world ends," she says in her smooth, prowling voice, "the caterpillar sees darkness. But something much more beautiful emerges."

She looks alive. Power radiates off her as she descends from above.

The light in the Mirror is like a blazing star. I have to squint to see that Pop . . . is gone.

Mom turns to Urma. "What in the world?"

Urma drifts and hovers just a few feet above the stage. She holds out a gloved hand toward the Mirror. The blue star leaps from inside the glass and levitates to her fingertips as though she called it to her. She tilts her head back, opens her mouth, and eases the star down her throat. She glows from the inside. The blue energy beams through her translucent skin and then blasts forth, exploding from the inside out like a thousand blue suns.

I'm blinded by it. I'm sure we all are.

When my eyesight comes back, there are fresh crystals *everywhere*. I mean, it's like we're on the North Pole all of a sudden. Blue-tinted white crystals cover every inch of the Mercury. They line the stage, the empty seats, the walls, the mezzanine, and even fill the hole in the roof. Everything is bright now, like Urma banished the summertime and made an ice cave.

The crystals even cover me and everyone else. I look around at my mom, V, Too Tall, Sol, and Sula—all of us are practically wearing suits of armor made of crystal that hold us fast to the crystalized floor. We're each like a human stalagmite.

I can't move. The crystal is like cold hard steel. My arms, my legs, my knees, my jaw are all locked up tight. It's even hard to breathe. The Lost and Found is on the floor between my feet, partially covered in crystal. I can just barely look down to see the Watch of 13. The hand inches to forty-five minutes away from the thirteenth hour. Mint appears from stage right. He stalks in gingerly on the crystal floor, careful with each step.

"You were right, Urma," he says. "The boy came through." He surveys the stage and forces a pleased smile. But I'm not so convinced this is what he had in mind.

Behind him, four more of his scarred goons haul out

the heavy, hog-tied bodies of my two uncles. Long Fingers and Crooked Eye groan and cuss into the gags across their mouths, hands twined tight behind their backs. Urma's goons drag my dad's brothers along the crystal floor and toss them beneath Urma's feet like they're hefting trash bags. My uncles struggle against their bindings until they accept it's hopeless.

The crystals hold me rock-still, but my stomach is doing backflips. A rage ignites in my chest. But I can't call out. My lips are clamped shut.

Urma Tan, still hovering in the blue light, is now slowly rotating like a figure in a snow globe. There's a serene smile on her face. The way someone looks when they're eating an insanely good meal. Mint and the goons just watch, entranced. Like they're waiting for words or a message. She doesn't seem to notice that any of us are here. I'm not entirely sure what's happening. It seems like this hunger for Realm energy has consumed her completely.

I think about how I held her crystal back at her place on Torrini Boulevard. Urma was turning gray. I dropped the crystal and left it for her because she needed it to live. Now it's like she just lives to feed. If I hadn't given her back the crystal, could I have stopped all of this from happening?

I want to help my uncles up. I just want to *move*, so bad. I want to free my friends.

But I feel the energy draining from me. I'm stuck thinking about how wrong things have gone. And how it's all my fault. The final pieces click into place. It was *Urma* who put the code on the marquee. She was around Maestro and Dad, she must have known the code from way back when. Then she must have found the box. But she couldn't open it. She didn't have the Watch of 13. She needed Long Fingers for that. Or, as it turned out, me. She said she wanted the box to recharge her crystals. But we did her one better and built her a whole portal and went and opened it for her. So she could do . . . *this.* Just drink and consume endlessly, not caring if she breaks our world.

I was so blind, so fixed on being the hero and rescuing my father, I ruined everything he sacrificed himself for.

I watch the energy gush from the Mirror.

I wonder, *Did she do this last time?*

Was she consuming the energy when my dad broke the Mirror?

As these thoughts lay me low, I realize I have to resist. *It's not over,* I tell myself. *It's not over.* It's the only thought that keeps me from giving up. *It can't be over. I won't let it be.*

My finger moves.

The index finger on my Realm hand.

It begins with that little finger wiggle. *It's not over,* I repeat to myself. The crystal that formed around my Realm hand cracks. I feel the hard crystal split down my arm. There's suddenly space around my hand. My fingers flex and it can *move.* I make a fist and summon all the concentrated force that I can manage. I put all that bad feeling of letting everyone down into that fist. I let it build and build. All the disappointment in myself. How I let down V and Tall, and all their faith in me. And Sol, who somehow believed in me, too. How I broke Mom's heart. And how bad I just missed Pop.

I see the clock click closer to 13 . . .

And I let it all go.

I flex my hand flat and shatter the crystal surrounding me into tiny pieces. I can somehow feel every little shard in my Realm hand, like they're all tied to strings looped around my fingers. I feel them like extensions of me. I hold each shard suspended, like hail frozen in time. I feel as though they're waiting for my direction. So I send them at Urma.

Every last crystal shard flies at her like a maelstrom.

She waves her hand and the shards come to an abrupt halt.

I fall to the crystal floor, drained, and land on top of the Lost and Found. I realize that was *all* of my power. And she stopped it cold.

She turns to me with a feline grin. I hear Mint's hoarse laughter. With a flick of her fingertips, she sends the sharp shards right back at me.

I hug my arms around the Lost and Found, and leap in the only direction I can.

Straight into the Mirror.

I'M FLOATING.

There's no ground beneath me, but also nothing pulling me down. I'm just *there*. Momentum carried me through the Mirror, and then I stopped. I'm in empty Realm space, hovering in the air, if air is even what you'd call it. I imagine this is what it's like with no gravity. I'm not even sure what I'm breathing, or whether I'm breathing. I just seem to be alive somehow.

I turn back the way I came. I can see through to the other side of the Mirror. There's Urma, looking after me. She doesn't like that I got away, but she's too busy feeding to care. There's Mom, V, and Tall, all locked up in crystal, with Sula and Sol. There's Long Fingers and Crooked Eye, tied up near Urma Tan's feet. And there's Mint and crew, looking dumbfounded. Their eyes are all on the Mirror.

I know what I need to do. Break the glass from the inside, like Dad did. But I don't know how. There isn't exactly a rock around for me to throw through the glass. Really, from this side it doesn't even look like *glass*. It just looks like a portal to reality itself, wreathed by blue flame.

I am in the Realm. I see other portals lit up in the darkness ahead of me, like mirrors tinted electric blue. They must lead to other echoes, other realities, just like Black Herman told me in the graveyard. Two portals are close to me. One is moving closer and the other is shrinking. The rest trail off forever, repeating and repeating until they're just like far-off stars.

I realize Dad must have been here, in this strange space, when he tried to return to us. Is his portal closed for good? I glance down at the clockface on Magician's Lost and Found. The little hand is maybe thirty minutes from the 13.

When my hand went through this box, I started a new echo and put Pops on the clock. Wherever his echo is in here, time will be up at the thirteenth hour. I might never be able to find him again.

As I stare from one portal to the next, I realize I'm

falling toward them. I have no clue what's up or down. I thought I was vertical, but it turns out I'm horizontal. My stomach feels like it's somewhere near my throat.

As I get closer, I can see through the entrance of each portal. It's like I'm looking through a window into someone's house. Except these aren't houses, these are echoes, new dimensions created the moment the Realm opens. Within the bigger portal to my right is the Mercury, dark and dormant, blanketed in ash and dust. It's just as it was yesterday, when I opened the Magician's Lost and Found. Within the shrinking portal to my left, speeding farther away, is the Mercury, bright and alive, a packed house, and a show on the stage . . . *The Mercury of four years and six months ago. It's not gone. Not yet.* Then I crash through the larger portal and I tumble to the Mercury's stage, covered in dust.

It takes a moment to orient myself. I'm in the Mercury. From *yesterday.* Well, not actually yesterday, but a copy of it. The Realm's echo of yesterday. It's a dead ringer for yesterday, anyway. Same shadows slanting across the audience. Same sunbeam spotlighting the stage. Same eerie quiet that's heavy with shows past.

I realize this is what Black Herman was talking about. I'm in an echo, and if I want to ride to another echo, to where my father disappeared, I must jump through this echo that I created when I opened the Magician's Lost and Found.

I glance to the Lost and Found in my hands right now. The clock says twenty-two minutes to go.

I hear someone coming. *Who's that now?* I wonder. *Mint?* I leap down to the orchestra section and stash the Lost and Found under one of the dusty seats and hide behind it. The footsteps come closer.

"Oh, hey, King. There you are."

It's Too Tall. He sees clear over my hiding spot. He's looking right at me.

My heart is beating a million times a second. *What do I do? What do I say?*

"Oh, um. Hey, Tall," comes out of my mouth.

"Why you hiding like that?" he asks. I realize *he* was expecting to see me.

"Um, I dunno," I say. "Just got spooked, I guess. Man, this place is creepy, huh?"

"You said it, man. Jeez."

I try to remember exactly what happened yesterday. Where am I now? Well, not me, but the other *me*, the Realm me.

"How'd you get those clothes?" asks Tall with his eyebrows scrunched up.

"Oh, I just, like, had these on, under my other shirt and shorts, you know?"

"Um, what? My dude, it's like eighty degrees outside."

"Well, I run cool, is all that is."

I close my eyes, realizing how lame all this sounds.

He looks at me like I'm from Pluto.

But it doesn't matter at all if this Too Tall thinks I'm crazy. He's a Realm copy and not the real Too Tall at all. Just like Urma. I just need to get to the *echo* before the clock runs out. But how?

Think, Kingston.

Another portal. That's how. That's the only way. Riding echoes. Like Black Herman said.

I opened the portal yesterday. The one that made this whole echo happen to begin with. I created the portal by accident when my hand went through the Lost and Found. I didn't see it, but then again, I was *under* all six-foot-plus of Too Tall at the time.

When the last portal opened up, you need to be there, and jump through. That's what Black Herman said. Riding echoes.

I look up at Too Tall, and panic hits me like a punch to the chest.

Yesterday, I opened the portal when I stuck my hand

into the Lost and Found, and Tall *fell on me.* But what happens if he's distracted, and doesn't fall on me, because I'm here talking to him?

"Um, Tall, have you been up on the stage?" I ask, my voice trembling with nerves.

He shakes his head.

"You see that wild mural up there?"

"Nah, it's cool?"

"Very."

He leaps up onstage. I grab the Lost and Found from where I stashed it under the seat. I hold it behind my back as I follow Too Tall. "Man, I already wrecked these kicks when I came down that chute," he says, eyeing the dusty stage steps as he climbs. "You know, I haven't even worn these OGs but three times. Dead-stocked out the box." He shakes his head.

Exactly what the real Too Tall would say. These Realm copies are *identical but they're not real.* So that means *I'm* somewhere down under this stage. Another me. The thought gives me a chill.

I see the open trapdoor in center stage, in front of him. I know he was looking at the mural when he fell on me.

"*Wow*, that's your pops, right? Man, that mural is excellent," he says, eyes fixed on the scene of my dad and

Maestro squared off as his feet keep walking, keep walking toward the door . . .

Get ready, I tell myself.

"Yooo—" he howls.

Sure enough, Tall slips and falls into the trap.

Here's my chance.

I watch from above as Tall crashes into me—well, the *other* me—and my hand is jolted into the box.

Blue light shoots from the box. From above, I see the infinite reflections of the Realm. This is the moment I created a new echo. I must jump. My echo self falls backward and pulls his hand from the box. A blue burning energy outlines the box. There's only so much space in this trap beneath the stage. Most of the portal seems to be under the stage where I can't see. I can't even make out what the portal leads *to.* There's only a little corner I could jump through.

It couldn't have been open for long, since I didn't even see it when I'd opened it. So here goes—it's my only shot.

I hold on to the Lost and Found and leap—

And I hit the side of the trap on the way down and land in the blue flame around the portal's edges.

AN EXPLOSION OF energy courses through me. My mind feels like it's breaking into little bits, spreading out, traveling like lightning, and forming back together. I'm able to think and see, but not feel. I'm not aware of having hands or arms or feet or even breath. But I do see things.

I see the Mercury, once again. But like I've never seen it before.

I'm on the stage. Maestro is just a few feet away. Pop is behind him. Urma is about to step through the Mirror. And I'm the Mirror. Literally standing in the Mirror.

Am I stuck in it? In between echoes?

I remember something Black Herman said. *When*

you ride echoes, you can miss and get stuck in the portal itself. I look out at a packed house. Everyone, even the ushers in the balcony, have their eyes glued to the performance. The lights are so bright, I have trouble seeing every face in the crowd, at first. But then I find the seat, center orchestra, three rows back. There's Mom, and there's me.

A good four and a half years younger. Smaller, hair much shorter. I look like a blank page.

I expect to see myself alert and concerned. That's how I remember it. I was one of the first to realize that something wasn't quite right. I remember the look on Dad's face. I remember the tremor of what was about to happen before it happened.

But it doesn't go down like that. There's no tremor. There's no look on Dad's face. There's no look on my face. I mean, I'm watching the show, but watching normal, like I'm waiting for a cool trick, just like everyone else.

I must have twisted it up in my memory. I must have told myself that I saw it coming.

I reach to pull myself out of the Mirror and step onstage, but my hand hits the glass from the inside. I can't reach into the scene in front of me. I look down at the Watch. *Ten minutes and time's up.*

And now, I'm stuck here, too. Does that mean when the portal closes, I won't make it back?

So instead of Dad stuck in the Realm forever, it's *me* . . .

There's Urma, staring into the Mirror. This is a different Urma, though. She looks scared. This must be the original Urma, Sula's mom. No cold eyes or purplish veins running through her neck. She makes eye contact, for just a brief second. She looks confused.

Then I look behind the curtain, stage left, and see the other Urma. She's visible for a moment, only to me, as far as I can tell. She's stepped from the cover of the curtain and makes this move with her hand like she's throwing a baseball.

Before I can take it all in, Sula's mom flies toward me, right into the Mirror. She goes through me, like a gust of wind that should knock me backward, only I can't seem to go backward. The force of her passing blurs my vision for a moment.

She's through the Mirror and gone behind me.

The other Urma starts drawing a flash of blue light to her behind the curtain.

If memory serves, Maestro is next.

From this angle, I can see the panic in his face. I guess he didn't expect Urma to go through the Mirror. He doesn't hesitate. He jumps through the Mirror now, too. He doesn't even seem to notice me. Am I that hard to see, somehow? He passes through me and I feel the force of it again as my vision gets cloudy.

Now it's Dad's turn.

I always remember him giving me that wink in the audience. The one so quick you barely know you saw it, like the flap of a wing. But I don't think he winks at me in my seat.

He sees me in the Mirror.

He's on the stage and he makes eye contact with me in the glass. He looks concerned. Then he jumps in.

Only he doesn't go right through me like Urma and Maestro. He catches me by my left hand, and I hold on and pull him toward me, like I'm saving him from falling through an open door. He stands beside me like he's joined me in the reflection.

"King," he says. Dad is just as he was four years ago, to a T. I know he's a Realm echo. He's not my real dad. But he looks just like him. Acts just like him. Probably thinks just like him. And he says, "What're you doing here?"

"I'm here to rescue you."

"Rescue *me*? I'm here to rescue *you*," he says, and knocks on the glass surface in front of us, testing its strength.

"You saw me," I say.

"In the reflection," he confirms.

I'm wondering, *Did he see me, back then? Did the real Pops see me when he leapt through? Is that even possible? Did I somehow show up in the Mirror four and a half years ago? Is that the logic of the Realm? Look forward and backward, it's all the same.*

"Pops, did you jump through to break the Mirror and close the portal? Or to save me?" I ask.

He seems surprised by the question. "It's a twofer, I guess."

I realize he couldn't possibly know what my real dad saw or didn't see. He only knows what he sees.

He's staring over my shoulder. "What's that behind you?"

What *is* behind me? I've been staring at the stage this whole time. I turn around and see.

There's the blue outline of a portal, only it seems far away. Inside the portal, I see the Mercury of *now*. In real time. With Urma Tan drinking Realm energy. With V and Tall, with my uncles and mom, with Sol and Sula, all trapped in crystal. The portal is getting smaller, almost like looking through a telescope. It's fading away with each tick of the clock.

I turn again. There's the Mercury of *then*. There's the packed house erupting in flames. Everyone panicking. My four-years-ago self holds my mom's hand and runs down the aisle.

My dad and I—we're *inside* the portal, straddling these two realities. In the far distance, there's the reflection of my reality, the Mercury of now. My family encased in crystals, Urma lit up like a blue goddess. Slowly pulling farther and farther away.

I look at the Lost and Found in my hands. The watch clicks four minutes away from the 13.

"King?" says my dad.

"That's my time," I say. "That's Mom. That's our family. They're really trapped. They're in trouble."

"King, don't be scared," he says.

"How do I help them?" I ask.

"What went wrong?" he asks.

"Did you know there's a second Urma Tan? A Realm copy?" I ask. I realize I can ask him all the questions I want to ask my real dad. Their answers would probably be exactly the same.

"*Yes,*" he says, amazed. "I just found out. Maestro confessed about the double-Urma act. He told me that the Realm Urma was draining the life from his kids. He convinced me to help him open this portal to send her back to the Realm. Only, something went wrong, and I'm the fail-safe. I have to make sure the Realm is closed. I wish we had time for you to tell me all about your life now. But you've got your own emergency."

"Urma. The Realm Urma. She's opened a portal."

"I see it," he says, looking over my shoulder. "It's fading fast."

He glances at the Lost and Found in my hands. "Good. You've got my box, and my watch." He looks closer at the Watch of 13. "Not much time left at all. King, you and I have the same problem."

There's a portal open in his reality, and a portal open in my reality. "I guess we do," I say. "With the same Urma."

"Just let me help get you out of here," says Dad.

"You know how I can get home?" I ask.

"Well, it's tricky, you might say. But I have an idea."

"Wait, Dad—I gotta ask. How do I stop Urma?"

"I sure wish I'd been able to stop her. But send Urma back to the Realm. Otherwise, she won't ever stop. She'll keep drawing the Realm through the open portal until your world, the real world, drowns. She belongs in the Realm."

"One more question," I say. "Will you come with me?"

"Come with you? Into your reality? I can't do that, Kingston."

"But why?"

"Don't you see? What's happened to Urma could happen to me. I wish we could spend some time together, King. You know I do. But you belong in your world, and me in mine," says Dad.

"But you *left* our world. You never make it back, Pop."

"I never make it back?"

"Not in four and a half years. But I never gave up on you. I came into the Realm to get you." I want to tell him everything. About my Realm hand, how I can do real magic, about how I met Black Herman, about Mom and the King's Cup café and V and Tall and I even want to tell him about Sol's murals and Sula's universe-size eyes.

"And that's why you're stuck here now?" he asks.

"Yeah."

Hearing that seems to crush him. "I'm so sorry, Kingston. I'm sorry I had to leave. I'm sorry it's taking me so long to get back, that you and your mom had to go all these years without me, that you had to come after me." He lowers his eyes and they land on the Watch of 13. "Ah, King. You're running out of time. The least I can do is set you free."

I look down at the Watch. Sure enough, thirty seconds to go. Thirty more clicks of the big hand and the little hand will hit 13. "But you won't come?" I ask.

"I'll make it back one day, Kingston. No matter what."

Pop takes the Magician's Lost and Found in his hands. He raises the box over his head. "When I say jump, take my hand, and jump toward the portal behind you," he says. "When I break the glass, that should free you. Your momentum from the jump should take you home."

And he smashes the box down, hard, just to my right.

"*Jump!*"

And I take his hand in my left hand and jump.

I feel the shards of glass falling down, all around me.

I feel like I'm the shards.

Like I'm breaking up into bits again, spreading out, traveling like lightning, and forming back together.

It's like being in the trunk of a car as it drives over speed bumps and *whams* into ditches.

I move through the portal, and spill headfirst onto the crystalized floor of the Mercury.

36

I CAN BREATHE again. Smell again. Feel again.

I make quite an entrance, coming back in through the Mirror the way I came, the Magician's Lost and Found tumbling through the Mirror after me.

Urma is there, drinking the blue Realm energy with a thirst that has no end. The blue light is glowing from her eyes, and it's like she can't even see me.

I concentrate all of my strength into my Realm hand. I can feel the energy burning through this Mirror. I feel like I can direct it. Control it.

I close my eyes, and I can sense Urma, hovering above the crystal. She feels light, somehow. As though I can just push . . .

"Where's she going?" Mint asks as she sails toward the portal.

Urma's eyes snap and she's suddenly aware of what's happening around her.

"No!" she shrieks, and halts in midair right in front of the Mirror, reaching a clawing hand toward me.

I'm only a couple feet away from her, willing her through. "Go back, Urma," I say. "You belong in the Realm."

"I need to *feed*," she says, resisting my effort to push her into the Mirror. This isn't about her survival anymore. Her appetite is bottomless.

I realize, Urma in or out, I *need* to destroy that portal.

The Magician's Lost and Found is open at my feet.

And I think back to what Dad did.

He used the box.

He smashed the Mirror from the inside with the Magician's Lost and Found.

I turn to the box. With my Realm hand glowing blue, I raise the box in the air, and send it hurling at Urma. It crashes into her chest and carries her through the Mirror with a shout.

Once Urma and the Lost and Found have cleared to the other side, I turn my wrist and pull my hand into a fist and will the box to come back to me.

It *shatters* the Mirror from the inside into a hundred bits, raining broken glass into the crystal floor like a waterfall.

The place goes dark. The blue light is gone. The crystals all fade to black.

I blink and my eyes slowly adjust. I reach to the dark crystals surrounding my family and shatter them with one push of my Realm hand. The crystals pulverize into dust. Then I turn to my uncles. Mint and his goons block the way.

"It's over," I say. "Your bootleg goddess is back where she belongs. Go and be on your way. Unless you want me to send you." Without realizing it, my Realm hand brightens the stage with a blue glow.

Mint digs a cold look into me. His nostrils flare. He and I both know he's got no hand to play. "Okay, boys. Let's be out."

One by one, they peel off and drop down off the stage. They make their way across the crystal-slicked aisles and toward the front entrance.

"King, that was amazing!" I hear as V tackles me and wraps me up in a hug.

"You the *man*, King!" says Tall, taking my hand in his. I feel him stuff something in my palm.

It's my *glove.*

Very slick. V's hug turned me just so no one could see.

"Thanks, guys," I say, slipping the glove back on my Realm hand. My hand was glowing when I came through the Mirror, so maybe my mom didn't see that it's actually invisible now. "But I didn't get Dad back."

"But King," says V, "you jumped through the Mirror— and *you* came back!"

With a little help from a Realm version of the man himself, of course, I think, but I keep it to myself. There's too much to explain, for now.

Sol gives me a big high five. He's got this goofy smile, like he's drinking a chocolate milkshake or something. Sula smiles at me with those big eyes. I hold out my hand and she takes it. Respect.

My uncles' bindings are actually tougher to break than the depowered crystals. My Realm hand doesn't really work on them. I pick a shard up off the floor and use its edge to cut the layers of twine wrapped around their wrists.

Uncle Crooked gives me a big, blubbery hug. "My boy, I'm *so* proud."

Long Fingers takes me by the hand and shakes it, looking in my eye and beaming. "I thought she had us." Then he looks at the shard I'm holding. "You and me got to talk. Boy, do we need to talk."

"We will, Unc," I say with a quick wink. It's sorta my version of my dad's wink. "Soon. Got lots to tell you."

I turn, and there's my mom. She's been hanging back, just watching. There's so many emotions knotted up in her face, I don't know whether to laugh, cry, hug, or run. I just open my mouth and say, "Mom. I am so sorry."

She shudders like she's about to cry.

"Did you see him, in that Mirror somewhere?" she asks.

"Yeah," I say. "I saw him. I got to touch him."

She hugs me. "I'm sorry, Kingston. I just wanted to protect you," she says.

"I know, Ma. I know."

"Does this mean he won't ever come back?" she asks.

"He'll come back. One day," I say. "He told me so himself."

I look at the husk of the busted Mirror and the shards piled on the floor. It looks a lot like the last Mirror from four and a half years ago, but no fire this time. All I set out to do was bring him back, and I don't have him back, once again. Instead, in a weird way, I finished his trick—though it wasn't ever really a trick. We both jumped through that Mirror, but I'm the only one who made it back. He was almost here, just now, so close. Now he's back somewhere in that *Realm*, that series of strange magic places and echoes—that *Echoverse*, I guess, riding echoes. I have so much to tell him, and now add that an echo of him saved me. And saved us all.

EPILOGUE

MY POPS USED to say I'd have to choose my own path someday. That I could only walk with him so far, and then I would have to decide which way to go.

It's been three weeks since I saw him in the echo or the Realm, or whatever you call that place. It's like somewhere I just visited for the day.

I can see the massive obsidian from our street. They're calling it the Black Rock of BK, formerly the Mercury Theater. Now it's a dark crystal almost a block long and six stories high. You can see it just peeking over the buildings like a setting black sun. Some news vans showed up, people started selling T-shirts—our neighborhood became a destination. Like Stonehenge or those Easter Island statues or crop circles.

The new normal—that's what Ma calls it.

It's also been good for business. We officially went with the name King's Cup. Ma put a King of Hearts on the logo. After everything we went through, she understands that magic will always be a part of our family. She's got a line of customers. All the worry about the brownstone and "foreclosure"—well, we're open, and sometimes way past four. Mom seems happy.

Today, we've got a good crowd. Crooked Eye is balancing a plate of fresh pastries.

"Customers," he says with a smile.

I grab some quarters one of the customers left on the table and flip them a few times over my knuckles, looking out the window.

Too Tall barrels inside. He's talking before I even get a chance to say hello.

"King, King—there's something you gotta see," he says, and almost runs over V.

"If it isn't Bigfoot himself," Veronica says as she drops off a few coffees to some customers.

"V, come look," Tall says. "Miss James, you too. All of you."

"We're a little busy here, Eddie," Ma tells him.

"Trust me, it won't take long," Too Tall says.

Long Fingers is ringing someone up at the register. "Go ahead, we got this," Long Fingers tells my mom.

He's been getting out a lot more since that night. He even got himself a haircut. He's less wolfman these days, but I still hear him in his lab tinkering into the late hours of the night.

"This way, this way," Tall says, motioning for us to see the back side of our building. We turn left down the alley and stop cold.

It's a new mural. The kid is at it again. And he's getting better. We haven't seen a new one of these since that night.

It's the inside of the Mercury, every detail just the way I remember it from last month. The pigeons nested near the holes in the ceiling. The charred stage, the broken light bulbs. In the middle of the stage is the Mirror. Inside the Mirror is Pops. Classic Pops, dressed to the nines. He's holding the Magician's Lost and Found in one hand. His other hand holds a hand that disappears at the wrist by the edge of the Mirror.

"It just appeared last night," Tall says.

V rests her hand on his shoulder. "Give them a minute."

Ma steps forward and stares up at the mural. She doesn't say a word. She takes my hand.

I look at her and I look at Pops in the Mirror within the mural.

He saved Echo City. Saved me, and reality as we know it.

Then I feel something grab my hand. My phantom hand.

And I look up at the mural. I swear the painting of him winks at me.

I look to Ma. Somehow, we're all here now. All three of us.

I'm holding both my parents' hands at once, across dimensions, for the first time in four years, seven months, and eight days.

ACKNOWLEDGMENTS

FIRST, THIS BOOK wouldn't have been possible without the original creator and third star in the SunnyBoy constellation, Michael White. Big thanks to Jane Startz, our shepherd; her faith in us and vision for what we had was beyond our own perception. To our editor, Stacey Barney: thank you for taking a shot on us, bringing the band together, making us better writers, and making the world we dreamed up greater than we could have imagined. With gratitude to our parents for putting books and ideas into our heads and hands. Love and endless appreciation to our wives, who carry and support us with their time, love, and energy. Thanks to Uncle Pat, our earliest reader, for sharing your wonderful, creative brain. Thanks to Dr. James and Mary for all the great magic books and space talk. Shout-out to Ted B. for lifting us up and making us believe in our ideas. Thank you to Sienne for the laughs, the drawings, and bringing the happiness all day, every day. To St. Francis College's MFA program for your creativity, your community, your courage, and all your favorite Cs. Big ups to the SunnyBoy crew for rocking the chairs on the best front porch in the universe. What would we be without the endless magical conversations, friendships, and adventures? To Ant for being a brother like no other. To the great Black magicians: your due will come. Most importantly, thanks to our kids—your lives are our greatest story.

The Sleuth
and the Scholar

Recent Titles in
Contributions to the Study of Popular Culture

The Baker Street Reader: Cornerstone Writings about Sherlock Holmes
Philip A. Shreffler, editor

Dark Cinema: American *Film Noir* in Cultural Perspective
Jon Tuska

Seven Pillars of Popular Culture
Marshall W. Fishwick

The American West in Film: Critical Approaches to the Western
Jon Tuska

Sport in America: New Historical Perspectives
Donald Spivey, editor

Screwball Comedy: A Genre of Madcap Romance
Wes D. Gehring

Buckskins, Bullets, and Business: A History of Buffalo Bill's Wild West
Sarah J. Blackstone

S. J. Perelman: A Critical Study
Steven H. Gale

The Rhetorics of Popular Culture: Advertising, Advocacy, and Entertainment
Robert L. Root, Jr.

In Manors and Alleys: A Casebook on the American Detective Film
Jon Tuska

National Styles of Humor
Avner Ziv, editor

The Sleuth
and the Scholar

*Origins, Evolution, and Current Trends
in Detective Fiction*

Edited by
Barbara A. Rader
and
Howard G. Zettler

MIDDLEBURY COLLEGE LIBRARY

Contributions to the Study of Popular Culture, Number 19

Greenwood Press
New York • Westport, Connecticut • London

Library of Congress Cataloging-in-Publication Data

The Sleuth and the scholar : origins, evolution, and current trends in
detective fiction / edited by Barbara A. Rader and Howard G.
Zettler.
   p. cm.—(Contributions to the study of popular culture,
ISSN 0198-9871 ; no. 19)
   Papers presented at symposium, Wesleyan University, Middletown,
Conn., 10/18/86, sponsored by National Endowment for the Humanities.
   Bibliography: p.
   Includes index.
   ISBN 0-313-26036-2 (lib. bdg. : alk. paper)
   1. Detective and mystery stories, American—History and criticism—
Congresses. 2. Detective and mystery stories, English—History and
criticism—Congresses. I. Rader, Barbara A., 1941-
II. Zettler, Howard G. III. National Endowment for the Humanities.
IV. Series.
PS374.D4S57   1988
813'.0872'09—dc19   87-24958

British Library Cataloguing in Publication Data is available.

Copyright © 1988 by the Southern Connecticut Library Council

All rights reserved. No portion of this book may be
reproduced, by any process or technique, without the
express written consent of the publisher.

Library of Congress Catalog Card Number: 87-24958
ISBN: 0-313-26036-2
ISSN: 0198-9871

First published in 1988

Greenwood Press, Inc.
88 Post Road West, Westport, Connecticut 06881

Printed in the United States of America

The paper used in this book complies with the
Permanent Paper Standard issued by the National
Information Standards Organization (Z39.48-1984).

10 9 8 7 6 5 4 3 2

Papers from a Symposium held
18 October 1986
at
Wesleyan University
Middletown, Connecticut

Sponsored by the
Southern Connecticut Library Council

Support provided by the
National Endowment for the Humanities

Contents

III. Down These Mean Streets

Foreword

Robin W. Winks

The link between scholarship and detective fiction has long been established. Any number of writers of successful mysteries, especially British, have been academics. The methods of analysis applied by the scholar are in many cases the methods used by the fictional detective to arrive at the right answer. Deductive logic, inductive reasoning, close textual analysis, the interrogation of evidence, the search for incongruities, patterns, and causal relationships: these will be found in literary criticism, philosophy, philology, history, indeed in a dozen disciplines in the social sciences and humanities. While few of the papers presented here draw these parallels close, each paper is a demonstration, in one form or another, of the affinities between the world that we take quite seriously and a world that much of the public sees largely in terms of entertainment. These essays, taken together, are meant at least in some measure to show how those two worlds are linked.

Those who do not live and work in the academy tend, on the whole correctly, to see the academy as something of a self-enclosed environment, not of the "real world" of selling shoes and missile defense systems, of meeting car payments and worrying about one's pension. This is a mistake, of course, not only because members of the academy are no less preoccupied with such worries than those outside its ivory wall, but also because detective fiction itself generally exploits, even celebrates, a closed environment. As John McAleer demonstrates with cunningly selected quotation, the English writer June Thomson views the English village as a closed world in which the breakdown of the old order may be seen most clearly—a point drawn home by Marilyn Stasio in her remarks on Sheila Radley. Both Dennis Porter, writing of P. D. James, and Peter Rabinowitz on Chester Himes, remind us that crime takes place in a self-aware social environment and that crime is socially defined. James's murders are, quite literally, an offense against good manners, and a reading of Porter's perceptive essay must remind us that the notion of manners, bad as well as good, is socially conditioned in relation to class, to a peer group, to national idiosyncrasies, just as

Rabinowitz shows how crime in black Harlem is defined in relation to white racism. Murder in a closed environment—the locked room, the English village, the snowed-in mountain cabin in the Adirondacks, the faculty club, or the rugby locker room—is solved, most likely, by a person who may be of that environment but who is nonetheless an outsider to it, able to view the closed environment with a healthy skepticism, even with a certain productive antagonism, precisely because he or she is equally self-enclosed, much like Chandler's Philip Marlowe.

Of course, these essays were originally written to be heard, to be taken in by the ear, not by the eye. Any student of the art of writing knows that an audience of the ear must be approached somewhat differently from the audience of the eye, so each author has provided a series of referent points. One might disagree with some of these—Dickens or Edith Wharton—or with some of the asides so essential to communication when an audience is seated before one, en masse. I certainly do. There is no tacit agreement here on the future of the mystery, though the majority of the essays hint at a future, but there is agreement on the obvious fact that the mystery story has become a prime vehicle for social criticism.

Three of the papers pursue this theme directly. To James, Himes, and Thomson one could add many others: James McClure, who attacks South African apartheid in a series of sometimes grisly, always blackly humorous, interchanges between the races, in counterpoint to Himes's own closed world; or Tony Hillerman, who illumines not only Anglo/Native American differences, but the gulf between Navajo and Zuni, for example, so as to remind the reader who may have thought that all Indians are just alike of the reader's unexamined bias; or Joseph Hansen in his earlier and less didactic novels about David Brandstetter, homosexual betrayed in love. Such writers lead us, as readers, to look again at unexamined lives, individually and collectively, as social criticism must.

Parts II and III of this collection may set up a false tension between women writers, who in the argument here appear to write primarily from inside society, in gentle social criticism of the "cozy" type (never underestimate Agatha Christie as a critic of the role of vicious gossip in the village community), and male writers, who alone are presumed to walk the mean streets. Once this division reflected a truth, and the analysis here thus reflects a historical reality, but it is no longer true. Today, in fact, there are many women writers (Liza Cody and Sara Paretsky are just two examples) who are part of the hard-boiled school. That fact in itself constitutes a criticism of the way in which popular culture and the genre of detective fiction are normatively viewed.

That critics as astute as these are turning their attention to the genre is a good sign. It is not a sign that detective fiction is now accepted by the academy, however, for most critics who take such literature seriously—indeed, who call it literature—are probably seen as rebels or, at best, refugees from the annales school of analysis. Whether detective and mystery fiction become part of the mainstream for literary analysis hardly matters, in any event, for too much effort

has been spent on trying to persuade departments to tenure a scholar for writing on Rex Stout rather than on Jane Austen. This is not the issue: how society defines, deals with, and internalizes what is conventionally viewed as crime is the real issue. Thus such fiction is an adjunct, and a most accessible adjunct, to the sociology of knowledge.

To be sure, detective fiction labors under a problem of expectation that much fiction is able to avoid. Consider Glenn Most's effective exposition on Elmore Leonard in this volume. Most begins with the observation that some word, some nuance, as spoken by a millionaire who has killed a Haitian refugee, has attracted the attention of a young squad-car officer. We are meant to be puzzled by what this may be. Yet as readers we are unlikely to be puzzled, for having the artifact, the book, the printed page directly before us, we too will spot that anachronistic word. The question is one of provenance: a millionaire who appears to be what Robbie Daniels wishes to appear to be would not have so readily used underworld slang. We know the moment Daniels says "tossed" that something is amiss. All Leonard's abilities with language will not keep us from being ahead of him: indeed, it is precisely because he has an ear for language as it is used by different subgroups that Leonard builds his own language trap.

Our reading of a detective story is, of course, in some large measure culturally conditioned. Were we to read in a news report the passages on which Most focuses, we would think nothing of them or would allow our perception of cultural "reality" in Miami to tell us what the passages mean: that a Haitian refugee tried to kill a millionaire who struck back in self-defense. Because we are reading a detective story, in which little can be what it is made to seem, we know at once that the straightforward interpretation is unlikely. Since readers, and scholars, tend to think of refugees, and blacks, as victimized by society, we are ready to believe that this Haitian has also been victimized; so even if we do not notice that anomalous "tossed," we are on guard. (Further, do we not know by now that any adult male who carries a diminutive such as "Robbie" as a first name is suspect?) Leonard has sought by his speech pattern to focus us away from the normative suspicions the inveterate reader of detective fiction will bring to the text. It does not work, but nonetheless the text operates at three levels as a result of such an effort, and this, at least, we can appreciate. In short, because we know that a particular person, Elmore Leonard, writes detective stories, we also know that we must be on guard with respect to plot, action, and language simultaneously.

So what? So the task of the writer of mystery and detective fiction is a difficult one, largely because of the conventions of the genre. This does not mean that such fiction is formulaic, though much of it is so; rather, it means that the creation of a truly good mystery—one that penetrates to the mysteries of the human condition—is difficult beyond the heralding of it and worthy of close attention for that reason alone, even were there no social criticism, no revealing

gender trends, no statement about the mean streets of the modern urban condition. "The sustained invention of a really telling lie demands a talent which I do not possess," says Joseph Conrad in the author's note to his Tales of Unrest. Although Conrad may have felt that he had no such talent, this skill is exactly what is demanded of writers of mystery fiction. In other words, good mystery writers are good because they write well.

From Antigone to the present, great literature has been about laws defined and laws broken and the consequences to society and to the individual of that breaking. To examine the broken fabric of the law, or of society, is to examine society itself. Thus detective and mystery fiction is concerned with ultimate issues of provenance: Where do we learn what we learn? How do we test what we have been told? What is the source of wisdom, or order, or hope? Derivation is what such fiction is about, cause and effect, and responsibility: the scholar's continuum, whatever the discipline. Just as the historian, the social critic, or the theologian must have the discipline to examine all of humanity's really telling lies, so must the reader who settles down to the quiet nightcap and the "good read." In examining how really telling lies are invented and sustained, we demonstrate our own talents. More, we examine our cultures.

Few subjects can be so basic to the nature of a culture as gender-specific work. Being a private eye was once, as the title to one of P. D. James's best books wryly noted, "an unsuitable job for a woman." Carolyn Heilbrun, distinguished scholar and—as Amanda Cross—author of superb and literate mysteries, takes on this question in the lead piece to this volume, asking the right questions about why the face of detective fiction is changing so rapidly and how those changes mirror society. Three scholars then develop the general issue of mystery fiction as social criticism, an issue to which Professor Heilbrun has introduced us, by examining two British women writers—P. D. James and June Thomson—and a black American writer, Chester Himes, who is widely regarded abroad (and most particularly in France) as an acute social critic of urban black culture.

The tension between Parts II and III is not, then, ultimately the false division one might have feared. The six scholars who take on the issue of how women write about crime and whether the mean streets still belong to men are acutely aware of the problem Professor Heilbrun has posed. Two of the authors, William Stowe and Richard Slotkin, quite explicitly relate those mean streets, male-dominated and dark, to the conventions of Western or "cowboy" fiction of an earlier generation, showing us the transition between the rider amongst the purple sage who arrives to right the wrongs done to society by its outlaws and the "private op" who, as vigilante, must do for society what it seems unable to do for itself. The theme shared between the two types of fiction thus raises yet another question: must fiction that demonstrates how society must be protected from its own restraining laws invariably be conservative in political impact?

No symposium could hope to resolve this last question, though the essays make it clear that men and women of every political hue populate the pages of detective and mystery fiction. What the essays do, in sprightly prose and with many new insights and much new information, is to introduce the reader to the range of issues that preoccupy scholars who examine such literature, sweeping— as Marilyn Stasio puts it—through the subgenres. We meet, in the work of B. J. Rahn, the figure of Seeley Regester, a strong claimant to being America's first detective novelist; we look again at Agatha Christie, who, under the lens supplied by Michele Slung, proves to demonstrate attitudes in keeping with feminist concerns of the 1980s; and we discover, through Glenn Most's perceptive inquiry into how Elmore Leonard uses language, that unattractive and perhaps unethical figures may, in modern society, stand as heroes. The symposium from which these essays come, itself the centerpiece of a year-long series of meetings devoted to the examination of the work of dozens of mystery writers, aptly illustrates the nature and the attractions of a style of fiction once dismissed as "merely sensational" and now seen as mainstream.

Acknowledgments

The National Endowment for the Humanities provided funding for "Poisoned Pens: Mystery Fiction from Poe to the Present," and, in so doing, made possible a unique experience for Connecticut residents. Using the familiar, comfortable setting of public libraries, mystery readers and scholars met to discuss mystery fiction. The project established a link between a widespread group of mystery readers and the growing number of scholars attracted to this popular genre.

The "Poisoned Pens" project brought one hundred scholar-led book discussions to twenty participating public libraries. In addition, a series of public conversations between scholars and highly regarded authors of detective fiction was held. The entire project was launched with a scholarly symposium, entitled "The Sleuth and the Scholar: Origins, Evolution, and Current Trends in Detective Fiction," held at Wesleyan University, Middletown, Connecticut, on 18 October 1986.

This book is a record of the formal content of the symposium. Support for its publication has been provided by the National Endowment for the Humanities. The editors wish to thank the Endowment and four Southern Connecticut Library Council staff members for their invaluable contributions to the publication of the proceedings of the symposium: Sharon W. Hupp, Director of the Southern Connecticut Library Council; Susan Davidson, Project Director for "Poisoned Pens"; Susan M. Carlquist, Assistant Director of SCLC; and Beth A. Murphy, Administrative Assistant, whose setting of the entire book made possible the existence of this record.

The Sleuth
and the Scholar

1

Keynote Address:
Gender and Detective Fiction
Carolyn Heilbrun

In 1973, more as scholar than sleuth but, as Robin Winks has so well demonstrated, inevitably as both, I published a book called Toward a Recognition of Androgyny. The term "androgyny" was very new then, and shocked a great many reviewers who would be marvelously ho-hum in a few years. By now androgyny has become a media event, and I have gone on, as a scholar, to discuss and teach gender in a much more sophisticated way, with all proper references to Lacan, semiotics, and psychoanalytic history, but I have never discussed androgyny in connection with the detective story. I would like to do that here, because it has recently occurred to me that there is a kind of gender division in detective fiction that has become quite unrealistic since, say, 1970, but which never carried very much conviction.

I was led to the decision to discuss gender and the detective story by a sudden bout of housecleaning. As those of you who have grown children well know, getting them to leave home is child's play compared to getting them to take their possessions with them. After a decade of storing objects about which children feel sentimental enough to keep in your space but not sentimental enough to store in their own, most parents rebel. Come and get it, they say, or out it goes. Recently, as most of the accumulation was going out, I rescued two paperbacks originally published in 1940 and 1964, entitled The Boys' Book of Great Detective Stories and The Boys' Second Book of Great Detective Stories, both edited by Howard Haycraft. The first volume's preface began thus: "This is a book for modern boys in their teens—for those active, growing, adventurous young minds that demand more robust fare than 'children's books.' At such an age boys turn naturally to the detective story." The collection begins with Poe and ends with Sayers, including Agatha Christie in between. Haycraft no doubt knew then what moviemakers know today: that girls will reverberate to stories about boys, but neither wants stories about girls. But is this really true with the detective story?

The English detective story from the very beginning, and the American detective story lately, is remarkably androgynous in the work of its more interesting practitioners. And what do I mean by androgynous? I mean the opposite of sex-

ual stereotyping. Here is how the psychologist Sandra Bem describes the androgynous person, who, interestingly enough, is characterized by an ability to cope. Those who are stereotypical males and females are unable to act when they do not know what the appropriate action is. Placed in an unprescribed situation, they sink into bewilderment and inaction. As Bem writes:

> Even if people were all to become psychologically androgynous, the world would consist of two sexes. . . . Thus, being female typically means that you have a female body build; that you have female genitalia; that you have breasts; that you menstruate; that you can become pregnant and give birth; and that you can nurse a child. Similarly, being a male typically means that you have a male body build; that you have male genitalia; that you have beard growth; . . . that you can impregnate a woman and thereby father a child. Precisely because there are biological givens which cannot be avoided or escaped, except perhaps by means of very radical and mutilating surgery, it seems to me that psychological health must necessarily include having a healthy sense of one's maleness or femaleness. But I would argue that a healthy sense of maleness or femaleness involves little more than being able to look into the mirror and to be perfectly comfortable with the body that one sees there. . . . But beyond being comfortable with the body, one's gender need have no other influence on one's behavior or life style. Thus, although I would suggest that a woman ought to feel comfortable about the fact that she can bear children if she wants to, this does not imply that she ought to want to bear children, nor that she ought to stay home with any children that she does bear. Similarly, although I would suggest that a man ought to feel perfectly comfortable about the fact that he has a penis which can become erect, this in no way implies that a man ought to take the more active role during sexual intercourse, nor even that his sexual partners ought all to be female.[1]

Let us notice that subordinate phrase "except perhaps by means of very radical and mutilating surgery." We have recently come to understand that the entire phenomenon of transsexualism is the result of defining sex roles as absolutely distinct, as at opposite ends of the old masculinity-femininity scale. Transsexuals are the ultimate victims of stereotypical gender behavior. The best example of this is from <u>Conundrum</u> by Jan Morris, who, before she became a woman, had been an adventurous journalist who had, among other exploits, more or less run up Mount Everest in sneakers. Jan Morris writes:

The more I was treated as a woman, the more woman I became. If I was assumed to be incompetent at reversing cars, or opening bottles, oddly incompetent I found myself becoming. . . .My lawyer, in an unguarded moment one morning, even called me 'my child'; and so, addressed every day as an inferior, involuntarily, month by month, I accepted the condition. I discovered that even now men prefer women to be less informed, less able, less talkative, and certainly less self-centered than they are themselves, so I generally obliged them. . . . If the condescension of men could be infuriating, the courtesies were very welcome. . . . I did not particularly want to be good at reversing cars. . . .

My view of life shifted too. I was even more emotional now. I cried very easily, and was ludicrously susceptible to sadness or flattery. . . . Let me see what everyday inessential sensations I conceive as specifically female. First, I feel small, and neat. I am not small in fact, at 5'9" and 133 lbs., and not terribly neat either, but femininity conspires to make me feel so. My blouse and skirt are light, bright, crisp. My shoes make my feet look more delicate than they are, besides giving me, perhaps more than any other piece of clothing, a suggestion of vulnerability that I rather like. When I walk out into the street I feel consciously ready for the world's appraisal, in a way that I never felt as a man. . . . And when the news agent seems to look at me with approval, or the man in the milk-cart smiles, I feel absurdly elated, as though I have been given a good review in the Sunday Times.[2]

Let us compare to this an account of how a "real" woman, in this case Marcia Yudkin, feels:

I have to confess that, in the sense in which transsexuals use the phrase, I do not feel myself to be "really a woman." I feel myself to be "really" just a person, sex unspecified. Of course, I know that I am female, just as I know that I am 5'6", have brown hair and blue eyes, and am 25 years old; but I do not let any of these facts define me and I prefer to be in circumstances where others do not define me by those physical facts. . . . I do not consider myself a "woman in a woman's body," as I should if the transsexuals' versions of womanhood as an inner reality which can match or fail to match biological facts were correct for everyone. This intuition too contradicts some philosophers' insistence that women are essentially women rather than human beings who happen to be of the female sex.[3]

This is an American woman speaking. But for many years, it was the English, even so unlikely a one as D. H. Lawrence, who supported what has come to be called androgyny. Here is Lawrence, quoted appropriately enough by Dorothy Sayers:

> Man is willing to accept woman as an equal, as a man in skirts, as an angel, a devil, a baby-face, a machine, an instrument, a bosom, a womb, a pair of legs, a servant, an encyclopedia, an ideal or an obscenity: the one thing he won't accept her as is a human being, a real human being of the female sex.[4]

The English novel, and certainly English mysteries, have accepted "androgyny" from the beginning. Indeed, the English detective novel has always boasted androgynous males, though they would certainly not have welcomed the phrase. When women as writers of crime novels entered the field of detective fiction in large numbers in the 1920s, they followed the males in making their detectives charming and effete.

These women writers' male detectives were even more gentlemanly, upper-class, and languid than their predecessors. This, while arousing all good revolutionaries to considerable and understandable ire, was, of course, a put-on. Criminals and others were lured into thinking that anyone that effeminate must be incompetent. For a number of years the women authors paraded their carefully dressed, gentlemanly heroes through case after case, as sales soared and the form became one of the most popular of genres, particularly with intellectuals. I need not remind you of how much money Agatha Christie made, nor of her detective, Poirot, who might be called many things, and frequently was, but "manly" was not one of them. Manliness, indeed, was left for the Watsons in the outfit. Let me merely point out, in passing, that the English, in their detective fiction from Holmes on, were the first, but perhaps not the last, to equate manliness and stupidity.

The United States has been slow here as elsewhere to move away from sexual stereotyping. It is a fact that Americans divide children by gender earlier and more emphatically than any other culture. Not only have our male writers produced tough detectives, they have produced women who are stereotyped and usually either dead or man-eaters as well. Robert Parker is one of the rare exceptions. Spenser is tough, to be sure, but he is also tender, and his views on women and poetry would terrify Rambo as well as the moral majority.

It is, however, women detective writers with women detectives who have brought about the greatest change. Carol Brenner, with whom I discussed this matter a short time ago—you all know, I am sure, that she runs that wonderful bookstore Murder Ink, and is both extensively knowledgeable and enormously kind about mysteries of all persuasions—Carol mentioned that when Amanda

Cross began publishing her novels in 1964 there were very few female detectives available in the novels on the shelves at Murder Ink. By 1972 we had, among others, the wonderful Cordelia Gray from England in P. D. James's <u>An Unsuitable Job for a Woman</u>. Today there are more than anyone but Carol and perhaps Marilyn Stasio and Michele Slung can keep up with, and most of them are American. Sara Paretsky's V. I. Warshawski, whose latest and most marvelous adventure is called <u>Killing Orders</u>, is a woman private eye, period. She is one of those women who has crossed the line from amateur to professional detective, she earns her living at it, and she's good at it. Lynne Jacobi, in Dorothy Uhnak's <u>False Witness</u>, is high up in the D. A.'s office, a public rather than a private eye, and a fine example of how an androgynous female can beautifully succeed in crime fiction. So, too, Carolyn Wheat's Legal Aid lawyer Cassandra Jameson avoids stereotypical thought as assiduously as most American male novelists, detective or straight, embrace it.

This move toward androgyny and away from stereotypical sex roles— away, more importantly, from the ridiculing and condemning of those who do not conform to stereotypical sex roles—has, I am proud to say, found greater momentum in the detective story than in any other genre, and has recently gone further in the United States than elsewhere. It is the sad truth that despite the efforts of the English women detective writers and a good many of the men, including Dick Francis, the English have recently embraced our machismo rather than our, or their own, androgynous tradition. Of course, this move toward androgyny in crime writing or anywhere else is not an easy one. The same Sandra Bem who did the studies of androgynous individuals tried, together with her husband, to raise their children free from what she calls "gender-schematic processing." To inculcate beliefs and values that deviate from the dominant culture, Bem tells us, one must begin to undermine the dominant ideology in the children before the ideology can undermine them. Bem and her husband tried with their own children to undermine the gender-schematic process, which assigns sex by all sorts of external signs rather than the single anatomical sign. They found this inspiriting if uphill work. Bem reports:

> Before we read our daughter her first volume of fairy tales, we discussed with her the cultural beliefs and attitudes about men and women that the tales would reflect, and while reading the tales we frequently made such comments as, "Isn't it interesting that the person who wrote this story seems to think that girls always need to be rescued?" If such discussions are not too heavy-handed, they can provide a background of understanding against which the child can thoroughly enjoy the stories themselves, while still learning to discount the sex stereotypes within them as irrelevant both to their own beliefs and to the truth.[5]

The Bem son, aged four, met up with phallocentrism in a more literal way. He decided one day

> to wear barrettes to nursery school. Several times that day, another little boy told Jeremy that he, Jeremy, must be a girl because only girls wear barrettes. After trying to explain to this child that wearing barrettes doesn't matter and that being a boy means having a penis and testicles, Jeremy finally pulled down his pants as a way of making his point more convincingly. The other child was not impressed. He simply said, "Everybody has a penis; only girls wear barrettes."[6]

I recommend the entire article to you; for after all we are all faced with those who see that everyone (who matters) has a penis; and we must all be pre-programmed against the sexual stereotypes of fairy tales. Unfortunately, most of the theorists and critics of the crime story have observed women's emergence in the contemporary detective novel rather as one responds in the early stages of any infiltration. The hope is that if one doesn't notice the invaders, and especially if one doesn't encourage them, they will go away.

I have served for two years running on a Mystery Writers of America committee to pick the best biographical or critical work on a mystery writer. Please do not think that my only or even major criterion was that the winning book be enlightened on the subject of "gender schematic processing." Both years the committee was intelligently and readily unanimous; the first year the prize was given to a biography of James Cain, the second year to a wonderfully well-written study of Le Carré, neither author noted for his original views on women. Le Carré is a bit better than Cain, but in any case, the question never arose. I mention all this to suggest that I am far from asking for a new party line in detective criticism. At the same time, one wishes someone would notice that women have not just been writing more books lately—"the ladies, God bless them"—but that they have done a certain amount to transform the genre. I have two shelves of academic, ponderous (I'm afraid) books on crime writing, and there are but a few of them that consider the new androgynous writers at all; when women are taken up, it is in a separate section, as though to say, Hey, fellows: look! The girls have a softball team too. No one has noticed that crime writing is changing in an important way.

There is, of course, a gender bias even to their not noticing. Dick Francis and Robert Parker, to stick to two of my favorite male novelists, have gone far along the road of anti-stereotyping, and they have both been honored by fame and fortune and awards. But androgynous women in male novels with a tough and resourceful hero are not as threatening, or unfamiliar, or dangerous as androgynous females in novels by women. And this fact has marked the whole history of

androgyny, as many commentators have noticed. Men may acquire "feminine" characteristics, but woe unto the woman who becomes "masculine." One need think no further than the theories of Jung and Norman O. Brown. Aggressive women frighten everyone: it's an idea we've been taught to be uncomfortable with; furthermore, we have defined men not as wonderfully human, but as "not women."

There is a plethora of books, romances and westerns, designed for those who want no surprises. These books relax the reader precisely because everyone knows what to expect, of men, women, and the plot. I am not altogether certain that the American classics by that sainted trio Hammett, Chandler, and Ross Macdonald do not always satisfy the same unexamined and unchallenged assumptions. Parker interests me and many others because, in that same tradition, he does challenge them. And recent writers, women and men, have begun to challenge them too. I think that this openness about the prison of gender is one of the detective novel's great claims to fame and has been ever since Holmes's Irene Adler put on men's clothing for her own purposes. I think, since I am throwing so many scandalous opinions around here, that the English, who began by being courageously androgynous, are passing that torch on to Americans who today have shown wonderful new possibilities for the genre.

It's a safe guess that every detective novelist has been asked why he or she writes detective stories and not "real" novels. There are many answers, but I think an important one has never been stated flat out: that with the momentum of a mystery and the trajectory of a good story with a solution, the author is left free to dabble in a little profound revolutionary thought. In my opinion, detective fiction, often called formula fiction, has almost alone and with astonishing success challenged the oldest formulas of all.

NOTES

1. Sandra Bem, "From Traditional to Alternative Conceptions of Sex Roles," in Beyond Sex-Role Stereotypes: Readings Toward a Psychology of Androgyny, ed. Alexandra G. Kaplan and Joan P. Bean (Boston: Little, Brown, 1976), 60.

2. Jan Morris, Conundrum (New York: Harcourt Brace, 1974), 149, 150, 153, 157.

3. Marcia Yudkin, "Transsexualism and Women: A Critical Perspective," Feminist Studies 4, no. 3 (1978): 103.

4. Dorothy L. Sayers, "Are Women Human?" in <u>Unpopular Opinions</u> (London: Victor Gollancz, 1946), 114.

5. Sandra Bem, "Gender Schema Theory and Its Implications for Child Development: Raising Gender-aschematic Children in a Gender-schematic Society," <u>Signs</u> 8, no. 4 (1983): 612

6. Ibid.

I

Mysteries as Social Criticism

2

Detection and Ethics:
The Case of P. D. James

Dennis Porter

Readers of detective stories are not nice. At least, in the act of reading, they are not as nice as most of them think they are or, if pressed on the matter, would probably claim they ought to be. The pleasures they take in their reading have an even more marked voyeuristic character than those found in average realist fiction and, more often than one might suppose, rival those of pornography. Moreover, this is true for the classic detective story as well as for the hard-boiled thriller. At the risk of sounding like a New England Puritan, I would suggest that, here as elsewhere, "innocent pleasure" is an oxymoron, if one means by that phrase a pleasure divorced from libidinal or aggressive drives. But I mustn't forget myself.

There is apparently in some quarters, including our funding agencies, resistance to the idea that "psychological approaches" to the detective story genre are legitimate. Yet one cannot begin to understand the mass popularity of the detective story genre if one is inattentive to reader response and reader pleasure. One cannot close one's eyes to the fact that there is a pornography of crime, in film as well as in literature, and it takes both soft-core and hard-core forms.

This is immediately apparent even if one limits oneself to the role that is the fundamental defining characteristic of the genre, the role of detective. Nothing distinguishes him more than the fact that he carries a license to snoop and to pry, to peep, eavesdrop, and interrogate. He enters other people's houses, often against their will, goes through their drawers, reads their correspondence, and analyzes the stains on their bed linen or their most intimate articles of clothing. In P. D. James's <u>Death of an Expert Witness</u> such activities are given particular emphasis—the scene of the initial murder is a forensic science laboratory, a place where post facto surveillance attains its greatest precision. Perhaps for that reason, a short paragraph in the novel suggested to me at least that the ultimate act of voyeuristic indiscretion is a postmortem examination: "He hadn't expected the colors of the human body would be so vivid, so exotically beautiful. Now he

saw again Kerrison's gloved fingers, slick as eels, busying themselves at the body's orifices" (56).

In short, because of the material on which it has to work, including particularly the soft, corruptible human body and what people are driven to do to it—to their own as well as others'—the work of detection itself is not nice. The young female investigator of P. D. James's <u>An Unsuitable Job for a Woman</u> is frequently reminded of this in the course of her investigation. As a result, one might appropriate P. D. James's title and suggest that reading tales of detection is also an unsuitable activity for a woman or, for that matter, any man who claims to have moral sensibilities above those of your average peeping Tom.

The interesting point is that in her fiction P. D. James turns out to be aware of the apparent "unsuitability" of both activities—of detecting and of reading about detection. On the one hand, she proves to be highly self-conscious in recognizing how morally ambivalent the work of her investigators might seem to be: "Yours is a filthy trade," an angry suspect yells at Superintendent Dalgliesh in <u>Death of an Expert Witness</u> (339). So "filthy," in fact, that the murderer who stalks his victim in <u>Innocent Blood</u> goes through many of the same routines as a fictional detective.

On the other hand, P. D. James goes to great lengths to underline for her readers the seriousness of the issues raised by her tales of crime and punishment. In spite of the fact that she mostly respects the conventions of the genre associated with mass entertainment, she does not permit her readers to take violent death lightly. It is as if her novels were haunted by a sense of guilt, the guilt of an author as well as of her characters, and, by extension, of her readers. As a result, one encounters an apparent need to justify the whole business of detection, both through the reflections her detective heroes and heroines make on their work, and through comments diffused throughout her text that are designed to set before the reader a code of behavior appropriate to the modern world. Her tales of violence and murder are nothing if not didactic; P. D. James has morally improving designs on her public.

The example of her work reminds us, in fact, how in one form or another mass popular literature invariably takes upon itself the ideological function of transmitting a *doxa*. Moreover, in a post-religious society like that of modern Britain, it is frequently the only kind of widely read material that attempts to distinguish between right and wrong or set up models to be imitated. And among all forms of popular literature, nowhere is this more true than in detective fiction in the broad sense. Where else outside detective fiction does it still seem appropriate to raise questions about such theological categories as "good" and "evil" or such philosophical ones as "truth" and "justice"?

In the first place, then, P. D. James sets up a situation in which the reader is made to feel that, in spite of the unsavory character of their work, it is in the end her detectives who lead exemplary, ethically upright lives. It is they who are the

heroes and heroines amidst the moral malaise and spiritual confusions of our time. More than any other characters in the novels it is her investigators who combine critical intelligence and a disabused knowledge of the world with sensibilities educated by the moral tradition in literature. Superintendent Dalgliesh is a sometime poet and Cordelia Gray knows her Blake.

If, as has often been suggested, such British predecessors as Dorothy L. Sayers and Agatha Christie embedded their criminal plots in novels of manners, P. D. James may be said to locate hers in novels of bad manners. Not the wise-cracking bad manners of the hard-boiled private eyes, however, but the bad manners of the new Britain of the 1960s and 1970s. Thus, where once it was possible to distinguish between classic British detective fiction and the American hard-boiled tradition on the basis of the relationship implied between the crimes committed and the environment, with P. D. James such a distinction breaks down. The typical ambiance of a Sayers or Christie novel implied the surprise of crime under circumstances of order and relative beauty. The world represented was that upper middle-class English world of the long weekend, interrupted temporarily by violence between the moment of crime and its solution. The hard-boiled tradition, on the other hand, posited not an antithetical, but a sympathetic relationship between crime and environment in the urban spaces of rapidly developing, unregulated American cities that, out West at least, were only a generation or two from frontier life.

The bad manners in P. D. James novels, however, are a function of a modern seediness that is familiar from the realistic tradition in fiction. It is, moreover, a seediness occasionally worthy of Graham Greene both in its power to disgust the reader and in its moral as well as material dimensions. In P. D. James's novels those country houses of the classic tradition are frequently referred to. But they have been tastelessly transformed into laboratories for forensic or other research, and only a plaster ceiling or a mantelpiece remains to attest to the lost beauty. At the same time the detective invariably discovers in the course of his investigation the messiness and waywardness of human lives pursued under circumstances so unpropitious that outbreaks of criminal violence seem a natural consequence.

Failure of one kind or another—in one's personal relations, one's career, one's moral or material ambitions—dogs the lives of the great majority of P. D. James's characters. Thus the frequent drabness and domestic tawdriness she depicts—she is very strong on closed spaces and disagreeable smells—are often no more than the material expression of loveless, anxiety-ridden lives. Her novels are inhabited by characters who are victims of personal and professional self-doubt, dead or departed mothers, foolish and irresponsible fathers, broken marriages, and failed love affairs. The complaint of the physician at the beginning of Death of an Expert Witness is typical: "I'm forty-five next week and what have I achieved? This house, two children, a failed marriage, and a job I'm frightened

of losing because it's the only thing I've made a success of" (13). It turns out at the denouement that he is the murderer, but his situation is not very different from that of his embittered first victim, Dr. Lorrimer—an individual whose earlier marriage went unconsummated and whose subsequent love affair ended in rejection.

Against the background of this particular fictional universe, P. D. James's investigators are designed to stand out. The young female private eye of An Unsuitable Job for a Woman, Cordelia Gray, suggests the form that heroism in the modern world might take. The significance of her first name is not meant to be overlooked by the reader, since the Shakespearean connection is made in the text by a playful reference to "her sisters." Moreover, the combined circumstances of a mother who was lost to her at birth and a foolish, irresponsible father confirm the allusion. The latter is referred to as "an itinerant Marxist poet and an amateur revolutionary" (31), who, we learn, took his daughter out of school to serve him in his wanderings. Yet P. D. James's Cordelia survives all the losses the novel records in order to play an actively heroic role. Incidentally, her motherless life suggests that it is surprising no Shakespearean scholars have, to my knowledge, speculated on the character and fate of Lear's consort, of Queen Lear. (And not necessarily along the lines of L. C. Knight's classic article, "How Many Children Had Lady Macbeth?")

The course of the investigation in An Unsuitable Job for a Woman is, of course, calculated to prove the opposite of the affirmation of the title. It turns out that this particular young woman on her first case has the intelligence, the curiosity, the persistence, and the mental and physical toughness to overcome male skepticism, an attempt on her life, and a shrewd adversary to solve her crime. Moreover, she also demonstrates a subtle moral flexibility at the denouement, when she becomes an accomplice in hiding the murder of a particularly reprehensible murderer. If Cordelia is posited as exemplary for our time, it is because she embodies the triumph of character over circumstance. Out of the deprivations of virtual orphanhood and a succession of foster homes, she salvages the lessons of a convent education—"an oasis of order and beauty" (63)—and learns how to remain morally upright as well as effective.

Where, on the one hand, P. D. James proposes through her investigators models of right conduct appropriate to modern living, on the other, she also promotes a kind of wisdom through the scattered comments and asides that abound in her works. A figure, a situation, or a piece of behavior is susceptible to eliciting a swift, generalizing judgment in the dialogue or in a character's reflective moments. Life's experience in young or old is distilled in maxims intended on the whole to suggest the paradox and complexity of the human animal.

On one level, these maxims are offered with a combination of irony and seriousness as the practical advice of an experienced investigator to the neophyte.

An Unsuitable Job for a Woman, in particular, is full of the sayings of Cordelia Gray's defunct mentor, Bernie Pryde. They take the form of quotations, attributed to a number of sources, such as "Never theorize in advance of your facts" (42), "Get to know the dead person" (43), or "When you're examining a building look at it as you would a country church" (70). Such quotations are expressions of the collective experience of a trade. Yet they are ironically reevaluated at the denouement as Bernie Pryde's "horrible platitudes" (284).

On another level, there are a great many formulaic comments dispersed throughout the work that are left uncorroded by any kind of contextual irony. They may be as unexceptionable as Cordelia Gray's reflection, "How inconsistent and how interesting human beings were!" (47). They may take the form of the received folk wisdom of an aging nanny: "If a man's good to one woman, he'll be good to another" (159) or "My mother used to say, 'Don't marry for money but marry where money is!' There's no harm in looking for money as long as there's kindness as well" (161). They may be as suggestive as the comment of a Cambridge undergraduate when asked if he had been in love: "I'm not sure. All sex is a kind of exploitation, isn't it? If you mean, did we explore our own identities through the personality of the other, then I suppose we were in love or thought we were" (111). They may be as arresting as the same undergraduate's assertions that "Death is the least important thing about us" (252), or "Beauty is intellectually confusing. . . .Every time she opened that delicious mouth I was expecting her to illumine life. And all she could talk about was clothes" (253).

Finally, at their most sustained, such comments find themselves located in extended Dostoyevskian dialogues between investigator and suspect. At such a moment as the final confrontation between Cordelia Gray and Sir Ronald Callendar, there occurs a kind of formalized exchange of maxims. The question raised here is precisely: How much is a human life worth, and under what conditions, if any, does someone have the right to take it? Sir Ronald Callendar had killed his only son because the young man's continued existence would have jeopardized the father's career and the advancement of science. It is an act that causes Cordelia Gray to exclaim, "I can't believe that a human being could be so evil." She then goes on to affirm, in a sentence that echoes a famous line of W. H. Auden, "But what is the use of making the world more beautiful if the people who live in it can't love one another?" At which point Sir Ronald pours out all the contempt he feels for the concept of love, ending his peroration with the counter-maxim, "Love is more destructive than hate. If you must dedicate your life to something, dedicate it to an idea" (226).

Nevertheless, what P. D. James underwrites here through the character of her crusading private eye is an ethic founded on an idea of love that is more closely related to charity than to sex. In any case, the response invented for Cordelia to Sir Ronald's affirmation is symptomatic of a notion that haunts all of P. D. James's fiction: "I meant love, as a parent loves a child" (227). The

sentence implies a demanding and traditional view of right conduct. In a world without God and the rewards and constraints of a religiously grounded morality, one is left with a form of <u>caritas</u>, of Christ without Christianity. The only salvation for all those teeming, lost souls that P. D. James's intrigues of crime and violence uncover in contemporary society is a religion of love, of devotion and sacrifice of self, the love of a parent for a child. But this is precisely what is lacking in the world projected in her fiction. Her novels are peopled with irresponsible or even murderous fathers, lost mothers, childless women, and abandoned children. It is, in short, no surprise if her plots recall both the bloody familial dramas of Greek myths and the tortured family romance of psychoanalytic theory.

In this respect the quest of the adopted Philippa Palfrey for her real parents in <u>Innocent Blood</u> is characteristic. In spite of the novel's realist trappings, which occasionally betray P. D. James into coming on like a British Joyce Carol Oates, it is to my mind most fascinating when it operates on the level of myth or fantasy as a search for the lost good mother—a fantasy that is, in fact, shattered in the end by contact with the real thing. Philippa's loss of innocence does not prevent her author from projecting onto her the vocation of a lay nun, in spite of all her modern woman's tough talk and sexual knowingness. First, she mothers the "real" mother whom she had set out to find. Then, after that mother's death, she discovers, like her author, that one suitable vocation for the charitable heart in the modern world is the writing of fiction. P. D. James would have us believe that writing and detection, equally as much as mothering, are suitable jobs for a woman. Moreover, all three may be combined in the writing of detective fiction.

It is thus consistent with an ethic of love if, in <u>An Unsuitable Job for a Woman</u>, Cordelia should in the end devote herself to preserving the memory of Mark Callendar unsullied by the perverse sexuality with which his father had decked out the murder scene. If she plays Antigone to the saintly Mark's Polynices—Mark, who devoted his time to the care of autistic children and senile old men—she also becomes in retrospect the mother he never had. Antigone's was after all also a maternal role.

Further, in the concluding discussion between Cordelia and Superintendent Dalgliesh, the reader is told that it is not such abstractions as "justice" that count but "the person." If the truth of neither Mark nor Ronald Callendar's murder is disclosed, it is because some things are more important than "truth" and "justice." And in the final maxim of the book, Superintendent Dalgliesh acquiesces, "there are some cases which are better left unsolved" (286).

That there may be a kind of love in the choices made by a novelist as well as by her leading characters is perhaps most obvious in <u>Innocent Blood</u>. The form "charity" takes there is in the reconstruction of the feelings and thought processes of not just one but two murderers. P. D. James employs her characteristic magisterial omniscience in order to adopt the point of view of a murderer in

pursuit of his quarry, and she does so because she wants to invest the abstraction "murder" with an ideology of "personhood." In the representation of Norman Scase one recognizes the injunction that attention must be paid to an ex-clerk in his anguish.

In short, P. D. James invests her tales of murder with a relatively consistent account of what constitutes appropriate conduct in some of life's more extreme situations. In an age without absolutes or the codified moralities of established religions, she clings to one central concept of Christian faith, namely Pauline caritas. That is why her sense of "personhood" is very different from E. M. Forster's liberal humanist affirmation of "personal relations." Whatever P. D. James's own feelings about religion—they are, in fact, irrelevant to my argument—the most sympathetic characters in her fiction tend to share the attitudes of Cordelia Gray, who is diagnosed as "incurably agnostic but prone to unpredictable relapses into faith" (247).

It is no accident that the sites of the two murders in Death of an Expert Witness are a country house transformed into a laboratory for forensic research and a so-called Wren chapel that has been deconsecrated. Two buildings that attest to the ideals of order, beauty, and faith of former times provide the settings for the acting out of homicidal violence and lust in the confused present. Such signifiers imply nostalgia for a nobler age of belief that manages to exist in the fiction alongside a modest hope in the individual's capacity to live the good life now against all odds.

In their final confrontation Sir Ronald Callendar responds to Cordelia Gray's expression of outrage with the statement, "If you are capable of imagining it, then I'm capable of doing it" (226). It is as close as P. D. James's "evil" man of science comes to the celebrated affirmation of Dostoyevski's Grand Inquisitor, namely, that if God does not exist, then everything is permitted. The conscious intention of her novels is, however, to refute such a thought. Like so many of her predecessors in the detective genre, this English writer offers her readers investigators who are men and women with a vocation and, in spite of appearances, models of right conduct. Their function is to limit in modest ways the damage caused by the apparent nonexistence of a deity.

Yet her own purpose seems less modest. P. D. James has designs on us as readers. Her books are baited traps. She wants to make us nicer in the very works that speak to our pleasures. She wants to make us better human beings. Her example should remind us, then, that the writer of detective novels is no more innocent than her readers. We do well to observe them both closely, though for different reasons. There are apparently some questions that both P. D. James and those who resist "psychological approaches" to the genre prefer not to raise. In any case, a casual reader should be warned that to read one of her novels is to risk a kind of conversion.

NOTE

References to the following novels by P. D. James are noted by page number in the text: <u>Death of an Expert Witness</u> (New York: Warner, 1977); <u>Innocent Blood</u> (New York: Warner, 1980); <u>An Unsuitable Job for a Woman</u> (New York: Warner, 1972).

3

Chandler Comes to Harlem: Racial Politics in the Thrillers of Chester Himes

Peter J. Rabinowitz

"When I went into. . .the detective story field," noted the black expatriate novelist Chester Himes, "I was just imitating all the other American detective story writers, other than the fact that I introduced various new angles which were my own. . . .I just made the faces black, that's all."[1]   And, indeed, Stephen Milliken has convincingly suggested that many of Himes's thrillers—which center on a group of sinister people competing in the search for a mysterious object—recapitulate the basic plot of Hammett's The Maltese Falcon.[2] But whether Himes was being disingenuous, or whether he was self-deceived, he wasn't just imitating other American writers. In fact, you cannot take the genre and simply "make the faces black"—not, at least, if you see the black experience as Himes does. More specifically, I'm going to argue here that—despite his own claims—Himes substantially changed the genre that he inherited from Hammett and Chandler; that he was forced, whether consciously or unconsciously, into these formal changes because of his political situation as a self-aware radical black writer; and that by looking at the ways in which he altered the genre, we can see some of the contradictions between the Chandlerian thriller and American racial reality. Because of my limited space, my argument will necessarily be schematic, but I hope that my simplification will be seen to distill, rather than distort, the issues I'll be discussing.

As the background to my argument, let me indicate what I see as the essential elements of the novels from which Himes apparently took his inspiration. Those elements are both formal and ideological. That is, the Chandlerian novel—which, for the sake of brevity, will have to serve as my exemplar of the hard-boiled genre—took on its distinctive shape in part because of its political vision of the nature of evil. This becomes clear if we contrast it to the classical British detective story, as typified by Christie. For Christie, evil springs from the diseased minds of disturbed individuals, and it is perpetuated primarily by deceit (which can be punctured by logic) rather than by raw power (which

requires social transformation for its uprooting). The detective's task is thus fairly easy, and resolution of the text's initial disorder can be readily achieved by a single intelligent, even unarmed individual. Following the thread of the initial crime back to its origins leads, however, not to a source in a single perverted individual, but rather to a complex weave of political relationships in which the detective becomes increasingly tangled. "Solving" the crime thus becomes a more difficult task, and the "solutions" proposed become increasingly sloppy and approximate. And even to the extent that the sources of particular evils <u>can</u> be determined, they are often so well entrenched in the political structure that nothing short of revolution can dislodge them. It's no accident that Poirot is characterized by his arrogance, Marlowe by his gloomy sense of despair—for Poirot succeeds in a way that Marlowe cannot.

As I've said, form is closely tied to ideological perspective, and this particular vision of evil as social in origin necessitates any number of structural changes in the genre.[3] I want to focus on one of them today: the disengagement of the hero. To be sure, as many critics have pointed out, most literary detectives are aloof. But Philip Marlowe has a particular kind of self-enclosed isolation that is different in kind from the solitude, say, of Poirot, or Holmes, or Nero Wolfe. Marlowe's isolation—which might have been called, in the loose but evocative vocabulary of the 1950s, his "existential" loneliness—is neither a "character trait" nor an individual psychological eccentricity. Rather, it follows more or less inevitably from Chandler's view of crime. That's because for a novel to work at all as detective story, it has to have at least some kind of "resolution." But given Chandler's world view, that resolution cannot come, as Christie's does, with the eradication of evil and the restoration of the initial peaceful order, since from Chandler's perspective, that order was not <u>interrupted</u> by evil, but was itself the very source of evil.

Nor could Chandler's novels find their resolution in political upheaval and still remain within the limits of the detective story genre: even Hammett's <u>Red Harvest</u>, which pushes the genre to its limits in this direction, does not reflect a substantial political change. Thus, some other kind of affirmation is required. In most of Chandler's novels, that affirmation takes the form of personal discovery. To put it in other terms, Marlowe follows the path of the first detective in our tradition, Oedipus, by finding that the "important" truth lies within himself; at the same time, through what Dennis Porter calls his "moral education,"[4] he comes to accept his own responsibility, recognizing that in following the tangles of the thread of the crime, he has gotten fouled in the web himself. "Me, I was part of the nastiness now," he admits at the end of <u>The Big Sleep</u>.[5] And his acceptance of that responsibility usually lies in an "existential" choice to maintain his principles even in the face of an absurd world. In other words, Marlowe's actions do not take on meaning because of their effects (indeed, the effects are

often explicitly trivialized—as when he suggests, at the end of <u>The Big Sleep,</u> that the primary effect of his actions is "to protect what little pride a broken and sick old man has left in his blood").[6] Rather, Marlowe's actions gain their stature because of their inherent—one might almost say "aesthetic"—quality as exemplars of a purely individual, self-created integrity.

This kind of affirmation—as we've seen in texts as diverse as <u>The Red and the Black, Enemy of the People, The Old Man and the Sea,</u> and <u>The Stranger</u>—generally goes hand in hand with personal detachment. That's because seeking individual integrity is a sufficient quest—and finding it is a sufficient end—only for someone whose personal relations to others are minimized. The message of Chandler's <u>The Long Goodbye</u> is poignant but clear: friendship and abstract principle conflict, and friendship can betray you as principle cannot. It's thus no accident that the heroes of the texts I've mentioned, from Julian Sorel to Meursault, are all males, or that Marlowe's marriage ends his career as a literary character. And it's probably no accident that, threatened with death, Marlowe finds himself apostrophizing on the romantic habits of worms. "And don't scatter my ashes over the blue Pacific," he tells Silver-Wig in <u>The Big Sleep</u>; "I like the worms better. Did you know that worms are of both sexes . . .?" He goes on to explain that "any worm can love any other worm," but a reader who knows Marlowe well is apt to see another meaning—for any worm is also self-sufficient.[7] Indeed, every one of Chandler's novels except for <u>Playback</u>—by most counts a failure—ends with an image of estrangement or death.

There is, however, a mystification behind this touting of Marlowe as a hero. I don't mean that Chandler tries to glide over the question of whether or not such conduct is really admirable; indeed, debate of this very issue lies at the center of his novels and gives them much of their power. What the novels obscure, rather, is the question of under what conditions this brand of heroism is possible. And when you hold up Chandler's novels against Himes's, you realize that Marlowe's model simply cannot be followed for many people, in many circumstances—specifically, once you "make the faces black." For Himes's detective protagonists, Grave Digger Jones and Coffin Ed Johnson, even though they are caught up in a world of Chandlerian evil, Chandlerian heroism is not an option. Indeed, the fact that they always appear as a team is itself a clue that individualism of the Marlowe sort is not available on the streets of Harlem.

I'm not suggesting, of course, that Coffin Ed and Grave Digger lack either physical stamina or the intellectual prowess that hard-boiled heroism requires. To the contrary, they're quicker thinkers than Marlowe is, and the scene in <u>The Real Cool Killers</u> where Coffin Ed hangs head downward from the roof of a building for twenty minutes, waiting to get a bead on the gang-leader Sheik, is only one instance of his physical endurance. Indeed, his primary physical characteristic—his scarred face—is a testament to his stamina: it's the result of

acid thrown in his face by a gangster in <u>A Rage in Harlem</u>, the first book of the series.

Nor am I suggesting that Coffin Ed and Grave Digger lack professionalism. True, they're insubordinate (but then, so is Marlowe). Still, except for a brief reference to bribe-taking at the beginning of <u>A Rage in Harlem</u>—written before Himes had really developed their characters—they do their thankless jobs unstintingly and with integrity. But the moment they articulate their professional code, as in <u>The Real Cool Killers</u>, you can see that their situation as blacks gives it a different shape and a ring of bitterness: "'I'm just a cop,' Grave Digger said thickly. 'If you white people insist on coming up to Harlem where you force colored people to live in vice-and-crime-ridden slums, it's my job to see that you are safe'" (65). Their situation, in other words, is inextricably tied up in racial politics.

In part, that connection between professional conduct and race derives from the personal commitments of Coffin Ed and Grave Digger. Although they are middle class, and live with their families in Queens, they have a strong identification with the poor black people among whom they work. Throughout the eight novels in the series, the detectives and the narrator gnaw relentlessly on the demeaning physical and psychological consequences of American racism:

> Blank-eyed whores stood on the street corners swapping obscenities with twitching junkies. Muggers and thieves slouched in dark doorways waiting for someone to rob; but there wasn't anyone but each other. Children ran down the street, the dirty street littered with rotting vegetables, uncollected garbage, battered garbage cans, broken glass, dog offal—always running, ducking and dodging. God help them if they got caught. Listless mothers stood in the dark entrances of tenements and swapped talk about their men, their jobs, their poverty, their hunger, their debts, their Gods, their religions, their preachers, their children, their aches and pains, their bad luck with the numbers and the evilness of white people. Workingmen staggered down the sidewalks filled with aimless resentment, muttering curses, hating to go to their hotbox hovels but having nowhere else to go.
>
> "All I wish is that I was God for just one mother-raping second," Grave Digger said, his voice cotton-dry with rage.
>
> "I know," Coffin Ed said. "You'd concrete the face of the mother-raping earth and turn white folks into hogs."[8]

And throughout the novels, Coffin Ed and Grave Digger do what they can to alleviate the pain suffered by the black community. In <u>Cotton Comes to Harlem</u>, Deke O'Malley has swindled $87,000 through a fraudulent "back to Africa"

scheme, but before he can take the money and run, it is highjacked. And through all the Chandlerian twists in the plot, their fundamental aim remains clear. It's not some abstract search for truth (à la Christie) or some acting out of abstract principle (à la Chandler). As Coffin Ed puts it, "Eighty-seven grand of colored people's hard-earned money got lost in the caper; and we want to get it back" (53).

In part, too, the increased commitment to other individuals comes from what might be called the accident of events, which often makes it difficult for Coffin Ed and Grave Digger to avoid personal involvement in the events they are investigating. At the climax of The Real Cool Killers, when Coffin Ed is hanging from the roof, Sheik is threatening a hostage—and she happens to be Coffin Ed's daughter, who has been engaging in her own adolescent rebellion by joining the gang.

But their commitment is, in the end, neither really a matter of free choice nor really an accident, for Coffin Ed and Grave Digger's inability to be Chandlerian heroes is not simply a matter of their individual situations. Rather, it is to a large extent imposed; that is, because their "faces are black," they do not have the luxury of the Marlowe option, of detaching themselves from the criminals and the victims among whom they work. You don't have to be a fancy reader to see Coffin Ed's rescue of his daughter as emblematic of his and Grave Digger's relationship to all black people—not so much because they "choose" to think of themselves that way, but because white power defines them first and foremost as black.

This theme is central to Himes's vision. As he once noted in an interview, "What else can a black writer write about but being black?"[9] And we see it as early as his first novel, If He Hollers Let Him Go, where his protagonist, Bob Jones, sums up his utopian wish—a wish the novel resolutely and relentlessly crushes:

> I didn't want to be the biggest Negro who ever lived. . . .Because deep inside of me, where the white folks couldn't see, it didn't mean a thing. If you couldn't swing down Hollywood Boulevard and know that you belonged; if you couldn't make a polite pass at Lana Turner at Ciro's without having the gendarmes beat the black off you for getting out of your place, . . . being a great big "Mister" Nigger didn't mean a thing. . . .
>
> I'd settle for a leaderman job at Atlas Shipyard—if I could be a man, defined by Webster as a male human being. That's all I'd ever wanted—just to be accepted as a man—without ambition, without distinction, either of race, creed, or colour; just a simple Joe walking down an American street. (153)

The same idea is put in a less flowery form in Cotton Comes to Harlem, when Grave Digger points out that the slums in Spanish Harlem are even worse than those in the black neighborhoods. "Yeah," Coffin Ed replies, "but when a Puerto Rican becomes white enough he's accepted as white, but no matter how white a spook might become he's still a nigger" (50). One need not accept Bob Jones's masculinist stance[10] or Coffin Ed's implicit anti-Latin bias—subjects for separate study on their own—to recognize the validity of their observations about being black in America. And the novels continually hammer away at this theme. In All Shot Up, when Coffin Ed needs to make an emergency phone call, he

> drove around Gramercy Square and stopped in front of a quiet, discreet-looking bar on Lexington. He got out and went inside.
> Well-dressed white people were drinking apértifs in a dim-lighted atmosphere of gold-lined wickedness. Coffin Ed fitted in like Father Divine in the Vatican. . . .The bartender informed him with a blank face that they didn't have a phone. (143)

And even after Coffin Ed shows his badge and threatens to close him down, the bartender directs him to the phone "without a change of expression." It's no accident that the scene toward the beginning of All Shot Up where Coffin Ed punches a white cop for using the word "nigger" is recapitulated later when the interracial group of gangsters is split apart for the same reason (44, 155). Race is a powerful and ever present bond in Himes; or, to be more accurate, blackness is an ever present bond, for it is precisely the asymmetry of American racism that makes blacks "black" while whites are free to be just "people." As Coffin Ed puts it when Anny identifies her race as "human" rather than "white" in Blind Man with a Pistol: "I got no reverence for these white women going 'round joining the human race. It ain't that easy for us colored folks" (90). And powerful bonds—as Marlowe learns in The Long Goodbye—make Chandlerian heroism all but impossible.

To put it another way, whereas Marlowe can be detached, Coffin Ed and Grave Digger are necessarily caught in the middle: they're black, but at the same time they are (as they explicitly put it) "the man," that is, a part of the oppressive power of the state. This contradiction in their position may be a partial explanation for the rage and violence that characterize their actions in these books. For one of the most striking features of these novels is the brutality with which Coffin Ed and Grave Digger go after information. The following description, from The Crazy Kill, exemplifies their interrogation techniques:

Suddenly, without warning, Coffin Ed stepped forward from the shadows and chopped Chink across the back of his neck with the edge of his hand. It knocked Chink forward, stunning him, and Coffin Ed grabbed him beneath the arms to keep him from falling on his face.

Grave Digger slid quickly from the desk and handcuffed Chink's ankles, drawing the bracelets tight just above the ankle bones. Then Coffin Ed handcuffed Chink's hands behind his back.

Without saying another word, they opened the door, lifted Chink from the chair and hung him upside down from the top of the door by his handcuffed ankles, so that the top part of the door split his legs down to his crotch. His back lay flat against the bottom edge, with the lock bolt sticking into him.

Then Grave Digger inserted his heel into Chink's left armpit and Coffin Ed did the same with his right, and they pushed down gradually. (125)

There are, of course, many levels on which to explain such violence, for it is probably overdetermined.[11] One could, for instance, make the economic argument that Himes, financially strapped, was simply knocking off thrillers to bring in quick cash, providing what would sell to the white French readers who were his immediate initial audience. Following another track, one might argue that, psychologically, Himes is working out some kind of desire to "get back"— that the oppressed is, by an act of imaginative will, turning himself into an oppressor. As he himself said, "I want these people [that is, the white people] just to take me seriously. I don't care if they think I'm a barbarian, a savage, or what they think; just think I'm a serious savage."[12] But at the same time, the violence can be seen to stem from the contradictions in the situation in which Coffin Ed and Grave Digger find themselves; that is, it's easy to see how being on both sides of the oppressive power structure portrayed in these books would produce the smoldering rage that marks Coffin Ed in particular, a rage that's ready to erupt at the slightest provocation.

Since the asymmetry of black and white in our culture rules out Chandlerian heroism for protagonists, the author is left in an artistically difficult position. As I've argued, his vision of evil is closer to Chandler's than it is to Christie's, so that his story line tends to be Chandleresque. The ingenuity of the crime itself (central to Christie's complications) is replaced by fast-paced plots and counterplots, crosses and doublecrosses, often involving people of considerable social and political standing. But since he recognizes that the Chandlerian resolution is a luxury that black cops in our society can't afford, he has to look elsewhere for a satisfactory means of closure. At first, he seems to have fallen back on the kind of comic Christie-esque resolutions that Chandler and Hammett

had more or less abandoned.[13] Granted, while Christie will occasionally set a criminal free in order to give her plot an extra jolt, it happens more often in Himes, largely because of his more complex sense of the world—either because his heroes decide that it wasn't really a "crime" at all (in The Real Cool Killers, for instance, Grave Digger decides that it's appropriate for the black victim of a white sexual pervert to kill her tormentor), or because it's a necessary part of a deal (in Cotton Comes to Harlem, it's the only way to get the money back), or because someone is too well-placed politically (All Shot Up).

Nonetheless, most of Himes's detective plots resolve themselves in surprisingly genial ways. Dennis Porter has pointed out that the "hard-boiled novel ends with the rejection of a woman and a retreat from intimate personal relations," whereas "the classic detective novel often couples the solution of a crime with an engagement or a wedding."[14] And in this regard, Himes often follows the classic mold.[15] At the end of A Rage in Harlem, the impossibly naive Jackson, who has gotten himself entangled with a brutal gang that manages to knock off several people far more experienced than he is, gets back both his job and his girlfriend; The Real Cool Killers ends even more sentimentally, with the impending marriage between the equally square Sonny and Sissie, who is pregnant with the child of the dead gang-leader Sheik; in Cotton Comes to Harlem, Uncle Bud the junk man ends up with $87,000 with which to buy himself a harem in Africa. And while All Shot Up lacks the element of coupling, it too is upbeat: the stolen money is stolen back by Coffin Ed and Grave Digger and sent as an anonymous contribution to the Boys' Club. Indeed, the last words of that novel are those of the anonymous telegram they sent to political boss and swindler Casper Holmes: "Crime doesn't pay" (170).

You can't, however, just slap a Christie ending on a Chandlerian novel, and the very incongruity of these finales seems a self-conscious questioning of the implications of the genre itself. In a sense, then, these novels make a political point about the asymmetries of white and black experiences through their internal contradictions, which show that the same literary forms are not appropriate to both. And from this perspective, perhaps, some of the violence in the novels—especially the violence of Coffin Ed and Grave Digger themselves—can be seen to undercut the genre, as well. Certainly, that violence (in contrast, say, to the violence in Spillane) is explicitly made problematic in the texts. Beneath the rapid-moving surface of the adventures, there's always something questionable: not only do people both black and white complain about their tactics, but for all their insistence that only the guilty have anything to fear, they often find themselves trouncing the innocent in their pursuit of justice. At the beginning of The Real Cool Killers, a teenage hood throws perfume at Coffin Ed, who, remembering the acid thrown at him in A Rage in Harlem, overreacts; in the

aftermath, not only is the prankster killed, but an innocent bystander is shot as well.

But even if the violence were never explicitly questioned in the text, we could still see that it is generated by the novels' contradictions—not only the social contradictions in the situations of Coffin Ed and Grave Digger, but also the formal contradictions in the genre that emerge when it is asked to attend to black life. For the only way to arrive at a Christie-esque ending in a Chandlerian world is precisely through violence—that is, when it is power rather than deception that protects evil, you can only hope to get to the bottom of things by violent means.[16] In a figurative sense, then, the violence is not only characteristic of the novels, but is also directed against them: the very incongruity of the genre and its subject matter produces a violent disruption. Perhaps that's why, in the last novel in the series, Blind Man with a Pistol, all attempt at a resolution is dropped, and the novel rips itself apart into chaos. A long goodbye to the detective story itself? Perhaps; but if so, it's a tacit recognition that when ideology and art collide, something has to give way. And since the genre stood in the way of Himes's own vision of what it meant to be black, who can say that his farewell was a wrong choice?

ACKNOWLEDGMENTS

Special thanks to Megan Wolf for her invaluable research assistance on this paper, and to Joan Wolek of the Hamilton College Library, who managed to track down a number of out-of-print texts quickly and efficiently.

NOTES

References to the following novels by Chester Himes are noted by page number in the text: All Shot Up (New York: Penguin Books, 1978); Blind Man with a Pistol (New York: William Morrow, 1969); Cotton Comes to Harlem (London: Allison and Busby, n. d.); The Crazy Kill (London: Allison and Busby, n. d.); If He Hollers Let Him Go (rpt., New York: Thunder's Mouth Press, 1986); The Real Cool Killers (London: Allison and Busby, 1985).

1. John A. Williams, "My Man Himes: An Interview with Chester Himes," in <u>Armistad 1</u>, ed. John A. Williams and Charles F. Harris (New York: Vintage Books, 1970), 49.

2. Stephen F. Milliken, <u>Chester Himes: A Critical Appraisal</u> (Columbia: University of Missouri Press, 1976), 217-18.

3. For a fuller discussion of these changes, see my "Rats Behind the Wainscoting: Politics, Convention, and Chandler's <u>The Big Sleep</u>," <u>Texas Studies in Literature and Language</u> 22, no. 2 (Summer 1980): 224-45.

4. Dennis Porter, <u>The Pursuit of Crime: Art and Ideology in Detective Fiction</u> (New Haven: Yale University Press, 1981), 39.

5. Raymond Chandler, <u>The Big Sleep</u> (New York: Pocket Books, 1950), 214.

6. Chandler, <u>The Big Sleep</u>, 211.

7. Chandler, <u>The Big Sleep</u>, 177. My appreciation to Donna Serniak-Catudal for pointing out the resonance of this passage to me.

8. <u>Cotton Comes to Harlem</u>, 34-35. See, in this regard, Angus Calder's claim that Himes differs from his predecessors because "environment . . . takes precedence over all character, including the characters of his detective heroes," in "Chester Himes and the Art of Fiction," <u>Journal of East African Research and Development</u> (Nairobi) 1 (1971): 124.

9. Williams, "My Man Himes," 71.

10.   For a further discussion, see Loyle Hairston, "Chester Himes—'Alien' in Exile," <u>Freedomways</u> 17, no. 1 (1977): 14-18, and John M. Reilly, "Chester Himes' Harlem Tough Guys," <u>Journal of Popular Culture</u> 9, no. 4 (1976): 941. Himes's homophobia is equally problematic.

11.   For an interesting discussion of the violence of these texts, see Edward Margolies, "The Thrillers of Chester Himes," <u>Studies in Black Literature</u> 1, no. 2 (1970): 1-11.

12.   Williams, "My Man Himes," 48.

13.   See Raymond Nelson's claim that the first five novels in the series are "classic detective stories" with a "single discovery of guilt, which restores [the] balance," in "Domestic Harlem: The Fiction of Chester Himes," <u>Virginia Quarterly Review</u> 48, no. 2 (Spring 1972) 265.

14.   Porter, <u>Pursuit of Crime</u>, 186.

15.   For a discussion of this point from a different perspective, see Calder, "Chester Himes and the Art of Fiction," 129-31. For a different view, see James Sallis, "In America's Black Heartland: The Achievement of Chester Himes," <u>Western Humanities Review</u> 37, no. 3 (1983): 195-97.

16.   For a further discussion, see Nelson, "Domestic Harlem," 269-70.

4

The Social-Domestic World of June Thomson's Detective Chief Inspector Jack Finch/Rudd

John McAleer

June Thomson, the recipient in 1983 of France's coveted <u>Prix du Roman d'Aventures</u>, has been identified by British critics as the writer best fitted, along with P. D. James, to carry detective fiction forward into the next century.

From the outset critics have commended Thomson's success in observing accurately the closely knit life of an English village even as she immerses us in a magnificently created pastoral atmosphere. But June Thomson has not written mere pastoral idylls or British cozies. Her sleuth's inquiries amply confirm Sherlock Holmes's oft-quoted dictum: "The lowest and vilest alleys of London do not present a more dreadful record of sin than does its smiling and beautiful countryside." And it is that world that June Thomson documents with a fidelity that will cause readers fifty years hence to go to her works to learn what life was like in English villages in the last decades of the twentieth century. Though sometimes called the Simenon of British detective fiction, Thomson, unlike Georges Simenon, is unfolding before us, in an expanding epic, a detailed, scrutinizing, sociological appraisal of a specific locale and the reasons for its decline. The crimes recounted are not superimposed on that society, but come about as a logical consequence of the blight that has befallen it.

Thomson's detective, Jack Finch (Rudd in the United States, to avoid confusing him with Margaret Erskine's Inspector Septimus Finch), is Detective Chief Inspector in the Chelmsford, Essex, CID (Criminal Investigative Division). "I called him 'Finch' because it's the name of an ordinary bird," June Thomson says. "When my American publishers asked me to rename him, I called him 'Rudd,' the name of an ordinary fish."[1] The Chief Inspector's commonplace names are our first clue to understanding his role. As an outsider, Finch would be kept at arm's length by villagers. Since that would never do, he must appear to be one of them, in every sense.

Most of Finch's cases (as recorded in twelve novels published since 1972),[2] have taken him into retired Essex villages—what his pedestrian, urban-bred assistant, Detective Sergeant Boyce, is wont to call "dead-and-alive holes" (DC, 35). Finch, however, is a product of the ordinary village world. He comes from farming stock. He lives with his sister, Dorothy, a farmer's widow. He looks like a farmer. He has a countryman's face, "his features undistinguished, more like a farmer's in their open-air bluffness" (TMK, 94). His "stocky, un-tidy" figure is unintimidating; he could pass as "a farmer at a livestock sale" (DF, 98). His "faint local accent" (SD, 156), suggesting "limited intelligence" (AT, 87), is also a useful cover. Visiting a village pub, he blends in, having "a ploughman's lunch," bread, cheese, pickle, a pint of bitter (CC, 61). As a member of the county constabulary, Finch, especially since he has a first-class intellect, has much to gain from these humble characteristics. Sergeant Boyce, we are told, "would never understand the country and the countryman's attitude to life" (DC, 35, 36). "Literal-minded" and "unimaginative," Boyce wears patterned ties, checked overcoat, and porkpie hat (SD, 221). These sartorial oddities alienate the villagers whose confidence he must gain.

Finch also has other "less directed impulses" which go back

> to his childhood . . . spent in a village . . . and to that much earlier
> training which had never been expressed in so many words, merely in
> a shake of the head or a folding of the lips but which, nevertheless,
> had made it quite clear that there were certain subjects which ought
> never to be discussed, certainly not with strangers. (DS, 98)

As a result he must put his own conduct under constant review. In The Dark Stream, for example, Finch realizes he has succumbed to his conditioning and has "unconsciously been sharing in the primitive and collective response of the herd-under-threat to group together against danger" (DS, 98). Sometimes, also, he is sweetly naive. In The Habit of Loving he finds it hard to accept the possibility that "a woman in her fifties could be in love with a young man thirty years younger than herself" (HL, 105). In Alibi in Time he finds it difficult to talk with Hilary Shand about her illicit love affair. In Sound Evidence he is so innocent he does not realize that Garston's alibi is his homosexual tryst with Terence Bentley until, not without amusement, the urbane Inspector Nunn points out that fact to him (SE, 139).

Finch's village origins would have no more significance than Chief In-spector Davy's farmer-like aspect ("looking like an old farmer discussing his stock and his land"), in Agatha Christie's At Bertram's Hotel, were it not for June

Thomson's village world.[3]   The world she writes about is not Miss Marple's St. Mary Mead. It is Sherwood Anderson's Winesburg, Edith Wharton's Starkfield. We call the roll of villages—Wynford, Barnsfield, Althorpe, Chellfield, Hawton, Frayling, Ashbourne, Barnston, Abbots Stacey, and Heversham—a whole society attacked by an insidious canker of decay. The names of the villages are legion, but the people who dwell in them are, in their common plight, all but interchangeable. Finch's tragedy is that he is aware of what is happening but powerless to intervene except in individual cases. In A Question of Identity, when Finch thinks of the harsh misfortunes that have befallen Betty Lovell and Nancy Fowler, he feels an "angry pity" (QI, 98). His brooding compassion for his fellowman is so consuming, indeed, it denies him an emotional life of his own. "I never had the time to get married," he says (NOU, 217). Romantically stirred, he cannot articulate his feelings adequately because "he would be sharing with someone else a private emotion" (AT, 146). When he falls in love with Marion Greave, in Sound Evidence (tenth book in the series and the first in which we progress to the intimacy of learning his first name) (SE, 147), his diffidence allows for only one outcome (DF, 154-55). The "gulf of reserve" yawning between the Shands, father and daughter, and between Shand and Kitty Fulton, is something Finch understands (AT, 146).

Even as his personal knowledge of the intricacies of the village mind and mores enables Finch to carry out his inquiries effectively, that very intimacy leaves him without a complete understanding of the origins of the murrain that has engulfed his world. Through the skillful manipulation of June Thomson, however, that larger perception is not withheld from the reader. One crucial fact is quickly evident. The wholesome alliance with Nature on which this society was built, has been sundered. With that loss other values essential to the peace and well-being of a rural population have also been lost. The materialism of the world beyond the village seems the ultimate good. Dazzled by that vision, many experience a craving for excitement that the village cannot provide. Ron Lovell, who darts away on his motor bike to the public houses of the neighboring town of Harlsdon, is "the local tear-away" (QI, 146). For Nancy Fowler, his sometime girlfriend, even Harlsdon is without appeal: "You could rot in this hole and no-body'd notice" (QI, 84-85). When Doreen Walker's adulterous lover tells her she must make do until Christmas with the present he has just given her, her retort is, "You'd be surprised how often Christmas comes round" (NOU, 227). The day after Doreen's murder, Pamela, her thirteen-year-old sister, her smile "already full of sexual significance," takes eager possession of the cheap finery Doreen's fatal alliance had brought her (NOU, 52). For the crippled Bland, sharp and knowing, Doreen's murder is a sporting event (NOU, 33), as it is for Mrs. Meyrick (NOU,

23), and for "the cluster of youths on bicycles, circling slowly round and round . . . all afternoon, like vultures at the scene of the killing" (NOU, 27). At fourteen Terence Bentley runs away from the village of Kinderly to become the lover of a ganglord (SE, 137). Marion Shand, in her thirties, kills herself driving her car at high speed (AT, 32).

Some struggle to accept their lot passively. Stanley Aspinell finds comfort in his elderly dog, which sleeps in a little bed next to his own (SE, 106). Melanie Thorpe's father's sole companion is an old dog (CC, 55). Cairn, a dog, is Francis Elliot's only friend. At his insistence it sleeps with him even in his jail cell (NOU, 204). Finch eventually brings Cairn home to be a companion to his sister, who also is alone much of the time, "cheated of years of loving companionship" by the early death of her husband (CC, 5-6; SD, 36). Out of loyalty to her father's memory, Maggie Hearn, living alone on the farm that had been his pride, has a "desperate need to be wanted and understood." She is, Finch perceives, "a tired, haggard woman, at the end of her tether, emotionally on her knees" (HL, 5). Others grasp for status by feeling superior to those around them. Even as a girl Amy Leacock "fancied herself a cut above everybody else because her father had a shop and she'd had piano lessons" (DC, 168). She belongs, Finch sees, to that class of women who are "always blaming their husbands for their dull and unrewarding lives" (DC, 67). Dr. Cotty, like Dostoyevski's Raskolnikov, looks on his fellow villagers as "lesser people" (AT, 197). Madge Bingham is sustained by her "sense of her own esteem" and "social superiority" (DS, 184). This method of dealing with the tedium of village life is evidently the least desirable of all. The three who adopt it all commit murder.

Though Finch is superior in intelligence to most of the people he deals with, he has only to recall his own village boyhood and his mother asking, when he looked up from his books, "Tired, Son?" to realize that "the books studied so diligently were his means of escape . . . . He had wanted to escape . . . . The life of the village was too cramped and confined" (NOU, 53-55). He feels only pity for those who want to break free from the village but do not know how. When he is challenged by a sharp village mind, even a devious one—by Stan Spurgeon, whose "stupid, country oaf" manner is only a defensive posture that can be doffed at will (DC, 52); by canny, old Mrs. Turnbull, who likes a chat (DC, 154); by quick-witted Geoff Lovell, whose "jeering manner" is merely defensive (QI, 110, 176); or even by the sly Wheeler, "not very eager to give away much" (QI, 144)—he rejoices. And he is quick to see merit wherever it is found: in Nancy Fowler's "courage and gallantry and . . . tough instinct for survival" (QI, 128); in Betty Lovell's "steely center"—Betty "would bend but she

would not break" (QI, 149); and in the buoyant assurance with which Stella Reeve faced life (DS, 164).

Others go through the motions of keeping up the rituals and forms that satisfied their forebears but draw no strength from them and, with no true comprehension of their plight, feel discontented and unfulfilled. In Alibi in Time, Patrick Vaughan, a London novelist who has settled in Chellfield, soon protests, "I don't know how I stand it some days. It's all so bucolic and bloody boring!" (AT, 33). In saying this Vaughan is saying what the villagers themselves think but are too inhibited to admit, even to themselves.

In Death Cap Finch perceives: "The old patterns were dissolving. . . .The county communities were breaking up. Young people especially moving on, seeking new jobs and new homes in towns and cities. Yet a nucleus still remained" (DC, 79). That nucleus consists of such people as old Mrs. Spurgeon, clothes dirty, body unwashed, and her son Stan, deserted by his wife and left with a retarded son to raise, harvesting mediocre crops, and forced, at last, to take a job outside the farm to pay his debts, even as his farmhouse decays into ruin. Stan's forced estrangement from Nature is written large when the spiteful Amy Leacock sows poisonous mushrooms in his mushroom field and he fails to recognize them. Visiting the home of the murder victim in Not One of Us, Finch "felt suffocated by the atmosphere of poverty, fecklessness, and greed that surrounded him" (NOU, 52). In The Habit of Loving, Vi Aston, worn and unkempt, toils at her husband's market garden while he slips away for an interlude of dalliance with one of his nubile currant pickers (HL, 28). In A Question of Identity, the Lovell brothers, Geoff and Charlie (the latter retarded), live in isolation on their farm, concealing both a criminal and a corpse. Sometimes the people themselves, as befits people guided by a "herd instinct," have taken on the appearance of their own livestock. Doreen Walker's father has a "brutish, unintelligent face" (NOU, 46). Mrs. Holbrook, whose husband is a constable oriented toward the land, is a "big placid," ruminating woman (DC, 7). Mr. Parsons favors Finch with a glance of "bovine casualness, like a cow looking over a gate" (NOU, 213). Acting to get a response from Reg Bartlett, a crippled, sullen gardener, whose life is "dull and routine," is "like prodding some great farm animal" (DS, 114, 116).

In Sound Evidence, the corner grocery, a village nerve center, is "now run by an Asian family" (SE, 10), a fact recollective of Edith Wharton's blighted Starkfield in Ethan Frome, where the village store has passed into the hands of an Irishman. An old neighborhood falls before the bulldozer to make room for a neon-lit filling station, multi-story car park, or "soul-less" shopping precinct (AT, 104). Alcoholic dropouts live in isolated houseboats (CC, 55-56). A shopkeeper

greets the public with a mournful, undertaker's face (DC, 65, 66, 70, 72). Next to the vibrant Nina Gifford, who had lived much of her life in London, her village suitor, Lionel Burnett, appears "very squeezed-in and deficient" (TMK, 97). Nina's mother, a farmer's daughter, had run away to London to be an artist's mistress. In time Nina also participated in this revolt from the village. Now again living in a village, Nina finds life closing in on her. Mrs. Walker has the look of someone "under constant physical fear" (NOU, 46). Betty Lovell's face is "drawn to the bone" (QI, 97). Nancy Fowler, in her dreary council home, lawn abandoned to knee-high weeds, telly blasting from the windows to the annoyance of neighbors, abandoned by her spouse, lives with her thirteen- and fourteen-year-old chain-smoking sons, amid "a rich patina of squalor," from which she escapes, at every opportunity, to the neighborhood pub (QI, 93). Nor can one forget the Parsons family, "sitting on a large settee, eating plums and custard with automatic gestures, their eyes never moving from the [television] screen" (NOU, 213).

With calculation June Thomson has created a village world with few of the recreations usual in times past, or even in the present day, in the towns. The cinemas have shut down. Local dances, sporting events, parades, and festivals seem inconsequential. There are no strolling players or conjurers, no local newspapers. Politics do not get talked about. Football pools go unnoticed. No one is observed playing darts at the local pub. Drugs are unheard of. Once or twice someone visits a neighboring town to go to a disco or play bingo. Otherwise, there is television. That is all. June Thomson, of course, exaggerates the sterility of this world to emphasize the crisis that has overtaken it. Since in this environment many families are childless, many marriages broken by death, desertion, or divorce, and many bachelors and spinsters live alone (the last survivors of once thriving families), loneliness, as an affliction, is all but universal. For some, promiscuity is the answer. Hilary Shand becomes Patrick Vaughan's lover. "Dry-as-an-old-stick" Dr. Cotty takes a mistress (AT, 194-95). Rex Holt brings his mistress from London to live in the village (DF, 11-12). Ron Lambert begets a child by his own daughter (HL, 167).

Others turn for solace either to drink or to the church and good works. The village of Wynford is typical. The Goat, the local pub, where the murder victim had just taken a job as barmaid, is at one end of Main Street, the church at the other. The principal elements of the village sprawl between. Few concerns of the village go unnoticed at the Goat, the Anchor, the Crown, the Dolphin, the Feathers, the Rose and Crown, the Bunch of Grapes. And there many find the assurance needed to get them through another day. The church does less well. Nina Gifford's father was a vicar and his severe, unforgiving sister his co-adju-

tor. The "small, and bright and perfect" village of Heversham fostered frustrations that drove Nina into the arms of her mother's lover, and her brother Danny into the arms of the sheriff (TMK, 26, 27). Claire Jordan, murdered in Shadow of a Doubt, was the daughter of a country rector, a man who "had a high opinion of his own rightness" (SD, 85). From his certitude her inconsequence inevitably followed. In The Dark Stream, Madge Bingham, a doctor's wife who saw herself as "lady of the manor," is, at forty-eight, a school governor, organizer of the Old Folks' Wednesday socials, a Parish Councillor, chairman of the Ladies' Church Guild, and a volunteer at the Oxfam shop (DS, 6). All her parochial activities avail her nothing. She feels superfluous. With her children at the University, "a restiveness and dissatisfaction" take hold of her (DS, 109). Otherwise, the church in a June Thomson village exists only as a physical point of reference, a tower visible above the trees (DF, 8). Traditional morality is only vaguely understood by the villagers and is invoked more out of vindictiveness than out of any desire to better the lot of humanity. Even as Nancy Fowler schemes to seduce another woman's husband, she virtuously complains, "Bits of kids, sleeping around. Having babies. It's all wrong" (QI, 96). Yet she is not a hypocrite. She is simply confused. Madge Bingham can commit murder, cast suspicion on someone else, and then, with perfect sincerity, long for past times when "people were more content," and "there was none of this desperation to acquire material things" (DS, 116). Even Finch finds country morals awry. When he says, "Country morals are still quite a bit different from the city's," he does not mean that they are closer to orthodoxy (QI, 55). The observation is occasioned by his reflection that the villagers, if they knew that Geoff Lovell slept with his brother's wife, would look upon it as incest. There is a still harder side to village morality. In Death Cap, because Amy Leacock had introduced an element of chance into her murder of Mrs. King, Finch is unable to bring her to justice. That does not faze him. Understanding the mentality of country people, he knew that "there was a justice that the village would mete out" (DC, 187). Traditional morality, if it survives at all, survives in people like Biddy Moxon in A Dying Fall, Rex Holt's retired housekeeper who counsels Martin Holt and reinforces his reasonableness (DF, 10-14). The one tradition that survives in this new village world comes under the heading not of morality but of hospitality. Rare is the villager so vexed or impoverished that he fails to offer Finch tea when he comes to call. Or so it seems. Certainly, in the course of the saga Finch must consume gallons of tea. It is the unfailing courtesy of the village household.

One sin Thomson's villagers never seem to recognize for what it is: the act of slander, which here we broaden in definition to include malicious gossip. In gossip the village finds the recreation it can find nowhere else. For Finch it is a

sober truth that "Women gossiped more easily than men" (DC, 60). That
statement should occasion no astonishment. They left to the men the forum of the
pub. Their outlet was gossip. Finch, while recognizing that some gossipers require careful handling, recognizes gossip as a valuable resource. Bland, the crippled storekeeper in Not One of Us, has a sharp mind and relishes feeding it with
unsavory speculations. Although Finch personally deplores Bland's nastiness, he
understands when Mrs. Bland tells him, out of her husband's hearing, "You
mustn't mind Harold too much, Inspector. He finds life a bit dull, just sitting all
day long. He doesn't mean any harm, really." Finch recognizes what is behind
Bland's viciousness but feels no sympathy for him. Even so, he makes "a mental
note to talk to the man again. He could be a useful source of information, if the
facts were sifted from the malicious gossip" (NOU, 38). In A Question of Identity, Finch goes to Len Wheeler for essential information, though conscious of the
note of malice that runs through Wheeler's confidences (QI, 28-29). In The Habit
of Loving he turns to his own profit the "sharp nose for gossip" possessed by
Mrs. Deakin, who denigrates, without mercy, the murdered girl whose body her
husband found that morning (referring to her in the present tense to circumvent
the impropriety of speaking ill of the dead) (HL, 62). Dr. Cotty avows his
"contempt for village gossip" (AT, 151). That is unusual but not surprising. As
a murderer himself he can hardly expect to gain by the inquisitiveness of his
neighbors. In The Dark Stream the unexpected return of Stella Franklin Reeve
proves a glorious moment for gossipers. There is no need for Madge Bingham to
disclose her curiosity openly. Soon enough, she knows, the reason for Stella's
return will "no doubt be common knowledge" (DS, 12). When Stella quarrels
with her estranged husband, Mrs. Armitage is passing the house. "It'll be all over
the village by tomorrow," sighs Stella's mother (DS, 36).

   In The Habit of Loving Finch is glad to learn that Constable Cookson can
count on his wife's mother to pass along necessary tidbits of gossip (HL, 47).
And he is grateful to intelligent, amiable gossips like Mrs. Leach, from whom he
learns essential facts (NOU, 58-60). When Finch outlines to Amy Leacock the
circumstances leading up to the murder of Mrs. King, he knows full well her
vulnerability when he tells her, "There was talk. There's always talk" (HL, 182).
Nonetheless, Finch is careful not to generate harmful gossip himself. When he
visits the Macey farm (where gossip has already preceded him though the farm is
a mile from the village), he takes pains not to stir Macey's animosity against the
tenant living in his caravan: "Having been brought up himself in a village, he
knew the capacity of local people to gossip about outsiders who were not part of
the established community . . ." (DS, 68).

Gossip would be of no use to Finch if he did not know how to draw people out. This is something he does superbly well. In <u>The Long Revenge</u> Bravington, a member of the Secret Service, tells him, "You have a good knowledge of human nature." "It's my job," Finch replies. "Like a carpenter gets to understand wood, I get to know people. It's my stock-in-trade, you might say" (<u>LR</u>, 85). Finch can "sum up a man's character by voice alone and adapt his approach accordingly" (<u>DC</u>, 43). By raising his eyes interrogatively he can get some people to speak (<u>DC</u>, 75). He adapts himself to his audience. With Dr. Cotty he resorts to "deliberate casualness to play down the official nature of the visit" (<u>AT</u>, 149). With his "quiet authority" and an "imperturbability which nothing seemed to shake," he impresses the cynical Alec Lawson (<u>DS</u>, 129). He has an "avuncular expression" he uses when appropriate (<u>LR</u>, 123). In a variation of this, to elicit information from Nancy Fowler he adopts the "sympathetic listening air of an older relative, preparing to give good advice" (<u>QI</u>, 90). Also in <u>A Question of Identity</u>, when he talked with the opportunistic Stebbing, we are told, "His face had relaxed into the friendly listening expression that his colleagues would have recognized as part of his interviewing technique. It fooled Stebbing as it had fooled many others" (<u>QI</u>, 13). In <u>The Dark Stream</u> we are advised that Finch, with simple villagers, was able to "settle down for a quiet chat, knee to knee," but not with the top-lofty Madge Bingham. Talking to Madge, he must use his "official, formal voice" (<u>DS</u>, 87). On a comparable occasion, however, he gets results that surprise him. He does not expect "his listening pose" to garner gossip from someone as sophisticated as Kitty Fulton, widow of a prominent MP; yet their conversation is well under way before Kitty realizes that the impression Finch gave, that he was "not very intelligent or particularly perceptive," was a pose (<u>AT</u>, 81, 87). As an audience to Finch's interview of the criminal Eddy Lisle, Detective Chief Inspector Monk of Scotland Yard is amazed: "He had seen various interviewing techniques but never this subtle, almost cruel yet friendly-seeming approach" (<u>CC</u>, 177). The perceptive Francis Elliot, talking with Finch after Finch has cleared him of the murder of Doreen Walker, recognizes that same complex makeup: "There sat the Inspector, with his kind, open countryman's face and his shrewd, sharp eyes; a strange mixture of a man, cunning, honest, cruel, and yet sensitive" (<u>NOU</u>, 181-82).

Nowhere is Finch's understanding of the subtleties of the village mind more germane to his purpose than in his handling of those situations in which villagers close ranks against an outsider who has come among them. In <u>The Long Revenge</u>, when Alec Mercer settles in the village of Barnston, the farmers at the Plough shoulder him out of their conversation. Finch, on hand, understands the situation: "Mercer was still very much the outsider." He wonders if Mercer real-

izes this (LR, 50). Mercer does not and Finch tells him: "It may take years. . . .Country people don't make friends all that easily" (LR, 58). At Wynford, for all his rapport with the village mind, Finch is himself made to feel an intruder by Madge Bingham: "Seated in her drawing-room he had felt very much the outsider, not one of the community" (DS, 88).

The title of the opening volume of the series, Not One of Us, emphasizes the importance of this theme. Francis Elliot has come to Freyling from London. He has settled at the outskirts of the village and kept to himself—a ready-made object of derision. Colin Edge, a local van driver, speaks for the majority when he brands him a "Commie, crank, snob, hippie, lay-about, Londoner." He equates Elliot's "beard, long hair, educated voice, and aloof behavior . . . with every quality of class, politics, and beliefs which he did not understand" (NOU, 90). To Mrs. Meyrick it is enough that Francis looks like an artist (NOU, 31). Under pressure to produce a murderer the villagers find in Elliot a made-to-order scapegoat. Yet, ironically, they repudiate even the victim herself since she, too, has been an outsider. Mrs. Bland tells Finch: "I've heard nothing . . . and I don't expect I shall. I mean, she wasn't from this village and people tend not to mix" (NOU, 147).

In Alibi in Time the outsider is another Londoner, Patrick Vaughan, a writer who wears jeans, a beard, and two-inch boot heels, by his very appearance inviting alienation. Neave, the local constable, "mentally categorized him as the arty type and consequently a bit odd" (AT, 42). Vaughan, too, lives at the outskirts of the community. Indeed, June Thomson usually endorses twofold the isolation of the outsider by placing him physically as well as socially outside the community. This is true of Mercer in The Long Revenge, Thorpe in Case Closed, Stebbing in A Question of Identity, the Lamberts in The Habit of Loving, Lawson in The Dark Stream, Max and Nina Gifford in To Make a Killing, and even of the nonconforming villagers Mrs. Spurgeon in Death Cap and Maggie Hearn in The Habit of Loving. Though she has lived all her life in the same village, Maggie herself realizes that she, owing to her difference in outlook, has "never properly belonged" (HL, 77).

Some outsiders appear to gain acceptance—Mrs. King, for example, in Death Cap. Yet she does not reckon with the "intricate web of blood relationships" that link several generations of the same families, going back three hundred years. Among such people she remains an interloper (DC, 79). The callow Stebbing, in A Question of Identity, courts acceptance with no appreciable results: "I go regularly to church. . . . Never miss a Sunday if I can help it. After all, when you come to live in a small community, like a village, it's as well to join in, make yourself known. Not that I believe it all, mind" (QI, 107). Patrick

Vaughan, of course, also courts acceptance and when he fails to get it schemes to get "his own back on all of them" (<u>AT</u>, 195). For his presumption, he pays with his life.

While villagers gossip freely about one another among themselves, Finch knows that they will "like a family . . . close ranks at the first signs of danger" (<u>DS</u>, 97). In both <u>Death Cap</u> and <u>Alibi in Time</u> the local constable is prepared to resign sooner than bring evidence against some respected villager (<u>DC</u>, 16; <u>AT</u>, 55, 70, 119). When Sergeant Neave tells Finch of Hilary Shand's liaison with Vaughan, he is embarrassed. That fact troubles Finch. A policeman cannot meet his responsibilities if he lets his private feelings stand in the way of his commitments to duty. Yet the time will come when Finch realizes "that part of himself, still loyal to the old pattern of village allegiance, wanted to respond" to "that closing of the ranks and the shutting out of strangers" (<u>DS</u>, 97-98). Once he acknowledges this fact, however, he is able not only to deal with it in himself but to cope with it as a factor conditioning the behavior of others.

In <u>The Dark Stream</u> the villagers are unwilling to admit that a murder has been committed. Finch reasons:

> "They were closing ranks against the idea of murder, shutting it out, because if they admitted to themselves that murder was a possibility, then they had to admit to something else—that someone from the village could be the killer. The reaction was probably instinctive . . . . It was a collective response to danger. Better for it to be an accident than to face the alternative" (<u>DS</u>, 97-98).

This defensive attitude takes on sinister dimensions, however, when the villagers, to save their own, determine that the outsider in their midst is the sought-for murderer. In <u>The Habit of Loving</u>, Bateson, the farmer, says it is natural for people to believe that an outsider killed Jess Lambert (<u>HL</u>, 77). So certain are the villagers that Francis Elliot killed Doreen Walker, they put his hut to the torch (<u>NOU</u>, 195). In <u>The Dark Stream</u>, the newcomer, Alec Lawson, becomes the inevitable suspect, with the victim's husband, Ken Reeve, also an outsider, a close runner-up (<u>DS</u>, 80, 97, 119). In <u>A Dying Fall</u>, Bea Chilton, Rex Holt's mistress, a new arrival in the village, seems a likely candidate (<u>DF</u>, 112-14). Lacking an outsider as their candidate for murderer, villagers will deny reality. In <u>Death Cap</u>, their embarrassment is heightened by their awareness that the manner of the crime bespeaks of "local knowledge," not a likely method to have been used, for example, by Mrs. King's nephew and heir, an aloof Londoner (<u>DC</u>, 87).

In the Finch saga the extent to which a character relates to the land serves as an index of his capacity for attaining peace of mind in a rapidly changing world. Stan Spurgeon is embattled but tries every stratagem to hold onto his farm (DC, 144). Martin Holt loves his smallholding and it is his love for what he has that exonerates him—his neatly folded fertilizer sacks, his neatly stacked lumber, his late-night labors packing tomatoes (DF, 161). The elderly Turnbulls maintain themselves in contentment symbolized by their well-kept garden, tended by Constable Holbrook and his friend, who know how essential a thriving garden is to old Turnbull (DC, 164).

The land seems to rebel against outsiders who intrude on the village world—repudiating them. Village youths come and destroy Francis Elliot's kitchen garden. Stebbing finds a body buried in his lower pasture (QI, 7). Chris Lawrence works as a currant picker and is accused of murdering Jess Lambert in the currant field (HL, 52). That the world of Nature, resisting encroachments, will not be reconciled to outsiders is symbolized by the settings in which violence befalls them. In Not One of Us, the shopgirl's body is found in woodland bordering a plowed field (NOU, 13). In Death Cap, death is carried to the shopkeeper, Mrs. King, from Spurgeon's mushroom field (DC, 173). In Case Closed the body of the hairdresser's apprentice is left behind a hedge in a roadside field (CC, 41). In The Habit of Loving, Jess Lambert's body is placed in a currant field (HL, 41). In A Question of Identity, Maguire's body is buried in a pasture (QI, 7). In Alibi in Time, Vaughan's body is left by a grassy verge on a country road in downpouring rain (AT, 40-41). In The Dark Stream Stella Reeve is left to drown in a brook that breaches a dark country lane (DS, 56). Rex Holt, descended from a farm laborer, but now, in his affluence, leasing his farmland to tenants and maintaining himself, aloof from others, at the outskirts of the village, meets violent death in a rose garden (DF, 63-64). And surely it is significant that all these deeds are carried out under cover of darkness.

June Thomson does not suggest that the urban world, with its new solutions, holds the answers to the problems the village is facing. Quite otherwise. Inspector Nunn perhaps is closest to the truth when he tells Finch: "Our generation has a lot to answer for" (SE, 140). No one, he says, has told boys like Terence Bentley "the difference between what's real and what isn't," so they come to the city "looking for a dream" (SE, 140), and instead are submerged in corruption (DF, 111). An unattractive world is replacing the old way of life. People live in sterile, toy villages, like the Cavendish estate (AT, 4), draw disability pensions, drink and fornicate to idle away their time, or retreat to the fringes of society to pine away in loneliness and bewilderment. There are safety nets to meet their basic physical needs but none to meet their basic emotional, intellectual, and spiritual

needs. The people who infiltrate their world are either in flight from broken marriages, failed careers, or sexual entanglements, or caught up in criminal activities. Rare indeed is the individual like Kitty Fulton whose "attitude to life" was "that it was to be taken joyfully with both hands, not treated with niggardly caution" (AT, 4). Her wealth does not account for her optimism. Kitty, we are told, "would have been the same even on a farm laborer's wages" (AT, 97). Surely the ending of <u>Sound Evidence</u>, the only Finch novel to take place chiefly in an urban environment, is symbolic. To escape death, Benny Costello flees the London underworld to seek a haven in the rural world. In a last, desperate flight, he makes a frantic effort to reach a <u>village</u>, and <u>safety</u>! (SE, 176). No less significant is Martin Holt's decision to spurn his father's elegant manor, a Queen Anne house built for some fox-hunting member of the now-vanished gentry (DF, 9) to live, close to the land, in an old mill (DF, 191). Martin's mother, daughter of an impoverished farmer, had spurned her husband's material plenty to cling to a poetic vision of reality glimpsed in girlhood when a young poet became fleetingly infatuated with her (DF, 186-87). That memory is besmirched for Martin when he discovers that others have manipulated it to contrive his father's murder and learns further that his mother had taken haven in a dream world of unreality. He does not intend to repeat his parents' mistakes and, with Hester Chilton, loyal and sensible, at his side, seems likely to succeed where they had failed (DF, 191-92).

How much of all this does Finch understand? Enough, at least, to know that the human condition is to be pitied, that in the world which modern man has fashioned for himself, love and idealism are lacking and are needed. And that is sensed also by June Thomson's most upright characters—Francis Elliot, Chris Lawrence, Betty Lovell, Nancy Fowler, Maggie Hearn, Nina Gifford, Martin Holt, and Kitty Fulton. They are <u>survivors</u>. No matter how much they are hurt by life, they are determined to go on. And we are left with the conviction that ultimately, somehow, some way, their trust will be upheld and they will prevail.

NOTES

1. June Thomson to John McAleer, at Chawton, Hants., 2 March 1985.

2. Citations and summaries from the Thomson works considered in this paper are noted by title abbreviations and the relevant page or pages, here described in alphabetical order:

AT	Alibi in Time (New York, 1980)
CC	Case Closed (New York, 1977)
DC	Death Cap (New York, 1973)
DF	A Dying Fall (London, 1985)
DS	The Dark Stream (London, 1986)
HL	The Habit of Loving (New York, 1978)
LR	The Long Revenge (New York, 1975)
NOU	Not One of Us (London, 1972)
QI	A Question of Identity (New York, 1977)
SD	Shadow of a Doubt (London, 1981)
SE	Sound Evidence (London, 1984)
TMK	To Make a Killing (London, 1982); U. S. title: Portrait of Lilith (New York, 1982)

3. Agatha Christie, At Bertram's Hotel (New York, 1965), 257.

II

Women and Crime Writing

5

Seeley Regester:
America's First Detective Novelist
B. J. Rahn

DEAR SIR:

It's too bad to disappoint you. Could not execute your order, as everybody concerned will discover. What a charming day!—good for taking a picture. That old friend I introduced you to won't tell tales, and you had not better bother yourself to visit him. The next time you find yourself in his arms, don't feel in his left-hand pocket for the broken tooth-pick which I lent him. He is welcome to it. If you're at the place of payment, I shan't be there, not having fulfilled the order, and having given up my emigration project, much against my will; so, govern yourself accordingly. Sorry your prospects are so poor, and believe me, with the greatest possible esteem,

"Your disappointed Negotiator."

—The Dead Letter

THE DEAD LETTER

Cast of Characters

Mr. Argyll	Father of Eleanor and Mary; lawyer in Blankville
Eleanor Argyll	Elder daughter of Mr. Argyll; fiancée of victim
Mary Argyll	Younger daughter of Mr. Argyll; in love with Richard Redfield; later engaged to James Argyll
James Argyll	Nephew of Mr. Argyll; secretly in love with Eleanor; member of Mr. Argyll's law firm; later engaged to Mary
Richard Redfield	Son of old friend of Mr. Argyll; secretly in love with Eleanor; member of Mr. Argyll's law firm
Henry Moreland	Son of a New York banker; fiancé of Eleanor; the murder victim
Leesy Sullivan	Poor sewing girl hopelessly but idealistically in love with Henry Moreland
George Thorley	Pharmacist who married and deserted Leesy's cousin and was forced to leave Blankville for malpractice
Mr. Burton	Private consultant to the police on especially difficult cases
Lenore Burton	Mr. Burton's clairvoyant daughter

It has generally been recognized that an American woman wrote the first full-length detective novel. In fact, most standard reference works on crime fiction cite Anna Katharine Green's The Leavenworth Case (1878) as the first detective novel in English, or alternatively, as the first detective novel written by a woman. The first indication I found that such might not be the case was a brief mention en passant in Jessica Mann's Deadlier Than the Male (1981) that a novel called The Dead Letter had been penned nine years earlier than The Leavenworth Case in 1867 by Seeley Regester, pseudonym of Mrs. Metta Victoria Fuller Victor, also an American. In pursuing this tantalizing hint, I subsequently discovered an entry in Steinbrunner and Penzler's Encyclopedia of Mystery and Detection (1976) identifying Ms. Regester as the first American woman detective novelist and describing The Dead Letter as "one of the most important detective novels published in the United States."[1]

The obvious next step was to locate a copy of The Dead Letter to see whether or not it lived up to this description. Imagine my delight when I telephoned Mysterious Books in New York and was told by the proprietor, Otto Penzler, that he had a copy of a recent facsimile edition published by Gregg Press.[2] I remember it was a wet Saturday afternoon in 1984—the perfect sort of day to curl up with a good mystery story. And once I began reading The Dead Letter, "I couldn't put it down." It seemed quite obvious to me that Ms. Regester had preceded Ms. Green in assembling and fusing the essential features of the detective story in her early novel. This essay will examine to what extent The Dead Letter fulfills the formula of the detective novel, in order to establish its claim to be considered the first full-length novel in the genre.

Features of the Genre

It would seem sensible at this point to identify the conventions of the genre in order to provide a context in which to evaluate the contributions of Seeley Regester. Most of the conventions governing the classical detective novel can be traced back to three short stories published by Edgar Allan Poe in America in the mid-nineteenth century: "The Murders in the Rue Morgue" (1841), "The Mystery of Marie Roget" (1842), and "The Purloined Letter" (1845).

During the one hundred and fifty years of the genre's history, emphasis has shifted from one convention to another, but the basic formula has remained unchanged: **(1)** A murder occurs within a closed environment—sometimes a locked room. **(2)** The police are called in to investigate the crime but remain baffled even after examining the circumstantial evidence and interviewing witnesses and suspects. They sometimes arrest an innocent person. **(3)** A gifted but eccentric amateur detective with encyclopedic knowledge, intuitive insight, and great capacity for deductive reasoning is consulted. **(4)** He then visits the scene of the crime, examines the physical evidence, conducts research, interviews the

crime, examines the physical evidence, conducts research, interviews the witnesses and suspects, and forms a hypothesis using logical deduction to explain how the crime was committed—including means, motive, and opportunity. **(5)** He tests his hypothesis by reconstructing the crime and confronting the villain— often the least likely suspect—in a dramatic climax. **(6)** The ending usually preserves the comic worldview, because the culprit is apprehended and the moral and civil order restored. **(7)** The denouement includes a full explanation of any unanswered questions or obscure points of the mystery. **(8)** Of course, the balance of the tale is devoted to discovering who-done-it. **(9)** The sleuth is sometimes assisted by a trusted but less able friend who, in addition to performing minor tasks, may keep a written record of the case and later publish it.

Poe's short stories were well received in England as well as in America. Charles Dickens, who was fascinated by Poe's work, included a detective subplot in Bleak House (1852-53) and would have presented the world with a full-length detective novel if he had lived to complete The Mystery of Edwin Drood (1870). Dickens's friend and collaborator, Wilkie Collins, experimented with the murder mystery in The Woman in White (1860) and with the detective novel in The Moonstone (1868), but the latter work cannot be considered a proper detective novel because the sleuth does not solve the initial crime. Instead, the solution is put forth by a minor character introduced for the purpose at the end of the novel. Moreover, the principal crime in the novel is theft rather than murder—although murder does take place.

The Dead Letter, while revealing suggestive similarities to the work of Poe and Dickens, is original enough to dispel the charge—should anyone put it forth—that Seeley Regester merely imitated the work of widely admired male predecessors in creating the first detective novel. Although The Dead Letter is not a novel of great literary merit, it is a workmanlike job as good as—or better than—many novels published in the period. The plot is well constructed; the characters are plausible and well drawn, though stereotypic; the setting is well contrived and rendered; and the themes are valid though morally commonplace. The worldview is typical of that of an educated middle-class American woman of the era. Let us consider how Seeley Regester has employed the conventions of detective fiction—such as they were—in The Dead Letter.

Plot Summary

It is difficult to discuss a book with which readers are unfamiliar, so I include a brief plot summary herewith:

One Saturday night in October 1857, Henry Moreland, the handsome young son of a New York banker, is stabbed in the back as he walks through a heavy rainstorm from the train station in Blankville to the home of his fiancée, Eleanor Argyll. When the inquest is held on the next day, examination of the body reveals

that the point of the weapon has broken off in the wound. Because Henry was not robbed, no motive for the crime appears. Inquiries among the townspeople and railway personnel produce information regarding two suspects: (1) a mysterious dark stranger who had traveled from the city in the same car as Henry and got off at the same station, and (2) a young seamstress, later identified as Leesy Sullivan. At this time, Eleanor's father, Mr. Argyll, discovers that $2,000 has been taken from his desk at home. No connection is made between the two crimes although there is some speculation on the subject.

On the advice of the victim's father, help is sought from Mr. Burton, a private detective consulted by the police on especially difficult cases. Mr. Burton is assisted by James Argyll and Richard Redfield, intimates of the Argyll family who are both secretly in love with Eleanor Argyll. No progress is made in tracing the mysterious stranger, and when Mr. Burton becomes convinced of Leesy Sullivan's innocence, the investigation falters. At that time, Mr. Argyll offers James a partnership in his law firm and dismisses Richard, who feels that Mr. Argyll suspects him of robbery and perhaps murder as a result of covert slander by James.

Richard gets a job in the Dead Letter Office in Washington, D.C., where he works for two years until he finds a dead letter which he believes to have bearing on the murder. He shows it to Mr. Burton, who deciphers its meaning. The letter leads to the recovery of the monogrammed murder weapon, which enables them to identify the murderer. At the same time Richard identifies the killer as the man who cashed the missing bank notes, so a link is established between the robbery and the murder. When Mr. Burton traces the murderer and confronts him with the evidence, he reveals that he was hired to kill Henry and names his employer. In a dramatic climax in front of the entire Argyll family, Mr. Burton accuses the primary villain, who then confesses. The denouement records the banishment of the culprit and the reconciliation between Richard and the Argyll family.

From this summary, it should be apparent that The Dead Letter does manifest many features of the classical detective story. Let us examine them carefully to discover how close the correspondences are.

Conformity to the Whodunit Formula

Condition #1: A murder occurs within a closed environment—sometimes a locked room.

The convention of the closed community is usually invoked to confine within reasonable limits the physical area to be investigated and the number of suspects to be interviewed. By limiting the scene of the crime and the individuals

affected by it to the environs of Blankville, Seeley Regester takes advantage of this convention; however, she enhances the use of the convention somewhat.

Blankville is very much a closed community, but the murder investigation extends beyond its limits because there is some evidence that the killer traveled with the victim by train from the city. The police assume that the killer returned to the city after the murder, and although they do try to find leads in New York, their investigation breaks down because they cannot trace the murderer from Blankville. Despite this assumption, Mr. Burton is never faced with the need to interview the entire population of metropolitan New York or scour its terrain for clues. The chief suspects—Leesy Sullivan and George Thorley—are local people.

Nonetheless, their efforts to trace the assassin lead Mr. Burton and Richard Redfield to Mexico and to California. But when they travel west pursuing clues, they have already identified their quarry; they have a specific destination; and they are carefully encapsulated within the closed society on board the ship. Although the author seems to violate the convention of the closed community, she never really enlarges the size of the canvas. She always works with a small number of characters within a limited locale. Actually, the Argyll household forms the principal narrative focus of the novel, while Mr. Burton's home in the city presents a second center of interest, and the action shifts back and forth between them.

Condition #2: The police are called in to investigate the crime but remain baffled even after examining the circumstantial evidence and interviewing witnesses and suspects. They sometimes arrest an innocent person.

Once murder has been established in The Dead Letter, the police assist in interviewing local villagers and railway personnel, in attempting to locate Leesy Sullivan, and in trying to trace the missing bank notes. They uncover some useful information but are unable to proceed beyond a certain point. Their only suspects are Leesy Sullivan and the dark, mysterious stranger who have both disappeared. They are baffled, and do not have enough information even to arrest a wrong person.

The Detective

Condition #3: A gifted but eccentric amateur detective with extensive knowledge, imaginative insight, and great capacity for deductive reasoning is called in.

When the initial police investigation proves fruitless, the victim's father, Mr. Moreland, requests the services of a talented secret police detective, Mr. Burton,

who, like Poe's Auguste Dupin, is consulted by the police in especially difficult cases. Mr. Burton, assisted by Richard Redfield, takes over the investigation and follows it to a successful conclusion.

Mr. Burton would not be considered eccentric in the sense that the term is applied to Dupin. Mr. Burton leads a normal family life and takes great delight in his children, especially his daughter Lenore (100, 256–57). A gentleman of private means, he is physically attractive and well groomed (57). He is companionable and charming—a good mixer with people in all walks of life from the penny grocer in Leesy Sullivan's tenement (106) to the proud, wealthy Mexican landowner, Don Miguel (263–64). Nevertheless, he has a strong personality. His voice, described as "searching though not loud" and "gentle yet penetrating," could assume a tone of stern command by which he subjugated people to his will—an invincible will with which he "magnetized" people (189).

Presumably Dupin's amateur status is based on the fact that he is consulted by the police only occasionally, because he does accept remuneration for his services. Although Mr. Burton works with the police on a regular basis, he refuses to accept financial payment and must also be considered a non-professional. Mr. Burton is motivated by a strong sense of public duty and a longing for justice rather than a desire for personal gain or fame.

Unlike Dupin, Mr. Burton is not a scholar and has no pretensions to learning. But he does have great intuitive insight and special talents, which, like his extraordinary gift for deductive reasoning, will be discussed in relation to his investigative methods.

Method

Condition #4: He then visits the scene of the crime, examines the physical evidence, conducts research, interviews the witnesses and suspects, and forms a hypothesis to explain how the crime was committed—including means, motive, and opportunity.

Mr. Burton may not resemble M. Dupin in physical appearance or life-style, but his detective method—logical inference based on acute observation—bears a marked similarity to that of Poe's hero. Moreover, when engaged in deductive analysis, Mr. Burton goes into a state of abstraction reminiscent of Dupin's trances as described in "The Murders in the Rue Morgue":

> His face glowed with a light which shone through from some inward fire. . . .A few moments he stood thus in silence, his countenance illuminated by that wonderful intelligence. . .when this man was pondering the enigmas whose solution he was so

certain to announce, sooner or later, he grew absorbed and taciturn. (79)

Almost the first thing Mr. Burton does upon accepting the case is to visit the scene of the crimes to collect firsthand impressions because, as he says, "A clear picture of these, carried in my mind, may be of use to me in unexpected ways" (70). Upon arrival, he examines the room in which the robbery occurred (80). Then, in attempting to imagine how the thief committed the crime, he looks outside for traces. Like Dupin in "The Murders in the Rue Morgue," he scrutinizes every inch of the exterior of the building and its grounds.

> Mr. Burton looked carefully about him, walking all over the lawn, going up under the parlor windows, and thence pursuing his way into the garden and around to the bay-window. It was quite natural to search closely in this precinct for some mark of footsteps, some crushed flowers, or broken branches, or scratches upon the wall, left by the thief. (81)

While Mr. Burton is engaged in his reconnaissance, Richard discovers a woman's handkerchief with the initials "L. S." under a rose bush and opines that Leesy Sullivan might have lost it the previous Sunday night when he observed her peering into the room where candles were burning by Moreland's body. Unlike Dupin's assistant, who contributes nothing to advance the investigation, Richard finds an important clue, but true to his type doesn't "see" what it means. Mr. Burton, whose observation is keener, interprets the evidence correctly:

> "You forget that there has been no rain since that night. This handkerchief has been beaten into the grass and earth by a violent rain. A thorn upon this bush has pulled it from her pocket as she passed, and the rain has set its mark upon it, to be used as a testimony against her." (82)

Thus the condition of the rain-beaten handkerchief was used to determine the time of its owner's presence, as was the condition of the missing woman's clothing in Poe's story "The Mystery of Marie Roget."

Of course the most spectacular example of Mr. Burton's analytical powers occurs when he examines the dead letter (see chapter title page) which leads to the location of the murder weapon. As eagerly as Dupin sought the purloined letter, Mr. Burton seizes upon the dead letter.

> He examined the envelope attentively, before unfolding the sheet within; and as he continued to hold it in his hand, and gaze at it, one

of those wonderful changes passed over his countenance. . . . His practical intelligence seized upon the date, the post-office marks, the hasty direction, and made the contents of the letter his own, almost, before he read it. For some moments he pondered the outside, then drew forth the letter, perused it with one swift glance, and sat holding it, gazing at it, lost in thought, and evidently forgetful of my presence. (204–5)

Following this close scrutiny, Mr. Burton makes his deductions.

"I have now made out all the meaning of the letter. In the first place, it is written 'by contraries'—that is, it means just the contrary of what it says. The contract was fulfilled. The price was expected, the emigration decided upon. The bright day was a rainy night; the picture taken was a human life. And, . . . the old friend was the hiding-place of the instrument of death, after which the accomplice is directed to look. That instrument is the broken tooth-pick. It was secreted in the pocket of an old friend. . . The arms are the arms of that old oak. Unless it has been removed, and that is not probable, since this letter was never received, the broken knife or dagger (of which I have the point which was taken from the wound), will be found in some hollow on the left side of that oak." (211)

The final pertinent example of deductive reasoning from circumstantial evidence concerns the murder weapon. As Dupin inferred from a bit of ribbon that the orangoutan's owner was a Maltese seaman, Mr. Burton arrives at the identity of the assassin from the nature of the murder weapon.

"This . . . is a surgical instrument. You see, it is quite unlike a common knife. It corroborates one of my conclusions. I told you the blow was dealt by a practiced hand—it has been dealt by one skilled in anatomy. There's another link in my chain. . . .A doctor—a doctor. . . .The fellow who married Leesy's cousin, and ran away from her, was a doctor. . . .Richard, I begin to see the light!—day is breaking!" (226–27)

Although Dupin revealed imaginative insight in dealing with the diplomat in "The Purloined Letter," he did not rely on intuition. Seeley Regester adds dimension to the detective's powers when Mr. Burton adds intuition to observation, knowledge, and analysis. However great Mr. Burton's powers of observation and logical deduction, nonetheless his extraordinary success is the result of his extrasensory perceptions. At the end, he tells Mr. Argyll:

"In the first place there is about me a power not possessed by all—
call it instinct, magnetism, clairvoyancy, or remarkable nervous and
mental perception. Whatever it is, it enables me, often, to feel the
presence of criminals, as well as of very good persons, poets,
artists, or marked temperaments of any kind. The day on which this
case was placed before me, it was brought by two young men, your
nephew and this person now present. I had not been ten minutes
with them when I began to perceive that the murderer was in the
room with me; and before they had left me, I had decided which was
the guilty man." (299–300)

Second only to his intuition is his amazing ability to deduce character from
samples of handwriting. Mr. Burton gives Richard a stunning exhibition of this
talent.

"I am glad I have a specimen of the villain's handwriting; it will
enable me to know the writer when I see him. . . .I have a very
good picture of him, now, in my mind's eye. He is about thirty
years of age, rather short and broad-shouldered, muscular; has dark
complexion and black eyes; the third finger of his right hand has
been injured, so as to contract the muscles and leave it useless. He
has some education, which he has acquired by hard study since he
grew up to be his own master. His childhood was passed in
ignorance, in the midst of the worst associations; and his own nature
is almost utterly depraved. He is bad, from instinct, inheritance and
bringing-up. . .I do not know his name, and I have never met him.
All acquaintance I have with him, I have made through the medium
of his chirography. It is sufficient for me; I can not mistake."
(205–6)

Mr. Burton's astonishing physical description of and insight into the character of
the letter writer, expressed with arrogant egotism, are confirmed later in the
narrative by Leesy Sullivan's account of George Thorley (241). This passage, so
reminiscent of the spectacular deductions of Sherlock Holmes from a bit of cigar
ash or a frayed coat sleeve, appeared twenty years before Conan Doyle introduced
his famous character. It may be the first time that this type of inference, so ably
satirized by Agatha Christie in The ABC Murders,[3] appeared in print.

Condition #5: He tests his hypothesis by reconstructing the crime and confronting the villain—often the least likely suspect—in a dramatic surprise ending.

At the climax, Mr. Burton assembles all the interested parties in the Argyll drawing room and relates step by step how the crime was committed, supplying evidence to support each logical deduction and ending with the formal accusation of the murderer. Mr. Burton begins by establishing <u>motive</u>. He states that two men jealous of Henry Moreland for different reasons conspired to kill him. In effect, one volunteered to do for money what each desired, so the second stole Mr. Argyll's money to pay for the crime. Having established motive, Mr. Burton describes how the assassin sought his <u>opportunity</u>, followed Moreland from the city and, under cover of rain and darkness, stabbed him. Then he hid the murder weapon (<u>means</u>) because it had become damaged in the wound and could tie him to the crime, escaped by stealing a boat, and wrote his accomplice identifying the location of the weapon and urging him to dispose of it. A great deal of tension is generated throughout this scene because it is not yet clear who is the hired assassin's employer. Mr. Burton has not been completely frank with Richard (or the reader) regarding Thorley's confession, so no one knows whom Thorley has accused. James or Richard—or even Mr. Argyll—might be named.

The final unmasking of the culprit is dramatic indeed, but it is dependent upon the ambiguity of Richard's position. The irony rests on a genuine confusion because Mr. Burton does not tell Richard what he intends to do; he does not prepare him for what is to come or give him a role to play in the final scene. Richard's role seems to be that of wronged innocence, but it might be a pose. His bewilderment and discomfiture produce tension which isn't resolved until—to everyone's surprise—Mr. Burton actually accuses James at the very last moment.

Condition #6: The ending usually preserves the comic worldview because the culprit is apprehended and the moral and civil order restored.

Contrary to what one might justifiably expect, at the end of the book both Thorley and James are free men. In conventional detective fiction, the conflict is often, but not always, resolved by the arrest of the murderer, who is taken to jail to await the meting out of legal justice, thus satisfying the demands of morality and literary decorum.

In other cases, however, lest the happy ending be tarnished by thoughts of prison or capital punishment, the criminal is dispatched quickly—that is, he is allowed to commit suicide or he is killed while trying to escape arrest. Mr. Burton has an opportunity to shoot Thorley as he tries to escape but holds his fire. One wonders why Ms. Regester failed to avail herself of this convenient method of disposing of a troublesome character, especially given the strong moral nature of

her novel and the nature of the culprit, who wasn't likely to reform. In fact, he loses little time before trying to kill Mr. Burton with a poisoned orange.

In more sophisticated detective stories, the villain is sometimes allowed to survive but may live a life constantly faced with the painful consequences of his immoral act. Thus some novels invoke punishments other than death. The Dead Letter sets the precedent for such novels.

Condition #7: The denouement includes an extensive explanation of any unanswered questions or obscure points in the mystery.

After James leaves under pain of death should he ever return from exile, and after apologies are given to Richard by Mary and Eleanor for their unfriendly behavior, Mr. Burton produces the surgical instrument with George Thorley's initials and fits to the shaft the broken point extracted from the corpse. He then shows Thorley's written confession, as well as the dead letter, and invites the Argylls to compare the documents so they can see for themselves that the handwriting is the same. He relates the curious circumstances by which the dead letter has come to light and its role in unraveling the mystery. He explains that although he knew intuitively that James Argyll was guilty, he had to collect evidence to prove it. Hence his pursuit of Leesy Sullivan in hopes of uncovering a link with James. He also clarifies why he did not take Richard into his confidence: lest "his impetuosity might cause him to do something indiscreet, and I did not want the guilty one alarmed until the net was spread at his feet" (301). Finally, he completes the reconciliation between the Argyll family and Richard by urging Mr. Argyll to adopt Richard as his son and offer him a partnership in his law practice. The final chapter records Richard and Mary's wedding as well as the deaths of Mr. Argyll and Mr. Burton.

Condition #8: Of course, the balance of the tale is devoted to discovering who-done-it.

In The Dead Letter, the murder occurs at the beginning of the story, and the investigation conducted to solve the crime forms the principal line of action of the book. No subplot exists. Although the plot of The Dead Letter is closely crafted along the lines of the puzzle novel, Seeley Regester mixes crime and romance and gets away with it for the same reason that Wilkie Collins was successful in The Moonstone—namely, the romance is at the heart of the conflict. The murder is a crime of passion whose motive is sexual jealousy. The romantic entanglements complicate the conflict. When James's hopes of marrying Eleanor after the death of her fiancé are defeated by her self-inflicted martyrdom, he transfers his attention to Mary, who has preferred Richard all along. Extra pressure is placed

on Richard by this development. Mr. Burton and Richard solve the crime just in time to prevent Mary's reluctant marriage to James.

Apart from implementing the whodunit formula, Seeley Regester reveals literary ability in contriving and structuring the plot of her novel. The novel is divided into two uneven segments: Part I consisting of two-thirds and Part II of one-third of the total narrative. In each part the conflict is developed skillfully and tension mounts steadily to a climax. Part I, which opens nearly two years after the murder with Richard's dramatic discovery of the dead letter, is actually a flashback relating the murder and tracing the ensuing events to the point where Mr. Burton pretends to abandon the investigation and Richard leaves Blankville after being rejected by the Argyll family. In Part II of the narrative—the final third—the action proceeds in a series of logical steps from the finding of the dead letter with its clue to the location of the murder weapon, to the confrontation of the hired killer, to the accusation of, and the confession by, the primary villain.

Narrative Viewpoint

Condition #9: The sleuth is sometimes assisted by a trusted but less able friend who, in addition to performing minor tasks, may keep a written record of the case and later publish it.

Perhaps the most important stylistic feature of The Dead Letter is the imaginative manipulation of the narrative viewpoint. Seeley Regester expands the role of the detective's companion/assistant and at the same time casts him as the murderer's scapegoat.

Richard is superior to most detectives' assistants, who only enter after the fact and have no knowledge of the principal characters involved in the crime; nevertheless, Richard fulfills many of the conventional functions of his role. He asks obtuse questions whose answers demonstrate the detective's superior intelligence and also advance the plot. Richard's trust and admiration for Mr. Burton encourage the reader to trust the sleuth also. And as with "I," Dupin's anonymous assistant, and others of his tribe, Richard's admiration of Mr. Burton leads him to publish an account of their adventure. However, Richard is not merely passive like Dupin's assistant. Very early in the novel he uncovers an important clue concerning Leesy Sullivan and later conducts an independent investigation of the haunted villa, which leads to the apprehension of the "ghost." He also discovers the dead letter, which results in the recovery of the murder weapon and the identification of the hired assassin. Finally, he identifies Thorley from his description as the man who cashed the missing bank note and links him with the robbery.

For creating verisimilitude, Richard Redfield is an ideal narrator because he is an intimate of the Argyll family circle as well as a participant in Mr. Burton's

investigation—he has a foot in both camps. He knows all the principal characters well, and his interactions with them prove his judgments of them are to be trusted. He is ideally placed to observe their reactions immediately prior to and directly following the murder. He is an eyewitness to all the events at the time of the murder, including the examination of the body. He even makes important independent observations.

Various character traits encourage the reader to trust his account, although he is not an entirely disinterested observer. He is maligned by a rival, unjustly falls under suspicion, and is cast out of the Argyll family. Hence he has a personal interest in the solution of the mystery and apprehension of the murderer. Although Richard is a sympathetic character with whom the reader identifies and empathizes in his disgrace and suffering, Mr. Burton's lack of complete candor creates doubts about him. Mr. Burton seems to trust him, and yet—like Holmes and Poirot in later years—he withholds information from his assistant and maintains a certain reserve up to the very last moment. Preserving Richard's credibility throughout the novel without sacrificing his innocence is a formidable challenge, and its accomplishment creates a climax fraught with ironic tension. The manipulation of his character is most ingenious and anticipates Agatha Christie's famous experiment with narrative viewpoint in The Murder of Roger Ackroyd by over half a century.

Conclusion

Thus it is clear that Seeley Regester's The Dead Letter is indeed a proper detective novel because it implements most of the classical conventions of the genre. Until another novel with an earlier copyright date appears, it should be considered the first full-length detective novel in English.

However, The Dead Letter is not merely a slavish imitation of Poe's short stories, because in addition to observing the essential conventions of the detective story, it *extends* and *enhances* them:

(1) Seeley Regester has contributed to the development of the crime novel by extending the character of the detective. Without sacrificing any of the rational skills of Dupin, Ms. Regester has augmented the abilities of the sleuth to include intuitive insight and extrasensory perception. Moreover, despite his extraordinary abilities, she has substituted a real flesh-and-blood person for Poe's bizarre caricature.

(2) Seeley Regester also enlarged the role of the assistant. Instead of merely recording events as a disinterested observer, Richard performs important tasks that contribute to the solution of the murder. His privileged position as an intimate of the Argyll family gives him insight into the principal characters and provides unusual opportunities to observe events and collect information. His personal plight as the murderer's scapegoat adds conflict and creates suspense.

The reader is always aware of the potential for ironic role reversal—a conversion from victim to villain.

(3) Seeley Regester lifted her novel above the sterile limits of the crossword-puzzle story by replacing its cardboard cutouts with flesh-and-blood characters whose personalities and problems engage the reader's sensibilities as do the characters in mainstream novels. This enhancement applies not only to the sleuth and his assistant, but to the secondary characters as well.

(4) Seeley Regester also contrived a complex and well-constructed plot in which she combined romance and crime in a plausible and artistically satisfying fashion. She shows ingenuity and control in the patterning.

(5) In meting out punishment to the villain(s), Seeley Regester set a precedent that satisfied the demands of morality and literary decorum, without marring the happy ending by leaving the culprit to face the inexorable demands of the legal code.

By drawing parallels with Poe's short stories and establishing the existence of a generic formula, I have demonstrated that The Dead Letter is the first detective novel in English. Anna Katharine Green's The Leavenworth Case was a runaway best seller and has long enjoyed the reputation of being the first detective novel; whereas The Dead Letter, a far better whodunit, was buried in obscurity for a century. Who knows why? The important fact to remember is that Seeley Regester did it first and did it better!

NOTES

1. Chris Steinbrunner and Otto Penzler, eds., Encyclopedia of Mystery and Detection (New York: Harcourt Brace Jovanovich, 1976), 340. In 1869, Mrs. Victor wrote a second successful mystery novel, Figure Eight; or, The Mystery of Meredith Place.

2. The Dead Letter (Boston: Gregg Press, a division of G. K. Hall & Co., 1979). Subsequent citations are noted by page numbers in parentheses in the text.

3. Agatha Christie, The ABC Murders (London: Collins, Fontana Books, 1971), 43–44.

6

Let's Hear It for Agatha Christie:
A Feminist Appreciation
Michele Slung

With all due respect to P. D. James and Ruth Rendell—to name two writers who have resisted inheriting the queenly mantle of Agatha Christie from over-eager blurb writers—there is no doubt in my mind that these women never should have been offered the honor in the first place. Bestsellerdom (in the case of James) or simply being British, acclaimed, and prolific (Rendell) just isn't enough to warrant succession to Christie's literary throne.

I should add here that in a recent <u>Time</u> magazine cover story (the international edition—it was Stephen King that week stateside), James has modified her previously stated distaste for Christie somewhat. "I write much better than she did" was how she'd once dismissed the comparison to Dame Agatha in an interview. Now, however, she has this to say: "She is a literary conjurer; she shuffles her cards with these clever hands and lays the cards face down. Each time you think you know the right one. And each time, you are wrong."[1]

That's certainly diplomatic, carefully conveying admiration but indicating, nonetheless, how she perceives as <u>limited</u> the nature of Christie's achievement. What's wrong with her assessment, however, is that it, too, is limited. As she slips sidewise to prevent the royal Christie mantle from being draped on what <u>Time</u> refers to as "her unwilling shoulders," James, in an effort to protect herself, neglects the bigger picture.

By this I mean that Agatha Christie, with all her flaws intact, is <u>sui generis</u>. And P. D. James, for all her virtues, never will be. Around the world, in dozens of languages, for several generations of readers, the two words "Agatha Christie" are synonymous with "mystery story" or "detective fiction." I find I am even oddly moved when I think of this—that such an unlikely and private woman is writ so large in the minds of so many.

From Oz as a child, I moved on to River Heights, where Nancy Drew dwelled with Carson, Hannah Gruen, and the rest; but quite soon, there came a moment when old attics and crumbling castles lost their appeal, when I stopped caring about the next annual appearance of Carolyn Keene's plucky and boringly

perfect heroine. (This isn't the moment to address the issue, but I want to go on record here as saying that taking away Nancy's frock and her roadster and giving her self-doubt, Calvin Klein jeans, and a Honda is as much of a defilement as putting a modern facade on any historic building, and I think the National Trust should have intervened.)

What happened was that I'd come upon a copy of <u>The Mysterious Affair at Styles</u>. In reading it, I'd entered a new stage. The following two or three years were spent tracking down the fifty or so Christie titles then available.

I also admit, without embarrassment, that, in the quarter of a century since, there have been almost no other authors—no matter how ardently I enjoy them or how avidly I seek out their various books—about whom that same thrilling joy accompanies the discovery of an unread volume by them.

And, of course, when I wasn't reading James or Proust, I went on from Christie to Doyle and Stout, Sayers and Allingham, Hammett and Chandler, Innes and Crispin, Lockridge and Rice, and so forth. Eventually, despite concerned college professors who steered my attention to Edmund Wilson's "Who Cares Who Killed Roger Ackroyd?" I turned my innocent amateur pastime into the sordid profession I demonstrate to you today: I became a commentator on the genre.

So I applaud Agatha Christie, and I'd even be willing to debate the proposition that we might not be convened here today had Agatha Christie never existed. Let me detail some of the reasons why I feel Agatha Christie is important to feminist readers and why I think it's so very wrong for serious critics to take a condescending or contemptuous tone when discussing her.

No one that I've ever come across has taken up the topic of role models in the work of Agatha Christie. Yet, in a rather obscure work of hers—I say "obscure" because it doesn't feature one of her series characters, such as Hercule Poirot, Miss Jane Marple, or Tommy and Tuppence Beresford, and because it contains no famous plot tricks—there's a heroine whose attitude and behavior, whose imaginative zest for life has continued to influence me in all the years since I first read about her. The book is <u>They Came to Baghdad</u>, the 1951 Christie; its heroine is the irrepressible Victoria Jones.

An adventuress in the making, now an unemployed typist with no outlet for her exotic yearnings, Victoria's "principal defect," Christie tells us, "was a tendency to tell lies at both opportune and inopportune moments. The superior fascination of fiction to fact was always irresistible to [her]. She lied with fluency, ease, and artistic fervour."[2] (One is reminded of Saki's daughter of the house in "The Open Window." Romance at short notice was her specialty, too.)

The wonderful thing, when you think of Christie's retiring, matronly presence, her prim, perfected public self (like the Queen Mum—if the Queen Mum wrote bestselling thrillers), is that this opening portrait of the mendacious Victoria is affectionate and anticipatory of the fun to come, not at all disapproving. (And here I should add that it's not Victoria's fibs that inspired me, but rather, as

Christie describes it, "her optimism and force of character.") What a flair for life Victoria has! And how beautifully flexible she is, when opportunity knocks. "One never knew, she always felt, what might happen."[3]

This philosophy is definitely not that of a passive or retiring stay-at-home! And, since Victoria does wind up saving civilization as we know it, then settles herself being useful on an archeological dig—as Christie herself was, accompanying her second husband—it's very easy to imagine the sixty-one-year-old Agatha recasting her youth in the figure of such a heroine. "To Victoria an agreeable world would be where tigers lurked in the Strand and dangerous bandits infested Tooting."[4] Now, isn't this just a penny-dreadful way of describing the world that Agatha Christie, living most of her life in luxurious suburban villas, could inhabit by writing thrillers?

Since Christie's notoriety, in 1926, when the strain of the breakup of her first marriage led to her mysterious disappearance, she shunned publicity and lived amazingly away from the claims of celebrity for someone of such global renown. Yet her books are filled with all manner of surrogates, highly active and ingenious female characters—no Nero Wolfes they, sitting home and getting clues secondhand—whether the redoubtable Jane Marple (more about whom in a moment), clever Tuppence Beresford, or the booming-voiced Ariadne Oliver who writes mystery stories about a peculiar Finnish (read Belgian) sleuth. In fact, in the 1936 Christie, <u>Cards on the Table</u>, this selfsame Ariadne Oliver, who voices many of Christie's own sentiments about writing and the writer's life, is depicted as a "hot-headed feminist"—one who wishes, despairingly, that a woman was the head of Scotland Yard![5]

It's true, to contradict myself briefly, that when we first meet Miss Jane Marple, in 1928, in <u>The Thirteen Problems</u> (known in this country as <u>The Tuesday Club Murders</u>), the format in which she functions is a sedentary one. Not un-Wolfean, that is. An informal club of village friends is attempting to stump each other with curious outcomes to curious tales, and the placidly knitting Miss Marple, with her black lace mittens, fluffy white hair, and faded blue eyes, is only included as an afterthought, so as not to hurt her feelings. However, alert to every human foible, she outguesses her fellow members every time.

But, to look at this debut in another light, Agatha Christie herself, whom most of us now see only as the distinctly dowager type she was from the 1950s onwards, was just a mid-thirtyish young woman when the character of Jane Marple was forming in her mind. I find it distinctly praiseworthy that, for her, a true heroine was not bound by cliches of age or physical attractiveness. Christie also puts across the idea of Miss Marple's worth continually in sly ways, even letting Miss M. herself do a bit of horn-tooting from time to time. In "Miss Marple Tells a Story," written when Christie was in her forties and hardly tottering out to pasture, here's how the tale begins:

"I don't think I've ever told you, my dears . . . about a rather curious little business that happened some years ago now. I don't want to seem *vain* in any way—of course I know that in comparison with you young people I'm not clever at all —Raymond writes those modern books all about rather unpleasant young men and women— and Joyce paints those very remarkable pictures of square people with curious bulges on them—very clever of you, my dear, but as Raymond always says (only quite kindly, because he is the kindest of nephews) I am hopelessly Victorian. . . .Now let me see, what was I saying? Oh yes—that I didn't want to appear vain—but I couldn't help being just a teeny weeny bit pleased with myself, because, just by applying a little common sense, I believe I really did solve a problem that had baffled cleverer heads than mine. Though really I should have thought the whole thing was obvious from the beginning. . . ."6

Anna Katharine Green had Miss Amelia Butterworth; Dorothy L. Sayers, Miss Climpson; Patricia Wentworth, Miss Silver; and so forth. Jane Marple, thus, isn't—as my mother would say—the "only pebble on the beach." But isn't there something <u>enormous</u> about her? Just as Christie is for many millions of people synonymous with the mystery story, Miss Marple is the archetype of the elderly lady detective. And to move on from Nancy Drew to Jane Marple, as I did, so long ago, gave me something to grow up <u>to</u>. Not a flat earth up to seventy!
With her own unfortunate experience—the faithless Archie Christie—in mind, Agatha Christie kept a cynical view toward men and marriage for most of her oeuvre. Yet in the first Miss Marple novel, <u>Murder at the Vicarage</u> (1930), Christie allows Miss Marple to reveal her method in these words: "It's really what people call intuition. Intuition is like reading a word without having to spell it out. A child can't do that, because it has had so little experience. But a grown-up person knows the word because he's seen it before. You catch my meaning?"7

Please notice that the word "women's" does not figure here. Her way of <u>knowing</u> is a human trait, regardless of sex but dependent on experience. Understanding people as she does she could be a shaman or a psychotherapist, but the seemingly conventional Agatha Christie was writing detective stories and so Jane Marple plies her perceptivity—that is, she detects—within those conventions.

Even if it's clear that the "psychopathology of everyday life" is what she's dealing with, still such case histories as "The Bloodstained Pavement" won't get the respect of "Combined Parapraxes," nor will "The Affair at the Bungalow" be accorded the stature of "Bungled Actions." Yet, if Sherlock Holmes could meet Freud, why not Jane Marple?

The problems of attempting to gain for Agatha Christie the vast honor I think she deserves—from feminists and misogynists alike, as well as Mr. and Ms. Intelligent Reader—are always being brought home to me. Just a few nights ago, I was at a dinner party and mentioned that I was working on this paper. But before I could explain, a Renaissance historian who was listening interrupted, claiming, "I can't read Agatha Christie. She's too tedious."

Sure, and for millions of others, she's anything but. And for many, many more, who've read her and thought about her work, their enthusiasm, if it exists, is often tempered by reservations about her blimpish social attitudes, her reliance on stereotypes when casting most of her parts, her less than limpid style, the repetition of some of her conjurer's tricks, her Never-Never Land of village teas and Blue Trains speeding through the night. Yet one could reply to those snooty folk who prefer Lord Peter to Hercule Poirot (and I grant you he's sexier, at least in his later incarnation) that Dorothy L. Sayers is only the Thinking Person's Agatha Christie!

I began this talk by deploring the comparison of such current writers as Ruth Rendell and P. D. James to Agatha Christie. They may believe it reflects ill on them; instead, I feel they should be so lucky. In regard to their series characters, Inspector Wexford and Adam Dalgliesh, I challenge anyone to be able to give me a really evocative word picture of either of these men. Will their first novels still be in print, translated into nearly as many languages as people speak, over half a century after original publication? I even have to ask, is it likely there'll be a cargo cult in Papua, New Guinea with either of them the object of Melanesian veneration? Finally, would anyone write an essay asking "Who Cares Who Killed . . . ?" Fill in the name of any victim in any of their books, if you can.

Moreover, no one can or need do again what Agatha Christie did in this century (something Anna Katharine Green is credited with doing in the previous one). She brought mass respectability to the genre, with an audience that ranged from presidents and queens to shop clerks, from nursery school teachers to university presidents.

I hope you understand that I'm not trying to equate ubiquity with quality, popularity with literary greatness. No, I'm talking about the kind of impact that's simply so large we can barely see it. Agatha Christie may not be Shakespeare, but then she's not Mary Roberts Rinehart or Judith Krantz either. She's a legend, not a mere phenomenon.

Rendell and James and their ilk, don't mistake me, are certainly truly talented writers, but in the end, genius, like murder, will out.

NOTES

1.   <u>Time</u> (6 October 1986): 52.

2.   Agatha Christie, <u>They Came to Baghdad</u> (1951; New York: Dell, 1974), 15.

3.   Ibid., 18.

4.   Ibid., 15.

5.   Agatha Christie, <u>Cards on the Table</u> (1936; New York: Dell, 1956), 14.

6.   Agatha Christie, "Miss Marple Tells a Story," <u>The Regatta Mystery and Other Stories</u> (1939; New York: Dell, 1964), 116–17.

7.   Agatha Christie, <u>Murder at the Vicarage</u> (1930; New York: Dell, 1966), 76.

7

A Sweep Through the Subgenres
Marilyn Stasio

I would like my contribution to this symposium session, entitled "Women and Crime Writing," to be that of an in-house pragmatist, one concerned with the practical side of theory.

This role comes with the territory, through my work as a reviewer of popular mystery and crime fiction. As a reviewer, I do not categorize books as written by (a) men and (b) women, or even (a) women and (b) men; rather, I tend to classify books as (a) good and (b) bad—with an occasional (c) promising.

In order to write a well-rounded monthly column, I try to observe all the various subgenres of the mystery. This seems to me necessary in order to offer my readers a comprehensive and fair selection of the kinds of books they most enjoy reading. To satisfy those who like American hard-boiled private-eye mysteries, I will include at least one good one in every column. At the same time, I also want to serve the reader who wants to know about the latest police procedural, historical crime novel, or village mystery. (To satisfy myself, I also try to include the work of a brand-new writer, either a first novel by a promising writer, or a second novel by a someone whose work I haven't yet read.)

One result of the way I work has been that I've come to appreciate excellence in <u>all</u> the subgenres of the mystery, including those which I wouldn't normally read for my own personal pleasure. (In fact, I'm fond of daring people to guess my own personal preferences, because I hope you won't be able to tell from my reviewing.)

Another by-product of this monthly cataloging and categorizing has been my own awakened interest in the performance of <u>women</u> authors in various fields. Like Carolyn Heilbrun, I am heartened by the recent appearance of women in those mystery fields where they were so rare as to be anomalous. But that's not what I'm discussing today.

Today, I want to talk about those categories of mysteries, those subgenres, that women have traditionally dominated. The reason I picked them is because they are <u>not</u> the up-and-coming genres that Carolyn Heilbrun covered this

morning. Just to be ornery, I want to go back to four classic subgenres that women have quietly, but efficiently dominated.

First is the Village Mystery, with its attendant sensitive detective, either amateur or professional; second is the Historical Mystery, often perceived as a romance; the third is the Puzzle Mystery, intellectual, but not bloody; and the last is the Suspense Mystery, often domestic. I chose these specific categories because I am interested in the way they are often dismissed today as old-fashioned and stodgy. I am also concerned, and I confess a bit alarmed, by the tendency to dismiss, as well, the significant literary contributions that women mystery and crime writers have brought to these fields.

Rather than forcing rigid definitions on these subgenres, I will simply illustrate them by referring to the work of four of my favorite authors in these fields.

The first subgenre, the Village Mystery, is often dusted off today as the "cozy," along with its sensitive detective-hero, frequently dismissed as a "bore." You will actually find these patronizing quotation marks used to designate village mysteries—the "cozy mystery," the "teacup mystery," the "cottage mystery" are probably familiar terminology.

Although I sometimes use the terminology myself, I do feel that something important is denied the village mystery when we reviewers denigrate it; namely, the author's clear moral vision and sturdy social conscience. The village mystery is traditionally set in a self-contained society whose way of life is threatened by crime. Within the mythology of this sort of mystery, crime is seen as a major disruption of the social order, a force of evil that often comes from within the community itself, as a sign of invisible corruption.

When we dismiss the village mystery as old-fashioned and out-of-date, we ignore its rather impressive power to portray a microcosmic universe struggling to maintain its values against an evil influence. This evil influence, whatever its form, must be rooted out by the detective-hero if the society is to be cleansed and restored to health. The "boring" detective so beloved by women authors of the village mystery is, indeed, not at all boring. He or she is, as a rule, more compassionate, more thoughtful, and more morally responsible than many detectives working in the hard-boiled genre. I regard this man or woman as a valuable hero in the literature.

Now, for my example: I could nominate Agatha Christie, of course, as master of this genre, but the author I would prefer to talk about today is a less well-known writer—Sheila Radley. Radley's hero, Detective Inspector Douglas Quantrill, conscientiously raises basic questions about morals and values, especially in the relationships between parents and children. He frequently questions the role of education and educators in instilling values in the young. He is also very conscious of the waning influence of established religion in this task. And,

finally, he is always fretting about the chances that young people have for a <u>real</u> future within a changing society that appears to have rejected all the old values.

I really do think that serious issues are dealt with in the village mystery, and I submit that Sheila Radley is one of the most socially conscious writers in this genre. Just to give you a few examples: In <u>Death in the Morning</u> (1978), her theme is young lives nipped in the bud—as the title says, in the morning of their lives—because the values that once sustained them have been weakened by corruption by the elders of the community. In <u>A Talent for Destruction</u> (1982), another picturesque little village is torn apart by a conflict between established church teachings and modern sexual mores. I found this also to be a very perceptive study of the pressures, the lack of privacy, the terrible responsibilities of being a model community leader, whether it's the local vicar or the Chief Inspector himself. As a matter of fact, the Chief Inspector's own family is endangered in another book, <u>The Chief Inspector's Daughter</u>. Both of Quantrill's children are in trouble in this one. His daughter is alienated from her family because of a disastrous love affair, and his fifteen-year-old son is arrested for vandalizing church property. Quantrill's dilemma is how to offer his kids moral direction in a world that no longer respects his precepts of behavior.

In <u>The Quiet Road to Death</u> (1984), we meet an interesting new Radley character. She's Hilary Lloyd, a police sergeant who helps Quantrill on a rather gory decapitation case. In her first appearance, the new sergeant makes this observation of her male colleagues' double standards: "If she showed any emotion in the course of her work they would despise her for being unprofessional. When she showed none, they thought her unfeminine."[1] (I'm happy to say, by the way, that Hilary Lloyd is not a beautiful woman. She's very realistically drawn and she probably looks more like Tyne Daly than Sharon Gless.) This character appears again in <u>Fate Worse Than Death</u> (1986), which takes a very compassionate look at the elderly, not only at the loss of their physical and mental powers, but also at the criminal inadequacy of social services for the elderly.

One last point about Radley's perceptive mystery-studies of East Anglian villages: they are not at all romantic or sentimental. Her books are all emphatically realistic about country life and country people. Her characters live close to nature, and, like other creatures of nature, they can be cruel, ugly, and bestial; in one of her novels (<u>Fate Worse Than Death</u>), she refers to this characteristic as "that streak of rural barbarism."[2] This is scarcely a sentimental view of the rural countryside. Her vision is far from "cozy," and it reflects human evil in a way that I think would curl your toenails.

The second subgenre I would like to call to your attention is the Historical Mystery, often misidentified as being a romance novel or some sort of time-travelogue. My subject here, Anne Perry, uses the historical time frame of Victorian London to make extremely perceptive and meaningful social commentary. (If you haven't already guessed, that happens to be very important to me; when I fail to

find some level of social awareness in a mystery, I find the reading a chore.) In Anne Perry's books, the subject is often the conditions of poverty, which she tends to relate to the low status of women and children in nineteenth-century society.

Inspector Thomas Pitt and his wife, Charlotte, are co-heroes in Perry's novels, because they truly share the detective work. Charlotte was born into the upper classes but renounced her privileges when she married into the lower working-class order—a policeman's lot, in those days, was about on a par with a shopkeeper's. Charlotte has the keener mind; but Pitt has got the tenderer conscience, along with a man's freedom of mobility within a restrictive society. They make a good pair.

Perry's novels all concern themselves with solid social issues. Her style is somewhat sentimental, and she does get preachy; but she draws extremely vivid studies of the social conditions of the period, and I find her sense of moral outrage very refreshing. In Bluegate Fields (1984), for example, she presents an appalling look at child prostitution. She takes the reader through the jails, the workhouses, the sweatshops, the match factories, and the slum dwellings where boys and girls are recruited for this thriving industry. The finer point she makes in the book is that nineteenth-century prostitution was a male crime—with women and children as victims—which the upper orders of society hypocritically deplored but actually condoned and, in effect, institutionalized. In the Pitt household, the compassionate Thomas is unnerved by the legacy of poverty, disease, and squalor that child prostitution engenders. Charlotte, however, gets angry and organizes a reformist group of upper-class ladies to confront the issue.

In Death in the Devil's Acre, Perry is back in the slums, examining another cottage industry—the private gentlemen's club. Her point here is that the private pleasures of the privileged classes—the gambling establishments, brothels, and sporting clubs beloved of respectable gents—were pleasures bought at the cost of human lives, usually those of women and children. In Paragon Walk, she writes about rape, showing how little hope for justice was open to women, whatever their social class, when they were victimized by rapists. (You just didn't let yourself get raped in Victorian society, ladies—forget it!) In Cardington Crescent, her subjects include illegitimacy, infanticide, and (a quaint Victorian custom I'd not known about) baby farms. In The Cater Street Hangman and Callander Square, she pursues the same subjects into the upper-class reaches of society.

Perry isn't a particularly subtle writer, and she has absolutely no sense of humor; but I dearly love to recommend her books to people who want a "nice, romantic history-mystery."

The third subgenre I'd like to mention is the Puzzle Mystery. Alas, I think the whodunit is dying out, victim of the modern notion that character and event and action are all that really matter for a good detective mystery. As a theater

critic, I am forever furious at playwrights who feel they no longer have to tell a good story. Sometimes, I think I can read their minds: "Oh, I can get away with it. I have this fabulous character, a young nun in a cloistered convent, and this wonderfully exciting event, the murder of the nun's illegitimate infant. What more do you want? A story? Don't be ridiculous."

The story element has also taken a beating in non-genre fiction, which makes me respect the puzzle mystery even more. Interestingly, it is another genre in which women have traditionally excelled. It disturbs me to see their well-plotted mysteries dismissed by critics who find their characters shallow, or their plots lacking in action. This strikes me as a serious misunderstanding of the quiet, chess-like nature of the genre. The puzzle mystery still has its place in genre fiction, and women, for whatever reason, seem to be extremely clever at concocting puzzles. Perhaps it's that love for detail that we're so often praised for. Along with P. D. James, who has often remarked on the phenomenon, I don't really know why so many women authors have chosen to work within the tight restrictions of the puzzle mystery—but I'm very grateful for it.

The writer I want to mention in this context, Patricia Moyes, is not really appreciated, in my opinion, for the careful, intricately detailed puzzle-plots that make her mysteries so satisfying. This might be because her hero, Chief Superintendent Henry Tibbett, and his cupcake-cute wife, Emmy, are rather too adorable for some tastes (including, on some occasions, my own). Nevertheless, she has written about twenty novels, all of them with devilishly clever, brain-teaser plots, and each set in a highly atmospheric locale.

Night Ferry to Death, for example, takes place on an overnight ferry crossing between Amsterdam and London, and it fairly reeks of that silent, sinister atmosphere one feels far out to sea. I read the mystery on a night ferry from Naples to Sicily, and will testify that the locale is perfect for murder. Season of Snows and Sins sets its tricky plot in a ski resort in the Swiss Alps, a locale rendered with appropriate cold, silent chills by Moyes.

For anyone who can still appreciate the puzzle mystery at its twisted best, I also recommend Who Is Simon Warwick? with its wheels-within-wheels story about rival claimants to a million-dollar inheritance, and A Six-Letter Word for Death, an absolute tour-de-force of plot trickery, in which a twenty-year-old mystery is solved when Superintendent Tibbett unravels the clues of a crossword puzzle.

I want to be clear, here: certainly, I believe that the mystery story has been enriched by modern authors' attention to character and psychological complexity. But I do feel that the heart of the mystery is still the mystery story. However much readers and reviewers respond to lively characters and fast-paced action, or are charmed by an exotic setting, we should remind ourselves that the essence of the mystery writer's craft is still the storyteller's skill.

My final subgenre is the psychological Suspense Mystery, at which women are absolute craftmasters. Ruth Rendell and Patricia Highsmith are no doubt familiar to you. To these, I would like to add Margaret Millar—again, an underrated writer. Actually, Millar is probably used to a certain amount of this because, as the wife and then the widow of Ross Macdonald, she has consistently been in the shadow of his career. (Personally, I find her a superior writer.)

Millar wrote her first novel, The Invisible Worm, in 1941; since then, she has written approximately thirty novels, most of them in the psychological-suspense genre. She is a subtle and, I think, genuinely original writer who creates suspenseful stories through her understanding of the pathology of crime. Her studies of the psychology of children are indeed extraordinary, and I direct you particularly to Banshee. Here she writes with exquisite sensitivity of a lonely child who invents playmates to console herself. The beauty of this portrait is its insistence on the child's honesty.

During an interview, I once asked her about her uncanny insights into the minds of her child characters. "Why is it that adults don't seem to take children seriously?" she asked me in return. I couldn't tell her, so she went on: "A kid will come home from school and tell his parents something important that happened; and the parents will say, 'Oh, the little bugger's lying again!'" This seemed to annoy her, because she said: "Adults always assume that the child is lying or having a fantasy. I, however, would always tend to believe the child and assume that the adult is having the fantasy."

I consider Millar one of the very few writers of suspense fiction who truly speaks for children's rights. Her young characters are always human beings, which is what makes her descriptions of childhood horrors so compelling. I think that Millar also understands that the essence of suspense involves the threat of evil to innocence—something which takes on extra frisson when the innocent is a child. There is also the drama, in suspense stories, when the victims are unable to communicate this threat of evil to those who might help them. With Millar's children, this becomes more poignant because they are doubly vulnerable, unable to communicate their fears to adults who either won't listen or won't believe them. That's genuine suspense—not those gory, pornographic, woman-loathing, slice-and-dice novels so often mislabeled "suspense" mysteries.

So—at the risk of sounding like an old fuddy-dud myself, I hope I've managed to make a case for some classical mystery traditions, and for a quartet of old-fashioned ladies who have done a splendid job of keeping up the standards and the values of their profession.

NOTES

This paper is an edited transcript of comments developed informally from notes. As its title suggests, it is to be considered a talk rather than a scholarly analysis.

Sheila Radley is published by Scribner's. Paperback editions of some of her novels are also available from Dell. Anne Perry is published by St. Martin's Press, which also publishes her in paperback. Patricia Moyes is published by Holt, Rinehart & Winston, which issues her novels in paperback, as well, under its Rinehart "Owl" imprint. Margaret Millar is published by William Morrow. Many of her novels are newly available in paperback edition, published by International Polygonics.

1.   Sheila Radley, <u>The Quiet Road to Death</u> (New York: Scribner's, 1984), 129.

2.   Sheila Radley, <u>Fate Worse Than Death</u> (New York: Scribner's, 1986), 20.

III

Down These Mean Streets

8

Hard-Boiled Virgil:
Early Nineteenth-Century
Beginnings of a Popular
Literary Formula
William W. Stowe

John A. Murrell, the Great Western Land Pirate, was arrested in February 1834 in Jackson, Tennessee, for slave-stealing. Virgil A. Stewart, Murrell's accuser and captor, testified in a straightforward manner to the specific charges brought against him. In the weeks that followed Murrell's arraignment, however, Stewart enlarged on his original testimony, creating from bits of legend, current fears, and romantic imagination an extravagant tale of organized crime and mystic conspiracy, of a gang of a thousand bloodthirsty criminals plotting to raise a slave rebellion and use the ensuing confusion to plunder the banks, plantations, and commercial institutions of the lower Mississippi Valley. What is more, people believed him. His wild tale of a mystic brotherhood using abolitionist rhetoric as bait for slaves, whom its members would sell, steal, resell, and finally murder, crystallized the fears of a broad, unsettled region of the country, providing a focus for ruthless vigilantism, the justification for a large number of lynchings, and the basis for the Mississippi Panic of 1835.

Since the publication of James Lal Penick, Jr.'s The Great Western Land Pirate: John A. Murrell in Legend and History,[1] the facts of this amazing affair have been available in a single fascinating volume. In The Fatal Environment, furthermore, Richard Slotkin has described the process by which Murrell was transformed from a local figure into "a national myth," and presented Stewart as an example of "the figure of the vigilante, a prototype of the private citizen detective."[2] Slotkin's analysis of the social phenomenon of vigilantism and its connection to the myth of the private detective is impressive; it does not attempt, however, to show in detail how Virgil Stewart transformed himself from a shadowy witness of a simple crime into a prototype thriller hero and created an early example of the power—and the danger—of popular fiction.

This transformation took a distinctly literary form: Stewart effectively wrote himself into heroism and history by inventing a complicated narrative, presenting it piecemeal in his oral testimony, and publishing it at last in a pamphlet alluringly entitled A History of the Detection, Conviction, Life and Designs of John A.

Murel, The Great Western Land Pirate, Together With His System of Villainy, and Plan of Exciting a Negro Rebellion. Also, A Catalogue of the Names of Four Hundred and Fifty-five of his Mystic Clan Fellows and Followers and a Statement of Their Efforts for the Destruction of Virgil A. Stewart, the Young Man Who Detected Him. The author of this opus was ostensibly one Augustus Q. Walton, Esq., of Cincinnati, but Penick has found no evidence that such a man ever existed, and confidently attributes the pamphlet as well as the testimony to Stewart himself (Penick, 3).

Regardless of who actually wrote the pamphlet, it is certainly a record of Stewart's testimony and a product of his imagination. It is also a forerunner of that quintessentially American genre, the hard-boiled detective novel, and of particular interest as a place where some of the elements of that genre came together as it were spontaneously, born of historical circumstances and literary conventions perceived and transformed by a more or less ordinary frontiersman of some reading, apparently, but no particular literary education or ambition. The "Virgil Stewart" of the pamphlet could count Natty Bumppo, Vautrin, and even Faust among his forebears, and Mike Hammer, Ned Beaumont, and Philip Marlowe among his descendants.

The link between the hard-boiled detective story and the frontier hero is familiar. It may have been Balzac who first transposed the denizens of Cooper's wilderness to the streets of the modern city, baptizing his criminals "les Mohicans de Paris" and pitting his own half-wild agent of justice, the criminal-turned-police-chief Vautrin, against them. The genre was soon Americanized, however, and the image of the hard-boiled detective as urban cowboy or citified Daniel Boone has become a commonplace.[3]

As it evolved from its frontier origins, the hard-boiled detective novel developed three paramount characteristics that helped give it form as a narrative and as a text, and definition as a moral and a cultural document. First, the hero of the hard-boiled detective novel has at least as much natural affinity for the criminals he is combatting as for the society he is defending. He could well have been a criminal himself, is often suspected of law-breaking, and is usually contemptuous of legal niceties and the failings of the judicial system. His crusade against crime can therefore also be interpreted as an assertion of his own hard-won moral position, a public acting-out of his espousal of the good.[4] This is particularly clear in the close association of the frontiersman and the Indian, the struggle of the former to maintain and assert his identity as a white man and a Christian in the face of his affinity for a people considered savages and even devils by his own friends and family.[5] It can also be seen in a character like Sam Spade, who is attracted by and at home in the world of Gutmann, the Maltese Falcon, and especially Brigid O'Shaughnessy, but defends himself against the attraction by interposing between himself and the world that draws him the rules of his trade, his

need for self-protection, and finally, almost reluctantly, his own private ethical code.[6]

Second, the hard-boiled hero's activities are dangerous. In accepting an active role in the fight between good and evil, he puts himself at risk. His adventures combine mental acumen and physical courage: he outwits his opponents, it is true, but then he must act on his superior understanding. He is first and foremost the agent of justice, though he sometimes also acts as its theorist. The Indian-hunter and the hard-boiled detective do the dirty work of the society and the ideology that back them. They make themselves vulnerable, in consequence, to physical danger as well as moral uncertainty.

Finally, the hard-boiled hero is defined as a loner defending society against an evil conspiracy.[7] Property, decency, civilization itself are threatened by savages, outlaws, and their silent allies in respectable society. The hero sees this evil for what it is, and stands up to it. If he is Daniel Boone, he wipes out the redskins to make the country safe for decent people. If he is Mike Hammer, he blasts the commies off the face of the earth to make the country safe for decent people. If he is Hammett's Continental Op, he may work a little more subtly and get rival exponents of evil to eliminate each other; the sense of a world made safe for decency may be slightly less secure at the end, but the gist and the shape of his operation will be the same. "In short," as John G. Cawelti puts it, "the hard-boiled detective is a traditional man of virtue in an amoral and corrupt world."[8] His narrative has the shape and the moral significance of a crusade, a righteous campaign against evil.

Stewart's actual history seems to have embodied the first two characteristics of the hard-boiled detective novel. He was in fact a borderline character, a routinely shady citizen of a developing region, who practiced a number of trades in a number of places before getting involved in the Murrell affair. He may well have been a counterfeiter, and when a Mississippi business associate named Clanton accused him of misappropriating goods, he claimed he was innocent but lit out for Tennessee "with a haste that was thought unseemly." Finally, it is not at all unlikely that he and Murrell were at least at one time in cahoots, and he was suspected of being a paid turncoat and informer (Penick, 34–35, 92–93, 97, 99).

Stewart also exposed himself to danger in the course of his adventures. His "detection" of the Great Western Land Pirate was not a matter of pure logic and "deduction"—Poe's "Murders in the Rue Morgue" was still seven years off—but of personal exploit. Whatever the precise circumstances, Stewart was at some point and for some time a spy in the enemy camp, and in danger of exposure. He was also at some risk after his accusations were made public, though whether his person or only his reputation was in danger is hard to tell (Penick, 102).

When he came to prepare his testimony, and presumably to write his pamphlet, Stewart emphasized both of these aspects of his adventures. He claimed,

first of all, that he had ingratiated himself with Murrell by pretending to espouse a romantic theory of crime:

> "Well, sir, if they have sense enough to evade the laws of their country, which are made by the wisest men of the nation, let them do it. It is no harm. It is just as honorable for them to gain property by their superior powers, as it is for a long-faced hypocrite to take the advantage of the necessities of his fellow-beings. We are placed here, and we must act for ourselves, or we feel the chilling blasts of charity's cold region; and we feel worse than that, we feel the power of opulent wealth, and the sneer of pompous show; and, sir, what is it that constitutes character, popularity, and power in the United States? Sir, it is property; strip a man of his property in this country, and he is a ruined man indeed—you see his friends forsake him; and he may have been raised in the highest circles of society, yet he is neglected and treated with contempt. Sir, my doctrine is, let the hardest fend off."[9]

When Stewart addresses Murrell's "noble and lordly band" he plays the romantic overreacher even more boldly, declaring that "members of this conspiracy are absolved from every other power or obligation to either God or man" and appealing to a crude version of natural law for his justification:

> "Turn your attention to the animal world; do we not see the beast of the field, the fowls of the air, and the fish in the sea, all in their turns falling a victim to each other; and last of all, turn your attention to man, and do we not see him falling a victim to his fellow-man? Yes, sirs, if there is any God, these are his laws: but, my noble sirs, we acknowledge no religion or moral instructions apart from the fraternity." (52)

The extravagance of these speeches is clearly intended to convince Stewart's readers that they were not meant in earnest, but rather calculated to deceive a group of "noble conspirators" so far gone in evil that they would have cheered a pep-talk from Satan himself.

Stewart also made literary hay of the dangers he had passed, describing, for example, the scene of his first meeting with Murrell in conventional romantic language:

> The smoke from the cabins had settled among the heavy timber of an extensive bottom in large black columns, and seemed to wrap all nature in deep mourning. Such a scene was calculated to impress the

idea that nature was weeping over the miseries of the inhabitants of so
desolate a spot. (21)

The author of these lines knows that the image of a mourning, weeping nature
raises conventional expectations of danger and of evil. He also knows on some
level that his central figure will cut a more convincingly heroic—if perhaps less
literally believable—figure if he holds surreptitious confabs with successive
hosts, collects an arsenal of pistols from them, and makes artful notes on
Murrell's confession in the most approved romantic fashion—"on his boot legs,
finger nails, saddle skirts and portmanteau, with a needle, as he would be riding
and listening to Murel's horrid account of himself" (50).

The danger Stewart undergoes and his way of responding to it are inscribed
in a well-defined melodramatic tradition. They are also early examples of another,
more strictly hard-boiled tradition of extravagantly heroic action. One putative
attempt on Stewart's life, for example, produces a page of narrative almost
worthy of Mickey Spillane in its violence, though far beneath that master in the
quality of its prose and its command of effective punctuation:

> The assassin on his right appeared to be the commander, and after he
> had ordered Mr. Stewart to dismount several times, and still
> advancing until he was within eight or nine feet of him, he then halted,
> and asked Mr. Stewart if he intended to dismount from his horse—to
> which inquiry he gave a negative answer. The assassin commenced
> levelling his piece on him, but Mr. Stewart being very expert in the
> use of a pistol, fired at the assassin's face; the ball struck him on the
> corner of his forehead; he fell back apparently lifeless, and as he fell
> his gun fired, but the muzzle had dropped nearly to the ground, and
> the contents struck the earth just after it passed under the belly of Mr.
> Stewart's horse. The assassin who was posted on his left, presented
> his rifle and fired, but without effect. The assassin who was stationed
> in front, with the horseman's pistol, seeing that Mr. Stewart had
> drawn no other pistol, only the one which he had fired, concluded that
> Mr. Stewart was then unarmed, so he, to make a sure shot, advanced
> within a few feet of Mr. Stewart, and leveled the pistol at his breast;
> but just as he was bearing on the trigger, Mr. Stewart threw his empty
> pistol, with all his power, at the face of the assassin, and struck him
> over one eye, and cross the nose—the assassin's pistol snapped, and
> fell from his hand. He spurred forward his horse, and made several
> strokes at the assassin, but he could not get near enough to him for the
> full force of his strokes to be received by the assassin: while he was
> engaged in trying to kill this fellow with his dagger, the other
> assassin, who had the rifle gave him two blows with his heavy rifle—

the last blow was received on the back part of the neck, just where the head and neck joins, which came very near unjointing his neck, though it did not disengage him from his horse. He found that he was badly wounded, and betook himself to flight; and after he had gone thirty or forty yards from the scene of action, the horseman's pistol was fired at him; one shot passed slightly through his left arm. Mr. Stewart had got about three miles from where he had received his wound when he was compelled to dismount from his horse from excruciating pain. (77–78)

From all we can tell, then, the historical Virgil Stewart did have some natural affinity for the outlaw, and he did put himself in jeopardy in the course of his pursuit of Murrell. His decision to emphasize just these features in elaborating his fictional version of his exploits helps make his pamphlet a prototype of the hard-boiled thriller.

He also emphasized, with far less historical justification, what was to become a third, more strictly ideological feature of hard-boiled fiction, casting himself as a crusader, a defender of decency, and a guarantor of the values of the community. His motive for doing this is not hard to imagine. Finding his own integrity impugned after Murrell's arrest, becoming indeed a kind of pariah, under suspicion of being an outlaw turncoat, and thus doubly reprehensible as criminal and as traitor, he went on the offensive, claiming to have acted in the community's interest, to have put himself in danger in order to enforce the community's standards and protect it against a dangerous conspiracy. His own sense of persecution led him to cast himself as the noble persecutor and castigator of the enemies of civilization. He thus became in his own narrative a crusader against evil, and a predecessor of such figures as Philip Marlowe, as well as the more egregious Mike Hammer and James Bond.

He did this by establishing an opposition between good and evil, and placing himself unequivocally in the proper camp. The third sentence of "Augustus Q. Walton's" preface takes this task at hand, vilifying Murrell and his band, and placing their enemies on the side of God and of "community":

There is no country under the canopy of heaven, which has, in any other age of the world, produced so formidable a banditti [sic], so extensive in its operations and so scientific in its plans, as the North American Land Piracy, of which John A. Murel was the leader and master spirit who directed its operations against community; but it was the will of heaven that this enemy of the human family and destroyer of the lives and happiness of man, should be stopped in his fiendish and destructive career; and that he should be delivered into the iron

grasp of the offended laws of his country, to satisfy the demands of bleeding justice. (17)

"Walton" is also careful to paint Murrell as an enemy of community in his own past history. "The infamous character which followed him" into western Tennessee from his birthplace further east "soon taught the citizens of that vicinity to abhor and dread him" (19). His frequent absences from home and the coincident cases of horse and Negro stealing "convinced the community of his guilt" (19). His arrest on a charge of "negro harboring" caused "all good men in the vicinity . . . to take some interest in the matter to get rid of so dangerous a character" (20). The bulk of "Walton's" narrative, indeed, is taken up with Murrell's own boasting of his offenses against community and property, his methods of slave-stealing, and the brutality with which he treats the slaves themselves once they have served his purpose. At sixteen he became a thief, and "by the time I was twenty, I began to acquire considerable character as a villain" (45). What is more, he defies the community's moral standards by becoming "a considerable libertine . . . rioting in all the luxuries of forbidden pleasures with the girls of my acquaintance" (46). In the end, he declares himself a partisan of evil and an enemy of all the people:

> "I will have the pleasure and honor of seeing and knowing that my management has glutted the earth with more human gore, and destroyed more property than any other robber who has ever lived in America, or the known world. I look on the American people as my common enemy." (41, emphasis mine)

As if to raise the value of his own exploits, and put himself even further out of blame's way, Stewart has made Murrell an incarnation not only of evil but of anti-Americanism. With this stroke he has unknowingly claimed as his heirs that particular tradition of self-righteous, jingoistic, violent crime fiction that descends from tales of Indian hunters and vigilantes through the exploits of the Pinkertons in the Pennsylvania minefields[10] down to Mickey Spillane's anti-communist super-patriotism and the post-Vietnam adventures of Rambo.

Stewart does not stop, furthermore, with general rhetoric. Like many of his hard-boiled followers, he links his own enemies with an unpopular political movement, making Murrell speak with the tongue not only of an enemy of America but more specifically of an abolitionist, and in the process lumping the enemies of slavery with the enemies of all property, community, and decency itself. The slave rebellion Stewart accuses Murrell of fomenting is of course no fight for freedom but rather a cover for his own nefarious plans. His method of recruiting potential rebels, however, is a vicious parody of abolitionist rhetoric,

which might well serve to crystallize the fears of backcountry slaveholders in an already unsettled time. Here is how he describes it:

> "We find the most vicious and wicked [sic] disposed ones on large farms, and poison their minds by telling them how they are mistreated, and that they are entitled to their freedom as much as their masters, and that all the wealth of the country is the proceeds of the black people's labor; we remind them of the pomp and splendor of their masters, and then refer them to their own degraded situation, and tell them that it is power and tyranny that rivets their chains of bondage, and not because they are an inferior race of people. We tell them that all of Europe has abandoned slavery, and that the West Indies are all free; and that they got their freedom by rebelling a few times and slaughtering the whites; and convince them, that if they will follow the example of the West India negroes, they will obtain their liberty, and become as much respected as if they were white; and that they can marry white women when they are all put on a level. In addition to this, get them to believe that most of the people are in favor of their being free, and that the free states in the United States would not interfere with the negroes if they were to butcher every white man in the slave-holding states." (40)

This tissue of truth, lies, and villainous insinuation was intended to bring down the wrath of the people on Murrell, and make a hero of his captor. The actual results were neither so simple nor so positive. Murrell went deservedly to jail, not for fomenting revolution but for stealing two slaves, a crime of which he may not even have been guilty in this particular case, but which he had pretty certainly committed in the past. Stewart had his fifteen minutes of fame, but they did him little good, for he was soon being denounced as an impostor and a slanderer, and spending much of his time soliciting affidavits of his good character (Penick, ch. 6).

If Stewart's original, imaginative, narrative self-defense backfired in practical terms, however, it marked an important step in the development of a popular type of American hero. Combining a literary romanticism still evident in Chandler's Marlowe and Parker's Spenser and the traditions of frontier heroism with the demands of his own exposed personal position, Stewart made his own fictional persona a prototype of the hard-boiled detective to come.[11]

More ominously, Stewart's narrative also foreshadows certain negative tendencies of the hard-boiled novel, and its practical results underline their dangers. When his public proclamation of his imaginary exploits during Murrell's trial failed to reestablish his reputation, he took his case on the road, hawking his pamphlet for twenty-five cents a copy in the backwoods area of Mississippi where

the revolt was supposed to begin (Penick, 108). The country was ripe for panic: whites were far outnumbered by blacks; memories of Nat Turner were fresh. The great scare began with rumor, was fed by confessions evoked by fear and whipping, augmented by an ill-timed postal campaign by the American Anti-Slavery Society. Before it was over it had claimed the lives of at least seven whites and probably fifty blacks (Penick, 150) and strengthened the slaveowners' hatred for abolitionists.

An 1836 New York edition of Stewart's pamphlet includes additional material concerning "the Trials, Confessions, and Execution of a Number of Murrell's Associates during the summer of 1835," which bears witness to the extent of the panic and the direction that it took.[12] The vigilante committee of Livingston, Mississippi, took upon itself the responsibility of causing "the lives of a number of their fellow-beings to be taken" without a legal trial, justifying their proceedings by "the law of self-preservation, which is paramount to all law." [13] The report of their proceedings in the case of a certain Angus Donovan, a gambler, a Kentuckian, and an opponent of slavery who happened to be in the district on business, is a good example of the confused thinking that contributed to the panic. According to one witness of the "trial,"

> "[i]t appeared that this man had brought down a boat-load of corn from Kentucky. . . , had carried it up the Yazoo river for sale, and had sold it, together with his boat. . . . There was not a particle of evidence implicating him in the guilt alleged, except that of two or three ignorant negroes in the vicinage, who had been seen once or twice near his boat, and from whose reluctant lips certain disclosures had been coerced under the severest infliction of the lash." (Penick, 136)

Despite the paucity of evidence,

> the committee was satisfied, from the evidence before them, that Donovan was an emissary of those deluded fanatics of the North, the ABOLITIONISTS. And, that while disseminating his incendiary doctrines among the negroes to create rebellion, he had found out that he was anticipated by a band of cut-throats and robbers, who were engaged in the same work, not wanting to liberate negroes but to use them as instruments to assist them in plunder. Being of a dissolute and abandoned character, as will be seen from his wife's letter to him, and ripe for every rash enterprise, he joined the conspirators with the hope of receiving part of the spoils.[14]

The committee condemned Donovan to death, and executed him. Its scribe clearly had no second thoughts on the matter when he inscribed the following sentence in the record: "Thus died an ABOLITIONIST, and let his blood be on the heads of those who sent him here."[15]

This, then, was what Virgil Stewart wrought. It is also an example of what popular fiction could do in the days of "The Detection, Conviction, Life and Designs of John A. Murel" . . . and in the days of Uncle Tom's Cabin . . . and in the days of The Clansmen . . . and in the days of I, The Jury . . . and of what it can still do in the days of Rambo. When a work of fiction gives form and focus to a popular feeling it can be a potent weapon, regardless of its literary qualities. Whoever wrote Virgil Stewart's pamphlet was a living example of the truth of the old saw about a little learning: he had read enough to cast his hero in the mold of the romantic overreacher and set his tale in an intermittently romantic setting, but he hadn't written enough to develop a felicitous style or a coherent use of commas. No matter. Mrs. Stowe was no great stylist, and as conventionally sentimental a romancer as can be imagined. Spillane's style parodies itself on every page. None of these writers created social movements, but all three provided a form and a focus for a set of feelings that already existed, and all three influenced the thoughts and the actions of their readers in very practical ways.

Once in a very great while the exigencies of a particular time, place, and set of circumstances link up with a set of pre-existing patterns of thinking (frontier hero legends) and modes of expression (heroic romance) to produce a powerful literary embodiment of popular feelings or fears or ideas. The text in question need not be particularly good: Wells's War of the Worlds is no masterpiece, nor, obviously, is Stewart's pamphlet. Both had practical consequences, however, because they embodied ideas that people were prepared to believe in a form that rang true to them because it was already part of their culture. Truly popular fiction, in whatever medium, is powerful because it affirms and gives form to previously existing cultural material. Spillane did not create violent anti-communism any more than Mrs. Stowe created abolitionism or Virgil Stewart vigilantism. Their work demonstrates, however, the power of artistic representation to channel feelings into action, and the efficacity of culture, however "low," in the contest between rival modes of thinking and behavior, between rival ideologies.

NOTES

1.   James Lal Penick, Jr., <u>The Great Western Land Pirate: John A. Murrell in Legend and History</u> (Columbia: University of Missouri Press, 1981). Subsequent references are cited by author and page number in the text.

2.   Richard Slotkin, <u>The Fatal Environment: The Myth of the Frontier in the Age of Industrialization, 1800–1890</u> (New York: Atheneum, 1985), 133, 135.

3.   See, for example, Slotkin, <u>The Fatal Environment</u>; George Grella, "Murder and Mean Streets," <u>Contempora</u> 1 (1970): 8; William Ruehlmann, <u>Saint with a Gun: The Unlawful American Private Eye</u> (New York: New York University Press, 1974), ch. 1; Dennis Porter, <u>The Pursuit of Crime: Art and Ideology in Detective Fiction</u> (New Haven: Yale University Press, 1981), 172.

4.   On this and other characteristics of the hard-boiled hero see John G. Cawelti, <u>Adventure, Mystery, and Romance: Formula Stories as Art and Popular Culture</u> (Chicago: University of Chicago Press, 1976), 139–61.

5.   See, for example, Richard Slotkin on Daniel Boone, in <u>Regeneration Through Violence: The Mythology of the American Frontier, 1600–1860</u> (Middletown, Conn.: Wesleyan University Press, 1973), 268–312.

6.   Dashiell Hammett, <u>The Maltese Falcon</u> (1929; rpt. New York: Vintage, 1972), 226–27.

7.   For more on the role of conspiracy in hard-boiled fiction, see Jerry Palmer, <u>Thrillers: Genesis and Structure of a Popular Genre</u> (London: Edward Arnold, 1978), 82–89.

8.   Cawelti, <u>Adventure, Mystery, and Romance</u>, 152.

9.   "Augustus Q. Walton," <u>A History of . . . John A. Murel</u> (Cincinnati, 1834), 23. Subsequent references are cited by page number in the text.

10.   See Allan Pinkerton, <u>The Molly Maguires and the Detectives</u> (1877; rpt. New York: Dover, 1973).

11.   The line of descent is not so obscure as it might at first seem. Stewart's story seems to have remained well known in the region for some time—Penick quotes a reference to it by Mark Twain in <u>Life on the Mississippi</u>. It was

published in New York, furthermore, by H. R. Howard, "in two paperback editions, and also in the National Police Gazette" (Slotkin, The Fatal Environment, 133). More recent attempts to revive the tale have not been as successful. See Harry H. Kroll, Rogue's Company (Indianapolis: Bobbs Merrill, 1943) and Gary Jennings, Sow the Seeds of Hemp (New York: Norton, 1976).

12.   H. R. Howard, comp., The History of Virgil Stewart and his Adventure in capturing and exposing the great 'Western Land Pirate' and his gang, in connexion with the evidence; also of the Trials, Confessions, and Execution of A Number of Murrell's Associates during the summer of 1835, and the execution of five professional gamblers by the citizens of Vicksburg on the 6th of July 1835 (New York: Harper and Bros., 1836).

13.   Howard, The History of Virgil A. Stewart, 235.

14.   Ibid., 251–52.

15.   Ibid., 252.

9

The Hard-Boiled Detective Story: From the Open Range to the Mean Streets

Richard Slotkin

In an essay called "The Simple Art of Murder" the American detective writer Raymond Chandler distinguished between two traditions in the writing of detective novels. One he called the puzzle tradition and he identified it mainly with English mystery writers like Arthur Conan Doyle and Agatha Christie. The other tradition, which Chandler claimed for himself and characterized as American, he called the realist tradition.

In the puzzle tradition the story centers on the resolution of an intellectual problem in the form of a murder which generally is framed in a remote and eccentric setting. The reader is invited to join with the detective in the play of resolution. In the realist tradition, on the other hand, the solving of a simple act of murder engages detective and reader with a real and realistically rendered social environment. The intellectual analysis of clues cannot be pursued in studied isolation. It is complicated by the milieu, and by the cross-conflicts born of family psychology, urban life, social divisions, the struggle between law and justice, and power politics at both the street and the board room level. In brief, where the puzzle tradition reduces crime to an intellectual game, the realist tradition makes the pursuit of the criminal the vehicle for active engagement with social life.

But there is a difference between the realism of the detective novel and the realism of, for example, a Victorian novel or a modern work of naturalistic fiction. The realism of the American detective story is defined not by documentary accuracy but by hard-boiled realism, which embodies a view of social life from the perspective of the underworld or, as Raymond Chandler put it, from the perspective of the mean streets. This is Chandler's description:

> The realist in murder writes of a world in which gangsters can rule nations and almost rule cities, in which hotels and apartment houses

and celebrated restaurants are owned by men who made their money out of brothels, in which a screen star can be the finger man for a mob, and the nice man down the hall is boss of the numbers racket. A world where a judge with a cellar full of bootleg liquor can send a man to jail for having a pint in his pocket. Where the mayor of your town may have condoned murder as an instrument of money making. Where no man can walk down a dark street in safety because law and order are things we talk about but refrain from practicing. It is not a fragrant world, but it is the world you live in.[1]

Streets in hard-boiled fiction are always mean, whether they are in slums or suburbs. It is their meanness that makes them seem realistic. The central mystery of the hard-boiled detective story is not the discovery of who killed Roger Ackroyd, but rather the discovery that our worst suspicions about our society are true, that behind the facades of prosperity and order the world is really run by criminal conspiracies, driven by greed, establishing themselves through violence: the discovery, as a Chandler character says in The Long Goodbye, that "there ain't no clean way to make a hundred million bucks."[2]

What interests me, and what I'd like to talk about, is just why it is that Americans seem to delight in this hard-boiled view which seems to run contrary to our cultural tendency toward optimism and our complacent pride in American democracy and achievements. And with that, I'd like to tell how it was that detective stories became the vehicle for this hard-boiled perspective.

From the beginnings of the American republic, popular culture has provided one of the primary means of public education. Mass-circulation journals and newspapers and popular novels and histories are often the first places where Americans have gone to acquire a knowledge of history and politics. And certainly people spend more time in that kind of reading than they do doing their homework while they're in school. Popular novels are particularly powerful because their teaching is so entertaining, and because the historical and moral concepts they deal with are described in vivid detail and linked to appealing personalities.

One of the earliest and most fundamental of American conflicts was that between settlers and Indians for control of the expanding American frontier. So it isn't surprising that among the most popular types of novel in the early nineteenth century was the frontier romance, as it was called, a genre whose form was established in the 1820s by James Fenimore Cooper. Cooper's novels used the conflict between Indians and whites as a metaphor for the basic conflicts of American society. The racial and cultural conflict between Indians and whites was echoed in Cooper by the opposition between whites and Negro slaves, or by the division in American white society between haves and have-nots, between traditional landowners and the ambitious lower classes that were trying to displace

them. According to Cooper, American history can be symbolically represented as a war of races in which white pushes against, and ultimately replaces, vanishing red men. The stakes in the conflict are economic (land and resources) and spiritual, and the struggle is fought on both levels. If white triumphs, then the resources of the New World become the basis of progress; if red triumphs, which the reader knows will not happen historically, then progress halts.

However, the struggle requires certain white men to learn enough of the Indian way so that they can bring about the triumph of civilization. These white men who learn the Indian way become spiritually isolated from the white society; they forget their place in the social hierarchy. Cooper calls one class of these people a kind of evil version of the "squatter" class: those who live like Indians but try to accumulate property by stealing marginal lands from rightful white landowners. In a series of novels, The Little Page Manuscripts, which he wrote toward the end of his life, he has a volume actually called The Red Skins, in which there are no Indians; the red skins of the title are the squatters, the white-skinned squatters.

The struggle is symbolized by Cooper in the rescue of a captive white woman from the polluting clutch of heathen hands, and the woman symbolizes the stakes of the conflict. She embodies all the civilized and Christian values that ought to dominate in a civilized society. To possess the woman is, in a sense, to control the essence of civilization itself. If this woman falls into Indian hands and is either killed or raped, then the core of civilization has been either lost or polluted, and it is in the nature of the Indian, says Cooper, to try to do exactly this. But Indians are not the only threats to the woman. There are those corrupt squatters and lower-class whites, and even corrupt aristocrats, who would also like to marry or possess the virtuous woman. Cooper's fictional solution is to provide each heroine with a romantic hero of her own race and class to marry. But the problem with this romantic hero is that he doesn't know how to deal with Indians. His hands are too clean. So Cooper invents another character, the character of Hawkeye or Natty Bumppo, who will never get the girl but who understands how to fight the forces that threaten the white woman.

Hawkeye is a white man who has been raised by a particularly noble race of Indians. He has acquired all of their skills and none of the racial vices of the Indians. He is loyal, above all, to his own color because he is by birth a white man. He is a man who lives in both worlds, understands both, but belongs to neither. He criticizes both whites and Indians from an independent moral perspective. His sexual attitudes define his social position: he is too white to fall in love with and marry an Indian woman, so he will never be a savage, and he is too aware of his low social status to propose marriage to any white woman, so he will never become a threat to the romantic hero and the propertied classes. His antipathy for marriage is a metaphor for his attitude toward property. Since he will never own a white woman, he will never own any land either. The two seem to

go together. Although he has an Indian companion, this figure is essentially a solitary man who is lonely in his integrity, belonging neither to the Indian nor to the white world but understanding both.

There are real affinities between this figure and the classic private eye. Here is Chandler's description of his idea of the private eye:

> Down these mean streets a man must go who is not himself mean, who is neither tarnished nor afraid. The detective in this story must be such a man. He's the hero. He's everything. He must be a complete man and a common man, yet an unusual man. He must be, to use a rather weathered phrase, a man of honor. He is neither a eunuch nor a satyr. I think he might seduce a duchess, and I'm quite sure he would not spoil a virgin. If he is a man of honor in one thing, he's that in all things. He is a relatively poor man, or he would not be a detective at all. He is a common man or he could not go among common people. He has a sense of character or he would not know his job. He will take no man's money dishonestly, and no man's insolence without due and dispassionate revenge. He is a lonely man, and his pride is that you will treat him as a proud man or be very sorry you ever saw him.[3]

The story, says Chandler, is this man's adventure in search of a hidden truth, and although their environments are different, Hawkeye and the detective have a similar kind of quest in mind: they are both rescuers. They are out to rescue people—usually women—from some kind of threat. They achieve the rescue by following a path of clues (or in Cooper's case of Indian tracks) to the hidden goal. In Cooper's novels there is often a kind of mystery to be solved as well, involving somebody who has been defrauded of an inheritance or is living under a secret identity or something like that. Hawkeye and a Chandler detective are both solitary men who can operate as Indians or as whites, on the common side—the mean street side—or on the polite side. Likewise, they serve a bourgeois society but never compromise themselves by accepting its most corrupting social value. They do not do what they do for money. And they are engaged in unmasking a hidden truth. In Cooper, this is the truth of racial and ethnic incompatibility which will require white and Indian to keep massacring each other until one of them has been wiped out.

At its earliest point of origin, as Bill Stowe has suggested in the preceding paper, the hard-boiled detective story focuses on a similar theme: the idea that society is divided between classes of congenital criminals (white savages) and the rest of the citizens. But the detective story developed toward the discovery of a different kind of social truth.

There are some stages which the story goes through, and I want to run briefly over the ones that Bill has already suggested. First does come the frontier romance. Then there is a kind of intermediate stage: stories about adventures that occur just behind the white-Indian frontier, in which semi-civilized whites form the basic criminal classes and have to be exterminated in almost the same way that the Indians were. Very often these criminals are represented either as allies of another non-white race, as in the case of Murrell, or as lunatics or psychopaths, as in the case of the notorious Harpe brothers. I call them Harpies (although the name is pronounced "Harp") because you need to think of them as kind of mythological monsters. If gangsters like Murrell and the Harpes could arise in the backwash of the frontier where life is still open and property can still be gotten not by robbing your neighbor but by simply clearing off a small piece of land, what sorts of crime might be expected to occur in cities?

Cities had traditionally been associated with crime and corruption, born of a contrast of haves and have-nots living side by side. Jefferson had even expressed the hope that America might somehow remain a land of farms and plantations, with cities few, culturally insignificant, and fenced off from the rest of society. There was also a popular literature of urban crime whose roots went back to English ballads and pamphlets about London thieves and murderers, collections of which were published in America under the title Newgate Calendar. And there were American equivalents, notably the narratives that were appended to execution sermons in colonial New England. However, these stories all center on the pathology of the criminal classes. They do not feature detectives or police officials or vigilantes as heroes. The criminal is usually captured because of his drunken excesses, or because of the routine operations of a faceless constabulary.

The first urban detectives emerged from a hybridization of the frontier romance and the story of the urban sociopath. A key figure here is a man named George Lippard, a best-selling author of sensational fiction of the type now called "bodice rippers," who was also an important spokesman for the Jacksonian labor movement and a writer of patriotic fables. Lippard's novel Quaker City, or The Monks of Monk Hall, one of the great lunatic masterpieces of American literature, was published in 1844. Monk Hall is a vast gothic castle or monastery which has somehow grown up in Philadelphia, the city of brotherly love, the model American city. Its presence marks the transfer to the New World of the crime and corruption of the Old. Monk Hall has been built by the wealthy classes as a place for luxurious debauches. And to supply it with prostitutes, the managers of Monk Hall engage in the systematic corruption, seduction, and rape of the virginal daughters of the working and middle classes. As a spokesman for labor, Lippard uses the machinery of the crime novel and the gothic horror tale for ideological purposes. He contrasts the virtues of the so-called producing classes with landlords, bankers, false aristocrats, hypocritical ministers, crooked politicians, and so on. Although the setting is urban, the plot is the same as that of a Cooper

novel, except that this time the wilderness is this huge building. We still identify the enemy by his attempts to capture and rape white women who are the symbols of social and moral value. Lippard emphasizes this structure by describing the inhabitants of the underworld of Monk Hall as "urban savages"—men who might once have been citizens and working men, but who have been so debased by their oppression that they have become both morally and physically deformed.

There are several rescuers who attempt to deal with Monk Hall, one of whom is a kind of urban Hawkeye, a common man of skill and wit who speaks in the vernacular and sees through all hypocrisy. But although Lippard draws on this vocabulary, even his heroes are corrupted by the knowledge that they acquire in the cellars of Monk Hall. Nobody escapes the corruption that lies below the surface of the city of brotherly love. A vision of apocalyptic doom strikes American society at the end of this novel.

After the Civil War, with the increasing pace of industrialization and urbanization, and with rising class tensions now augmented by the fact that many of the working classes were immigrants from non-English-speaking countries or slaves coming up from the South, this imagery of the urban savage becomes very much a part of newspaper language. I will give you just one quotation that sums up this way of thinking. It is a quote from a magazine called The Nation (which is still publishing) in response to Custer's last stand (1876).

> There is, among the more rabid country papers just now, a loud demand for the extermination of the Indians, a course for which there is something to be said, if by extermination is meant their rapid slaughter. But if they are to be exterminated, why any longer pauperize them and then arm them? What would be said of the city of New York if, after lodging its thousand tramps in comfortable idleness over the winter, it were to arm them on leaving the almshouse with a revolver and knife and a tinderbox for firing barns? But why should it be worse to do this to savage whites than to savage Indians?[4]

In this environment, with the transfer of the frontier, in a certain sense, to the city, changes occur in popular writing—in the dime novels, for example. Many popular dime-novel figures who began their careers as either Indian-fighters or Wild West figures, begin to be called detectives. Deadwood Dick, for example, is originally the outlaw of the Black Hills but he ends as Deadwood Dick, detective. Buffalo Bill first appeared in dime novels as the man who got the first scalp for Custer, but by the end of his career there are titles like Buffalo Bill, Detective and Buffalo Bill and the Nihilists (in which he saves a Russian grand duke from an assassination plot).

In this context, in which the race war has now become a class war in the cities, there is one preeminent detective figure who is capable of fighting the urban war as the Indian war had been fought, and this is Allan Pinkerton. He was the head of the first and largest detective agency in the world, and former head of Union army intelligence and counterintelligence during the Civil War—at which he did an absolutely comically execrable job. At one point, he represented General Lee as commanding an army of a quarter of a million men, at a time when there weren't a quarter of a million men under arms in all of the Southern Confederacy. He convinced the head of the Union army that he was perpetually outnumbered. Pinkerton was, however, the nemesis of train robbers and embezzlers, the pursuer of Jesse James, against whom he made his reputation in part. He was the inventor for Americans of the labor spy and of the agent provocateur who broke labor unions. And, not incidentally, he was the author (or the putative author, I should say) of several books, some of which were offered as true accounts, some of which were offered as works of fiction. His most interesting books set the Pinkerton detective against various groups. Of particular interest is one about the breaking of the great coal strike of the mid-1870s, which pits the detective against the Molly Maguires, and Strikers, Communists, Tramps and Detectives, which recounts the great railroad strike of 1877.

According to Pinkerton, prevailing practice in the work of police and detective agencies before him had been to set a thief to catch a thief, to use corrupt people as informers. This resulted in an important alliance between law enforcers and the criminal classes. But Pinkerton proposed to train and employ detectives of the highest moral character, chaste men who would forswear drinking and smoking except when on duty! Their task would be to adopt the disguise of the criminal and the working-class malcontent, and to ferret out evil from within society. Pinkerton, in fact, was also running a large-scale vigilante operation. Many of his detectives were involved in fomenting lynch mobs to finish off criminals whose convictions the case would not sustain. The Reno gang in Indiana is one of the first cases of this, but Pinkerton also tried to frame I.W.W. leaders like Bill Haywood. And Dashiell Hammett, who was a Pinkerton man at one time, claimed that he was asked to assassinate a labor leader named Frank Little. But none of this vigilantism ever appears in a Pinkerton novel. His fictional detectives are very straight, they always get their man, and the criminal is always convicted by legal means. In these novels Pinkerton is not an actual operative, but a paternal figure who tells the story and very often gives you his introduction to the life of a detective. He teaches the detective the way to do things and then sends him out to have the adventure.

The heroes, through whose eyes the adventurous part of the story is seen, are also latter-day Hawkeyes. They are men who can live and deal with the criminal classes and seem to be at one with them, but whose pure hearts are firmly on the side of law. McParland, the detective hero who infiltrates the Molly

Maguires, is chosen because he's an Irishman. To recruit him, Pinkerton convinces McParland that the Molly Maguires are actually a corrupt extension of a certain type of Irish nationalist group, against whom McParland's family had worked in the Old Country. Much is made of the fact that the Mollies have weird rituals and a kind of tribalist ethic. Pinkerton compares them to the thuggees of India, a sect of supposedly murderous fanatics who worship the goddess Kali. One action wing of the Mollies is called the Modacs, the name of an Indian tribe which had recently been at war with the United States and had assassinated a brigadier general at a peace conference. As Pinkerton's son later wrote, "The case required something more than mere pecuniary reward to secure the right sort of person. McParland doesn't do it for money. He has to feel he's serving his church, his race, and his country" (just like the Deerslayer).

As a test, Pinkerton requires McParland to do research on secret societies and present a report. The report reveals that McParland is a wretched historian, but that his political prejudice lets him see the Molly Maguires as something after the fashion of the Ku Klux Klan, a group which initially, according to McParland, served a liberating function but which later became an excuse for robbery and murder. McParland disguises himself as a miner, infiltrates the Molly Maguires, and not only exposes them but provokes them to actions that will get them arrested. As the story unfolds, he is tempted by the Mollies—they are his Irish brethren, after all—but he always overcomes the temptation and remains true. This is all, of course, phony. McParland fabricated evidence, as he did again later in his testimony against the I. W. W. But for purposes of the novel, none of this appears. McParland does his job well.

Pinkerton, like Cooper and Lippard, was using a received vocabulary of myths and symbols to create a new model of American society. The stakes in the battle are still the survival of the civilization, with the savage proletariat replacing savage Indians. But where Cooper's story is open-ended and holds open the possibility of a redemptive triumph, the Pinkerton formula story is much more narrow in its possibilities. You can wipe out one criminal, but there will always be a sequel because there will always be another class of criminal to deal with.

The Pinkerton formula story also has the problem of representing only one side of politics and social life in America in the 1880s. It shows only the corporate side. And the fact is that American society in this period was deeply divided between those who sympathized with the position of labor and those who took the point of view of the trusts and the so-called robber barons. If you look at dime novels published in this period, you see a much more representative sample of story types. There is one series called "New York Detective" that, interestingly, included under the title "Detective" stories about both outlaws and detectives. One of their most popular figures is Jesse James, the Robin Hood of the Old West, who stands for justice where law is not equal to bringing justice to society. And on the other hand, there is a man called Old King Brady, an urban detective, a

master of a thousand disguises who puts down smugglers, criminals, and gangsters.

It is interesting that as the series unfolds over a span of about twenty years, the stories begin to blend and merge. At first, Jesse James turns up in New York and is pursued by Old King Brady. Then Old King Brady goes out west and pursues Jesse James. Then Jesse James goes to Mexico and discovers a poor but virtuous woman who is being cheated of her ranch by a wicked banker—and Jesse James turns detective. Then Old King Brady turns up facing a situation in which the law is in the hands of gangsters, so he has to turn into Robin Hood in order to solve the mystery. The detective and the outlaw, in other words, over this twenty-year period, begin to inhabit the same space and finally begin to swap roles. And this, for me, is the root of the modern hard-boiled detective story. It is the combination, in a single figure, of the outlaw and the detective. The inner life of the figure is that of the outlaw, whose perspective is that of a victim of social injustice. He has seen the underside of American democracy and capitalism and can tell the difference between law and justice, and he knows that society lives more by law than by justice. Yet he also embodies the politics of the police detective, the belief that we need order, some kind of code to live by if we are to keep from degenerating into a government of pure muscle and money. And he is willing to use force to impose order and strike a proper balance between law and justice.

The modern hard-boiled detective story arises from a combination of the world view of the Pinkerton novel (society is imperiled by conspiracies reflecting class conflict) and the vaguely populist style and ethic of the frontier outlaw-hero. Dashiell Hammett's work bridges the gap between these two worlds, in two detectives particularly—the Continental Op and Sam Spade. Hammett shows each of them as a person who finally ends up doing the work of law, but who stands finally outside and against law as well. In the novel Red Harvest, the Continental Op is supposedly a Pinkerton detective who goes into a town which has been taken over by a corrupt partnership of gangsters and factory-owners who have banded together to break a strike. The Pinkerton ends up acting as an agent provocateur not against the union but against the bosses. He turns the Pinkerton story inside out and on its head, to restore justice from the bottom up. It falsifies the history, but it is a wonderful fantasy and shows the potential of the detective. Again, in The Maltese Falcon, Hammett's next novel, the detective is described as a blond Satan. The setting is a little more abstract. This time he is a private entrepreneur; he does not work for a corporation. And we are never quite sure which side of the line Sam Spade is going to come down on. He acts like an outlaw, he acts like he could be a criminal—the cops treat him that way, the criminals treat him that way—yet somehow he comes out on the side of law.

For me, this is the essence of the hard-boiled detective and the secret of his appeal. We are in love with authority, we know that on the one hand we need

authority and hard lines of value, and on the other hand that authority is often corrupt and misdirected and that those hard lines of value are often blurry. The detective allows us to enjoy both of those features simultaneously, to play imaginatively at being both policeman and outlaw.

NOTES

1.   Raymond Chandler, The Simple Art of Murder (New York: Ballantine Books, 1972), 19–20.

2.   Raymond Chandler, The Long Goodbye (New York: Ballantine Books, 1971), 227.

3.   Chandler, The Simple Art of Murder, 20–21.

4.   "Our Indian Wards," The Nation (13 July 1876): 21–22, quoted in Richard Slotkin, The Fatal Environment: The Myth of the Frontier in the Age of Industrialization, 1800–1890 (New York: Atheneum, 1985), 493.

10

Elmore Leonard: Splitting Images
Glenn W. Most

Toward the beginning of Elmore Leonard's Split Images, a rather odd thing happens. A multimillionaire named Robbie Daniels has shot and killed a Haitian refugee who has broken into his house in Palm Beach. This, unfortunately, seems not to be odd at all, at least not in Leonard's world. What is odd is what happens next. Gary Hammond, the young squad-car officer who questions Daniels, asks him whether the woman accompanying him had entered the house together with him, and the millionaire replies, "'Yeah, but when I realized someone had broken in, the way the place was tossed, I told Miss Nolan, stay in the foyer and don't move.'" "The squad-car officer paused," continues the narrator. "One of Mr. Daniels's words surprised him, bothered him a little." We wonder: which word? why? Leonard does not tell us, and we must read on, hoping that this tiny perplexity will at some point be resolved.

This perplexity is in fact the only mystery at the beginning of this novel—which is surprising, considering that the first sentence announces that a murder has been committed and that a conventional murder mystery would be devoted to solving the question of who had done it. That question is not in dispute here—no one doubts that the millionaire shot the Haitian—but it will turn out that the circumstances are less clear than we might have thought. The millionaire claims he shot the burglar while the latter threatened to attack him with a machete; the Haitian, before dying, says that he was unarmed and that the millionaire ordered him to approach and shot him in cold blood. Faced by these competing versions, we are likely to respond the same way the patrolman's superior, Walter Kouza, does when Gary Hammond discusses the case with him: of course the Haitian tells it differently; we would expect him to. What could be more natural, Kouza thinks, than that a starved and vicious Caribbean should break into a house and try to kill its owner with a savage native weapon? What could be more absurd than that a wealthy American businessman should shoot a man in cold blood? When the opposing versions are estimated according to the calculus of social probabilities, the choice of the likelier one seems easy.

But that calculus is founded upon stereotypes and prejudices. How true are they? How confident can we be that our clear sense of the differences between a Haitian and a millionaire is not radically defective? Gary Hammond, the squad-car officer, has been bothered by something, and we are about to find out by what. His dialogue with his stolid superior continues:

> Gary Hammond was patient. He was going to say what was bothering him.
> "He said something to me, Mr. Daniels. He said he come in—he realized somebody was there from the way the place was tossed."
> "Yeah? . . ."
> "He used the word *tossed*."
> "So?"
> "I don't know, it seemed weird. Like he used the word all the time, Mr. Daniels."
> The detective said, "He say it was going down when he got home? How about, he looked at the guy but couldn't make him? TV—all that kind of shit come out of TV. They get to be household words. *Tossed*, for Christ sake." (16–17)

What had bothered the squad-car officer had been a linguistic anomaly, a stylistic break he was sure he had observed in the millionaire's speech: he would not have expected a rich and presumably well-educated white man to use a word from underworld slang like "tossed." To his hypersensitive ears, the anomaly was odd enough to suggest that this millionaire might not be everything he seemed to be: that, in other words, the stereotyped contrast between millionaire and Haitian might not correspond to the realities of this particular situation. So too, a few pages earlier, Gary Hammond had been talking with the Haitian's widow in the hospital while they waited for him to die:

> She said, "I go home tonight and fetch a white chicken and kill it."
> Gary said, "Yeah? Why you gonna do that?"
> The woman said, "Because I'm hungry. I don't eat nothing today coming here."
> Gary said, "Oh." (14)

Why does Gary ask her what she intends to do with the white chicken? Elmore Leonard does not tell us, but there can be no doubt that Gary imagines she intends to perform some weird voodoo ritual requiring the use of a chicken—and of a white chicken, at that. But her answer repudiates his unintentionally racist

fantasy and indicates merely that she is a human being just as he is, one who suffers hunger and eats chickens. True, she may speak a little oddly, and she may kill her chickens herself rather than purchasing them frozen in a supermarket, yet the point of the dialogue is that she is not as different from him as Gary had thought. But not only as Gary had thought: as we had thought too. For Leonard is careful not to hint at Gary's fantasy of a Haitian voodoo ritual by even a single word: we readers must supply such a fantasy ourselves in order to make his question intelligible.

Thus Leonard has tricked us into injecting our own racial stereotypes into our reading of the novel and has shown us at the same time how unfounded they really are. But if the Haitian is not so different from the policeman, and the millionaire uses the language of criminals, what remains of the calculus of social probabilities upon which we had based our estimation of the competing versions of the circumstances of the Haitian's death? Kouza rejects the patrolman's intuition, arguing that mass culture has blurred linguistic boundaries, and by implication social ones, yet he does not realize that his own argument destroys his foundation for instinctively preferring to believe the millionaire. Eventually he will pay for this error when, near the end of the novel, Robbie Daniels, the millionaire psychopath who dreams of committing murder on television and who had in fact shot the Haitian only for target practice, kills him too. Gary Hammond, on the other hand, suspects that Robbie, like many Elmore Leonard characters, has been so influenced by popular culture that he has begun to enact the violent fantasies he has been consuming. Gary will turn out to have been right in his suspicions, but his being right will do no good at all: it will neither prevent murders nor solve murders, but remain as a sad and sterile wisdom.

This dialogue between the patrolman and the millionaire is a curious encounter. It brings together symmetrically a member of the upper classes who descends to the language of the underworld, and an ordinary street cop who momentarily rises to the height of a considerable stylistic sensitivity—yet it brings them together without purpose or consequence, and allows them first to intersect at a moment of truth in which the criminal cannot help but betray himself and one policeman cannot help but understand, and then drift on as though that moment had never happened. Such intense and futile intersections define the fictional space of Elmore Leonard's novels.

The elements of that space are familiar from the crime novels of many other authors. The characters that populate it are a Hobbesian congeries of clever or unscrupulous egotists on the one hand and stupid or cautious ones on the other. The best that strangers can hope for from one another in this world is distrust; the likeliest is malice. Altruism is unknown, self-interest is taken for granted, greed is the most common motive. People's actions veer between coercive force and manipulative shrewdness; their lives are stretched taut between fantasies of whose

implausibility they are not quite unaware and are punctuated by the exclamation point of violent, sudden death. The large and colorful cast of secondary figures is drawn from the extremes rather than the center of economic and social life, and primarily serves to furnish spectators and victims for a central duel, which pits against one another a man who kills and a man who, often (but not always) with the blessing or at least the connivance of the state, kills men who kill. Women can enter this terrain, but—a generic weakness in Leonard's style and moral vision—almost always as victims. If they become the object of lust, that is only another form of the attempted exercise of power: true love is as rare in these novels as true friendship, and as surely doomed.

But if the elements of this narrative space are all familiar, its structure and boundaries are in fact quite different from those of most other novels: an Elmore Leonard novel resembles nothing else in the world except another Elmore Leonard novel (indeed, any one Elmore Leonard novel bears far *too* strong a resemblance to most other Elmore Leonard novels). There are three especially distinguishing features in these novels.

First, from the side of the detective figure, it is remarkable that there is almost never any process of detection. We readers generally know from the very beginning who the murderer is, and often the detective figure finds out soon after, but he is always prevented from arresting or killing his man at once. What prolongs his pursuit, and thereby gives the novel its necessary length, is generally not a process of investigation, with the careful gathering and sifting of evidence and the drawing and testing of tentative conclusions, but rather a frustrating combination of legal procedural constraints that are often portrayed as arbitrary, and the killer's own animal wiliness and absurd good luck. By and large, there are no clues in an Elmore Leonard novel.

Second, from the side of the killer, it is striking how frequently Leonard's criminals are straightforward psychopaths, borderline or full-fledged homicidal maniacs who kill simply for fun or for the most immediate forms of greed and revenge. This is a remarkable fact, one that cannot be explained away as social realism. Rather, the phenomenon of the psychopathic killer is best seen as related to another oddity in these novels: the almost total absence in them of the family. For the detective to be familyless, typically a divorced or widowed male, was, of course, traditional in the crime novel: this was thought to ensure his incorruptibility and the single-mindedness of his dedication to solving the mystery. But on the other hand, the crime itself, at least from Aeschylus through Ross Macdonald, always found its most fertile matrix in the prolonged tensions and covert violence of the ordinary nuclear family. In Leonard, not only is the detective figure usually a bachelor; so too is the murderer, and his victims are most often people he hardly knows. The result is that both of the central characters operate for the most part

as detached and isolated individuals, free-floating agents. They are monads with guns.

Finally, and most importantly, in the absence of both the rational necessity of an investigative process and the biological necessity of a family context, what ends up organizing the plot of an Elmore Leonard novel is largely chance. The characteristic form of these novels is not detection but pursuit. But it is a particular type of pursuit. There are, for example, few if any one-sided chase scenes—with the policeman hot on the heels of the fleeing malefactor—of the sort loved by the movies and television. Instead, the pursuit is always mutual: the man who kills and the man who kills killers circle around one another, hovering, waiting for the chance to strike, and each hopes that his attack will be so overwhelmingly forceful and so unpredictably timed that it will kill the other even though he has been anticipating and planning for it from the beginning. This means that an intimate bond links the two figures in this central duel, a bond expressed in Leonard's fondness for heroes who have served in prison or for plots that show the two males competing for a single female. But it also means that the narrative sequence of these novels becomes a broken temporality, one rationalized by no redeeming progress toward a goal. Without a *telos*, Leonard's novels could go on forever; what breaks them off and provides a conclusion is usually a fluke of chance, and these endings are almost always flamboyantly artificial, deliberately unsatisfying. Thus Robbie, the lunatic millionaire of Split Images, possesses an enormous gun collection, but the only reason another policeman (not Gary Hammond) can succeed in the end in pinning a murder on him is that, with unaccountable stupidity, Robbie happens to use the same gun on two different victims.

Or consider City Primeval. Here the policeman has been tracking the psychopath Clement for the whole novel and finding himself blocked constantly by legal constraints and bad luck; at the end, there is a showdown between the two in which the policeman shoots the murderer when the latter reaches for a can opener! Even when the novel is about to close with an apparent success for that character who has least alienated our sympathies, Leonard is careful to add a bitterly ironic twist. The title character in LaBrava, who has knowingly fallen in love with an aging actress because of the seductive roles in mystery films he had seen her play in when they were young, helps her to pull off a murderous swindle for which she finally has the chance to write her own script. Of course she ends as the big winner, and he is left saying the curtain line she had always had to mouth: the patsy's "Swell" (246, cf. 45). The title character in Stick kills and is almost killed for revenge and $73,000—just enough, he learns on the novel's last page, to cover exactly the back payments on his alimony (303).

How can such novels be structured before their off-key endings? During its course, this broken temporality is articulated above all by Leonard's most

important innovation in the mystery genre: the irony produced by constantly shifting the point of view from which the story is told. Leonard never employs first-person narration and his use of the limited third-person point of view is extraordinarily sophisticated. Any chapter in an Elmore Leonard novel can be narrated from the perspective of any character; even a murder victim, as in the second chapter of Glitz, can furnish the viewpoint from which the story of his death is told. But, as we might expect, the viewpoints Leonard prefers are those of the detective and the murderer, and for most of their course his novels oscillate uncannily between the one and the other. It cannot be stressed enough how innovative this technique is within the mystery genre. For in the traditional mystery novel, the author's control over an unvarying and sovereign viewpoint, whether it is first or third person, guarantees the closure and the intelligibility of his story. Of course, there have been rare exceptions of a shift in narrative viewpoint—one thinks of Agatha Christie's Murder of Roger Ackroyd or Ten Little Indians—but these were unrepeatable experiments in wit designed to confirm the code they momentarily violated. In terms of the history of the genre, Leonard's shifting viewpoints conflate the use of the first person from the viewpoint of the detective, common in the whole tradition of Hammett, Chandler, and Macdonald, with the use of the first person from the viewpoint of the schizophrenic murderer, a specialty of Patricia Highsmith. Many readers find such Highsmith novels as This Sweet Sickness or the Ripley tales disturbing, for one cannot be told a story from a certain perspective without at least conceiving of the possibility of the legitimacy of that perspective, and many of us feel uncomfortable sharing, even if only in part and only in a fiction, the goals and desires of a homicidal maniac. The choice of a narrative perspective is never merely a technical question, but rather always also a moral one, and Leonard's use of point of view is in fact more radical, and more disturbing, even than Highsmith's. For the consistency of Highsmith's perspective means that it can be rejected en masse: even if we read her novel to the end, we have long since concluded that the restrictiveness of the point of view from which the story is being told is part of the very sickness of the schizophrenic who is telling it; his expression in fact aids our therapy. But in Elmore Leonard's society, both evil and good have become equally respectable alternative points of view from which a story can be told. How can we bestow our sympathy upon the hero from whose perspective one chapter is narrated and then withhold our sympathy from the psychopath whose viewpoint shapes the next one?

There is something profoundly troubling here, and it is to this I would like to turn in conclusion, by examining a final oddity in Elmore Leonard's novels.

With obsessive frequency, the murderous gunshot in these novels is accompanied by the sound of shattering glass. Glitz begins and ends when Vincent is shot as he carries mostly liquid groceries: the first time, "Hearty Burgundy, prune juice and spaghetti sauce. This time chablis, J&B Scotch, Puerto Rican

rum and a family-sized bottle of Coca-Cola" (349). Both times the bottles fall and shatter and he collapses, wounded, into a pile of broken glass. Clement performs his first murder in City Primeval by shooting a judge through a windshield, "the windshield taking on a frosted look with the hard, clear hammer of the evenly spaced gunshots, until a chunk fell out of the windshield" (17). So too, the bullets Robbie shoots into Curtis for practice in a garage in the middle of Split Images shatter an automobile's windshield (88) and those he fires when he kills Chichi toward the end of the novel make a bottle on the side-table shatter and several windowpanes in the French door explode (240). In Unknown Man No. 89, Virgil's shotgun blast kills Lonnie, "making a terrible noise and shattering a full-length mirror, wiping it from the wall . . ." (69–70). In Gold Coast, Ed Grossi watches his own death in the splitting images of a shattered mirror:

> In his mind, in that moment, Grossi heard Vivian saying, "You're getting old," and his own voice saying, "Oh my God," and heard the heavy muffled gunshot hard against him, jabbing him, and saw in the mirror blood coming out of his shirt front and on the mirror itself, his blood sprayed there as from a nozzle, seeing it in the same moment the sunburst pattern of lines exploded on the glass, his image there, his image gone. (147–48)

And, in perhaps the most striking instance of all, in 52 Pick-Up, Bobby goes out of his way, for no apparent reason, to shoot his accomplice Leo through a plate glass window. He has been talking with Leo in the latter's nude-model studio, and could have killed him there at any moment, easily, privately, and safely. Instead,

> Bobby steered Leo over to the desk and gently, with his hand on his shoulders, sat him down. . . . Bobby walked away from the desk to the front door counting one, two, three, four and a half steps. He opened the door, gave Leo a nod and a little smile and walked outside. . . . Glancing at the street, at the few cars going by but not studying them or worrying about them, he walked back to the front door of the model studio, counted one, two, three, four and a half steps past it, stopped, faced the black-painted plate glass in front of the D in NUDE MODELS, raised the revolver belt-high and fired it at the glass, getting the heavy report and a hundred and twenty square feet of shattering glass and the D disappearing in front of him, gone, all at the same time. (166–67)

Why does the bullet that kills break glass so often in Leonard's novels? We

might think of explaining this as a dramatic device which provides a striking acoustic accompaniment to the sound of the gunshot, or as a visual effect underlining the power of the shot more forcefully than its impact on the human body alone could show, or even as an ironic moral emblem suggesting the brittleness and insubstantiality of the lives of so many characters in these novels. Such explanations may well capture part of the point of this motif; but there is another aspect to it I would like to suggest in conclusion here.

In the nineteenth-century realistic novel, the most traditional image for describing the relationship between the author and the society he depicted was glass. Whether the novelist was described as looking out from a corner window upon the crowds passing below him in the street, or as holding up a mirror to society, or as walking on the city's sidewalks carrying a mirror, his contact with society was not direct but was mediated by a pane of glass. On the one hand, of course, the barrier imposed by this medium implied the aesthetic distance which was necessary if the novelist was to be understood to be providing us, not with reality itself, but rather with some version of or comment upon it—from Plato onward, the looking glass is a recurrent feature in theories which emphasize the artwork as a mere image of real things. But on the other hand, the logic of this metaphor enforced a correlation between the sovereignty of the author's point of view and the unity of the society he represented: just as only one man, the author, stood before the window or held the mirror, so too all of the events and circumstances he saw, however disparate and unconnected they might have seemed to be on their own, became inextricably linked to one another by forming part of the single image visible in and through the glass. By their shared presence within the frame of the looking glass, two events which the merest chance might have juxtaposed in reality seemed to enter into mysterious connection with one another; suddenly, they became parts of a whole, communicating by subterranean channels which were all the more potent the harder their traces were to discern. Thus, in the traditional realistic novel, the narrator's unfailing control over point of view entailed the dream of an ultimately unitary society, and the novel's mission became inevitably that of uncovering hidden connections.

This was the formula the classic detective novel not only had followed with bland fidelity, but indeed had exaggerated and perfected. Yet while the detective novel did so, for many decades it was being left behind by developments in other kinds of novels. While the detective novel continued to provide its readers with unitary viewpoints, organic societies, and the investigation of the traces of hidden links, the "high" novel had for most of this century been exposing these very conceptions to searching criticism. How could one retain faith in the unitary viewpoint after Joyce, or in an organic society after Dos Passos, or in the full discoverability of hidden links after Conrad? Measured against the novels of early twentieth-century modernism, let alone against those of more recent movements

like the French "new novel," detective stories could come to seem increasingly artificial and distant from the very social realities they often purported to analyze.

In recent years, there have been numerous attempts to reform the detective novel genre from above by such high-culture authors as Robbe-Grillet, Butor, and Borges. Elmore Leonard's novels may represent the most successful attempt so far to transform it from below: and the first step in such a transformation must be a shattering of the traditional looking glass of realistic fiction. For on the one hand, once popular culture has permeated so fully into all domains of social behavior that the border between image and reality becomes irremediably blurred, the glass which had always prevented the novel from actually becoming reality and kept it instead a merely aesthetic artifact must inevitably break down. If Robbie in Split Images has read so many detective novels and seen so many murders on television that the language of crime has seeped into his vocabulary and his dream has become that of starring in the videotape of a murder he really commits, if Jean Shaw in LaBrava stages the heist she had always been prevented from pulling off in her films and uses for that purpose a man who has fallen in love with her because of her movie roles as a dangerous, manipulative temptress—then reality is imitating art and we can no longer confidently draw the line between what is fiction and what is truth. And on the other hand, Leonard's jaggedly shifting narrative perspectives, his sense of the sheer chance and blind arbitrariness of social encounters, and his repudiation of classical investigation and detection as modes of acquiring knowledge, cooperate not only to provide a sustained critique of the conventions of the traditional murder mystery, but also to create thrillers whose texture and rhythms are closer to the lives we are led, by television and the other mass media, to believe we actually lead. The evident popularity of his novels is the best evidence for his success.

But there is, or should be, a price for this success. For the glass that separated the traditional novel from reality also protected its reader from full moral complicity in the evil it had represented. But both of the innovations I have just mentioned converge in a single, profoundly disquieting question: Why do we read Leonard's novels? If the line between popular culture and social reality can become blurred beyond recognition, and if we share, even if only intermittently, the perspectives and goals of a psychopathic killer, then what are the possibilities for evil within ourselves that respond to Leonard's narratives, and what forms might our response one day take? What reason do we have to believe that our own capacity for evil will be, not exacerbated, but purged by these novels? This, I would suggest, is the glass that the bullets in Elmore Leonard are really aimed at: the looking glass of the reader's moral complacency. Leonard shatters that glass; its fragments give us splitting images of ourselves.

NOTE

The following novels by Elmore Leonard are referred to by page number in the text; the first date is that of the original publication, the second that of the edition used here: <u>City Primeval: High Noon in Detroit</u> (1980; Avon 1982); <u>52 Pick-Up</u> (1974; Avon, 1983); <u>Glitz</u> (1985; Warner, 1986); <u>Gold Coast</u> (1980; Bantam, 1985); <u>LaBrava</u> (1983; Avon, 1984); <u>Split Images</u> (1981; Avon, 1983); <u>Stick</u> (1983; Avon, 1984); <u>Unknown Man No. 89</u> (1977; Avon, 1984).

Annotated Bibliography
Susan Steinberg

It is fortunate for the mystery monger that, whereas up to the present there is only one known way of getting born, there are endless ways of getting killed.

—Dorothy Sayers

General Reference Works, Essays, History, and Criticism

Barzun, Jacques and Taylor, Wendell Hertig. A Catalogue of Crime. New York: Harper & Row, 1971 (2nd impression corrected). A bibliography, arranged by author, with brief and sometimes highly critical annotations from 125 years of the genre. An example: "The worst cock-and-bull story ever put together by a rational being." Worth reading on its own merits.

Hagen, Ordean. Who Done It? A Guide to Detective, Mystery and Suspense Fiction. New York: Bowker, 1969. A bibliography of mystery fiction 1841–1967 which, though not annotated, includes an unusual subject guide (mysteries featuring bees, railroads, or libraries, for instance), a filmography, and other intriguing special features.

Haycraft, Howard. Murder for Pleasure: The Life and Times of the Detective Story. New York: Appleton-Century, 1941. An early, and still classic, discussion of detective fiction as a literary form.

Johnson, Timothy W., and Johnson, Julia, eds. Crime Fiction Criticism: An Annotated Bibliography. New York: Garland, 1981. Includes a section on

---

[1] This bibliography was prepared in support of Poisoned Pens: Mystery Fiction from Poe to the Present, a series of book discussions in Connecticut public libraries from September 1986 through April 1987. Complete publishing information is cited for secondary works. Date of original publication only is given for mystery fiction because current paperback editions change frequently.

general references, and a second part of critical references on particular authors.

Keating, H.R.F. Whodunit? A Guide to Crime, Suspense & Spy Fiction. New York: Van Nostrand Reinhold, 1982. A fascinating reference work, including specialists' essays on genres and techniques, brief author entries with critical ratings of works, and a guide to well-known characters.

Landrum, Larry N.; Browne, Pat; and Browne, Roy. Dimensions of Detective Fiction. Bowling Green, Ohio: Bowling Green University Popular Press, 1976. An anthology of essays, in part advocating the view that mysteries are appropriate subjects for literary criticism.

Melvin, David Skene, and Melvin, Ann Skene, eds. Crime, Detective, Espionage, Mystery & Thriller Fiction & Film: A Comprehensive Bibliography of Critical Writing Through 1979. Westport, Conn.: Greenwood, 1980. Exhaustive listings but not as useful for individual annotations.

Most, Glenn W., and Stowe, William W., eds. The Poetics of Murder: Detective Fiction & Literary Theory. New York: Harcourt Brace Jovanovich, 1983. A well-chosen collection of post-World War II critical essays on detective fiction.

Porter, Dennis. The Pursuit of Crime: Art and Ideology in Detective Fiction. New Haven: Yale University Press, 1981. A critical study of how writers of detective fiction use standard literary devices to fulfill the dual mission of forwarding action while prolonging suspense.

Pronzini, Bill, and Muller, Marcia. 1001 Midnights: The Aficionado's Guide to Mystery and Detective Fiction. New York: Arbor House, 1986. A hefty, highly readable book of plot summaries.

Reilly, John, M., ed. Twentieth Century Crime and Mystery Writers. New York: St. Martin's Press, 1980. Handy collection of critical and biographical essays, with lengthy bibliographies.

Steinbrunner, Chris, and Penzler, Otto, eds. Encyclopedia of Mystery and Detection. New York: Harcourt Brace Jovanovich, 1976. Very useful and comprehensive encyclopedic treatment including authors, characters, book lists, plays, and films.

Symons, Julian. Bloody Murder: From the Detective Story to the Crime Novel: A History. New York: Viking, 1985. A revised, updated version of an important history of crime fiction originally published in 1972 by a noted critic and creator of the genre.

Winks, Robin. Modus Operandi: An Excursion into Detective Fiction. Boston: Godine, 1981. A witty, graceful personal essay by a master critic of crime/mystery fiction and, it is alleged, a practitioner of the art.

Winks, Robin, ed. Detective Fiction: A Collection of Critical Essays. Englewood Cliffs, N.J.: Prentice-Hall, 1980. A collection of some of the early and best-known essays, including criticism by W. H. Auden, Dorothy Sayers, Edmund Wilson, and Jacques Barzun.

Winn, Dilys. Murder Ink: The Mystery Reader's Companion. New York: Workman, 1977.
Murder Ink: Revised, Still Unrepentant. New York: Workman, 1984. Wonderfully readable collections of far-ranging articles, lists, and curiosities about murder in all its guises. There are significant differences between the two and both are well worth reading.

_____. Murderess Ink: The Better Half of the Mystery. New York: Workman, 1984. An equally readable collection which focuses on women in real life and fictional crime.

The Evolution of the Detective

Critical Works, Histories

Baker, Robert, and Nietzel, Michael. Private Eyes—One Hundred and One Knights. Bowling Green, Ohio: Bowling Green University Popular Press, 1985. On the development of the private eye novel in the United States.

Bakerman, John S., ed. And Then There Were Nine: More Women of Mystery. Bowling Green, Ohio: Bowling Green University Popular Press, 1985. Continuing the coverage of 10 Women of Mystery (see Bargainnier, below).

Ball, John, ed. The Mystery Story. San Diego: University Extension, University of California, 1976. Noted writers/aficionados, including Hillary Waugh and Otto Penzler, deal in separate chapters with amateur, ethnic, and women detectives, private eyes, and the police procedural.

Bargainnier, Earl F., ed. 10 Women of Mystery. Bowling Green, Ohio: Bowling Green University Popular Press, 1981. Includes essays on Sayers, Tey, Ngaio Marsh, P. D. James, Ruth Rendell, Emma Lathen, Amanda Cross.

Bargainnier, Earl F., and Dove, George, eds. Cops and Constables. Bowling Green, Ohio: Bowling Green University Popular Press, 1986. Discusses a number of the most important British and American detective fiction authors, including Tony Hillerman.

Craig, Patricia. The Lady Investigates: Women Detectives and Spies in Fiction. London: Gollancz, 1981. Unearths some lesser-known examples of the "elderly busybody female sleuth" personified by Miss Marple, and a wealth of other relatively unknown characters and types.

Davis, David Brion. Homicide in American Fiction: 1798–1860. Ithaca, N.Y.: Cornell University Press, 1957. Based on a dissertation by a first-rate American historian.

Dove, George. The Boys from Grover Avenue: Ed McBain's 87th Precinct Novels. Bowling Green, Ohio: Bowling Green University Popular Press, 1985. An engrossing study of the police procedurals of Ed McBain (pseudonym for Evan Hunter), one of the masters of the type.

_____. The Police Procedural. Bowling Green, Ohio: Bowling Green University Popular Press, 1982. Includes bibliographic references.

Haycraft, Howard. Murder for Pleasure (see earlier listing).

Murch, A. E. The Development of the Detective Novel. London: Peter Owen, 1958. Good on pre–World War I books, less satisfactory thereafter.

Ousby, Ian. Bloodhounds of Heaven: The Detectives in English Fiction from Godwin to Doyle. Cambridge: Harvard University Press, 1976. A revised doctoral thesis but a major contribution to the study of early detective fiction.

Panek, Leroy. Watteau's Shepherds: The Detective Novel in Britain, 1914–
    1940. Bowling Green, Ohio: Bowling Green University Popular Press,
    1979. An Edgar Award–winning study of the popular genre.

Penzler, Otto, ed. The Great Detectives. Boston: Little, Brown, 1978. An an-
    thology of famous detectives of fiction by the writers who created them.
    Includes bibliography and filmography.

Queen, Ellery. Queen's Quorum: A History of the Detective-Crime Short Story.
    Boston: Little, Brown, 1951; New York: Biblio and Tanne, 1969.
    Indispensable discussion of short crime fiction which the later edition covers
    through 1967.

Sandoe, James. The Hard-boiled Dick: A Personal Checklist. Chicago: Arthur
    Lovell, 1952. Annotated list of more than thirty "hard boiled" writers and
    their works.

Works by Authors Discussed

Chandler, Raymond. The Big Sleep (1939). Philip Marlowe, private detective,
    tells his story in the first person, and thus the reader becomes the detective
    in the step-by-step investigation of blackmail and gambling debts in a
    wealthy Los Angeles family.

Christie, Agatha. Miss Marple: The Complete Short Stories (1985). Stories
    featuring the most famous of the elderly lady sleuths.

_____. Murder on the Orient Express (1934). One of the best-known of the
    works by a most prolific (and uneven) author, this is a mobile version of the
    English country-house tale, a known group of suspects, isolated and locked
    in together.

Collins, Wilkie. The Woman in White (1866). The liveliest of Collins's crime
    stories, with an unimaginably convoluted plot.

Hammett, Dashiell. The Glass Key (1931). Hammett was perhaps the most in-
    fluential of the hard-boiled school of fiction writers. A tale of violence and
    political corruption.

_____. Red Harvest (1929). The Continental Op sets out to clean up a rotten town by manipulating members of two bitterly hostile gangs, with more than 30 people dying in the process.

_____. The Thin Man (1934). The most financially (though not the most artistically) successful of Hammett's books. The Thin Man chronicled the semi-humorous exploits of the glamorous Nick and Nora Charles.

McBain, Ed [Evan Hunter]. 'Til Death (1959). Instead of a series detective, McBain has created a whole series precinct, the 87th, located in a grimly pictured city, like New York.

Sayers, Dorothy. Whose Body? (1923) and Clouds of Witness (1926). Sayers was famed in the world of crime fiction for her creation of Lord Peter Wimsey, aristocrat and amateur detective, who was introduced in Whose Body? but gained popularity in her second mystery, Clouds of Witness.

Works by Other Authors

Allingham, Margery. Coroner's Pidgin (1945). Allingham's super-sleuth, Albert Campion, now mature and no longer an echo of Peter Wimsey, reveals a rare intelligence and skill.

Chesterton, G. K. The Innocence of Father Brown (1911). First of five collections of stories about Father Brown, a gentle priest whose intelligence and understanding of the sinful human soul place him among the supermen of detection.

Constantine, K. C. The Rocksburg Railroad Murders (1972). The first book by a talented but so far underrated author introduces the series policeman Mario Balzic, working out the gritty problems of an ethnically mixed small American city.

Dickens, Charles. Bleak House (1853). Features the first significant English fictional detective, Inspector Bucket.

_____. The Mystery of Edwin Drood (1870). The first six chapters, completed before Dickens's death, give promise that in his hands this might have been one of the greatest mystery novels. Many authors have attempted to supply a satisfactory ending.

Doyle, Arthur Conan. A Study in Scarlet (1887). In this first Holmes tale to be published, Dr. Watson introduced the gentleman detective Sherlock Holmes, whose scientific methods of deduction were often as ingenious as the crimes he solved.

_____. The Hound of the Baskervilles (1902). Doyle's best known attempt to write a mystery novel rather than a brief story.

_____. The Memoirs of Sherlock Holmes (1894). The first important collection of Holmes stories.

Durrenmatt, Friedrich. The Judge and His Hangman (1954). In this exploration of moral justice the author has his Inspector Barlach use criminal means to trap the master criminal he has been hunting for forty years.

Francis, Dick. Banker (1982). Beginning with the immediate success of Dead Cert (1962), Francis, a former jockey, has regularly produced compelling stories, always somehow connected with horses or racing, although the connection has become more tenuous in recent books. With no wasted energy or words, Francis in Banker captures the reader's interest as a typically strong but feeling and principled hero unravels a complicated plot in the world of high-stakes horse breeding.

MacDonald, John D., A Tan and Sandy Silence (1971). A representative novel from a long series, each with a color in the title, featuring the tough but compassionate (and sometimes preachy) Travis McGee as he explores the quirks and shortcomings of Florida and its inhabitants.

Macdonald, Ross [Kenneth Millar]. The Zebra-Shaped Hearse (1962). Macdonald's Lew Archer sees both California's rich face and its dirty underside, using hard-boiled plots and exquisitely precise language.

Poe, Edgar Allan. "The Murders in the Rue Morgue" (1841). The first of Poe's detective stories was a locked-room puzzle which introduced his eccentric hero, C. Auguste Dupin, and his anonymous companion and chronicler, the precursor of Holmes's Watson.

_____. "The Mystery of Marie Roget" (1842). The second Dupin story, based on the actual murder of Mary Cecilia Rogers in New York City in 1841, emphasized reasoning from the evidence to find the solution.

_____. "The Purloined Letter" (1845). In the third story, the most artistically satisfying of the Dupin trio, Poe used the device of concealment in plain sight, a gambit used over and over again by mystery writers thereafter.

Queen, Ellery [Frederick Dannay and Manfred B. Lee]. The Greek Coffin Mystery (1932). As an exercise in rational deduction, this is among the best detective stories ever written, with a brilliant surprise ending.

Rendell, Ruth. A Sleeping Life (1978). Rendell, one of the most accomplished and prolific British crime writers of the last decade, created her series figure, Inspector Wexford, a middle-aged detective with a full complement of family, aides, and residents of the richly pictured town of Kingsmarkham. A Sleeping Life explores some women's issues, and follows the continuing development of members of Wexford's family.

Slung, Michele B. Crime on Her Mind: Fifteen Stories of Female Sleuths from the Victorian Era to the Forties. New York: Pantheon, 1975. An anthology of stories featuring female detectives which includes a detailed and useful chronological survey of fictional women detectives.

Waugh, Hillary. Last Seen Wearing (1952). An early police procedural, about the disappearance of a Massachusetts college girl.

The Mystery Novel as a Reflection of Its Time

Critical Works, Histories, Reference

Many works cited in previous sections are also useful here.

Champigny, Robert. What Will Have Happened. Bloomington: Indiana University Press, 1977. Studies the relationship of the fictional genre to the society from which it grows.

East, Andy. The Cold War File. Metuchen, N.J.: Scarecrow, 1983. Covers the spy novel of the 1960s with biographical information on 73 authors, alphabetically listed.

Fiedler, Leslie. Love and Death in the American Novel. New York: Stein and Day, 1960. Includes discussion of the reflection of gothic elements in Poe's detective stories.

Keene, Carolyn. "Nancy Drew" in Penzler, ed., The Great Detectives (see earlier listing). The creator of the famed series comments on rewriting of earlier titles to bring them into line with modern attitudes of race and sex roles, among other things.

Madden, David, ed. Tough-Guy Writers of the Thirties. Carbondale: Southern Illinois University Press, 1968. Discussion of the hard-boiled hero as a vision of Depression America.

Merry, Bruce. Anatomy of the Spy Thriller. Dublin: Gill and Macmillan, 1977. A scholarly study of the structure and content of spy novels, with much good sense despite occasional pretension.

Ousby, Ian. Bloodhounds of Heaven (see earlier listing). Includes discussion of the figure of the detective as a reflection of social history.

Panek, Leroy. The Special Branch: The British Spy Novel, 1890–1980. Bowling Green, Ohio: Bowling Green University Popular Press, 1981. Critical essays on seventeen of the most popular writers of British spy fiction.

Skenazy, Paul. The New Wild West: The Urban Mysteries of Dashiell Hammett and Raymond Chandler. Boise: Boise State University Press, 1972. Traces the origins of the tough, street-wise detective to, among other things, the American ideal of the Western hero.

Smith, Myron J., Jr. Cloak and Dagger Fiction: An Annotated Guide to Spy Thrillers. 2nd ed., Santa Barbara: ABC Clio Information Services, 1982. Lists more than 3,000 works, with thousands of plot summaries.

Varma, Davendra. The Gothic Flame. New York: Russell, 1957. Sees the influences of Gothic elements in the work of Doyle and Christie.

Works by Authors Discussed

Cross, Amanda [Carolyn Heilbrun]. The James Joyce Murder (1967). The series figure, Kate Fansler, like the pseudonymous author, is an

accomplished academic. Often in a university setting, the novels feature a modern woman of high intelligence and wit and are studded with literary allusions.

Doyle, Sir Arthur Conan (see earlier listing). The Annotated Sherlock Holmes. Edited by William S. Baring-Gould (1967, 2 vols.). Includes the sort of annotations Sherlockians relish.

Hammett, Dashiell (see earlier listing).

Hansen, Joseph. The Grave Digger (1982). Today's acceptance of a wide range of sexual practices is reflected in Hansen's mysteries featuring a homosexual detective. In this novel, Dave Brandstetter investigates a death claim by a financially and sexually unstable father whose missing daughter may be the victim of a Manson-like mass murder.

McClure, James. The Blood of an Englishman (1980). Two South African detectives, Afrikaner Lt. Kramer and Zulu Sgt. Zondi, search for a murderer in the sordid underworld of Trekkersburg in this tale of psychological revenge.

Poe, Edgar Allan (see earlier listing).

Sayers, Dorothy (see earlier listing).

Wahloo, Per, and Sjowall, Maj. The Laughing Policeman (1970). Series policeman Martin Beck investigates the murder of eight people on a Stockholm bus, while the novel explores the boredom of his disintegrating marriage and the frustrations of a man only happy at work. (A 1973 film version transferred the action to San Francisco.)

Works by Other Authors

Deighton, Len. The Ipcress File (1963). An elliptically told spy story with an anonymous, sometimes puzzled hero, in which the technology of the period is functional and not merely flashy as in the James Bond tales.

Francis, Dick (see earlier listing). The Danger (1983). A very characteristic Dick Francis hero seeking to thwart an international kidnaping.

Futrelle, Jacques. Best "Thinking Machine" Detective Stories (1973). A collection of stories originally published in 1905 and 1906, which feature the intellectual detective Prof. Augustus S.F.X. Van Dusen, known as the Thinking Machine, one the great scientific detectives.

Gaboriau, Emile. L'Affaire Lerouge (1866). Published in America as The Widow Lerouge (1873), this was the first in a lengthy and immensely popular series featuring the scientific detection methods of his series figure M. Lecoq.

Green, Anna Katharine. The Leavenworth Case (1878). One of the earliest detective novels by a woman, one of the best-selling mysteries ever written.

Greene, Graham. The Quiet American (1955). Greene's novel, set in French Saigon, focuses on a skeptical British journalist and an idealistic American caught up in the turmoil of disintegrating French power.

Hillerman, Tony. The Blessing Way (1970). The first of three novels featuring Navaho policeman Joe Leaphorn. Highly and deservedly praised.

Hornung, E. W. The Amateur Cracksman (1899). Hornung created A. J. Raffles, gentleman thief, as a contrast to Sherlock Holmes, the brainchild of his brother-in-law Sir Arthur Conan Doyle.

Iles, Frances. Malice Aforethought (1931). Based on an actual murder case, the protagonist is a thoroughly unlikable doctor who murders his equally repellent wife. Critic Julian Symons said of it: "If there is one book more than another that may be regarded as a begetter of the postwar realistic crime novel, this is the one."

James, P. D. An Unsuitable Job for a Woman (1972). Considered by some to be P. D. James's masterpiece, it introduces a truly satisfying woman detective, independent and intelligent, about whom James's series figure, Dalgliesh, says: "I don't think that young woman deludes herself about anything."

Le Carré, John. The Spy Who Came in From the Cold (1963) and The Looking Glass War (1965). Not the romantic vision of espionage in James Bond novels: LeCarré's spies are weary victims of the complicated, ruthless, largely pointless espionage establishment of which they are part.

Leonard, Elmore. Glitz (1985). Detective Vincent Mora thrusts himself into the world of con men, hired killers, and high rollers in Atlantic City to solve a complex murder case.

Meyer, Nicholas. The Seven-Percent Solution (1974). One of the best selling of the many Holmes pastiches, on the collaboration of Freud and Holmes to cure the great detective's drug addiction and solve an international con-spiracy.

Van Dine, S. S. The Bishop Murder Case (1929). Features Philo Vance, some-times called Peter Wimsey's American cousin, a young aristocrat of rather greater erudition than Wimsey, who here solves a series of murders keyed to nursery rhymes.

The Reader, the Writer, and the Detective:

The Eternal Triangle

Critical Works

Many works cited in previous sections would also be useful here.

Brean, Herbert, ed. The Mystery Writer's Handbook (1956). Fifty members of the Mystery Writers of America write about all aspects of their trade, and although some articles are how-to's for writers, others are quite illuminating for readers also.

Cooper-Clark, Diana. Designs of Darkness: Interviews with Detective Novelists. Bowling Green, Ohio: Bowling Green University Popular Press, 1983. Interviews with thirteen leading mystery writers, including P. D. James, Ross Macdonald, Ruth Rendell, Amanda Cross, and Dick Francis.

Mason, Bobbie Ann. The Girl Sleuth: A Feminist Guide. Old Westbury, N.Y.: Feminist Press, 1975. A devoted reader of the teenage series detectives in her youth analyzes their images and influences.

Prager, Arthur. Rascals at Large. Garden City, N.Y.: Doubleday, 1971. Studies of the Hardy Boys, Nancy Drew, and other teenage favorites.

Winks, Robin, ed. Colloquium on Crime New York: Scribner, 1986. Eleven noted mystery writers, including Robert B. Parker, Tony Hillerman, and

K. C. Constantine, write about how they do their work and what they admire in other mystery writers' work.

Works by Authors Discussed

Chandler, Raymond (see earlier listing).

Francis, Dick (see earlier listings). <u>Odds Against</u> (1966) and <u>Whip Hand</u> (1979). Both feature Sid Halley, physically damaged jockey-turned-detective. The long gap between the books allows the reader to assess Francis's developing talents as a writer and increasingly subtle vision of his heroes.

Hillerman, Tony (see earlier listing).

James, P. D. <u>The Skull Beneath the Skin</u> (1982). The further adventures of Cordelia Gray, the woman detective introduced in <u>An Unsuitable Job for a Woman</u> (see earlier listing).

Marsh, Ngaio. <u>Enter a Murderer</u> (1935). "A classic of the murder in full view, with all clues and actions fairly presented in the tersest, most lucid way" (Barzun and Taylor). Inspector Roderick Alleyn is pictured in a more subtle, rounded way than in many of the novels.

Parker, Robert B. <u>Looking for Rachel Wallace</u> (1980). Spenser, the tough Boston detective/gourmet cook/jogger, is hired to guard a lesbian author on a publicity tour. All the Spenser novels include wit of a high order, and all but the first include the intriguing character of Hawk, the black enforcer and friend of Spenser.

Rendell, Ruth (see earlier listing). <u>A Demon in My View</u> (1976) and <u>A Judgement in Stone</u> (1977). In addition to her Wexford/Kingsmarkham series, Rendell has created many studies getting inside the minds of murderers. These are two of the best.

Tey, Josephine. <u>A Shilling For Candles</u> (1936). A more traditional whodunit featuring Allan Grant, whose historical detecting comprises <u>The Daughter of Time</u>.

Van Gulik, Robert. The Chinese Gold Murders (1961). Van Gulik first translated eighteenth-century Chinese detective stories featuring seventh-century
magistrate Judge Dee, then went on to create his own tales of the Judge.

Works by Other Authors

Bentley, E. C. Trent's Last Case (1913). An acknowledged and enduring classic, with "masterly development of the problem and . . . brilliant conduct of
the detection," although the detective discovers finally that "his ingenious
solution is completely wrong" (Barzun and Taylor).

Berkeley, Anthony. The Poisoned Chocolates Case (1929). Expanded into a
novel from a short story, the novel suggests six different solutions to the
crime.

Christie, Agatha (see earlier listing). The Murder of Roger Ackroyd (1926).
One of Christie's most famous novels, still controversial as to whether the
author "played fair" with the reader in supplying all information necessary
for solving the crime. Hercule Poirot, one of Christie's famed sleuths,
learns that his Watson, a local doctor, is the criminal in a book that was a
best-seller in the late 1920s.

Cross, Amanda (see earlier listing).

Eco, Umberto. The Name of the Rose (1980, translated into English in 1983).
Set in a fourteenth-century Franciscan abbey, laden with erudition, religious
ritual, and theological argument.

Fleming, Ian. Casino Royale (1953). The first book about James Bond,
smooth, sexy, and ruthless intelligence operative, licensed to kill. A figure
of fantasy to an American generation, including at least one American
president.

Hammett, Dashiell (see earlier listings). The Continental Op (1945). An un-
named operative for a detective agency, a prototype of the tough, hard-hit-
ting private eye. Hammett said he did not intentionally leave him nameless
but said, "He's more or less of a type, and I'm not sure he's entitled to a
name."

Keene, Carolyn. Secret of the Old Clock (1930). The first appearance in print of
Nancy Drew, the independent, blue-eyed, teenage detective whose many
adventures influenced more than one generation of growing-girl readers.

Fascinating changes in social view are evident when original versions are compared with rewritten modern ones. The male equivalents were the Hardy Boys stories, written under the name Frederick Dixon. Both were produced by the Stratemeyer Syndicate.

MacDonald, John D. (see earlier listing). All of his novels featuring Travis McGee, the tough but tender adventurer, also include eloquent, if sometimes excessive, commentary on commercialism, corruption, and decay in American society.

Macdonald, Ross (see earlier listing). The Underground Man (1971) and The Far Side of the Dollar (1964). Continuing themes in Macdonald's books are the social and ecological waste of California, and loss or lack of communication between parents and children.

Queen, Ellery (see earlier listing). The Roman Hat Mystery (1929). With others from the early Queen period, this complicated plot is a fine example of the Golden Age of deductive crime fiction. All the facts—rather too many of them—are there, if the reader can but find his way through them.

Spillane, Mickey. I, the Jury (1952). This best-selling novel introduced the quintessential tough and sexy detective, Mike Hammer.

Poisoned Pens:
Book Discussion List

The following books were discussed in the book discussion series <u>Poisoned Pens: Mystery Fiction from Poe to the Present</u>, which took place in twenty Connecticut public libraries from September 1986 through April 1987. The series was funded by a grant from the National Endowment for the Humanities.

Series 1: The Evolution of the Detective

1. Wilkie Collins, <u>The Moonstone</u> (1868).

2. Dorothy Sayers, <u>Strong Poison</u> (1930).
   Agatha Christie, <u>The Body in the Library</u> (1942).

3. Dashiell Hammett, <u>The Maltese Falcon</u> (1930).
   Raymond Chandler, <u>Farewell, My Lovely</u> (1940).

4. Chester Himes, <u>A Rage in Harlem</u> (1965), originally published as <u>For Love of Imabelle</u>, 1957.
   Ed McBain, <u>Ice</u> (1983).

5. Sara Paretsky, <u>Deadlock</u> (1985).
   Elmore Leonard, <u>Glitz</u> (1985).

Series 2: The Mystery Novel as a Reflection of Its Time

1. Edgar Allan Poe, "The Murders in the Rue Morgue" (1841).
   Sir Arthur Conan Doyle, <u>A Study in Scarlet</u> (1887).

2. Dorothy Sayers, <u>The Nine Tailors</u> (1934).
   Dashiell Hammett, <u>Red Harvest</u> (1929).

3. Per Wahloo and Maj Sjowall, <u>The Terrorists</u> (1976).
   Adam Hall, <u>The Quiller Memorandum</u> (1965).

4. Amanda Cross, <u>Death in a Tenured Position</u> (1981).
   Liza Cody, <u>Dupe</u> (1984)

5.   Joseph Hansen, <u>Troublemaker</u> (1975).
     James McClure, <u>The Steam Pig</u> (1971).

Series 3: The Reader, the Writer, and the Detective:
The Eternal Triangle

1.   Josephine Tey, <u>The Daughter of Time</u> (1951).

2.   Ngaio Marsh, <u>Death in a White Tie</u> (1938).
     Dick Francis, <u>Reflex</u> (1980).

3.   P. D. James, <u>An Unsuitable Job for a Woman</u> (1972).
     Raymond Chandler, <u>The Big Sleep</u> (1939).

4.   Tony Hillerman, <u>Dance Hall of the Dead</u> (1973).
     Robert Van Gulik, <u>The Chinese Bell Murders</u> (1958).

5.   Robert B. Parker, <u>The Judas Goat</u> (1978).
     Ruth Rendell, <u>Wolf to the Slaughter</u> (1967).

About the Contributors

CAROLYN HEILBRUN holds the Avalon Foundation Professorship in the Humanities at Columbia University. A specialist in modern British literature and feminist criticism, Professor Heilbrun's scholarly publishing ranges from <u>The Garnett Family</u> (1960) to <u>Reinventing Womanhood</u> (1979). As author Amanda Cross, she has followed the career of fictional literary scholar Kate Fansler from <u>In the Last Analysis</u> (1964), through <u>The James Joyce Murder</u> (1967), <u>Poetic Justice</u> (1970), to <u>Death in a Tenured Position</u> (1981), and <u>Sweet Death, Kind Death</u> (1984). Her eighth novel, <u>No Word from Winifred</u>, was published in 1986.

JOHN McALEER, a member of the English department at Boston College since 1955, teaches "Literary Biography," "Eighteenth Century Fiction," "The Novel of Manners," and "The Concord Idealists." In 1971, he introduced into the curriculum "Crime Fiction and Folk Myth," the first course in detective fiction to be offered as a part of the regular program at an American university. (It is interesting to note that today more than 700 colleges and universities offer such courses). He also teaches a course with noted criminologists entitled "Crime in Literature," which examines crime in the works of Sophocles, Chaucer, Shakespeare, Browning, Dickens, Hardy, Dostoyevski, Hawthorne, Dreiser, and Greene. His book <u>Rex Stout: A Biography</u> (Little, Brown, 1977) won an Edgar Allan Poe Award in 1978. Currently editor-publisher of two journals, <u>The Thorndyke File</u> (devoted to the works of British detective-fiction writer R. Austin Freeman) and <u>The Rex Stout Journal</u>, Professor McAleer recently finished his first detective novel, <u>Coign of Vantage</u>, a novel-of-manners mystery set in the Boston Brahmin world of the present day. He is serving his fourth term as a vice-president of the Mystery Writers of America and has recently been appointed to the Society of Fellows at the University of Durham in England.

GLENN W. MOST specializes in ancient and modern literature and literary theory. He has published books and articles on a number of topics in these areas and related fields, including The Poetics of Murder (Harcourt Brace Jovanovich, 1983), co-edited with William W. Stowe. He has taught classics and comparative literature at Yale, Princeton, Heidelberg, Siena, and the University of Michigan, and is currently Professor of Classical Philology at the University of Innsbruck.

DENNIS PORTER is a graduate of Cambridge University and the University of California at Berkeley and a former Visiting Professor at the University of Freiburg. He now holds the Germaine Brée Professorship of French Studies at the University of Massachusetts at Amherst. Professor Porter has published widely on nineteenth- and twentieth-century French and British fiction. He is the author of The Pursuit of Crime: Art and Ideology in Detective Fiction (Yale University Press, 1981) and a recently completed study of European travel literature, Haunted Journeys. He is currently translating, from the French, two seminars by Jacques Lacan.

PETER J. RABINOWITZ was educated at the University of Chicago, where he received degrees in Russian and comparative literature. He has written widely on a number of subjects, ranging from opera and detective fiction to literary theory; his study of interpretive convention, Before Reading, is published by Cornell University Press. An Associate Professor at Hamilton College, he is also active as a music critic for such publications as Fanfare, Ovation, and American Record Guide.

B. J. RAHN, a member of the English department at Hunter College, has been teaching courses on "The Detective as Hero" and "British and American Women Crime Writers" for several years. In March 1986 she organized a conference on women mystery writers, "Murder at Hunter: Whodunit?" In addition to panel discussions, the conference featured a book fair, a *tableau vivant* of popular sleuths, a library exhibit of novels and important critical books on the genre, and a whodunit play offering attendees an opportunity to play sleuth. Professor Rahn's forthcoming book, Speaking of Murder: English Women Crime Writers Discuss Their Craft, includes interviews with Antonia Fraser, P. D. James, Ruth Rendell, and June Thomson.

RICHARD SLOTKIN has been teaching at Wesleyan University since 1966, and is currently Olin Professor of English and director of the American Studies program. He teaches courses in American literature, myth and popular culture, film, and cultural history. Professor Slotkin's first book, Regeneration Through Violence: The Mythology of the American Frontier, 1600–1860 (Wesleyan Uni-

versity Press) received the Albert J. Beveridge Award of the American Historical Association as the "best book on the history of the Americas" in 1973, and was nominated for a National Book Award in history. A second volume of this study, The Fatal Environment: The Myth of the Frontier in the Age of Industrialization, 1800–1890, was published by Atheneum (1985). In 1980 he published his first work of fiction, a historical novel called The Crater, which recreates the complex military and social circumstances surrounding a significant battle of the American Civil War. The novel was the first work of fiction to be adopted as a selection by the History Book Club.

MICHELE SLUNG has written and reviewed widely in the mystery genre. Her books include Crime on Her Mind: Fifteen Stories of Female Sleuths from the Victorian Era to the Forties (Pantheon, 1975) and Women's Wiles (Harcourt Brace Jovanovich, 1979), the Mystery Writers of America anthology, which she edited. Her reviews have appeared in the New York Times Book Review, the Washington Post Book World, Newsday, the New Republic, and USA Today. Her column of mystery reviews, "Mystery Tour," has been appearing irregularly in Ms. since 1974. She has contributed new introductions to three nineteenth-century reissues: The Leavenworth Case by Anna Katharine Green (1981), The Dead Letter by Seeley Regester (1980), and The Experiences of Loveday Brooke, Lady Detective by C. L. Pirkis (1986). Her essays can be found in The Mystery Story, Twentieth Century Crime and Mystery Writers, Murder Ink, Whodunit? and The Penguin Encyclopedia of Horror and the Supernatural.

MARILYN STASIO, theatre critic for the New York Post, also writes a nationally syndicated monthly book review column, "Mystery Alley," which appears in fifteen major newspapers, including the Boston Herald-American, the Baltimore Sun, the Cleveland Plain Dealer, the Philadelphia Inquirer, and the Seattle Times. Ms. Stasio's broad knowledge and keen appreciation of contemporary detective fiction was evinced in her "Lady Gumshoes: Boiled Less Hard," a survey of contemporary women crime writers and their works, which appeared in the Sunday Book Review of the New York Times in April 1985. Her features and reviews of mystery fiction have also appeared in Newsday and the Miami Herald.

SUSAN STEINBERG is American and Commonwealth Studies Bibliographer in the Yale University Library, a position she has held since 1970. She is a graduate of Smith College and holds two graduate degrees from Yale.

WILLIAM W. STOWE teaches English, comparative literature, and detective fiction at Wesleyan University. The Poetics of Murder, an anthology he co-edited with Glenn W. Most, was nominated for an Edgar Allan Poe Award by the Mys-

tery Writers of America in 1984. Since then he has taught graduate and under-graduate courses on detective fiction and literary theory, lectured on the subject, and published related articles in College English and the Canadian Review of Comparative Literature. He has also published a book on Henry James and Honoré de Balzac (Princeton University Press, 1983) and is working on a study of nineteenth-century American travel writers.

ROBIN W. WINKS is Master of Berkeley College and Randolph W. Townsend, Jr. Professor of History at Yale University, where his specialty is the history of the British empire and comparative British and American history. His avocation is detective and spy fiction, on which he has written or edited five books: The Historian as Detective (Harper & Row, 1969), Detective Fiction (Prentice-Hall, 1980), Modus Operandi: An Excursion into Detective Fiction (Godine, 1982), an Edgar Allan Poe Award finalist, and Colloquium on Crime (Scribners, 1986). His most recent publication is Cloak & Gown: Scholars in the Secret War, 1939–1961 (Morrow, 1987), detailing Yale's involvement in the creation of the O.S.S. and the C.I.A. Professor Winks is a regular mystery columnist for the Boston Globe, reviews for the Washington Post and is a member of the Crime Writers Association of Great Britain, the Mystery Writers of America, and the Explorers' Club.

Index

ADG-6230

PS
374.D4
S57
1988

10/22/96

Middlebury College

0 00 02 0672729 9